THE SECOND BOOK OF CATACLYSM

THE SECOND BOOK OF CATACLYSM
THE ΩMEGA

G.A. Finocchiaro

THE OMEGA Copyright © 2021 G.A. Finocchiaro

ISBN: 978-1-7373536-2-1

First Edition November 2021

writingbloc.com
www.gafino.com

Edited by Cari Dubiel
Cover Design by Rachel Perciphone
Interior Design by G.A. Finocchiaro
Author Photo by Ashley Griffin Photography

SCALES is a shared universe of stories written by G.A. Finocchiaro.

Chapters bearing SCALES symbols are connected to the larger story arc set within the SCALES universe. It is not required to have read these stories to enjoy The Raptor—however, having read the below will provide additional insight not provided within this book.

List of books within the SCALES series:

- I The Knightmares
- II Quibbles
- III Grace Falls
- IV Bogey
- V The Raptor

For more information, please go to gafino.com and click on SCALES.

Dedication:

For all those who have found and lost love.
May you find that brilliant spark once again.

Music that Inspired **THE OMEGA**:
https://spoti.fi/2WOUaZy

prologue

Someone. Somewhere. Somewhen…

"Confession has been accepted," said the voice.

"Wait," I said. "I'm not done."

"Confession has been accepted."

"If you consider yourself righteous, how can you accept only half of what I intend to confess?"

"Confession has been accepted. The Host recognizes your conflict and moves to sentencing."

"What kind of court is this? What kind of judgment are you passing? Haven't you learned anything? I am not the same being I was when I committed my crimes. I accept them, I own them, but you all don't understand. Life is complicated! It's blood! It's pain! You sit up there on your golden perch and judge! That's exactly how this mess began! If you cannot understand what I, your brother, went through, how can we expect to understand them? Humans. We need them. We will need to fight beside them when the Cataclysm comes, and trust me, it's coming sooner than we think. The Unbecoming is calling our names, lest we find a way to work together."

After a long pause, the voice said, "…continue."

MALUS
Somewhere…
Then.

I had walked the Earth from end to end, sea to sea, valley floor to mountain top—one cannot count nor track the many millennia, but a life this vast had brought many lessons. I have breached the walls of the greatest kingdom and slayed kings of kings. I have tricked the deadliest manipulators and toppled the greatest underworld ever built. I have studied everything from alchemy to black magic, necromancy, genetics, cryptomancy, and enchantments—I even learned to drive an automobile.

But the most important lesson I had ever learned?

Never piss off angels.

When an angel comes to visit, brandishing threats and flaming Empyrean weapons—you might be up to no good.

However, when angels attack with the wrath of Heaven spilling forth into a vomitous blitz of cleansing fury—you might have struck a sensitive, sanctimonious nerve.

The powers of the dead were not meant for me. They were a gift for those with the wisdom to use it judiciously, if not shrewdly, and to be used in the name of all that was good and holy. When I stole them, I became someone to be watched—something to be feared.

For years I searched, digging into the past and future, for a passion that might become my next obsession. The Old Ones, The Thirteen, and the Crawling Chaos became that obsession, for a time…

When I started poking in the wrong spot, a war battalion of angels descended on me. Led by Uriel, the archangel, they were sent to destroy the "usurper" before I learned too much, and my followers too many—

In defense, I unleashed the full fury of the Necromancer Ring.

Another lesson learned; If one does happen to piss off pious, imprudent angels, make damn sure they learn to fear you.

When the angel battalion did not return, they were left with no other choice than to avoid my affairs. To wait for my inevitable fall, like Icarus flying too close to the sun.

For six straight days I tortured Dolios, the war battalion's messenger. I tormented him, siphoning information of the Heavenly Host and pillaging secrets the messenger had curried throughout his time as part of Uriel's inner circle.

Uriel, Archangel Prince, was privy to many divine secrets, and his personal messenger would have been at the center of it all.

On the morning of the seventh day, Dolios finally broke.

"I can smell your defiance, Dolios," I said. The tortured angel was crucified upside down, lashed to an old oak tree covered in moss. We were somewhere in Greenland, within a thicket of trees surrounded by fireweed. It was cold, late in the year when the temperatures began to plummet, and the frost collected onto every surface before the sun rose. Dolios had never felt cold, never felt uncomfortable or experienced pain, until he came into my possession. He was breaking, his divinity leaving his celestial body. The angel was wearing light armor with sections of overlapping interwoven metal plates that resembled broad silver scales. Beneath the scales was a golden mail like braided silk—twice as hard and more durable than Empyrean steel. The mark across his forehead was all but removed, torn from his skin. The side of his face had been mangled in such a way that it would never grow back, not even when healed.

However, no matter my attempt, I could not crack the golden halo upon his head. It was a hovering crown, a simple band of incorruptible gleaming metal, only visible behind the Veil. If it could be broken, the method of doing so was beyond my current understanding.

"If I tell you," wept the messenger, "I will never be welcomed back."

"If I were you, Dolios, I would be more concerned with life than whether or not Daddy will ever let you go home." I walked toward him, my power shimmering in the air between us. "Just tell me what I want to know. Tell me, and I will let you live."

Dolios sobbed. His choices were dire. He was being asked to forsake his maker, betray his prince and expose his brothers and sisters, all for the opportunity to live. He did not want to die, to cease existence as a celestial, coasting through the cosmos in service to his maker. Every creature that ever lived, that took breath and felt pain, wanted to remain alive. Dolios was no different. He was breaking. He saw his end and would do anything to ensure the next breath would not be his last.

"Tell me what you are hiding!" I shouted as I jabbed a clawed hand into his chest and threatened to rip out his heart. "If you will not tell me your secrets, I will crack open your head and sift through your brains until I uncover them!"

I had asked Dolios many questions about my obsessions. I expected him to unload his heavy heart. I expected the pathetic angel to tell me who and what The Old Ones were, and why the Host had wiped the world clean of their names—every shred of their existence had been destroyed, except those places hidden to even the Host.

When he answered, he unburdened his spirit with information beyond expectation.

"The Dyad has been lost!" squealed Dolios as my claws began to break the muscle that surrounded the angel's heart. His words stayed my hand.

"Be very precise when you speak," I said, needing clarification.

Had he actually admitted that? It was shocking if true.

"They are missing," mumbled the angel.

"Gone missing? How?" I asked.

"I do not know," cried Dolios. I reapplied my claws—I could feel his heart flutter with desperation as he wailed and begged. He was damned no matter the choice.

"Tell me!"

With a flustered cadence fixed with pain and fear, Dolios muttered, "A girl! A girl has it! That's all I know!" As those secrets left his lips, his golden halo cracked and faded forever.

Dolios wept.

A girl has the Dyad? How could that be?

"You could let me go," she said, her voice a whisper only I could hear. "You tried and failed before."

"Not this time," I replied.

"Please," she begged, "let me go."

"Who are you speaking to?" asked Dolios between sobs. "I told you what you wanted to know. Please, let me live."

I smiled. "So long, messenger," I said, then disappeared behind the Veil.

"Wait!" screamed Dolios, still crucified to the tree. "Take me with you! My halo is broken! I cannot go home! Take me with you!"

It took another century to devise and enact my plan.

My obsessions were my inspiration. I traveled the world and through time in search of Fallen I could manipulate into signing their rights to me, in exchange for whatever they desired—should they survive.

With those Thirteen contracts signed, I could tear down Mt. Sinai and torture the holy prophet, steal a Fae Augur, or abduct a Seer. What good was searching for a girl across all time when we could torture someone into telling us where she was? Perhaps to the exact second of her birth, whereabouts, even her name.

I had little doubt it would be that easy. But I was immortal, and I had all the time in the world.

THE OMEGA

innocence

JACINDA
October 13th, 1986
Then.

Your face was covered in something thick and warm and red, like the color of your hair. The air smelled tinny and the unsettled calm of tragedy was taking shape. The silence after chaos was perhaps the most unnerving part of any accident. The calm after the storm, but before the rescue, was as disorienting as waking from a deep sleep.

Hey Jace, it's me.

I'm watching you. I know that sounds creepy, and maybe it is—*a little bit*—but my intentions are honorable. I came here to figure you out, because I realized there were too many secrets. Too many things I didn't know about the woman I loved.

Were you an angel? A monster? Something in between?

Were you innocent? Trapped? A creature of circumstance?

I needed to know.

You were only a little girl—so young—and my heart was already breaking for you.

I watched this moment wondering if it was the beginning of the madness. Was this the moment that unlocked your dark secret? Or was your destiny inevitable?

I don't know what I intended to discover or to what end this would go. I only sought the truth. I deserved that much, didn't I? Traveling through time, hidden behind the Veil—another world beneath the real one, was like watching you from behind an invisible curtain—I came to learn all I could about your life.

There were rules, though—I was only allowed to watch.

To walk a mile in one's shoes, they say—and we were only six miles in.

Jacinda Moira O'Neill, *you* were born on November 11th, 1980, to parents James and Saoirse O'Neill. They had been married five years when you came into their lives. Saoirse only ever wanted one child, and they'd already been blessed with the baby they always wanted—the lovely daughter they'd prepared for since the day they married, while James was finishing law school. They named her Jane, after James's grandmother on his father's side.

Two years later, you were born.

Jane always had a leg up on her younger sister. She was older, obviously, with long blonde hair and bright blue eyes. You, on the other hand, had a mop of reddish curls that never seemed to lay straight and green eyes that went unnoticed. While Jane received compliments and praise for every perfect smile in her Sunday dress, you were largely ignored—especially by your own mother.

Before the age of four, you were locked in a sibling rivalry that neither of you asked for, but both of you participated in, nonetheless.

Jane beat you at every game, every challenge, and every accomplishment. She received better grades, ran faster, and had a better imagination than you, and there were days when all you ever wanted was to be just like your older sister. From a very young age, it was clear to you that your mother favored Jane. By the age of five, you never knew what it was like not to live in your sister's shadow.

Like all sisters, you and Jane fought, and on some occasions, they were downright nasty affairs. Tears would be shed, threats would be screamed, and sometimes hair was pulled. But twenty minutes later you'd be as thick as thieves once again, giggling in a corner. No matter how angry you were with each other, you would always find your way back to being the best of friends.

Then every Saturday, when your Grammy came to visit, was a day for adventure. Moira Flannery was a special kind of woman—a true saint without the title. She showered both of you with more love in one day than you had received all week from your mother, and most importantly, she spread that love equally between you and your sister. During her visits, your Grammy sang and played guitar. She took you both to the park playground and occasionally the zoo or museum. You saw your first Georgia O'Keeffe painting when you were five years old, and to hear your Grammy glow over the color and beauty of her paintings inspired you to appreciate them too. And a visit from Grammy was never complete without plenty of arts and crafts, then story time before bed.

"I wish I was like Jane," you said one Saturday evening as Grammy tucked you in. "I don't like being Jacinda." Your comment shocked your grandmother, a sad profession of a situation that had spiraled out of control. Moira had plenty of talks with her daughter, criticizing her unabashed favoritism, but to hear it verbalized through the mouth of a five-year-old sent Moira into a tizzy.

"Why do you say that?" asked Moira, hiding her anger. Her daughter had gone too far.

"Because Jane is pretty. She's better at everything. She can play guitar better too."

"Darling," Moira responded in her strong Irish brogue, "your dear sister is two whole years older than you. She got a head start, but eventually you'll catch up to her, just like the tortoise always beats the hare."

"I want to be better than her at something," you said. "So Mommy and Daddy will love me most for once."

Moira thought about her response for a moment, weighing her

words carefully, then said, "Tomorrow's not a promise, my dear. Gotta earn each one. If you want it bad enough, you can make it happen. But remember, you will always be my special little flower. Do you understand?"

You nodded, and after a goodnight kiss, Moira was ready to unleash her Irish fire upon her daughter. Sometimes innocence was the best mirror, reflecting back the damage done.

However, October 13th, 1986 was the day everything changed. Your innocence was shattered by an accident that would change your life forever.

Jace, I wish I had known. I wish you had told me. Why did you hide this from the one and only person who loved you unconditionally? I, of all people, would have understood.

After you took your own life, twenty years later, it was obvious that you harbored serious trauma, but I never thought that trauma was buried so deep into your past. The woman I loved was an enigma—a disguise—and I was looking for the truth. Why did you take your own life? Why didn't you share your inner torment with me?

The front end of the car was all but completely missing. Smashed and torn, unlike the modern cars that safely collapsed like an accordion to protect passengers. It looked as if the entire engine had busted through the passenger side dashboard, and it didn't stop there.

A few minutes after impact passed before the passengers within the tan four-door regained consciousness. It was the truck driver who called in the accident on his CB radio. He vomited on the side of the road immediately after, his grief seizing his entire body. It was not his fault. The accident was unfortunate happenstance—but as I had already come to learn, nothing was a coincidence.

It resembled an act of God.

A young man named Jonah Johnson—a peculiar guy I once met—had lost control of his aging VW Bug and swerved into oncoming traffic. His transmission blew just moments before. The truck driver tried to avoid the collision and ended up crashing head-on with the tan four-door carrying three.

It wasn't until the fire engine's siren came blaring into focus that you stirred from the

backseat, behind the driver. You had blood on your face, but very little of it was your own. You panicked and started to cry.

You were so little. So innocent. Not even seven years old. God dammit, why didn't I know about this?

"Stay still darlin'. Stay still," said the fireman, testing the jammed door. He was wearing one of those terrified looks on his face, despite the words and the tone he was speaking.

Your red ringlets hung in your face, and you were covered in something warm and sticky. You fingered the laceration on your forehead, a divot that slowly oozed and throbbed, and began to cry—more from the experience than from pain.

"Jane? Where's my Janie? Jacinda?" your mother asked hysterically. She was in great pain, with a broken leg and several broken ribs, but like any true mother, even the bad ones, she was worried about her children. They were the first thing that came to her mind, and their names came instantly to her lips as she regained consciousness. She struggled in the driver's seat, attempting to free her leg so she could turn to her children. She needed to see them, to know that they were alright.

What happened? How could she let anything happen to her babies? You could see the thoughts, the shock and fear and alarm on her face as she twisted painfully in her seat.

In the end, it was the guilt that hurt the most.

"I'm here, Mommy," you said. "My head hurts." Your tears washed bloody streaks down your pale cheeks.

"It's okay, honey. Hold still," your mother said with a fake calmness in her voice. It was courage she didn't know she had as she panicked on the inside.

"We'll get you out, ma'am," said the firefighter.

"No, get my daughters first," she growled. "Leave me! Get them first! Jane, baby? Are you okay? Talk to Mommy?"

But there was no response.

The driver's side back door gave way. A team of firemen removed the little redhead quickly, whisking you away delicately and left you in the hands of the emergency care staff, who had set up a ward on the road's narrow shoulder. Traffic was backing up both ways, and people stood beside their cars to watch the scene unfold.

The tractor-trailer had just stopped smoking when the bone-chilling cries of a mother in mourning began to shatter every bystander's heart.

"Hey, hon, what's your name?" a young woman asked you, her little patient, trying to distract you from your mother's cries. So much was happening so fast.

"Jacinda Moira O'Neill, ma'am," you said like you had practiced in kindergarten, in case of emergency.

"I want you to follow the light with your eyes, Jacinda," said the young EMT as she held a small flashlight in front of your eyes, moving it left and right, then up and down.

"Nobody calls me that. Everybody calls me Jaycie," you said with a hint of sass, and I couldn't help but smirk.

The EMT probed at the deep cut that blended with your fiery hair, staunching the bleeding with a piece of gauze.

"Nice to meet you, Jaycie. My name is Carina," said the EMT with a twinkle in her gray eyes. She looked familiar, like I had met her once before. Like the kind of face you'd recognize in a crowded room, unable to place how or when you knew them.

"What's that?" you asked, pointing to something shiny around her neck.

"This?" asked Carina, holding it up. "It's a key."

"What does it unlock?"

"Secrets," Carina responded with a smile.

A gathering of crows cawed loudly overhead, capturing your attention. You looked up at them and asked, "Where did they come from?"

Had they gathered to witness death? A murder of crows congregating over tragedy? There was something ominous about those crows...

"Don't mind them, darling," said Carina. But your surroundings were overwhelming you—the crash, the audience, the crows, the throbbing pain in your forehead, it was all too much—and when the firemen began shouting, the sound stole your attention once again.

Your mother was free from the wreckage and was being ushered on a stretcher toward the ambulance.

"Jaycie? Stay with me, darling," said Carina, gently guiding your chin toward her with a kind hand.

"Where's Jane?" you asked. "She was right beside me in the back seat." The innocence in your eyes shook Carina. You were too young to understand.

"Something happened to your sister," Carina said, hesitantly at first. "I need you to understand, it wasn't your fault."

"She made me so mad," you said as you started crying. "She kept teasing me about my freckles and I just wanted her to stop. I wanted her to stop and never talk like that again."

"It's not your fault," said Carina, but you shook your head and cried harder until your eyes met your mother's as she was being loaded into the ambulance. Her lower body was wrapped in a blanket to hide the injuries she'd sustained. As soon as the doors slammed shut, the ambulance moved urgently away.

"Is my mommy okay?" you asked, but when you turned back to Carina, the EMT was gone.

You looked all around but couldn't find her anywhere. It was like she had vanished, leaving you all alone, sitting on the edge of a stretcher behind an ambulance at the scene of the most devastating event of your life.

I watched your world spin out of control, like a twister behind your eyes, as you sat there watching the rescue crew remove the body. You were robbed of a sister, and you replaced her with a sadness you never learned to conquer.

I watched you, an angel upon your shoulder, until your father swallowed you up in a sweeping embrace and took you home.

There were other moments. Days I attempted to view, but it was as if I was locked out, like they were redacted from reality. April 4th, 1987 was one of those days, and I wondered what could have happened that kept me away.

May 5th, 1988

"Your hat is on crooked, dear," said your mother. You tried to straighten it, but even that wasn't good enough for her. Saoirse promptly straightened it for you, and your head was embarrassingly jostled about in the process, flushing your cheeks in front of all the people you didn't know.

The procession was long, but everyone who approached you told stories of your Grammy and how much they loved her. All you wanted to do was go to your room and cry. At seven years old, you had already learned a lot about death, and yet you could not grasp the permanence of it. At least, not yet.

When the procession was over, your mother asked you to say goodbye to Grammy, even though you weren't quite sure how to do that with someone who was dead. She was lying in a wooden box and surrounded by the most flowers you had ever seen at the front of the church, just below the altar. You were scared, because even from afar, the body didn't look like Grammy at all. It looked like a cheap imitation of the woman you knew and loved with all your heart.

One by one, the remaining members of your family went up to the altar and kneeled before the casket, saying their goodbyes as the church emptied. By the time it was your turn, the last to go, the church was silent and empty. Your parents didn't even wait for you. Your mother was crying too hard and needed to be escorted from the church, leaving you all alone.

"What's wrong, child?" asked the priest. He noticed you sitting alone in the front pew, struggling with an uncomfortable decision.

"I'm scared."

"What are you scared of?" he asked. "There is nothing to be afraid of in the house of God."

You considered his words for a moment before you looked at the priest and asked, "Where do you go when you die?"

Oh Jace, the look on his face! He should have been prepared for that, but you caught him off guard. You always did have a knack for asking the tough questions.

"If your soul is free from sin, you get to go to Heaven," he responded. It was funny watching a priest distill a complicated Catholic answer into a simple statement.

"I know that," you said. "But where? Where is it? What does it look like? Why can't I go visit?" It was all the questions that were spinning around your head. Questions that nobody could answer, or at least, nobody listened to. Nobody gave you that time.

Grammy would have listened.

"My dear, you can only visit Heaven when it's your time to go. Nobody knows what it looks like. You only know when you arrive at the pearly gates and St. Peter welcomes you home." The priest noticed your confusion and quickly attempted to fix his answer. "You can't visit her in Heaven because that's not how it is. Sometimes I forget that children need, and deserve, more direct answers. I truthfully cannot answer many of your questions. I don't know what it looks like, I only have faith that it exists."

"Why do people die?" you asked, your eyes filling up with tears.

"As my father used to say," said the priest, "all good things must come to an end."

You did not appear satisfied with his answers, but you accepted them, along with all the other great mysteries of the world. It always seemed like grownups didn't really know the answers, but only pretended like they did.

Then the priest leaned forward and said, "I think it's time to say your goodbyes. I believe they'll be looking for you."

"Who?"

"Your parents," he said with a smile.

"Oh, yeah."

"Go on," he said with a nudge. "Everything is going to be okay."

"Thanks, Father Monaco," you said.

You took a deep breath, stood up, then strolled toward the altar. You slowed your approach when you neared and looked over your shoulder, where Father Monaco watched with a gentle smile.

You were never alone, Jace. Not even then. I was right there beside you, the whole way.

When you got to your Grammy, your heart thumped loudly in your throat, and you felt uncomfortable. Your Grammy was wearing her favorite dress, her wedding ring, and her hair was done up just as she liked it, but there was something wrong about her. Something you didn't like seeing. She didn't look like Grammy. She looked like an imposter. She looked wrong. Unsure what to do, or what was proper, you reached out and touched Grammy's hand, and the moment you touched it you jumped—it didn't even feel like Grammy. It felt wrong.

That's when you cried. When you realized Grammy, just like your sister, was never coming back, not ever. You cried so hard—a deep cry, that came from the deepest parts of you—that you shook and wilted right in front of the casket. You loved Grammy more than words, and the person in the casket was just a fake, and you could never say a proper goodbye, not ever.

You learned a lot that day, a lesson you would always remember. You learned that a person isn't the body they inhabit—the person resides within the soul, in their spirit, in their very essence, and there was no person without it.

November 11th, 1988

As a child, every birthday was special. It was a day to celebrate, filled with cake, ice cream, and every child's favorite—presents.

You spent most of your day practicing on Grammy's guitar. After begging your mother for lessons, you were finally getting better, starting to put simple songs together. Grammy left you many things, including her guitar and all her old records, but it was the memories that you cherished most. You kept a framed photo of her by your bed at all times.

"Daddy," you asked as you caught him by the front door hanging his coat after a long day at the office, "want to hear a song?"

"Of course, dear," he said, "in a minute."

You had been practicing all day so you could show your mom and dad just how much you had learned. Grammy would have been so proud, and like every little girl, you wanted nothing more than validation and acknowledgment.

"Where's your mother?" your father asked.

"In the bedroom," you said.

"Still?" he asked. "Has she been downstairs at all? Looked after you?"

"No," you said. "But Mrs. Berry came by and gave me a cupcake."

"That was nice of her," said your father, frustration grinding his jaw.

"Daddy?"

"Yes, love?" he said, as he stood at the bottom of the stairs, ready to have a very uncomfortable talk with his wife.

"Are we doing anything for my birthday?"

"When is it?" he asked.

Your heart sank. "It's today, November 11th."

"Oh, right," he said. "Listen, hon, your mother is going through a very difficult time right now. I don't know if celebrating a birthday is going to be the best thing for your mother."

"Okay," you said sadly. "Did I do something wrong?"

"What?" he asked. "No, no, not at all. Let me check on your mother. I'll be right back."

As your father ascended the stairs, you sat on the couch and practiced the chords you learned from your lessons. In the middle of stretching your fingers for the second chord, you heard your mother screaming.

"Will you leave me alone, James!"

"Your daughter spent the entire afternoon all by herself. No supervision. She said Alice brought her a cupcake."

"So what? She's almost eight. She doesn't need me taking care of her."

"She's a fucking child, Saoirse! And it's her fucking birthday!"

"Don't be so dramatic, it's not her birthday. Her birthday isn't until the eleventh."

"And what day do you think it is, huh? Did you even get her anything?"

"We already got her guitar lessons. That's good enough."

"Lovely. Do you even want to be a mother?"

"I wanted to be her mother, James! I had the daughter I wanted. She even looked like me…"

"Oh, that's great. You still have one daughter. And she's a brilliant little girl, if you so much as care to open your fucking eyes. She loves you and wants nothing more than your affection."

That's when James realized he had left the door open and promptly slammed it shut, but you had heard enough. There was no cake, no presents, no special birthday dinner. You were eight years old and had finally caught up to Jane, and yet you were still living in her shadow.

The next week, they sent you off to private school.

reunion

TONY
December 22nd, 2013
Now.

My subconscious played out imaginary hypotheticals whether I wanted it to or not. They were fantasies I never thought I'd ever have the opportunity to experience—like winning the lottery or being drafted by a big-league team. For six years, there was one hypothetical that played out in every wishful daydream—one hypothetical that tortured me when I let my guard down and allowed it to creep in—and I was experiencing it, for real.

"What's going on?" asked my dead fiancée.

What would I do if I ever saw her again?

Her vibrant red hair lit up the cold gray of winter, and her green eyes sparkled. Memories, ghosts, and photographs had nothing on the real thing. No dream, no fantasy—this was like stepping barefoot into a puddle, licking both palms, and firmly grasping an electrified fence.

We were in a dark corner of the Grace Falls Cemetery by the weeping willow she was buried beneath. Fog permeated the air around us, and the temperatures had plummeted so far below freezing that the hot sweat on my brow was running cold down my forehead.

A million thoughts and questions crossed my mind, all with equal amounts of trepidation. The first, and the most important: was she real?

I suddenly found myself mentally devolving into an anxious mess, reminiscent of the night we first met, and the awful word vomit I suffered through in her presence—only now, every word I attempted to speak evaporated before it could leave my mouth.

"Tony? What is going on!?" she demanded while I stuffed the brass key dangling from my old silver chain into my pocket and brushed the dirt from my hands.

This was a gift. An opportunity.

What would I do if I ever saw her again?

I stepped forward, and in one fluid motion I placed both hands on either side of her face and kissed her. I didn't care about the circumstances. I didn't care about the legit mental ramifications if this was all just another delusion. I didn't even care what-in-the-zombie-girlfriend-hell was going on. The one and only thing my soul cared for was to kiss Jacinda O'Neill.

It had been more than six years since the last time I kissed her.

Six long years of absolute hell that saw me torn down to nothing, struggling to rebuild any semblance of life—the life after *her*.

With that kiss, I felt hope again. With that kiss I found strength.

The same beautiful pain nearly crippled me when our lips touched, and after each and every night spent alone, hoping that one day I'd feel her lips again, it was nothing less than paralyzing. She kissed me back, her arms wrapping around me instinctively, soaking up my warmth and clutching me close.

When we were out of breath, we stopped and held each other, tightly wrapped together and inseparable. Whole. We fit together perfectly, like interlocking pieces of a puzzle. In her arms was my only home, the only place I had ever felt secure and comfort—the only place I ever felt like I belonged.

With the impulsive hypothetical out of the way, next came unsurety and doubt.

I needed to know. For sure.

"Queen?"

She looked at me, puzzled at first—as if to say, "what an odd time to play this game," before she hummed the chorus to "Crazy Little Thing Called Love" with a lip curl that would have made the King jealous.

It was definitely her. And I dove back in.

"Why," she said, coming up for air, "does it feel like I haven't seen you in a very long time?" Her forehead scrunched like it always did when she was confused.

Pulling away, I stole a long look at her, studying her face as she studied mine. I admired her constellation of freckles as she lifted her hand to trace the scar across my forehead and cheek with the tips of her fingers. Then she ran her hand through my hair.

"You haven't aged," I said. I couldn't hide my bafflement.

She was barefoot, wearing a dirty dress that may have been white once upon a time, with yellow and green embroidered flowers. It looked old, vintage, but not her style.

"What?" she asked. She was lost in her assessment, trying to pinpoint what was different about me, besides the obvious. I could tell she knew something wasn't right.

"You still look twenty-seven," I said.

"Uh huh, I am twenty-seven, dork," she responded, her tone riddled with sarcasm. "You were there with me, remember? The party with Anne and Marsh and everyone." She raised her hand to my scar again and felt its rough edges. "What happened to your face, babe? Does it hurt? Nice haircut, by the way."

"No, Jace," I said, unsure how to explain the situation. And where would I begin? *Hey babe, so, you died? Don't you remember?* "I'm thirty-three."

"Sure, you are," she said playfully. "And I'm Freddie Mercury."

"If true, that would be awkward," I deadpanned. "Look at me, hon. We haven't seen each other in six years." I stepped aside and gestured for her to take a look at her own headstone, then watched her reaction carefully.

If it wasn't so heartbreaking, it would have been a fascinating experiment—show someone their grave and see how they react. Jaycie read the inscription, and at first, she scoffed and shrugged it off like coincidence. This reaction was quickly followed by a second, more serious look full of denial.

"I don't understand," she said. "Is this a joke?"

"I wish it was."

She looked like she was going to fall, then winced as a thought passed behind her eyes. "Please," she said, looking woozy, beginning to shake. "Take me somewhere. I don't want to be here."

We had been driving for a few minutes in silence when she began to play with the radio. She was wrapped in my leather jacket and an emergency blanket I found in the trunk. The car's heat was on full blast, but it didn't ease her shivers. She flicked the car radio to a classic rock station that was once her favorite and found it was now a crappy top-forty station playing music she had never heard before. Out of frustration, she channeled around and found each song as unfamiliar as the next. Jaycie's musical knowledge was legendary. She knew nearly everything. Music was like her compass; without its familiar tones, she was lost.

I reached over and dialed to the new classic rock station while she balled herself up into a fetal position to warm her frozen toes.

I wanted to be there for her. I wanted to comfort her, but I knew she needed to transition to this new reality on her own. Jaycie didn't enjoy being doted on while she was processing—she had to come to me.

"They changed it a few years ago," I explained, then paused and clarified. "Your station, I mean."

"Oh." She rubbed her left ring finger, like it hurt. Before I could begin to analyze what that meant, she said, "I remember."

"How much?" I asked.

"A lot."

"Where did you come from?" It was the most obvious question that I had been waiting to ask. Seemed like the kind of thing she would have already offered if she knew.

"I don't know," she responded. "What happened to my ring?"

"I don't know," I replied. "Marsh promised me it was with you when…I wasn't there. I wasn't allowed to be there when they—" I gestured ridiculously downward. How was I supposed to say *when they buried you?*

"How?" she asked. "How'd this happen?"

The look on her face told me she was speaking specifically to the miracle. I shook my head. I didn't have answers, only questions.

I could smell the saltiness of her tears beginning to roll down her cheek. She grabbed my hand and shifted in her seat to place her head on my shoulder. I imagined all the thoughts running through her mind and prepared myself to make this transition as easy on her as possible. I decided it was best to comfort her until everything could be worked out.

"Where are we going?" she asked.

"To find clothes," I said, placing my arm around her while I drove. "And a hot shower to get you warmed up."

We drove to a thrift shop next to the China King, where Jaycie grabbed a pair of boots, jeans, a warm sweater, and an old corduroy Sherpa jacket. The next lot over had a pharmacy and a gym. We grabbed soap and all the essentials, then I went into the gym and distracted the receptionist as a new customer while Jaycie slipped inside.

Right before we parted, I asked, "Are you going to be okay?"

"Yeah," she replied. She sounded like she was plummeting. Like the dark thoughts were catching up to her.

"You'll come back to me when you're finished?" I asked.

My words must have hit something solid. She looked up at me like my words hurt, but she realized they didn't hurt her nearly as much as it hurt me to ask them.

"Yes, I'll be back," she said. "Love you." Then she kissed me.

As she showered and dressed, I waited impatiently in the car. Everything was quiet. Too quiet. The brain-trust hadn't been that quiet since they showed up—after I went human-flambé on the floor of my apartment.

"Sir," said Henry, breaking the ice, "let me begin by saying we are all very pleased with recent events. However, one must be vigilant. Do not let down your guard."

Just what I needed—a buzz-killer.

"It's really her," I said. "This isn't some dream. This isn't a fantasy I concocted inside my head. She's here. She's alive."

"Agreed on all accounts," said Henry. "Yet there are so many questions left unanswered. How? Why? Where did she come from?"

"My man," said Montoya, "it does seem fishy. She died six years ago."

"I know," I spat. "I was there."

"Then you clearly need someone to smack some self-preserving-sense into that thick head of yours," said Jamaal. "We've seen some crazy shit over the last thirty-six hours. This is by far the craziest."

"Are you suggesting it's not her?" I asked. "I know that woman. I'd know an imposter. I'd know if I was being tricked!"

"Would you?" asked Doshin. "The heart may cloud the brain on the sunniest occasion."

I sighed, not just because I was frustrated, but because I knew they were right. I'd been a sucker for that girl ever since I met her. Was I giving her too much trust? Was I being a fool?

"What if this is a trap?" suggested Jamaal. "That guy on the phone, he wants to break you. What if he did this? What if he set this whole thing up?"

"Or," added Henry, playing devil's advocate, "it really is Ms. O'Neill, and we are only seeing the tip of the proverbial iceberg."

"You're talking about two complete extremes," I argued. "In one scenario she's an evil agent in disguise. In the other, she's the real McCoy."

"Who is McCoy?" asked Doshin.

"Perhaps," said Chappy, "both scenarios are true."

"How so?" asked Jamaal.

Chappy stroked his gray beard. "Everything is possible. After all we have already witnessed, how could we discount anything? It is true she died and was gone for six long years. It is true that there is an evil maniac out there who wants to destroy Tony, and we do not know to what lengths he is capable of going." Then Chappy leaned forward to speak directly to me. "The only one of us who knows this young woman is you, Tony. Be careful. Not just because she might not be all she seems, but because if she is, you must protect her heart as staunchly as you have protected your own since she has been gone."

Jaycie met me back in the parking lot thirty-five minutes later, looking like her normal self. When she got into the car, I was smiling ear to ear.

"What's that grin for?" she sassed, smiling herself. The shower and fresh clothes seemed to brighten her mood. Everything felt like it did back then—before it happened. It was like we hadn't missed a single beat of our own drum—it was our way, like it always was.

"I never thought I'd experience this again," I said honestly, even with ten sets of imaginary eyes watching me.

"Oh, yeah, those trivial weekdays sneaking in and out of public showers. Such great memories." She grabbed my hand and threaded her fingers through mine, then sat back and sighed. "What happened?"

"When?" I asked.

"After," she said. She was ready to hear it—as I said, on her time.

"Well, the Phillies won the world series, and Michael Jackson died. And—"

"No way," she said. "Wait, MJ died?"

"Yeah."

"And your team, the one that never wins anything, won the World Series?"

"Yeah, but I wasn't really there to see it."

"Tell me."

I took a deep breath and tried to find the best place to begin. "I was arrested. They thought I did it, and my prints were on the gun. Marshall bailed me out. Mr. Berry, my lawyer—I guess you know him," I said, and she nodded. "He argued that the only evidence was my prints, and that given the way they found us, I picked the gun up...*after*. I was acquitted but threatened and harassed. Everything fell apart, including me. Then I lost it and attacked a cop. I didn't know where I was or what I was doing, and they admitted me to Northcreek Psychiatric Hospital. While I was in there, my dad died."

Jaycie squeezed my hand, and I could see the flash of guilt in her eyes. She was blaming herself for it. Parts of me had blamed her for a long time. Why did she do it? Didn't she know it was going to destroy me? But blame disappears when you miss someone so much.

"I'm so sorry," she said. "How long were you there?"

"Four years."

She was squeezing my hand so tight, as if the harder she squeezed, the faster she could atone. She cried and attempted to stifle the sobs that shook her entire body. Then she leaned over and kissed me passionately, using our connection as a sedative.

"I don't remember much from that day," she said. "I remember the ring. I remember an ambulance, but not much else. I know you have questions. You're holding back. I can see it on your face."

"I don't want to ask them and ruin things," I said. "I have never and will never stop loving you. Not for a moment."

"Keep me warm?" she asked after she straddled my lap, fitting carefully between myself and the steering wheel. The look in her eyes was all the invite I needed to relive the only fantasy I ever had or wanted, the fantasy I thought was lost to me forever.

She was scared. I could see it in her eyes as she could see it in mine. Neither of us knew how much time we had left together. Everything seemed so fleeting and borrowed. If I was going to lose her all over again, I wanted one last memory. One last time to say a proper goodbye.

I held her for hours, until the night broke and the sun rose behind a gray veil of clouds. We were huddled together in the backseat, her head resting on my chest, when she finally spoke.

"How did you do it?" she asked.

"How did I do what?"

"How did you survive without me? I don't think I could have survived without you."

We weren't codependent. We had bad moments, but we didn't have an unhealthy relationship. Jaycie and I had a bond. We were best friends, lovers, inseparable. Lock us in a padded cell and we'd have the time of our lives together. She was my complement—my other half—we were stronger together. Yet without her, I crumbled. Words could not accurately describe the void she'd left in my life, nor the misery that arose in its place.

"I didn't. Whatever my life has become through the last several years, it's not been anything worth living," I explained, then added, "I wished it was me."

Jaycie sat upright and glared at me. "Don't you dare. I know you suffered, and I would do anything to take that away from you, but if you had died instead of me, what good would that have done? I would have suffered just the same without you. Would you have wanted that?"

"No."

"I don't remember why I did what I did, but I feel deep down inside that I did it for the right reasons. I won't abandon you again," she promised. From the moment those words left her lips, I knew she was wrong.

We sat there in silence for several minutes. I was caressing her hand when she propped herself up and looked at me.

"Does it hurt?" she asked, touching the scar on my face. Luckily, my deformity didn't scare her off. They say chicks love scars, but I'd be willing to bet chicks don't appreciate being squeamish.

"No."

"What is it?"

"I don't know."

"Do you think it's connected to me? Whatever that is?"

"No, I don't think so," I lied. Jaycie was like my personal lie detector, but whether or not she caught my untruthfulness, she didn't let on.

"Do you think it's magic? Witchcraft or something?" she asked.

"The scar?"

"No," she laughed. "Me. Being back."

"Funny you mention that."

"Why?"

"Nothing," I said, shaking my head. "Just something dumb."

"How dumb?"

"Brad sucking cake crumbs through a straw," I replied.

As she laughed, something strange happened. Something that caught my attention immediately and made every inch of my skin break out in goosebumps.

"Yeah," said Montoya. "I know you saw that too."

"What happened?" asked Jamaal. "I missed it."

Jaycie's face flickered. Not like a television flicker, but like it was sagging—not grotesque, or anything sinister—into something else for the briefest second.

"Are you okay?" I asked her.

"Yeah, why?" she replied.

"Nothing." I sat up and stretched my back.

"My man, I know you saw that," said Montoya. I could sense he was feeling skeptical from the very moment she appeared. This event did not help to put those fears to rest.

"Sir," said Henry. "Be careful. There is undoubtedly more to your lady friend than her appearance."

"I don't care how dumb it was," argued Jaycie. "It could have been Marshall singing the Gummi Bears theme song after shots of saké-level dumb." She was recalling his twenty-fifth birthday celebration at a sushi bar in Mercy Point. All video evidence was destroyed, unfortunately. "What was it?"

I wanted to laugh, but the memory of what had happened to Marshall made me grimace instead. Whether Jaycie saw it or not, I tried to move the conversation onward, but how was I going to say, "Tori Martin thought you were a witch," without it sounding absurd?

Instead, I took the easy way out. "That's a long story." It was a story I didn't wish to discuss, especially not after what I had just witnessed. There was something supernatural about Jaycie, and as much as I loved her, I needed to know what it was.

Tap tap tap!

There was a cop standing outside the car, tapping on the window. I half expected him to arrest me for driving around with a stolen vehicle—though, stealing was an obnoxious word for what had transpired. I commandeered it to escape the clutches of an evil pair of deranged goddesses—see? Much less obnoxious.

"You can't park here," he demanded with an irritated groan, and we agreed to move. Like it or not, I had to choose a destination.

"Where are we going?" Jaycie asked once I settled behind the steering wheel.

"We need to check on an old friend."

THE OMEGA

III

prelude to evil

JACINDA
Then.

What had I learned about you, Jace?

I was beginning to feel like I never really knew you at all. You were tortured, but you were a fighter. You had the kind of unrelenting spirit that fought back when things were tough, even when you were just a kid. However, the trauma was adding up.

You blamed yourself for the tragedy that took your sister's life.

Your mother was a piece of work. An abusive user who went through life in a cloud of lithium and misery.

Your father was a workaholic.

And your Grammy passed away and left you all alone and unloved.

These elements by themselves were enough to send a girl to therapy. Yet I believed they were all the start of something larger—a prelude to evil.

December 26th, 1988

It was the day after Christmas, and you were bored. The O'Neill household had emptied of cheer twenty minutes after presents were unwrapped the morning before, when your mother retreated to her bedroom and your father disappeared into the study for work. It didn't feel like Christmas without your sister and Grammy there. You could even still remember Grampy, always snapping photos and dozing off next to the fireplace. You and Jane would put leftover tinsel on him as he slept, pretending he was a snoring Christmas tree.

But those days were gone.

You'd spent the last month at a private boarding school in Mercy Point and only arrived home a few days before the holiday. You missed your parents and your own bedroom, but when you returned, your mother hardly acknowledged you were there, and your father was too busy with an open case to spend time with you.

You felt like a ghost in your own home, wandering the rooms to spare yourself the boredom. Eventually you settled into your bedroom, picked up your guitar, and played until that too became boring. At some point, you began staring out the window into the woods behind the house, and then you caught sight of the neighbor kids hanging out by the tire swing at the forest's edge. It was cold, and there were still banks of snow on the ground, but joining them was better than sitting inside, alone.

You and Amanda Hemmels were friendly, but the boy, Robbie Maynard Morris, acted strangely whenever you were near. Times change, but some things, like Maynard's aversion to you, never did. Maybe he didn't like girls, you thought? Or maybe he didn't like you?

You grabbed your coat and ran through the hedges, dodging patches of icy, half-melted snow that had refrozen where the drifts had deepened. There were five houses in the small neighborhood a few miles from town and a few miles still from the waterfalls on Cross Road— each in opposite directions. Your house was the last in the row, followed by the Berrys, the Hemmels, the Morrises, and the finally the Reeses at the far end. Each house was bordered by a combination of shrubs and fir trees that provided a modest amount of privacy.

Ducking under a few branches, you emerged out the other side into the Hemmels' backyard, where Amanda was attempting to stand on top of the tire swing.

"Hi, can I play too?" you asked. You hadn't seen Amanda since you left for boarding school. You didn't even have the chance to say goodbye.

"Oh brother," groaned Morris at your arrival.

"Jaycie! Sure!" cried Amanda. "We're about to go on an adventure."

"We were?" Morris continued to groan.

"Well, now that we have a new adventure companion, of course," she said.

"Wait up, you guys!" screeched the voice of another girl, jumping through the hedge and trailed by a German Shepherd that was twice her size. "Can Pajamas and I come too?"

Morris skittered behind Amanda, shielding himself from the giant dog, who was more interested in playfully licking faces than eating them. You could tell Morris was deathly afraid of the dog and moderately afraid of you. He looked faint. Morris—Maynard—the same person, but a far cry from the guy I knew. When I met him, he was as cool and smooth as a horror movie survivor, with a "been there, done that" personality.

"Of course, Whitney," said Amanda. "A loyal knight and her trusty steed are always welcome to join our party."

"Party," groaned Morris. "A party sounds like fun. This isn't fun."

"Why not?" asked little Whitney Berry, removing some wild hair from her face. She was three years younger than the others and tried to play with the neighbor kids whenever they'd let her.

"Because," said Morris, looking at Amanda for validation, "you're too young."

"Am not!" screeched Whitney.

"Let her come," said Amanda. "Besides, we can't turn down an escort from the Behemoth of Cross Road."

"The what?" you asked.

"Pajamas! He's the Behemoth. And we're the Cross Road Crew! C'mon, you guys! We have to talk like adventurers if we're going to go on an adventure into the Black Forest."

"I thought your mom said no adventuring into the woods?" said Morris as he wiped his glasses. They'd fogged up the moment the dog arrived, who had been sniffing in Morris's general area from the end of his leash.

"She did," said Amanda as she grabbed a stick and tested its sturdiness. You did the same, followed by Whitney, who didn't want to be left out. Pajamas instantly thought it was a game and started chewing on the other end of Whitney's stick.

"Stoppit, Pajamas!" said Whitney, and he immediately complied.

"Where are we going if we can't go into the woods?" asked Morris.

Amanda looked at you and smiled, then shrugged at Morris. "We're not going into the woods."

"Oh, good," said Morris, relieved.

"We're going into the Black Forest!" said Amanda. "Sally forth, cadets!"

Amanda checked to see if her mother was watching before she dashed beyond the forest's threshold, past a series of pines that hid them from view on the other side.

Amanda led the way, followed by you, then Whitney and Pajamas, with Morris grumbling in the back. You each carried walking sticks that doubled as wizarding staffs or swords of legendary power, depending upon the need. Amanda politely sparred with you, pretending the sticks were lightsabers as you all paced into the unknown.

Where Amanda and Morris had explored from their house all the way to Highway 13, you never so much as stepped thirty feet beyond the boundary. You were amazed by the world just beyond your back door—a whole mysterious place to explore—a place to get away whenever you were home from boarding school.

There were huge evergreens and windy paths, even a rushing stream down the hill, and those was only the first few things you saw as you looked out across your new kingdom.

Seeing the two of you together, Jace, it made me teary. The two most impactful women on my life: you and Amanda. What I would have given to have you both here with me.

"What are we looking for?" asked Whitney.

"That depends," said Amanda.

"Depends on what?" groaned Morris indignantly.

"The adventure, obviously!" replied Amanda.

"What kind of adventures are there?" asked Whitney.

The question made your fearless leader stop dead in her tracks. She spun around to face you, looking shocked that anyone could be so devoid of ideas for intrepid escapades. She exasperatedly said, "All kinds," then shrugged, as if prompting the rest of you for your own recommendations.

"We could look for treasure?" you suggested.

"We could search for ancient ruins?" suggested Amanda as you continued on the journey, brainstorming for the proper adventure.

"Or we could track down villainous spies?" you offered. The proposition drew wide-eyed anticipation from Amanda.

"Or we could go home?" added Morris glumly.

"Or we could hunt foul, hideous monsters?" said Amanda as you climbed over a fallen tree, Pajamas and Whitney crawling beneath.

"We already found a big hairy monster," said Morris under his breath, still unhappy that Pajamas had accompanied you.

"One time I found a monster under my bed," said Whitney. "And Pajamas killed it."

As if on cue, Pajamas huffed, accepting his accolades proudly, as you and Amanda exchanged a suspicious glance.

"Of course he did," grumbled Morris.

"What do you mean you found a monster under your bed?" asked Amanda.

"Are you sure you didn't imagine it?" you asked. You had yet to see real monsters, even though I knew they existed. Although I had no way of knowing if Whitney had actually seen them or not.

"No!" said Whitney as she stomped around in her bright red galoshes. "My whole family saw it too!"

"There's no such thing as monsters," you said, and I shook my head as you and the others passed beneath a series of low-hanging evergreen branches and wandered through a patch of thick brier. Morris danced through it as if the sharp thorns were poisonous, with a look of pure dread on his face.

"That's not true," said Morris. "Amanda fought one just over there. Tell her, Amanda, how you wasted a Breacher."

"A what?" asked Whitney.

Everyone stopped, and Amanda looked mortified. Amanda had once told me this story, a long time ago. But she'd told me she had dreamed it all, fighting a monster with a laser cannon and saving the world with someone who looked like her brother.

"Yeah, you said you saw your brother that night," added Morris.

Bingo.

"But your brother's dead," you said. You said it casually, like the word "dead" was nothing more than a simple adjective. You, having gone through so much death already in your young life, seemed desensitized to the finality of it. I know you didn't mean it, but ouch, Jace. It was a brutal start to a friendship.

Amanda looked at Morris and said, "Robbie Maynard Morris, what on earth are you talking about?"

Morris flinched at his full name. "That night two summers ago, when you saw the flashing light in the woods, and you said you went out and wasted a Breacher from another dimension."

"What's a Breacher?" you asked.

"Yeah, what's a Beech-cher?" said Whitney, tongue-tied.

"That was a secret, Morris!" growled Amanda. "Why are you being such a jerk?"

"I'm not being a jerk!"

"You saw your brother?" you asked. "How?"

Uh oh. I could see where this was going.

"I don't know. I thought I did. I didn't know it at the time, but it looked like him in the dark. He left before I could find out."

"But your brother's dead," you said again, as if Amanda needed another reminder.

"That's what we were led to believe," she said, sounding like a true conspiracy theorist.

You shook your head. "When people die, they don't come back."

"I saw my brother," said Amanda. "He came back."

"No!" you screamed. "People die and don't come back." Then you started crying. Morris looked uncomfortable again, while Amanda looked stunned. Whitney was having difficulty following the conversation, but Pajamas knew. The dog galloped over to you and licked your hand. When you looked at him with his big dopey smile and his tongue hanging out, it was hard to be upset.

"Pajamas doesn't like it when people cry," said Whitney. "He always cheers them up."

"I know what I saw," said Amanda.

"Why would your brother come back?" you cried, and Jace, I knew what you were thinking.

"I don't know," replied Amanda somberly.

"Why didn't Jane come back? Why didn't Grammy come back to me?" You sobbed and covered your face to hide the tears. My heart broke for you all over again. It was unfair, wasn't it? Despite the impossibility of it all, you didn't like thinking that other people got the one thing they wanted, while you were left missing your loved ones forever.

"Maybe her brother was a ghost," said Morris.

"He wasn't a ghost!" scolded Amanda.

"My mommy said that ghosts aren't real," added Whitney. "But the monster under my bed was real. I saw him."

Amanda rolled her eyes and started to reply but stopped when you stormed off.

"Where are you going?" asked Amanda.

"Home." You were too embarrassed to stay with them, too confused and hurt to go on adventures through the woods. You had run halfway home when you spotted your mother watching from her bedroom window on the second floor. She didn't yell at you for adventuring into the woods; she didn't even seem to care.

You wiped the tears from your eyes, but you didn't break your stare. You were daring your mother to do something. Daring her to pay attention.

To scold you.

To ground you.

To yell if she must.

Instead, your mother turned away and closed the curtains.

You cried so awfully it was like you were grieving—grieving for your failures and your losses, the unfairness of your reality. You wanted to belong. You didn't want to feel loneliness. You fell into depression so young, and every time you found reprieve—a grandmother's love— potential friendship—something to hold onto and hope for—it slipped through your fingers like dry sand.

Drifting over to the back-porch steps, you sat down as the world blurred behind your tears. You didn't want to be home. You didn't want to explore the woods. You didn't want to be anywhere.

And then, magically, you got your wish.

Jace, you disappeared from reality.

A girl, a human girl, slipped into the Veil—the mirror-world—the place between spaces on Earth. You were unaware of your surroundings, lost within your sobs. But if you had lifted your head and dried your tears, you would have found yourself in a world of trouble.

The Veil was like a pocket—out of the way, collapsed, hidden. Step into the Veil, and you were in the world behind reality, where angels and demons dwelt—and worse. Inside the Veil was like an upside-down world, where the senses muted and light inverted—and sometimes, if you were in tune with someone on the other side, you could even hear their thoughts. It wasn't meant for mankind, and only the most power- ful Fallen could pass through the barriers between the two worlds. Light was dark and dark was light, two realities out of phase and fighting over the same physical space. For those with the inability to break through from one world to the next, it was like a prison—they were damned to see reality but could never touch it. Most of the imprisoned pretended reality was never even there, lurking and rotting until the very end.

When little Jacinda O'Neill, you, willed yourself into the Veil with thought alone, it was like sending up a nuclear flare. All creatures in tune with the Veil were notified that something wrong and noteworthy had just transpired. Your action awoke every awful thing that slept and ceaselessly wandered, jostling them from their distant deep sleep.

I watched from nearby, debating my involvement. This was the past, and what happened had already happened. You'd survive this brush against the supernatural, and yet, I wondered *what if?* Could I influence the future? Had I already played this part, affecting the past to preserve the future that already was? The possibilities were like trying to decipher a David Lynch movie—the more I thought I knew, the less I actually knew in the end.

And then there were paradoxes. I could intervene and end the world—like a game of Russian roulette—a random punishment for attempting to exist in two places at once.

As you cried, the dark things closed in, if nothing more than curious as to what kind of creature had breached into their world—was she Fallen? Unnatural? Or something else? Some creatures crawled, others hovered, some flew, and a few even dragged themselves up from the muck, all for a glance at the creature that woke them.

Once they realized it was merely a girl, their curiosity became hunger. I stepped forward, putting myself between them and you, and ignited both hands in hellfire—a warning that you were protected—

—screams.

Shrilling screams cut through the muted drafts of the Veil. They were the kind of screams that meant trouble, like something terribly wrong had transpired, and like a stage hook to a bad act, those screams yanked you back into reality.

You left the Veil at will with panic in your lungs. You hyperventilated and shivered as a cold sweat mixed with your own tears. Shock could have overcome you, the exertion of moving between realities pulling you under, when an eerie sensation crawled up your spine at the sound of a faint call.

"Help!"

It was twilight—a whole hour had coasted by in a matter of minutes behind the Veil.

"Help!" yelled Morris.

You ran to them. You ran through briar bushes, climbed over fallen trees, and ducked under low branches. You ran without stopping, straight for your target, like you knew where they were. You felt a calling in your gut, like you were needed. Jaycie, I know you were never afraid of much—you were afraid of long car rides and saying goodbye—obvious childhood traumas, but you never believed in true evil, not yet. The shadows in your room at night were friendly, and the basement under your house with the old boiler and the hidden damp corners never terrified you. Jaycie, you didn't know danger, and when you heard those screams, you only thought of helping. That's who you were—kind, brave, and generous, a true example of humanity.

"Help!" cried Amanda.

When you came running out of the forest, the scene unfolded in abstracts. They were nestled onto a bank beside a flowing creek. Half a dozen dead crows lay on the ground around them, one of which was slowly floating downstream. Amanda was cut, with streaks of red running down her face and neck. She was swinging her stick around like she was fending off an invisible threat. Whitney was holding Pajamas and crying uncontrollably, while Morris stood shockingly pale and covered in mud—his eyes bulging from behind his glasses. It was only after a second look that you noticed Pajamas was limp and lifeless—his big furry body draped across Whitney's lap, the blood staining his handsome fur coat.

"What happened?" You dropped from the ridge above and onto the embankment with a big splash of semi-frozen mud. Before anyone could answer, there was a rustle from the thick brier on the opposite bank—a whole span of rushing water between you—in the direction of Amanda's stick. It sounded like a moan mixed with a pleasant coo of surprise. The moan was followed by a grinding chewing noise, like a person imitating a coffee grinder.

"I don't know," cried Amanda. "Something attacked us from the bushes and grabbed Pajamas. It bit him and I hit it with a stick."

"He's not breathing," cried Whitney, as she held Pajamas in her arms.

When you stepped forward to inspect Pajamas—his body as lifeless and wet as a bathroom rug—something shifted in the briar behind you.

"What attacked you?" you asked. Morris shivered at the question, then raised his hand and pointed at the gently swaying mass of thorns and weeds. On cue, the headless corpse of a crow was tossed into the air and landed at your feet, making you and the others yelp in surprise.

Then the creature, whatever it was hidden in the shady bush of thorns, spoke.

"Little girl," it said. "I can taste you from here. Come closer, please?"

Morris raised his stick with both hands, the end of it shaking erratically.

You squealed and backpedaled beside Morris. The voice sounded oddly familiar. You grabbed Whitney's stick from the mud and pointed it at the brier, like the others.

Amanda cried, "Leave us alone."

"Little girl," it said, "you remind me of someone—from long ago, long ago, long ago? Time is a construct, not a constant. It's all relative."

"Leave us alone," you shouted.

"I came from so far away," it said. "You put me there. You sent me far away, and just now I crawled back home. Naughty girl. You stepped beyond the Veil and called all kinds of dark things. Like Pandora opening her box."

"Does it know you?" asked Morris. "It didn't talk until now." Morris, for his part, wasn't crying. He was deathly afraid, and every inch of him shook, but he was always afraid—maybe he was a high-functioning fear-a-holic and could handle it better than the others.

"Red hair like fire. Green eyes like grass," it said. "I have a secret to tell you, my dear." A bony old hand slammed into the dirt, and in the failing light they could see the tracings of paper-white skin and a mouth.

Amanda and Morris screamed as it dragged itself from the thorns. It wasn't quite a man, yet it had all the basic parts and proportion of one. Except the eyes, which were like black holes devouring the light from its face. The creature crawled forth and unfolded itself into an upright position—bones and vertebrae realigning—a shapeless thing finding its form once again.

Jace, that thing was evil. I could taste it and feel it down to the very core of me. He wanted you. He was drawn to you. I wanted you to run away, but you stayed there, with your new friends. You wouldn't leave them, not even if I stepped out of the Veil and tried to drag you away.

"Who are you?" asked Amanda.

"I have many names, child," it said as it wriggled forward on disjointed legs.

"Stay back," you warned.

"Tsk tsk, child," it said, limping forward to the water's edge.

"Stay back!" you yelled.

"Yeah, stay back!" yelled Morris, stepping forward next to Amanda. The three of you defiant in the face of true danger.

"Extraordinary girl," it said as it scanned the area. "So many allies came to protect you."

Could he see me? I stepped closer, ready for a fight.

The man was like a fever dream—like a memory that had blurred—but you had the creeping suspicion that you knew him and had forgotten.

Amanda picked up a rock and chucked it, striking the man in the shoulder. He looked over at her as if he hadn't seen her standing there—as if he only had eyes for you, Jace.

"Leave us alone!" screamed Whitney.

"You're the fulcrum, dear child. The means to an inexplicable end." His old rotting shoe touched the edge of the icy waters. "Come with me, child. Others will come. Surely, they will. I can end it all for you."

You were as terrified as the others, Jace, if not more so. The man spoke to you as if you knew each other, and it was more than enough to send a chill up your spine. And mine.

Then the old man let out and awful groan as if he was gathering immense strength, and the ground started to shake beneath your feet.

This wasn't normal. This was awfulness that no child should ever witness. This was nightmare fuel. All you wanted was for the man to leave and never come back, and inside your chest, something gave way. You closed your eyes and screamed, "Leave us alone and go back to where you came!"

The world listened. All was quiet. All was still, but you swore you heard a door slam shut inside your head.

"Where did it go?" said Morris, after catching his breath. The creature was there one moment, then gone the next. Even I had no idea what happened, and I never blinked.

You opened your eyes, peered back and forth for some sign of the old man.

"I don't know," said Amanda.

"I think he's dead," said Whitney, drawing their attention back to her best friend.

Amanda's tears streamed down her face as Morris's legs finally gave way, and he fell onto the bank and broke down.

"What was that?" asked Morris.

You could tell by the way you looked back at the spot where the old man disappeared that you felt somehow responsible. Had you called him there? You were already blaming yourself, but it wasn't your fault, Jace.

You and Amanda went over to Whitney and knelt beside her—you needed to see Pajamas for yourself—and you took the dog's paw in your hand. It was cold, and from the moment you touched his fur it felt empty, and you were reminded of seeing Grammy, lifeless within her shiny wooden coffin.

"Pajamas protected me," said Morris. The shock of it overwhelmed him.

"He protected all of us," said Amanda. "That man tried to get us, but Pajamas jumped in front and barked at it."

"No," you cried. "No no no!"

Your cries made Whitney cry harder, and Morris began whimpering like he was half his age.

"He's a hero," wept Amanda.

The look on your face—grief, determination, sorrow, frustration. Is this when it happened, Jace? Is this when you finally realized you were different?

Angels could perform miracles, couldn't they? Could I do something about this? Where would I begin? How could I bring something back from the dead?

That's when something happened. I'd seen it once before—like the August heat rising off blacktop. Something changed—things rearranged—and when it was finished—

"What are you guys doing?" asked Whitney. She was standing at the top of the bank, looking down at them, with Pajamas wagging his tail beside her. "We heard you yelling. Pajamas wanted to come rescue you."

When you looked down, you realized you were no longer holding a cold furry paw, but Amanda's mittened hand. The two of you looked at each other, shaken and confused.

"What just happened?" asked Morris. "I don't understand what happened?"

"You guys! Why are you crying?" asked Whitney. "C'mon, the sun's going down and my mommy's gonna be mad."

That was the day you and Amanda became best friends. It only took a miracle for you guys to bond, but without it, I worry what you would have become, Jace. Would you have fallen into despair like me?

Sometimes, things really did come back from the dead.

July 4th, 1989

Independence Day was never one of your favorites. You enjoyed holidays like Halloween and New Year's Eve the most. Those were holidays spent with friends rather than family, which was why you liked them so much. Thanksgiving, Christmas, and Fourth of July were the toughest. Those holidays were for family.

Thanksgiving was when Grammy used to make her famous yams and stuffing, and your mother would make you and Jane set the table. Even at eight years old, you had too many painful memories of Thanksgiving—some you couldn't even remember, but they were there. At Christmas, Grammy and Grampy would spend the whole week with your family. Her and Grampy with armfuls of gifts knocking at your door and singing "ho ho ho."

But it was 4th of July you liked the least. It was always uncomfortably hot, and after being slathered in sunscreen lotion, you'd still end up getting burned in the summer heat. You remembered Grammy's potato salad and Grampy flipping burgers at their house in Mercy Point.

You and Jane would run around in the backyard, throwing a frisbee or blowing bubbles after watching the parade pass on the front sidewalk.

Oh Jace, I wished I could take this pain from you. It was unfair. And what was about to happen was going to change the course of your life. Maybe I could do something? Could I change history? Could we avoid the toxic people that tried to ruin our lives, together?

"This year is going to be different," your dad said as everyone loaded into the car. It was noon and didn't feel like a holiday. You were strumming away at Grammy's guitar when your mother popped into your room and told you to get dressed. She picked out your clothes, which was something she hadn't done since Grammy's funeral, and gave you fifteen minutes to get downstairs.

"Where are we going?" you asked.

"Mind your father," said your mother.

"My new boss invited us to his barbecue," said your father.

"Will there be other kids at the barbecue?" you asked. There was nothing worse than being the only kid your age at a party where you didn't know anyone.

"Yes," said your father. "In fact, I believe my boss's son is about your age."

After struggling for many years to make ends meet with his law partner, Brian Berry—Whitney's father—James O'Neill came into some luck when he met Everett Jansen. Brian told him not to represent that "crook," but James wasn't going to let ethics get in the way of a big payday.

Sure enough, the payday landed, and James and his family were moving up in the world.

When your family arrived, dressed in their Sunday best—James in slacks and a polo, and Saoirse in a sundress with a hat right off the Kentucky Derby concourse—it was you, Jaycie, not your mother, who felt antisocial. You hated the dress your mother picked out. It was itchy and looked like something a little girl would wear. You hated wearing it and wanted to be home with your guitar while you had the time to practice. The stuffy nuns at the boarding school didn't appreciate your strumming at night before lights out, and when you played you felt close to Grammy. But you were stuck, about to meet one of the worst things that ever happened to you.

The Jansens' house was one of the largest homes in Anemone Manor, the most affluent section in all of Grace Falls. Their house looked like a small hotel, with a drive-up pavilion and a four-car garage. It was three stories high, and every part of the lawn was meticulously cared for by a team of landscapers. There were ten cars parked outside, all of them worth twice as much as your father's sedan.

When your father rang the doorbell, you stood behind them, despite your mother tugging at your arm.

"Be good tonight, Jacinda. No whining like usual," said your mother.

"I don't whine," you said.

"Oh no? You just whined about whining. Be on your best behavior tonight so mommy and daddy can impress some people, okay?"

Jace, your mother was insufferable. How did you put up with it? You were old enough to know that she was being rotten. You knew the difference. You remembered a time when she was caring, if only a tad overwhelmed by parenthood. Could you snap your fingers and send her far away like the old man?

You were so different than them. How did you get that big golden heart of yours? How did you grow up into the most amazing woman I ever knew?

Everett Jansen answered the door—a smarmy fellow with a smoker's jacket and a glass of scotch in hand. He looked as if he'd stepped right off the back nine and sauntered into the country club for a good hobnob and soiree with finger foods served on silver platters by waiters in tuxedos. "James! Glad you could make it," he said.

"Everett, this is my wife, Saoirse, and my daughter Jacinda," said James.

"Hello Saoirse, I've heard so much about you," said Everett.

"We brought this for the barbecue," said Saoirse, handing Everett a bottle of wine.

"Oh, why thank you," said Everett. "You shouldn't have. I've never even heard of this." He said it with enough fakeness that even you could tell he wasn't fond of their inexpensive offering. "We'll have to get it open right away."

"Say hello to Mr. Jansen," said Saoirse, tugging at your arm.

"Hi, Mr. Jansen," you said.

"My my! Aren't you a cutie! How old are you, dear?" He squatted down to your level to ask.

"Eight," you replied.

"Well now, that's the same age as my son," he said, then turned over his shoulder and yelled, "Richard! Come out here!"

A boy wearing an exact replica of his father's clothes walked into the foyer. He had blond hair and blue eyes, and he was already much taller than you.

"Introduce yourself, son," said Everett.

"Hi, I'm Richard," he said confidently. "But you can call me Rick."

"Well now, looks like they're becoming fast friends," said Everett. "There may be some wedding bells in our future, huh?"

Your parents laughed and followed Everett into the next room, as Rick continued to stare at you, like he was mesmerized.

"Why are you staring?" you asked, taking the words right out of my mouth.

"I never saw a redhead before," he said. "Even your eyebrows are red."

Eight years old, and he was already an astute asshole.

"So?"

Then there was a long pause, and Rick smiled like he had a brand-new toy.

"I won't marry you," he said.

"Why not?" you asked, semi-offended.

"Because," he said snidely, "I'm only going to marry the prettiest girl."

Even back then, Rick was a total shithead. Jace, you should have run right then and there. Instead, Rick denied your acceptance, and in doing so made you want it more than anything. It was manipulative and rotten, but it worked. I wish it hadn't. I wish you could have seen right through it, but maybe, this was how it had to be.

Then, from that moment on, you wanted nothing more than Rick's attention.

THE OMEGA

fear and terror

MALUS
Now.

How was evil defined? Was it merely the opposite of good? Or was it the extreme lack morality? Depravity? Corruption? Throughout my existence, I have often found myself pondering the idea of malevolence.

Was I evil? Can an insane man view his own passions as evil? Or did one need their sanity in order to see the truth of their actions?

Did it take the opinion of the masses to bestow such a label? And what if the masses cannot see the intent and the reason behind the actions?

Are we not all the hero of our own story? The protagonist striving to better their own life?

If evil was simply profound immorality, what about the complexities of the moral compass? What was moral to one may not be moral to another. What if my immoral behavior had reason? What if it was for noble intentions, but immoral by someone else's method? Could one be both evil and good, depending on the point of view?

Once upon a time, I thought I was good. I was a righteous man who was wronged and would stop at nothing to make it right. Eventually, my desire to right that wrong became a selfish quest—to destroy everything in order to assure the wrong was righted. There was no doubt that evil had rested its sorrowful, icy grasp around my beating heart.

It was then, and only then, that I came to admit it to myself.

I am evil. I am deranged. I am the wicked.

But I did not do what I did, for myself.

After all, the road to hell was always paved with good intentions, and it was indeed a bumpy, lonely road.

I had two open contracts. With the voids left by Summanus and Mammon, I needed to find two Fallen—two powerful Fallen who could aid me in my quest to corrupt the girl's mind. There were two such beings on my list. Two such gods who could break her defenses and reconstruct her memories in whichever way I desired.

September 7th, 1962
Point Pleasant, NJ

Some gods hid away. Others lived in plain sight, blending in as an indigenous people of their chosen region. There were others who lived in temples and ruins, the old places where humans had abandoned. A few existed elsewhere, in worlds parallel to our own. Some of them needed to be coerced into meeting with me. None, as of yet, had turned down my offer.

Although most would rather sign my contract than experience the alternative.

It was the dead of night, in a suburban town along the eastern shore of the United States. Only there could you find people with warm beds and soft pillows. These modern times had made the dreams of men richer, as the great masses comfortably slumbered in their first-world bedding.

The richer the dream, the easier it was to send a message. And what better way to send a message than through the dreams of an innocent.

I was told by the spirits that she was special to him. Little Holly Harrison. Morpheus liked children. They imbued him with the most power. When children dreamed, their imaginations created the most lucid vibrant constructs of unreality. Grown men and women lacked the innocence of a child's imagination, and their unreality suffered for it.

Holly's bedroom was decorated in pink and lavender and the redolence of sugar. There were knickknacks on a table beside the bed, which was adorned in soft toy animals she appeared to be swimming in. Her room was her sanctuary, bringing meaning to the little princess who enjoyed ice cream and porcelain dolls. She was the epitome of innocence and comfort, surrounded by toys and love that many children had died desiring. How awfully corpulent humans were, soaking up valuable resources and comforts while others drowned in poverty.

Positioning myself beside Holly's bed, I gently placed my hands on either side of her head and brushed the fine silk hair from her face. She stirred but did not wake. She was much too deep in fanciful dreams to wake for me.

Leaning close, I whispered into her ear.

I spoke directly to him.

"I call upon winged Serapis, the god who carries dreams.

I speak to one sweet Somnia, the god who whispers sleep.

I bid master Morpheus, the god of all who slumber.

The Sandman come, when I call thrice.

Morpheus. Morpheus. Morpheus."

When nothing happened, I placed my hands to the child's throat and threatened to rip it open like a gift-wrapped present.

"Stop."

Sometimes, threats are all we had to bargain with.

"When did summoning our brothers become so contemptuous?" I asked.

"Why do you believe you are my brother?" asked Morpheus. He was no more than two white eyes in shadow. "I have no interest in listening to a mad man and his mad plan."

"You consider me mad?" I asked with a slitted smile. Morpheus and I had crossed paths once before, and it was slanderous to consider me anything less than ambitious. I may have been insane, but was I truly mad? Or was I just willing to go to extremes to right a wrong?

"I can see the madness in your eyes. I can taste the sourness of discontent and anguish upon the air you inhabit. Qualities I saw in my brothers before they locked Somnia away in the land of dreams, and bestowed The Nightmare King with untold power. They made a deal with the Boggleboo, and the silver gate was opened. They were mad, but your plight reeks of worse."

"When we succeed," I said, moving away from the girl and into the center of the room, "you will have the chance to right the wrongs done upon you and Somnia."

"I do not believe you intend to keep that offer."

"Brother," I said, but was instantly cut off.

"I am not your brother. I am an Oneiroi. I am no Fallen, nor was I ever an Angel. Erebus died defending our kind from the Omens and megalomaniacal Fallen. I will not bargain with you." He said it calmly. Unafraid, almost bored.

"We are the same, you and I. Our goals are as similar as blood to wine," I said.

"No. We are not the same," he said as he left the shadows and stepped into the beam of moonlight that fell into the room from a window on the opposite wall. Morpheus wore silken robes of black, his icy cold white skin wrapped taut around his wiry body. His head was bald, but stoic, if not kind. Despite his life of darkness, there was no evil within him. He was right: he wasn't like the rest of us. He could wear his wings openly without the fear of vindication, a prime rule for Fallen if there ever was one. "You forget, I know you. I know your fears and your desires. I know your soul and the delicate yearnings of your heart. You forget I once walked the halls of your fantasies and shook the pillars of your nightmares. Do not offend me with your comparison, as I am all too aware of who you are and where you come from, boy."

Without another word, I lashed out and threw all the powers of the dead at him. The combined spool of ectoplasm and psychic anguish would have made the almighty Ra bend a knee and should have obliterated Morpheus from existence. To end Morpheus was to wipe out the last existing memory of me and what I was, the price worth every ounce of accumulated power I had gathered.

Morpheus needed to die, and with him all of my secrets.

The spool slammed into him and grabbed hold, then against all their attempts to bring Morpheus down, the ghastly forms dissolved and broke apart. Morpheus did not smile, nor did he lash out in anger. He merely stepped toward me and allowed the dead to wither behind him.

"Dreams are all the slumbering dead have left."

Morpheus stood before me and stared deep into my eyes. I saw it all. He knew every truth, and every fear I kept.

"Do you still dream? Do you still think of her? Or has all of what you were been torn apart in your selfish search?" he asked.

I fled behind the Veil and watched him. He leered at me, as if he knew I was still there. As if he knew what I was intending to do, he sat down on the edge of the bed and protected little Holly from any form of retribution. When the anger finally resolved itself within me, I leapt through time and space in search of someone else.

Someone with more reason to trust.

Someone with more reason to trust me.

February 22nd, 634 B.C.
Lemnos, Greece

There was a rumor he might be there.

A long-lost island in the middle of the Aegean Sea was the perfect place to hide. After the War of the Gods, some attempted to live a human life. Others hid, wasting away in solitude at the fringes of civilization.

When I arrived on the island of Lemnos, it was all but abandoned. Livestock roamed the streets and moldy food rotted on clay plates. The villagers were gone, but the port was full—every boat still docked in the harbor. It was a mystery I intended to unravel as I marched inland, then north along a well-traveled path into the mountains.

The small isle did not have much vegetation. It was a rock with craggy nooks and loose coarse sand, which made it difficult for the villagers to have disappeared inland. From a certain height, one could see from one side of the island to the other, and it was empty of all human life.

Along the northern shore was a crack in the earth—a narrow pass split the mountain in two at its thickest. Beyond the crack was a small grove of brightly colored poppies, surrounded by six stone pillars bearing three large stone slabs. Upon them was the same inscription repeated six times.

"Somnia Portae Terrae," I said aloud. "Gate of the Dream Lands."

The gate, hidden within the poppy grove, was a great hole that corkscrewed straight into the earth, burrowing down into the mountain so deep that the air drifting from its depths was cold and damp. As the sun began to set, I sat upon a nearby rock and smiled. The poppies, although alluring, were a trap.

The dead had told me so.

Unlike the rest of the island, the soil within the grove was rich and fertile.

It was littered with the villagers' remains.

The caves were not meant for man.

Like Morpheus, Hypnos was nocturnal, the god of slumber. Combined with my own mastery of mesmerism, his abilities would put Lilly into a reconstructive hypnotic state—a trance that would allow us to rebuild her glamour and chip away at her resolve. Time had always been my ally. However, time was no longer on my side.

I needed an immediate solution to fix my problem. I needed to penetrate the girl's mental defenses, to tear them down and build a series of glamours on top. Her soul was mine, but her mind? Her body? Her heart? These would fall in order, one by one.

Once she was under my complete control, there was only one obstacle left. One last impediment that would be leveled by the tide of my wrath—I had to recollect the stolen key.

Every moment since Nemesis stole the Key of Capricorn was like a sharp hot poker jammed into my eyes. I'd trusted her. I saw the potential. I understood the rage within her. Of them all, she had earned my confidence—faithfully following me into battle and guarding Lilly—and look where that trust got me.

There were things I would do when I found her. Terrible things, the worst atrocities one could do to another celestial. It was said there were ways to pierce the very Grace of a Fallen—to puncture it like splitting an atom. The pain followed by the explosive disaster would be an extraordinary sight to behold.

Just for her…

"Sometimes I wonder," said her voice, "what thoughts travel through your mind when you go still."

"Do you care to know?" I replied. When she did not answer, I stood up from my perch and walked toward the poppies under the moonlight. The sun had set in the middle of my revenge fantasy, and it was time to see if the god of slumber was home.

Down into the earth, the cave entrance led me into an antechamber lit by torch. The chamber, though natural, had a spring of water pooled at its center with passageways branching in every direction. Along the wall was a great slab of silver. At its center was a keyhole surrounded by assorted messages in many languages—some long since dead—describing the destination beyond the gate.

Alterumterra—the Dream Lands.

The silver door was cracked at its base, leaking the pooled water into the room. The water appeared as silver as the door, surrounded by an evaporating wispy fog.

"The Lethe," I said. The River of Forgetfulness—I remembered it well, from long ago, before I had ascended into the creature I had become.

A voice said, "Pale Traveler." It was a hiss—wispy and devious.

"Hypnos," I said, "I have come with an offer."

The walls were moving.

No, not moving…

Sections of the wall were shifting. Each slithering slowly, slipping into position on either side of me. The movement was slow, but methodical, preventing me from grasping the size and shape of the threat. They were like insects, altering their coloration to match the rocky walls.

"No," spoke the one on the right. "Not Hypnos."

It suddenly made sense. Hypnos hid away to remain in anonymity, obliterating the mind of the traveler who came upon his home. These creatures, however, were predators—the way they moved to surround me, blocking my exit—they were hunting.

They killed the villagers.

Could they have killed Hypnos as well?

With a snap of my fingers, I bade the dancing torch flame to rise, filling the room with light. The shadows gave away their position, and together they emerged from the walls, unfolding their insectile bodies to address me like men. They were both inhumanly slender and tall, but their similarities stopped there.

One had tough, shark-like skin as black as oil, with blood-red horizontal lines along its body. The second had pale rubbery skin with jagged yellow markings.

They were like poisonous frogs or insects—marked for danger.

But the strangeness of them was amplified by their co-dependent features—the dark one was gifted with only a great big tooth-filled mouth upon its face. The other's face was equally as blank, with two white orb-like eyes.

Sight and speech split between them, reliant on the other half to fill in the missing senses.

"My, my," I said, "What are you?"

I had never seen such ghastly beings. My Thirteen were an assorted lot of horrors—some humanoid, others less than—but these two were only mimicking a bi-pedal being.

"This subterrane is home to Phobos and Deimos," said the one with the mouth. "You are trespassing, Pale Traveler."

Phobos, god of fear. Deimos, god of terror.

"Is this no longer the dwelling of Hypnos, god of sleep?" I asked. Their presence in the room was dominated by the sensation their markings made upon me. They were fear and terror personified, connecting to some far corner of the mind, the id, that begged me—beware.

"No longer," said Phobos, with a mouth full of perfect teeth. His smile was like a frown—somewhere between both, making all his words appear as a threatening gloat. "The god of sleep slumbered with his eyes wide open, so that he might look upon his beauty in a mirror. We distracted him and swapped his mirror with those that burned the ships assailing Syracuse. Hypnos burned himself to death. His own vanity was his ultimate end."

"Why?" I asked, as Deimos circled his brother like a moon. The more I looked upon them, the more they appeared like insects—creatures that could poison with a single touch or bite. Did they always appear like this? Or was it part of the fear they instilled? Was it magic?

"We wanted to learn his secrets," said Phobos.

"Did you?" I asked.

"We did," said Phobos, as I noticed his brother's orbit around him growing larger, nearing himself to me. "We wonder, what secrets do you possess, Pale Traveler?"

Deimos's movements were hypnotic. He converged and touched the skin at the back of my neck before I knew what was transpiring, and I immediately shivered. A terror overwhelmed me, and I witnessed wild smoky tendrils extending all around me, like vaporous versions of Dagon's great cephalopod arms.

"What is this?" asked Phobos, as he and his brother approached to inspect my hallucinations. I was wracked in fear, stricken with terror and unable to move. "Secrets you hide. We like secrets. We ate the sleep god's bones, sucking the secrets from the marrow. We will devour your secrets too."

"Netron," I said. The god's power over me vanished, vanquished upon the revelation of his true name, and I struck at once. Deimos immediately cowered under the wrath of the dead. I pinned the god down beneath the fury of every man, woman, and child the brothers had slain and eaten since they destroyed Hypnos, threatening to dunk the fear god into the Lethe, to obliterate his mind. Deimos's bones creaked and popped under the duress before I gave them both an offer. "Do you truly own the pathways of sleep? Taken from Hypnos himself?"

"We do," hissed Phobos. The worry for his brother was evident.

What good was Fear without Terror?
    "Then let us strike a deal," I said with a smile.

V

friends

(III)

JACINDA
Then.

I've watched you for years, Jace, but I still haven't found the truth. What are you? What secret are you hiding? Could I have missed it? Has it yet to reveal itself? I want to know. I want to know so I can do something about it.

June 21st, 1993

Ever since your family moved to Elm Way Acres, an up-and-coming neighborhood in Grace Falls, you saw less and less of Amanda. Summers allowed for sleepovers, mostly at your house because your mom was never around, and you girls would have the whole house to yourselves.

From the moment school let out, till the very last days of summer, you and Amanda were inseparable. At twelve years old, you were both coming into your own, leaving childish things behind as you ventured into the first steps of adulthood. You spent countless hours talking and laughing and snacking on sugary sweets. When you weren't together, you talked on the phone, planning your next sleepover.

You both took every opportunity you had to be seen together in public. You got rides to the town square or the new local mall, hoping to see friends or run into cute boys. You shared a similar taste in pop music and classic rock, and you laughed for hours on end, being goofy together. You read books, watched scary movies, and put on musical performances—you on guitar and Amanda on drums. Though Amanda was never any good at anything with rhythm except being a backup dancer—and even that was disputable.

The two of you even went to the drive-in movie theater together, near Northcreek. You saw *Hocus Pocus* and *Jurassic Park*, geeking out on witches and dinosaurs. You inspired each other's weird like two silly twelve-year-olds should.

When you weren't being silly, you talked about boys. Jace, you only knew one boy your age that wasn't Morris, so Amanda did most of the talking. Besides, I don't think you felt comfortable calling Rick a crush…

…At least not yet.

Amanda told you about all the cute boys, especially Grant Gross, and about all the cool stuff that the kids at Grace Falls Middle School enjoyed. In some ways, this was your only connection to the real world—private school was so isolated that it was like living on a different planet.

Seeing you both together, Jace, it made me smile. I immediately recognized the commonalities that brought Amanda and me together—the same traits that were planted by the two of you building pillow forts and watching movies. I wish I could have known you back then. I wish I could have been a part of it.

"What do you want to do?" asked Amanda. She was wearing a Frankenstein mask that was once her brother's Halloween costume, staring up from her bed. The glow-in-the-dark stars stuck to the ceiling had browned over time and barely glowed anymore.

It was a rare sleepover at her place. You'd needed to get away for a night. Your mother was on the warpath and being extra sensitive about noise.

Taking a break from painting your fingernails lime green, you said, "I don't know. Want to write another song?"

You had already written two songs earlier that day. One of them was awful, but you had a great time writing it. Your guitar teacher, Dylan Jacobs, had agreed to jam out with you guys. He was better than a babysitter and took you both seriously when you wanted to start a band. Not many adults did that.

"Nah," said Amanda. "Let's go on an adventure."

"Out in the woods?" you asked.

"No," said Amanda. "I'm thinking we should explore the jungles of retail," she said with a great big grin.

It was late afternoon, and Mrs. Hemmels wasn't available to drive you to the mall, so Amanda snagged her walkie talkie and called for backup.

"What? Over," replied Morris over the walkie.

"We're looking for adventure, Morris," said Amanda. "We need a ride. Over."

"Why are you asking me? I don't drive. Over."

Amanda rolled her eyes while you facepalmed with an audible smack. "Not you, dummy! Your mom! Over."

"Why would my mom take you to the mall? Over."

"We're inviting you too, Morris. Over."

"Okay, fine," he said, then paused and added, "but only if you stop calling me Morris. Over."

"Uh, whatever shall we call you? Robbie?" sassed Amanda. "Over."

"My middle name. Over."

"Why on earth would anyone call you Maynard?" yelled Amanda.

When you and Amanda met Robbie Maynard Morris and his mother next door, she loaded you all into the mini-van and drove you across town to the mall. She dropped you off in front of the Macy's department store and promised to pick you up in three hours as she ran errands, leaving just enough time for a half-dozen laps around the mall.

The Grace Falls Mall was a two-floor, figure-eight behemoth with more than two hundred twenty stores and a food court that fed nearly half the tweens and teens of Grace Falls on a weekly basis. The three of you entered the mall and made an immediate march to the food court, despite the allure of the video game store that nearly swallowed Maynard whole.

On your way, you passed several kids your age, and Amanda gave you the inside scoop on every one of them.

"Erica's nice, but she's a total drama queen," said Amanda.

"Yeah, she was great in last year's play," offered Maynard.

You giggled. I knew that giggle well, Jace. That was the giggle you always gave me when I was being daft.

"Ugh, Morris!" groaned Amanda.

"Maynard!" he corrected her.

"Okay, fine," she said, "May-nerd." After she rolled her eyes in a complete three-hundred-sixty degrees, she said, "That's not what drama queen means."

"Oh," he said, as he rolled up his flannel shirt sleeves and removed a long clump of hair from his face.

"You need a haircut," said Amanda.

"No way," said Maynard. "I'm going grunge."

"What's that?" you asked, and I actually rolled *my* eyes at you.

"You know," he said with a shrug, "Nirvana? Pearl Jam?"

You didn't know what he was talking about. Away at school, nobody ever talked about music. It was such a sterile environment that you fell out of touch with everything. You thought Maynard was just looking sloppy, when in reality, he was expressing himself.

"I don't know them," you said, and Maynard's jaw dropped.

"She's at private school!" growled Amanda. "Leave her alone."

"Can you show me?" you asked. "I'd like to hear them."

"Yeah," said Maynard, nodding his head. "We can go to the record store." He looked excited, like someone was finally speaking his language.

The food court was swimming with long queues of people in line for various fast foods from burgers to pizza to salad, even froyo. Beyond the chaos was a sea of tables, most of which had been gobbled up by shoppers.

"Nard!" yelled someone in the crowd, and other people waved.

"What did they just say?" you asked.

"Nard," said Maynard. "My nickname."

"I thought Maynard was your nickname?" you said.

Amanda rolled her eyes again, exaggerated and overly dramatic, and I thought they might roll right out of their sockets. The both of you followed Maynard toward the table in the back corner.

"Jaycie," said Amanda, "this is Jess, Kurt, Cyndi and Trent."

Of course, Amanda knew them all—they were her friends too.

"Hi," you said. It was a lot to take in. A whole group of friends you had no idea existed.

"Hey," groaned Cyndi. "We can't add another girl. It'll be unbalanced." She was wearing more eye makeup than most adult women you knew. It made her gray eyes pop, and I could sense your jealousy. She looked older, and you still felt like a little kid.

"We're not," said Amanda. "She goes to private school."

"Oh, lame," groaned Cyndi.

"Hi, Jaycie," said Jess. "Amanda talks about you all the time. Welcome!"

"Wait, aren't you that girl whose sister died in that car accident?" asked Cyndi. She had the kind of look on her face that begged for your tears, and as the question lingered between you, a smirk began to sprout on Cyndi's face.

Interesting…

Did they all forget about her?

"Leave her alone," said Amanda, then to you, "Don't answer her."

"Whatever," groaned Cyndi.

It wasn't your first experience with how mean kids could be, but nobody at your school knew about the private things you suffered through. There were only six other girls in your class at boarding school, and none of them paid much attention to you. This was different. Cyndi wanted you to hurt. She wanted a response, to see that she had gotten under your skin, and you were too confused to give her one.

"Jaycie, want some fries?" asked Trent. It was a peace offering, with optional cheese dipping sauce.

"Heck yeah," you said, and I laughed. Of course, you wouldn't turn down fries, Jace. They were your favorite food, even if you'd never admit it.

After a quick bite, the group traveled the mall, checking out every appealing store, from scented candles to video games to clothing. When they approached the record shop, Maynard ushered you over to the CDs and began leafing through them all, starting at the top of the alphabet. His first stop was Alice in Chains, and he made sure to cue up their album, *Dirt*, at the listening station with headphones. A whole new world opened up to you that included more than just the classics Grammy played and the 80s tunes you and Amanda loved—like Madonna and Michael Jackson.

"What do you think?" asked Maynard.

"I like it," you said. You were overwhelmed. The style of the music was so different than the pop and classic rock you were familiar with. This music was darker, heavier, and moodier than what you were used to. It made you feel some kind of way that you liked but couldn't understand—not yet, anyway.

"Yeah, but wait till Nard gets to the letter N," said Cyndi as she passed you by, "Nine Inch Nails will melt your brain."

"Nine inch what?" you asked.

"Nails," said Jess, sneaking up beside you. "My sister—"

"Half-sister," corrected Trent.

"Half-sister," repeated Jess, "can't stand them."

"Forget Tori," said Kurt. "She's so fucking annoying."

Hearing someone swear made your eyes go wide. Funny, some things never change, Jace. You weren't used to such cavalier language. It made you squeamish. Still does. *Did. Does?*

"That's your cousin," scolded Amanda.

"Oh, I know she is," he said. "That girl can't live without a spotlight. It makes me gag."

Maynard caught sight of your confusion and decided to elaborate.

"Tori's a popular girl with a mean streak. It's hard to believe she shares the same DNA as Jess."

"Nobody's perfect," said Jess with a grin.

"She sounds awful," you said.

Don't worry, you'll meet her eventually, Jace.

"She's a Heather," said Cyndi.

"A what?" you asked.

"It's a movie reference," said Cyndi. "For fuck's sake, were you raised in a bomb shelter?"

"No," you said, feeling obligated to answer.

"Don't worry," said Trent. "Cyndi just pretends to be a bad girl too."

"Pretends?" growled Cyndi. "I'm the real thing, sugar." Then she wandered away and started flirting with the guy at the cash register, who was clearly over the age of consent.

You spent the next half hour listening to every song Maynard proclaimed was essential to your musical re-education. From Smashing Pumpkins and Nirvana to Type O Negative and Tool. You were blown away by them all and hungered for more. If it was up to you, you would have spent all day and night inside the record store, exploring new music.

"Hey Jace," said Amanda, with Maynard and Jess standing by the entrance. "Come on, we're going to the Cinnabon."

"Okay," you said, removing the headphones and placing them back on the shelf next to the audio controls, when someone bumped into you. I always wondered why Cyn had it out for you, and this was probably the moment that started it all.

"Hey," said Cyndi. "Put this under your shirt." She was holding a CD in its white plastic anti-theft packaging.

"What?" you asked. You were confused and couldn't understand why you were being asked. It seemed like a silly notion, to put something under your shirt.

"Take it, put it under your shirt," said Cyndi in a patronizing tone, "and follow me outside."

"Wait," you said, "no."

"Just do it," grunted Cyndi.

"No, I can't," you replied. You may have been naïve, but you knew what theft was.

"What are you, some perfect angel?" said Cyndi. "You're dressed like a ten-year-old and you act like you're a fuckin prissy princess."

"No, I don't," you spat. You didn't understand why this girl was being so mean. You didn't do anything wrong to her, Jace. Some kids just needed to put others down to make them feel better about themselves.

"Where did you come from, prissy princess?"

The store clerks were starting to notice your argument, and it made you feel uncomfortable. You didn't want to get in trouble—your parents wouldn't react well to receiving a call from mall security. Your heart thumped and your eyes watered, and you didn't know what to do. You were feeling panicked, Jace, and I could see you start to hyperventilate and break out in a cold sweat.

"Just take the CD and put it up your shirt before we get caught," said Cyndi, looking around. She jammed it into your hands and chest, as if to force you into compliance.

"No," you said, backing away from her—but you weren't looking at Cyndi. You were looking at something else. The blood drained from your face, and I'd seen that fear once before—the moment you said, "I thought you were the moon," fifteen years into your future.

"What's going on?" asked Amanda. She walked back into the store to see what was keeping you from leaving.

"She's being a total bitch," said Cyndi under her breath as she scrolled her eyes from side to side to see if anyone was watching.

"No! Leave me alone!" you screamed, startling the whole store. Was this some elaborate scheme to get out of a bad situation, Jace? Or were you actually being threatened by something other than the little Courtney Love wannabe?

"What's going on?" asked a clerk, while his coworker picked up the phone and dialed an emergency extension.

"Leave me alone!" you screamed again.

There was nothing there—not even with me behind the Veil.

"What the fuck!" screamed Cyndi.

You were shaking and staring off into the distance at the far wall, but there was nothing there. Whatever the fuck was going on inside your head, Jace, I wasn't sure if it was real. Along the wall was a display with new releases and posters, with an angled mirror above it, and you were staring into that mirror like you were peering right through it. Whatever you saw reflected there, nobody else could see it, and it frightened you so severely that every single inch of your skin developed goosebumps, and you peed yourself right there on the spot.

I couldn't see it, Jace. I paused time, checked back and forth between reality and the Veil, and there was nothing there. What could you see? What was it?

Then two things happened simultaneously—the first was the shattering of that mirror and the glass raining down onto the floor, followed by you running for the exit with the CD still in your hands.

You bolted through the entrance as everyone braced themselves against the loud crack and crash and ran straight for the nearest stairs. As the record store alarm went off, you ran down the up-escalator, slicing through the crowd, then ran through the nearest exit, into the parking garage, and out the other side. You ran across the road, splitting traffic, and cut through an old strip mall. You climbed over a fence and ran through the town square, then up over the Elm Way Bridge, and through the gates to Elm Way Acres. You didn't stop running until you had slammed the door shut to your room, dropped the CD you accidentally stole, and cried into your pillow.

You cried for hours.

When Amanda called that evening, you answered the phone in a daze.

"Hello," you said. You had only stopped crying a few minutes before.

"Hey, what happened?" asked Amanda. She was upset. "You ran and set off the alarm and they caught Cyndi shoplifting. My mom had to pick me up from the security desk."

"What are you talking about?" you asked.

"From the mall," said Amanda. "At the record store."

You looked at the clock. It was almost six in the evening, but you had no idea where the day had gone. You remembered waking up and going to Amanda's house, but nothing else.

"I don't remember," you said.

"What do you mean you don't remember?" Amanda was frustrated and sounded like she was about to say something regrettable. "We went to the mall. You were listening to music with Maynard. Remember?"

"Who's Maynard?"

"Morris! Robbie Maynard Morris! He wants to go by Maynard now," she growled.

"That's stupid," you said.

"It is, but that's beside the point!"

"I'm sorry," you apologized.

"Sorry for what?" asked Amanda. "For bailing on me?"

"Let's just forget it," you said. You felt like you were going to vomit.

"I can't forget it," groaned Amanda. "I got in trouble!"

"Please, forget it," you begged as you squeezed a few tears through clenched eyes. "Just please, forget it."

There was something behind that desperate plea, Jace. It was like you knew something was wrong, and you just wanted to ignore it. That's what you always did: you ignored confrontation. You were afraid, and what you experienced wasn't normal. Whatever transpired, you didn't want to be reminded of it. You forgot about it, and you needed Amanda to forget too.

That's when the air thickened, like a pulse of humidity that made the hair on my arms stand up as if zapped by a burst of static electricity.

"What were we talking about?" asked Amanda once the pulse subsided. She sounded confused.

"The record store," you said, as you spotted the stolen CD inside the white plastic security case on the floor and wondered how it got there.

"Oh," she replied. She sounded confused. She was no longer angry, and her tone immediately changed. "Hey, want to go to the mall tomorrow?"

"Sure," you replied, as you hummed the tune to an Alice in Chains song that was stuck in your head.

And like that, everything was forgotten. Amanda couldn't remember any of it.

Friends are hard to come by, Jace. If it was you that manipulated Amanda's mind, I don't blame you. You were so alone, and you couldn't afford to lose the one person who had your back. It was a small thing. Innocent. Did you know what you were doing?

If it wasn't you, who was pulling those strings?

I need to know. I have to know.

July 28th, 1993

After spending all Friday morning chatting away on the phone, Amanda's mom picked you up and drove you both to the park for soccer practice. Your coach, Dahlia Darby, led the Grace Falls Marauders—the twelve-to-thirteen-year-old girls' Summer League team. You had your third game scheduled next week, and the girls were excited, if not a bit overconfident after a 2-0 start.

"Listen up, ladies," said Dahlia, twirling a whistle around her forefinger as the team gathered on the metal bleachers. A few of them were still tying the laces on their cleats and chugging Gatorade from water jugs. "We have our third game in less than a week, and I need to know what we're made of before we go up to Northcreek to face the champs."

"We've got this, coach," said Amanda. She was the jokester of the team, always finding ways to make the other girls laugh.

"Do you girls know what the word hubris means?" asked Coach Darby.

"Isn't that the stuff they make from chickpeas?" replied Amanda.

"That's hummus!" you corrected her, then laughed.

You were happy, Jace. Young and carefree. I could see the spark of the woman you'd become. Even that silly little sideways grin you had when you were trying to be cute.

"Overconfidence, ladies. Hubris means you're overconfident," said Coach with a half-hearted facepalm.

"Coach Darby," asked Amanda once the team had stopped laughing at her expense. "Why are the boys practicing on the other side of our field?" She was already sweaty after spotting Grant Gross within a hundred yards of her for the first time since the last day of school. It was a robust three-year crush, and she was sure he didn't even know her name.

"Very perceptive, Manda," said Dahlia. "We're scrimmaging the boys' team today."

"But they're the boys' team," you said, ignoring the draining color from Amanda's face. The boys were running drills and appeared to be much more efficient than your team was at running them.

"Astute," said Dahlia sarcastically. "What's the problem, Jace?"

"Nothing, it's just—"

"Just what?"

"They're boys," whined another girl.

"You're all so observant," said Dahlia, looking annoyed. "Tell me, what can a boy do that you can't?"

The girls looked back and forth at one another, when one of them said, "Open a jar of peanut butter?"

"Sometimes," shrugged Dahlia.

"Grow a mustache?"

"Oh honey, give it time." Dahlia winked.

"Pee standing up?"

"Ewwww!" several of them screamed.

"Yeah, got me there," said Dahlia. "What else?"

"Nothing," you said. "They can't do anything we can't do."

"Exactly!" hooted Dahlia. "That's why O'Neill's my striker." Then Dahlia eyed them up and said, "Take a knee." The Marauders hopped off the bleachers, leaving their thermoses behind, and knelt by their coach. "Amanda, you're my Keeper, get in there and stop everything. The rest of you," she said with a smirk, "let's beat up on some boys."

When they took the field, you were lined up right across from a tall boy with a shaggy mop of brown hair and bright blue eyes. He smirked at you and said, "Hey, Red."

"Red's not my name," you replied coldly.

"So, what is your name?" he asked.

"Jacinda," you replied, thawing. "What's yours?"

"Kick," he said with a straight face.

"Kick?" you questioned.

"Yeah, cuz I'm gonna be all over your ass," he said, and a teammate high-fived him aggressively.

Damn, Jace. You fell for it.

"That's not even funny," you said, and I agree, but they weren't listening. They were too busy planning their kickoff.

The game started rocky. The kid named "Kick" took the ball right past you, dribbled up field, passed off, then made a break behind the defense. He was met with a perfect pass for an easy goal. He slid it right by Amanda without much effort, then high-fived his teammates and took a breezy jog back to mid-field.

Amanda looked mortified.

"You'll get it next time," you said, trying to get Amanda's overconfidence back on track, but she just shook her head and moped.

"That was Grant," said Amanda.

"Which one?" you asked, looking back up field.

"The striker. The boy that scored."

"That boy?" you scoffed.

Yeah, me too, Jace. Amanda's taste in men was notoriously awful. We shook our heads in unison.

"Yeah," Amanda nodded.

That kid was a jerk.

"Really?"

A total douche-nozzle.

"Girls!" yelled Dahlia. "What are you doing? Stop gossiping and get in there!"

You jogged back to mid-field, where you took the kickoff. You passed it to the wing and bolted down-field. You were cutting past the defense when the winger tried centering the ball. As it floated down, you leapt, attempting to head the ball further down field—

Jace, in all my life, I only saw one other person get hit like that— and she was a bloodthirsty vampire slammed by a bull-god...

The world went spinning as your legs were taken out beneath you.

"Foul!" cried Dahlia.

"Is she dead?" asked one of your teammates. They had surrounded you and were trying to help you up. Half of them were shocked you weren't concussed. Me too, honestly. You had never been hit that hard in your life and were still brushing grass clippings out of your hair when Grant wandered over.

"Sorry, Jacinda," said Grant. "Didn't see you there." He smirked and ran off as you inspected the cut on your elbow and felt a bruise forming along your shoulder.

"Are you okay?" asked Gretchen, one of your teammates.

"I think so," you groaned, and I could smell the scent of your adrenaline, taking away the pain and focusing your anger.

"Take the free kick! Jaycie! Take the free kick," shouted Coach Darby from the sidelines.

You walked over to the spot of the foul and set the ball, then waited for your teammates to get into position. You had scored from twice that distance before and were feeling good about your chances. You lined up your kick and sent the ball soaring into the upper corner—a sure-fire goal against any other team your age—when out of nowhere came the extended arm of the biggest goalie you had ever seen, knocking your shot away.

"How are we supposed to score against that?" said one of the girls.

The boys' goalie was already tall enough to jump and hang from the crossbar, and just in case they weren't aware of this unique skill, he leisurely showed them all moments later.

"Hey, are you sure that kid's only twelve?" shouted Coach Darby. "He's got a freaking five o'clock shadow!"

Amen, Coach.

Over the next five minutes, the boys taunted the Marauders like a cat with a helpless mouse, playing an elaborate game of keep-away. Eventually you got angry, made a play and stole the ball, then streaked out ahead of everyone—no wonder you ran track in college. The goalie charged, but you deftly sidestepped him, then sank the ball into the back of the net.

Fuck, yes!

As soon as you stopped running, you were knocked to the ground viciously. Grant stood over you and smiled as he held out a helping hand. You slapped it away and said, "Might as well drop the kick from your name, because you're just an ass."

Jace, you have no idea how big the grin was on my face.

Competition always brought out the beast in you. I was so proud, watching you stand up to them. You wouldn't back down to anyone—not even against impossible odds—so why did you give up fifteen years later? Why'd you leave me? We could have taken on the world together.

You didn't stick around for some dumb, boyish retort from Grant. You got up and jogged back to half-field and waited for kickoff. The next twenty minutes were a mixture of frustration and pure resilience as the girls managed to hold the boys off. The boys scored only two more goals, and you assisted on one for the girls.

When it was over, Dahlia rounded her team up by the goal, where they collectively guzzled Gatorade. You were exhausted, and Amanda was covered in dirt and grass stains, having spent most of the scrimmage flopping from one end of the goal to the other.

"That was good, ladies," said Dahlia.

"No, it wasn't," said Amanda. "We got our butts kicked."

"Yeah, you totally did," said Dahlia with a laugh, still twirling her whistle. "But that's not the point. You stood up to them."

Coach usually ended practice with a few laps around the field, but she gave them all a reprieve this time, since they were spent.

You and Amanda left at once, walking from the park to grab ice cream from the town square a few blocks away. It was your normal Friday practice routine, and Amanda's mom would pick you up from there in fifteen minutes.

"Grant is gross," you said. "I'm not even trying to make a joke about his name."

"You don't know him like I do," said Amanda, despite the fact that she didn't know him at all.

"He's a jerk," you replied bluntly.

"Of course, you'd say that."

"What do you mean?"

"Because all the boys like you."

"That's not true."

When you arrived at the ice cream stand, there was already a line of people, most of them from various teams and practices from the recreation park. Amanda spotted a few of the boys and immediately tried to hide amongst the line.

"What's wrong?" you asked. Amanda was never bashful, and it seemed odd to start now when she was all set to order her usual triple fudge sundae.

"Some of the boys' team is here," responded Amanda.

"Maybe we should hide?" you suggested. You didn't know what the proper protocol was. What did Amanda want to do? Whatever it was, you were willing. She was your best friend. You'd do anything she needed of you.

"You've got bright red hair. How are we going to hide?" said Amanda matter-of-factly.

"Red!" said someone from behind.

"Hi, Grant," said Amanda, glowing. Her whole body went on like a fluorescent lightbulb, strobing until firmly lit, from uncomfortable and awkward to the star of the show.

You slowly turned to face your nemesis. He was tall, lanky, and held two scoops of ice cream in a waffle cone he was dedicatedly slurping on.

"Hi, ass."

"Whoa whoa whoa," said Grant, as a few of his friends gathered around. "I feel like we got off on the wrong foot."

"We didn't get off on the wrong foot," you said. "You stuffed them both into your own mouth when you acted like a total, violent jerk."

"What are you doing?" said Amanda, mortified.

"I guess it's true what they say," laughed Grant.

"What they say about what?" you asked.

Ugh, you asked for it, Jace.

"That redheads are feisty." Grant's friends laughed as the other kids took notice. A few parents tried to ignore the situation.

"Leave us alone," you growled.

"Stop, Jaycie," pleaded Amanda.

"I don't want to leave you alone," said Grant, forcefully.

"Amanda, why do you even like this jerk?"

"Oh my god, Jaycie!" she shouted. She was turning shades of red that made her blend right in with your hair.

"What?" you asked, oblivious. When you saw the look on Amanda's face, it suddenly clicked. You had just outed your best friend in front of the guy she liked.

"Whoa, Amanda Hemmels likes me?" laughed Grant, proving that he did know her name after all yet didn't seem to care for her feelings. At least, not the way he should. Amanda was the best. Fuck this shaggy haired fuckwad for not noticing.

"Ew!" yelled one of his friends, and I fought the urge to pop his head off like one of his bulging zits.

Amanda stormed off. You didn't mean to upset her, Jace. I know that. It was a slip-up in a high-pressure situation. It's happened to the best of us. You remember our first meeting, right? It took me a long time to forgive myself for that word-vomit.

When you caught up to her, you didn't know what to do.

"I'm sorry," you said. "I didn't mean to."

"They're going to make fun of me," said Amanda, tears forming in her eyes.

"Why would they make fun of you?" you asked.

"You don't understand," said Amanda. "You don't know what it's like."

"I don't understand," you admitted.

"I get teased all the time," said Amanda.

"Why?" you asked. "You're my best friend, and the most awesome girl in the world."

"Because I'm different!" Amanda's tears were like razors, cutting a thousand shallow cuts across your skin. "You go to private school. Everyone wears the same uniform. It's different for me. I don't own expensive clothes. I'm not as pretty as other girls."

"What do you mean? You're so pretty, Amanda," you said. It was true, you thought the world of your best friend, and I think it's an awful lesson to learn that there are those in this world who hold such superficial things important when judging others. I used to feel the same way when Amanda cried on my shoulder, Jace, just a few years from now.

I was lucky that you saw the beauty inside of me. Not many ever did.

"They think I'm weird, because I like comics and science fiction, and because I thought I saw my dead brother."

"Amanda…"

"Hey Red!" shouted Grant, catching up to them. "Hey *Amanda!*"

The jerk made sure to say her name, didn't he? It was like a game. In his defense, boys never know how to talk to girls, but even this tool knew he was antagonizing you. Sometimes I think my half of the species ruins it for the rest of us.

"Leave us alone," you shouted back to Grant and the other boys. They were across the street and Amanda wasn't slowing down.

"Now it's just going to get worse," said Amanda.

"What's going to get worse?" you asked.

"C'mon ladies," said Grant, catching up. "I just want to talk."

The boys were laughing, and they were relentless. They kept coming, following you down the street as you retreated. It was dark, and Amanda's mom would be picking you up soon, but Amanda just wanted to get away, and the boys wouldn't let her. Every time she glanced over her shoulder, they were closing in, several of them, hounding her with Grant in the lead.

"I just wanted him to like me," said Amanda. It was an overreaction, but she felt it. "He's more interested in you than he is in me."

"He's a jerk," you argued. "You deserve someone better than him."

"They always notice you," said Amanda. "Last week in the mall, all the boys noticed you. They don't even look at me."

"That's not true," you said, but you understood, didn't you? It was how you used to feel about Jane. You didn't notice all the attention, or how little attention Amanda received. In a lot of ways, you felt unnoticed too.

"Hey Red!" said Grant after giving his ice cream an extra loud slurp like he was kissing a cartoon. The kid was as annoying as silly-string next to an open flame.

"Leave us alone," you shouted, but they kept on coming, making Amanda more and more upset. You wanted to make them stop. Things were spiraling out of control.

"See? He's only talking to you," said Amanda.

"He doesn't even know my name," you argued.

"Does it matter?" Amanda snarled. It was the most upset you had ever seen her. She was livid and scared and sad and everything was just getting worse. Jace, you were always empathic, always felt what your friends were going through as if it was your own troubles—not that you needed any more of your own. Seeing Amanda like that did something to you, and you would have done anything to make it go away.

That's all you wanted. To make it go away.

"Hey Red!" yelled Grant, from a few short feet away. He was too close to be yelling like that, but he did it to get under your skin—and it worked. You felt it, like an electrical hum in your ears. A snap, and a pop, and the next thing you knew, you were spinning back to him with hot impulsive anger flaring from your eyes and mouth.

"I said, leave us alone!" you shouted, and something moved. A shift in the ether—a subtle commotion, like an unknown object falling in the next room—we could all feel the motion, even if we never saw it.

And Grant was flung twenty feet away.

A force—a formless shadow—snatched him up and tossed him from the end of your outstretched hand. When he landed, he was immediately struck by a mini-van, driven by Amanda's mom.

It all happened so fast. It was like you were watching a movie, and you didn't even react.

How did it happen, Jace?

There was blood. There were shrieking cries. It took a long time for anyone to actually respond to the accident.

"What did you do?" cried Amanda.

Your hand was still outstretched. You hadn't lowered it.

"I didn't mean to," you said, whispering. You weren't even sure you had done it, yet you were taking the blame. "I didn't mean to. I didn't mean to, I swear."

Grant Gross died on the spot.

Was that you, Jace? Did you do that? There were crows nearby, watching. There were always crows. Grace Falls was infected with them. Was there some nefarious plot? Or was it only you all along?

A month later, to avoid harassment and start a new life—away from the place that had brought them two tragedies—the Hemmels family moved to a small New Jersey town to start over. You wrote Amanda letters and called frequently, but Amanda very rarely responded, until one day she stopped responding altogether.

THE TAMING
OF MOLOCH

1265 B.C.

Fear was an emotion of instability. Fear destroyed men, burned cities, and toppled kingdoms. Eliciting fear amongst the mighty was problematic—to enlist an entity with such power as to strike fear within the powerful, meant searching for brainless brawn. Beings with might, but little intellect.

No fearsome faction could endure without the muscle to impose their will, and Malus knew exactly where to find it.

Moloch, the bull-headed god of sacrifice and war, was imprisoned by King Minos of Crete for copulating with Pasiphae, his wife. Daedalus, indentured master-inventor to the crown, was tasked with creating a grand labyrinth beneath Crete. The labyrinth was Moloch's prison, and the King's favored way to dispose of his enemies or win favor of the gods through ritual sacrifice.

Ariadne, the king's adopted daughter, had been entreated with the task of luring the monster into the labyrinth. She needed nothing more than her beauty, as few were as fair as Ariadne. Entranced, Moloch was placed into chains, bound forever to his prison, forced to eat the flesh of mortals in service to the king.

There the minotaur wasted away and became nothing more than a ferocious beast.

Until the day Malus strolled through the labyrinth's dank halls.

"Minotaur!" cried Malus. His flaming spear lit the dark passage. "Show yourself! I have an offer!" It was well after midnight, but long before the sun rose in the east. The labyrinth was humid and quiet and stank like rotted meat and filth. Stone walls, some carved and others built from loose rock and mortar, created an intricate maze that wound and twisted deep into the earth. Layer upon layer, the labyrinth drove down into the dark, but unlike other labyrinths there was no end, no way out. There was no escape upon entering. All hope ended with bloody death and bone-chilling screams. "Minotaur! Find me!"

The rattle of chain and the low rumble of a stampeding giant shook the labyrinth, and Malus knew the beast was near, tracking him down from somewhere beyond the next turn. The quaking tunnel shook grit and sand loose from the walls, unearthing dried bones. The dead were everywhere—mostly young Athenian maidens, marched in sacrifice as an official penalty for the death of the Cretan prince, Androgeos.

The rattling chains grew louder, and when the minotaur charged at Malus from around the corner with its massive black horns lowered, ready to gore its prey with either of its two-foot-long twisting spikes of menace, Malus did not flinch. With a small nod from their master, the newly risen dead took hold of the mighty chains that bound the beast. The chains snagged, drawing the roaring, manic beast to an immediate stop.

A sticky foam splattered across the wall as the minotaur raged against its bonds, spraying hot saliva in every direction. The creature's face was misshapen, long and narrow, but not quite the shape of a bull's face. There was obvious deformity: a shallow, flattened nose; animalistic eyes; a wide mouth with sharpened teeth that jutted from its lower lip; and a low-hanging, brutish brow that gave the beast a facade of pure nastiness. Its two black horns rose high above its head like curved, twisting pikes. The minotaur's skin was tanned and rough like hide, and his height and breadth were twice that of a man. His shoulders were as chiseled rock, carved down his arms into hands with great hooked talons that sprung from his fingertips. His legs were like the hind legs of a great attack dog, built for speed and power.

The beast was nothing but sheer rage and rippling muscle. Thick metal rings were embedded deep into his skin, looped around the large bones at the clavicles, and twice on each side along the ribs. Those metal rings were then attached to great lengths of mighty chain that kept the minotaur within the labyrinth but allowed him free reign of all the winding halls and tunnels.

To free himself of his chains meant tearing himself to pieces.

The minotaur raged and bucked, attempting to gain another foot or two, intent on goring or disemboweling his unwelcomed visitor. It had been some time since his last feeding. Malus may not have been a maiden, but he would do just as well to satiate the hunger.

"Are you finished?" asked Malus.

The beast calmed and dropped its head, ready to pounce should the opportunity arise.

"Ripping you apart, straight from the genitals to the throat, will bring me great satisfaction," it growled.

"Moloch," said Malus, addressing the creature directly. His own name forced a wince from the minotaur—it had been so very long since he last heard it. "I have an opportunity for you. The chance at power unlike anything you have ever seen. Join me, accept my terms, and I will set you free."

Moloch laughed hideously.

"You offer me great power, but there are none more powerful than I," gloated Moloch.

"Then free yourself from this labyrinth," stated Malus, who then walked away.

"Wait," grumbled Moloch, just before Malus disappeared into the inky gloom around the next corner. "What are your terms?"

VI

old friends

TONY
December 23rd, 2013
Now.

Robbie Maynard Morris was always an interesting guy. He started off as a geeky, cowardly kid, but grew into a tall, lanky, long-haired fellow with a genius IQ and a taste for good music. Amanda used to call him Morris—her adventure companion, and eventually he decided to go by Maynard. Nard to his friends, Maynard was the kind of guy you could rely on. We were friends who drifted apart, and though we hadn't spoken in years, I felt obligated to check up on him if he was still in town.

Someone had killed Amanda, and he'd threatened to kill everyone I ever knew to get even with me. Whatever my transgressions, I felt I owed Maynard to help steer him clear of any harm. The people I cared about, although few, were now fewer. Though I wouldn't say we were close, I was fond of Maynard, and there was a good chance he might still be local.

We pulled up at his parents' house around 10 a.m. and knocked on the front door. His old black van was in the driveway by the garage, with the words *"Under Consideration"* in red spray paint still scrawled across its side.

My eyes glanced to the spot just beyond their mailbox where Tori's car had been sliced in half as she pulled out onto Cross Road, more than ten years ago. The thought danced at the back of my mind as we wandered up onto the front steps.

Jaycie had her own memories here—she grew up three doors down and knew everyone who lived, for a time, in this short stretch of houses. She looked uncomfortable, like someone who might be accosted by the past at any moment.

"I still don't understand why we're here," said Jaycie.

I didn't tell her. I didn't want to freak her out that there was some evil fucker out there who was murdering people because of me—at least not yet.

"I need to warn him," I said as I knocked three times on the front door.

"Warn him of what? He's thirty-three, right? Why would he still be living at home?" she said.

The front door opened, and a sweet little lady wearing a lot of make-up answered. She had a great big smile and seemed thrilled to say hello.

"Hello," said Mrs. Morris. "How can I help you folks?"

"Hi, ma'am," I said.

"Oh dear!" she exclaimed. "What on earth did you do to your face?" She said it in the most supportive, motherly sort of way.

Jaycie snickered under her breath.

"It doesn't hurt," I said. "I'm fine."

Then Jaycie said, "Mrs. Morris, we're looking for Maynard. Do you know where we can find him?"

"Oh honey, you look so familiar," she said. "Do I know you?"

Jaycie shot me a glance and said, "No, sorry."

"You're a dead ringer for the gal who grew up next door," she said. I could hear Montoya and Jamaal laughing inside my head. There was, after all, some comedic charm to all this. "Anyways, how can I help you, hon?"

"Maynard," I said. "Do you know where we could find him?"

"Who?"

"Maynard."

"Oh! Robbie!" she said with a laugh and a playful swipe. "I don't know why he has everyone calling him Maynard. That was his great-great-grandfather's name, you know."

"Oh, I see," I replied, and Jaycie reached out and squeezed my hand. It was our secret way of saying that we were uncomfortable or wasting time. I'd once utilized this secret communication technique when I first met her father, and she purposely ignored it to get even with me for hogging the bed covers the night before.

"You're in luck, though," she said. "Robbie's inside getting breakfast before work. Come on in." Then she waved for us to follow her inside the house.

"Robbie still lives here?" I asked.

"Yes! Well, he lives in the apartment over of the garage. Please, take a load off! Make yourself at home," she said, gesturing to the couch, though neither of us did. Then she paced into the next room. "Robbie! You have friends!"

Jaycie walked over to the fireplace, where there were pictures hung on the mantle. One of them was a picture of her, Maynard, and Amanda. They couldn't have been older than ten, each of them in raincoats and rubber galoshes. The girls were laughing with their arms over each other's shoulders, while Maynard looked downright miserable.

When Mrs. Morris came out of the kitchen with a confused look on her face, I got the worst feeling—as if a monster was about to crawl its way out from inside her.

"I don't know where he is," she said, as we heard the sudden squeal of an old fan belt. By the time we got to the front door, the old black van was roaring down Cross Road at fifty miles per hour.

"Looks like you just missed him," said his mother. "That boy, always in a rush."

"I don't understand," asked Jaycie. We were almost to the Elm Way

Bridge when Jaycie asked the million-dollar question. "Why are we chasing him? What are we warning him about?"

Maynard's mom told us he managed the record shop at the Grace Falls Mall and would be working from noon till close. If we'd "find him anywhere, it was there," she said.

Jaycie eyed me carefully, and I couldn't help but look guilty when she scrutinized me like that. "What aren't you telling me, Oscuro?"

"Uh oh," said Montoya, laughing. "Girlie used your last name."

"You're in trouble," sang Jamaal.

I smiled despite myself. There was a method to my omission, and I didn't want to unload more crazy and depressing stuff on top of everything she was already going through.

Wiping the smile from my face, I said, "To protect him."

"Protect him from what?"

"I don't know."

"What aren't you telling me?"

"Amanda's dead," I said and pried my eyes off the road to view her reaction.

"Amanda? Hemmels?"

"I hadn't talked to her since high school," I said. "But someone is going around killing the people I care about. He killed her."

The look on my face must've told her something. She could read me like a children's book—all big type and simple illustrations. "Who else is dead?"

There was no sense in keeping anything else from her. "Marshall and Anne," I said as my voice cracked. "Yesterday."

"How'd it happen?" When I didn't reply, she asked again. "How did it happen?" Then the car's electrical systems flickered, followed by a stalling motor. It happened conveniently, seemingly at Jaycie's request. We coasted onto the road's shoulder, and I flipped the flashers on.

"What's wrong with the car?" I said, putting it in park and trying to restart the unresponsive engine.

"Answer me."

Taking a deep sigh, I said, "It's hard to explain."

"Try," she demanded, placing a hand onto the steering wheel next to mine.

I hadn't realized how tightly I had it gripped until she showed me. My knuckles were white, and my arm had a nervous tick—which explained the mystery tapping noise I was hearing. I thought it was the emergency flashers, but it was actually me.

"How do I explain something to you that I don't even understand myself?"

She sighed sadly, as if she knew that all too well. "Did they suffer?"

"I don't know. It was bad, but quick."

She nodded and wiped a stray tear from her cheek. It was then, without warning or even an attempt on my part to restart the car, the motor roared back to life.

"Did she just do that?" asked Jamaal. "Did she turn the car off and on?"

Jaycie twisted in the passenger seat to look into the back, then out the window as if searching for something.

"Did you just hear that?" she asked.

"Hear what?"

"A voice," she said. "Something about turning the car off and on."

In the rearview mirror I caught Jamaal's eyes growing as big as walnuts, as Chappy stroked his gray beard in thought.

"What the fuck is happening? Tony, my man, can she hear us?" asked Montoya.

"It just happened again," she said, looking at me, then into the back seat. There was nothing there, just a few bags from the drug store. "I swore I just heard your name."

"What are you?" I asked. It came out like an accusation, even though I didn't mean it to.

She looked at me and peeled away the accusation, followed by a softening that led to guilt. I could feel it building within her. I could smell it. She kept secrets, and for us to stay alive I needed to know everything about them.

"I don't know," she said, as tears filled her eyes.

Damn.

"I'm sorry. I didn't mean it that way."

"No," she said, wiping the tears away. "You have every right to ask."

I put the car in gear and pulled away from the shoulder as we approached the Elm Way Bridge. She squeezed my arm as I drove, and it was my turn to feel guilty—even I was still withholding information.

The two of us had no idea what we were as individuals, but we knew what we were to each other. We suffered because of it, just as much as we thrived. We had mysteries between us, and sooner or later we needed them solved.

It was a dreary day. Overcast and drizzly with a cold bite. It felt as cloudy as our uncertainty. What future did we have? Could we survive this?

As we crossed through town, Jaycie took note of the holiday decorations hanging from the telephone poles, and the decorated tree as we passed the town square. "Christmas," she said. "Of course, it had to be Christmas."

She hated Christmas—though, she never could explain why.

The decorations around town included banners strung across the main roads, printed with the lyrics to "Silent Night." They made me think of a question.

"What does *I thought you were the moon* mean?" I asked. Were they lyrics?

"I don't know," she replied, her head resting on my shoulder. "What's that from?"

The mall was empty that Saturday morning—however, that close to Christmas, it was sure to fill up fast. We entered through the food court and took the stairs to the second floor. Jaycie knew exactly where the record store was located, and I followed her until we found it tucked beside a vitamin shop. The mall had seen better days—floor tiles were dirty and cracked, the escalators were broken, and there were quite a few units closed with the previous signage still hanging in the windows. The mall reflected the rest of town: tired, decaying, and past its prime.

From outside the store, we spotted Maynard at the register, inspecting a clipboard. He was wearing a black t-shirt and his long hair was pulled into a ponytail. He looked older, but still the same guy I remembered.

"Maynard," I said, approaching with Jaycie following me a few steps behind. She was understandably apprehensive, so I took the lead.

"Yeah? How can I help you?" he replied in his best customer service voice without looking up from the clipboard. He was tapping his pen to the beat of the music playing in the store. His mind was a million miles away, and I was prepared to rock him like the hurricane playing over the speakers.

"Been a long time, pal," I said.

Without moving a muscle, his eyes slid in my direction. When he saw me, he gently nodded and said, "Tony. Of all the people I never thought I'd see again..."

"That's probably not true," I said, as Jaycie stepped out from behind me.

Maynard dropped his clipboard and the pen flipped into the air, followed by him shouting, "Shit! What the fuck?" and falling backward into a cardboard cutout of Gene Simmons.

"Hey Maynard," said Jaycie pleasantly.

"How? How are you back?" he asked.

"No idea," she said, shrugging.

"Oh god, it's the zombie apocalypse, isn't it?" His eyes were closed, and he took several deep breaths, as if on the cusp of an anxiety attack.

"Ehhh? Not the zombie apocalypse," said Jaycie, shaking her head. "It might just be the default apocalypse, though."

"No special flavor of the week, just apocalypse," I said.

"I mean, there is a touch of *dead rising*," she added with a smile, "but nothing more sinister than that."

"Well yeah," I agreed, "but just a touch. Anything more than that might be considered a *smidge* sinister."

"Is a smidge bigger than a touch?" she quipped. "I feel like it should be the other way around?"

Maynard shot us both a glance, then groaned, "Fuck, it really is you two. The lame banter gave it away."

"Hey, our banter is anything but lame," I said.

"I mean, it's got a limp at times," she added.

I shrugged playfully and shot her a smile.

"Why are you here?" he asked as I offered him my hand. Helping him out of the ruins of cardboard Gene Simmons was more difficult than it looked, as if Gene didn't want to let go.

"We came by the house to see you," I said. "To warn you."

"That's ironic," he smiled.

"Why's that?" I asked.

"Hey Tracy," shouted Maynard. A short goth girl was doing inventory on CDs and not paying us any attention. "Can you cover for me?"

Moments later we were in the service tunnels behind the stores, desperately trying to keep up with Maynard's long, lanky boot strides. He was moving purposefully and didn't say a word until we exited the back door by a loading dock, where his black van was parked.

"You know, Jaycie, this isn't the first time you've been connected to the rising dead," said Maynard.

I could feel Jamaal lingering like he had a bucket of popcorn, listening to everything like it was an episode of his favorite show.

"What?" I asked. I shot them both a confused look.

"Long story," said Jaycie.

"And what happened to your face?" asked Maynard.

I kept forgetting about the scar. Without a mirror, I hardly knew it was there.

"Oh this?" I said, pointing at it. "Cut myself shaving."

Maynard chuckled as we crossed the pavement. "C'mon." He waved. "Into my van."

Jaycie shot me a glare—the kind that said she was equally as confused as I was about Maynard's van. Other than it having the most flagrantly noticeable paint job I ever saw, we had no clue as to why he was taking us here—or inside it.

Despite the creepy vibe about the van, I couldn't help but feel complete having Jaycie back. We could easily communicate without speaking a single word. That was the dream, wasn't it? To know someone so well that just a look could articulate whole ideas.

Maynard's van may have looked exactly the same from the outside, but when he slid the door open, I was hit all at once with strange exotic scents that made me gag, my olfactory senses overrun.

"After you," he suggested, followed by a theatrical gesture, and Jaycie hopped in. When we were both inside, Maynard climbed in after us and shut the door.

The entire van went black, followed by a click and a sudden blueish glow that lit the back half.

Maynard had been busy.

The back of the van had been converted into a kind of lab. There was just enough height to stand with a bowed head as Jaycie and I stepped deeper inside to investigate. There were symbols spray-painted onto the interior of the doors and artifacts taped to the walls and ceiling. Some of them were dream catchers from indigenous tribes, as well as an assortment of native arrowheads and tools. There were wreaths made of various plants, and even cloves of garlic hung from the ceiling. A table spanned the full length of the back, holding a computer terminal and surveillance equipment, as well as a few test tubes and petri dishes next to a microscope that was bolted in.

"Okay," said Maynard after a second, "you didn't spontaneously combust. That's a good sign."

"What?" I asked as he removed a shotgun from behind his back and leaned it against the wall. I never felt like we were threatened, but the moment I saw the shotgun I was on edge, ready to protect Jaycie with my life.

"Sorry, can't be too careful these days in Grace Falls," he said.

"What is all this?" asked Jaycie. She was particularly distracted by the knives in the back. A few of them looked old, and some appeared downright demented with curves and jagged hooks.

"My life's work," he said as he began rummaging through a bin on the wall. "You really think I'm just a record store manager?" Before we could answer, he tossed objects at each of us. "Here, catch."

Mine looked like a rabbit's foot, with claws—and Jaycie's was some kind of metal. It smelled sweet and tasted like iron from several feet away—my senses were in overdrive, but concentrating on something, like the metal in her hand, seemed to focus them.

He watched us carefully then said, "Okay, switch."

After we swapped items, he looked almost shocked.

"Alright," he said to me, "I'm convinced you're okay." Then he turned to Jaycie and said, "But you, I'm not as convinced."

"Convinced of what?" she asked.

"That you're human," he said, erasing the smile from Jaycie's face.

I decided to reiterate that, "we came to warn you."

"Of what?" he asked as he looked around his van for something to strike his fancy.

"There might be someone after you," I said. "He's looking to hurt my friends."

"We haven't seen each other in what? Five years at least. Are we still friends?" he asked.

"I don't think they care about that," I replied, as he found something dangling from the back of the van. It looked like a grimy pouch of pot-pourri when he snagged it and handed it off to Jaycie.

"Hold this for thirty seconds," he said to her.

"What is it?" she asked.

"A hex bag," he answered. "It'll prove once and for all if you're actually a witch."

"A witch?" she shouted. "I'm not a witch."

"I never thought so," said Maynard as he grabbed a flat rock and stared at her through a hole in its center. "But Tori and Cyn were convinced."

"What?" she growled.

"They tried to convince us," said Maynard, pointing back and forth between the two of us, which made me cringe.

"The both of you? You knew about this?" she asked me.

I shrugged. "I didn't believe them." I felt like I was letting her down, like she was learning more about my suspicions than I was trying to solve her mysteries. To her credit, she took it in stride. The tests were as welcomed as they were irritating—a little reassurance never hurt.

Maynard was staring at his watch—it looked military-grade—and after thirty seconds he gave Jaycie a once-over with squinted eyes.

"Okay, not a witch," he said, but looked unsatisfied.

"I told you I wasn't," she groaned angrily.

"You passed the hex-bag test, the iron test; I even looked at you through a hag stone. Nothing. You're clean," he replied, sounding almost disappointed.

"Anything else?" I asked sarcastically.

"Got any extra nipples?" he joked with a shrug.

"Nope. The standard two. I can vouch for that," I said with a grin, and Jaycie punched me in the arm.

"Okay, good," said Maynard. He looked relieved. I was too, although we'd only managed to rule out that she wasn't actually a witch. "When you showed up at my house this morning, you tripped a proximity alarm. I snuck out the back and left. Never even stopped to think you might be a friendly."

"A friendly?" I asked, but he ignored me.

"I should have just peeked into the living room," he said. "Can't be too careful. Debt collectors are everywhere."

"Debt collectors?" asked Jaycie.

"Yeah, fucking taxes," he groaned.

Jaycie looked livid. "You set up security to prevent being served by debt collectors?" she asked.

"Yeah," said Maynard. "I mean, there are other reasons too."

"Like?" I asked.

"Never can be too careful in Grace Falls. It can be a dangerous place if you're not too…*careful*."

"So," started Jaycie, irritation riddled throughout her tone, "you ditched and let your poor old mother answer the door for you?"

"I mean," said Maynard, shrugging, "nobody's gonna hurt her. You could be the fucken Mum Killer and she'd invite you inside for brownies."

Jaycie looked livid, and I had to admit, that level of negligence made me feel uneasy. We went out of our way to warn him, and he was willing to risk his own mother's life?

"Oh!" said Maynard, as if finally catching up. "No, she's not in any trouble."

"You just said—" growled Jaycie.

"—yeah, I said it can be a dangerous place if you're not too careful," explained Maynard. "A few years back a friend put a tattoo on my neck." He flipped his hair up and showed us. It looked like a wheel at the base of his skull, with eight symbolic spokes, intricate squares, and circles. "It's called Hulinhjálmur. It's a symbol of disguise and protection, and it's supposed to make the wearer invisible. U-Nats can't sense me, and if they can't sense me, they won't come looking. Besides, I warded the house too."

"What the hell is a U-Nat?" I asked.

"Unnaturals," he explained, then paused. "You guys aren't looking at me like I'm crazy."

"Well," I said, looking over to Jaycie.

"That's because," she said, finishing my thought, "there's a lot of crazy going around."

"You guys really thought I'd leave my mom and dad vulnerable?" he scoffed. "C'mon. While everyone else was playing Hungry Hungry Hippos, I was learning to play Three-Dimensional Chess."

"That explains a lot," said Jaycie with a smile.

Maynard looked at me and said, "Sarcasm. At least we know she's not an android."

"Comforting," I joked.

"When did this happen?" he asked as he leaned against the back of the driver's seat. "When did you come back?"

"Yesterday," replied Jaycie.

"Where?" he asked.

"Grace Falls Cemetery," I replied, then gestured throughout the van. "What is all this?"

"My life," he said as he slipped on his trademark trench coat and hopped into the front of the van. "Let me take you to the lab."

"This isn't your lab?" asked Jaycie.

"Nope," he said. "You know the storage facility up on Gossamer Drive? The Store-It?" I nodded, but Jaycie didn't. It was built after she died. "My family rents one. Dad moved all his war memorabilia up there years ago and forgot about it. I use it as my lab."

"Don't you have to work?" asked Jaycie.

"When an old friend comes back from the dead, I think it's a good fucking excuse to take the day off from work, don't you think?" he replied. "Besides, don't you wanna find out what the fuck is going on?"

She shrugged. "I guess so, yeah."

"Then let me help you. I live for this stuff."

"That was you out there," I said, recalling my drive into town, "that spray-painted the welcome billboard."

"I see my reputation precedes me." He smiled as he stuck his key into the ignition and twisted. "Welcome to Grace Falls! Where Angels Fall and Demons Soar!" He said it theatrically as the van roared to life. "How fucking true is that, right?"

"Yeah," I said, not sure I understood what I was agreeing with.

"Let's go," he said. "Anybody hungry? The China King is on the way."

The ride over to the Store-It facility took us across town. After a quick stop at the China King, we loaded two bags of food into the van while Maynard gave us a little background on life as an amateur X-Files investigator.

"Right after Tori died, I hit rock bottom," he said as he pulled out of the parking lot and stopped at a red light. Jaycie squeezed my hand from the front passenger seat, and I knelt on the floor behind them. "I didn't know I was in love with her until it happened. I took it hard. Started drinking. It was bad shit, man. One night I found myself up by the Hallows House just staring at the Mkateewa River, and I could hear her voice. *'We're the cursed children of the Mkateewa.'*

"What does that mean?" asked Jaycie.

"Black," I said. "It means black."

"Good," said Maynard. "You remember."

"I know that," she grumbled. "I grew up here too, ya know? What did she mean about the *cursed children*?"

The light changed, and Maynard pulled out onto Main Street.

"Do you guys remember all the stories about this town? Thirty-three or so years ago, something happened here. Who knows what it was—you won't find it in the papers—but something definitely happened. Whatever it was, it was like a lightning rod for the weird and unexplained. Our high school class," he said, gesturing to Jaycie, "was ninety percent left-handed."

"That's really strange," said Jaycie. She and I were both left-handed too. "Is that true?"

"Does a gremlin love misery?"

"Yes?" she shrugged, unsure of the comparison.

"It's deeper than that," continued Maynard. "It's in our blood. Do you know what the rarest blood type is in the country?" We both shook our heads. "AB negative. Less than one percent. Want to guess the percentage in Grace Falls?" When we didn't answer, Maynard told us. "No less than seventy five percent—but it seems more prevalent in those born around 1980.

"Weird things happen here, man," he continued. "Being left-handed and AB negative blood are just symptoms. Remember those stories? Tommy Lee? Veronica Green? The Mum Murders? Nikki Twist? The list goes on and on. Young people and strange phenomena. We're cursed. If you're born in this town, or drawn to it, you've been ensnared in its web."

"I don't remember those stories," said Jaycie.

I remembered the few things Maynard and his friends shared with me about the Mum Murders, but not much more. Was this town really as weird as they all claimed?

"Tori's words got me thinking about a lot of shit. She was right, you know? We are cursed. This whole town is a cancer beneath our feet. The Shawnee knew it. Their warriors, my ancestors, settled all around this land, but not on it. They kept their tomahawks sharp and ready," he said as he pulled up to another red light.

"What do you mean?" asked Jaycie.

"Jace, how much do you remember about our childhood?"

"Like what?" she asked. Her memory was still spotty. I could tell.

"Do you remember the day after Christmas, 1988? The old man in the bushes?" he asked. "In the woods behind our houses?"

Jaycie shook her head. "No. I remember Whitney's dog got hurt, but he was okay."

Maynard looked over at her and said, "The dog fucken died. He was dead in Whitney's arms. You, me, and Amanda were there." Jaycie squeezed my hand again at the mention of Amanda. It probably wasn't a good idea to tell Maynard—at least not yet.

"I don't remember that."

"I remember it," he said. "It became all swirly in my head, but I remember it two ways. I remember the dog dying, and I remember Whitney and her dog finding us huddled on a bank by the creek, with sticks in our hands like we were defending ourselves."

Jaycie shook her head. "Parts of my memory aren't there."

The story sounded like something I should know, but I wasn't going to push for it. Jaycie's head must have been spinning, and I couldn't decide whether this conversation was helping or hurting.

"That day," continued Maynard, "I remember going back to my room and being so scared—like every sound in my house, every creak and pop as someone walked by my bedroom door, was something out to get me. Then, I became immune. I just stopped."

"Just stopped what?" I asked.

"Being afraid," he said. "Took me a long time to start putting pieces together, but all of us who grew up here remember the stories. Kids gone missing. Things happen here. The Mum Murders were high profile, but it wasn't just that." He pulled onto a side street, moving toward the edge of town. "I wasn't the only one. At first it was just me, but then I met others. Dylan Jacobs, Jonah Johnson, the Padre, Detective Blaise—before he died—and Doctor Celestine, to name a few."

"I know most of them," said Jaycie. "Dylan gave me guitar lessons. Jonah sounds familiar too. But Doctor Celestine? The theology professor?"

"Yeah, the guy's a genius."

"What do you guys do?" I asked. Seemed like a random bunch from my perspective. "Pay dues and play bingo?"

"For a while we just shared notes, but after a time we started working together. Shook the pillars of hell," he said with a smirk, but the smile quickly faded. "Did you know this town was built upon the site of a mass murder?" We both shook our heads, and Maynard pressed on. "You won't find it in any history books or official town records, but the original families of Grace Falls—the Jansens, the Hallows, and the Miltons—settled this town in the 1850s. They didn't even have to fight for the land. As I said, the Shawnee wanted nothing to do with it, claiming it was blighted long before they got here. Then in 1892, once the Hallows House was built, Godfrey Hallows had every mason, architect, and hired hand killed. Their bodies were dumped into a mass grave." Maynard pulled up to a stop sign on Gossamer Drive and continued. "The Jansens and the Miltons were appalled, but their families' success was predicated on the three families working together. It was all swept under the rug."

"That's awful," said Jaycie. "I had no idea."

"Most people don't," he said, as the road narrowed. We were out past the fairgrounds, heading into rural land. The skies were overcast and darkening, and I could sense the temperatures dropping below freezing.

"How'd you find out about it?" I asked.

"The Padre," he said. "Father Monaco."

"Wait," said Jaycie, "The priest from St. Mary's?"

"Yeah," he said. "The same. He's one of us."

"He was the priest at my Grammy's funeral," she said. "He was always really sweet to me."

"Speaking of—" said Maynard. "You're back from the dead. Have any weird symptoms?"

"Like what?" asked Jaycie.

"I don't know. Headaches? Bad taste in your mouth?"

Were these actual symptoms of the rising dead? Or was Maynard just making it up?

"No, nothing like that."

"Anything you can share that will tell us a little more about why you're back?"

She shrugged. "I remember some stuff, but they don't make sense. They're abstract, like a snapshot memory out of focus."

"Like?"

"The Mercy Point Mall?" she said. "A warehouse? Like the one up by the falls."

"Anything else?"

"Sometimes things happen."

"What do you mean?" I asked.

"Sometimes, in the past," she said after taking a deep breath, "things happened."

"What kind of things?" I asked, but Jaycie shrugged.

"Bad things, usually. Unexplained things."

"Interesting," said Maynard. He didn't want to press for answers for the same reasons I didn't. It was clear she was uncomfortable talking about it. "Like Pajamas."

"Like what?" I asked.

"Pajamas," said Jaycie. "That was the name of Whitney's dog."

"Anything else?" he asked.

"Sometimes I can hear voices inside other people's heads," she said, as she glanced at me with a guilty look.

Maynard said, "That's an odd one. How do you know they're in other people's heads?"

"I just know," she said, and looked at me.

"Fuuuck," said Montoya, eliciting a look from Jaycie.

"Well then, why are we bothering to be so quiet?" asked Jamaal. They were behind me. Doshin was inspecting some of the knives, but the others gathered close to listen in.

"The love of his life doesn't need to know he's got voices in his head," said Chappy.

"Typically," said Henry, "the subconscious offers what one might call a voice, but I do not believe the lady is referring to those kinds of voices."

Jaycie shot me another glance, this one filled with concern, and stroked my hand when she noticed something there—something I had forgotten all about, the mark on the inside of my left wrist.

"What's that?" she asked as she thumbed it.

Maynard looked over and added, "Looks like a keyhole. Like something out of a Bugs Bunny gag."

He was right. It did look like a keyhole—a circle with the classic trapezoidal box attached. I admitted, "It does," when a thought struck me.

"What if?" said Henry.

"Might as well try it, my man," added Montoya.

I removed the key in my pocket and showed it to Jaycie.

"Mini golf," I said with a smile, and she beamed at me. Her eyes watered, making a fresh connection to the memory. There was something about that smile that I would do anything for. It made me fearless, which was why I thought nothing of what I was about to do.

"What is that?" asked Maynard.

"The key to my heart," I said, looking at Jaycie.

Before Maynard could ask another question, I took the key and brought it to my wrist. Like a magnet, the key snapped into the hole, embedded halfway into my wrist, and the windows began rattling.

"What the fuck?" yelled Maynard. He swerved, preventing the van from soaring off the road and into a drainage ditch.

The key seemed to glow, like it was begging me to twist and open the lock, when Jaycie reached out and removed it.

"Don't," she said with tears. "Not yet." She had a knowing look in her eyes, like she could see the future.

When her face flickered again, my heart sank—her freckles moved, as if rearranging themselves, and her nose changed shape. Her green eyes washed away, and the red vibrancy of her hair dulled. Then as quickly as the shifting began, it sprung back into place, and she was once again Jacinda O'Neill.

Tears welled up in her eyes.

"Something's wrong," she said.

Maynard saw the whole thing and had taken his eyes almost entirely off the road. We were traveling through a stretch of old country back-roads, where the forest grew right up to the edge of the pavement. The roads were empty, and the skies were so dark that Maynard was driving with the headlights on.

"What the fuck was that?" asked Maynard.

"I'm not a witch," said Jaycie, trembling, "but I'm also not ordinary."

"Of course, you're not," I said, trying to lighten the mood. I could see a darkness take form inside her. It was true darkness, the kind people hope to never see inside someone they love. What she was digging up was deep, from fathoms so bottomless, the light of hope never shined there.

"You don't understand, Tony," she cried. Her mood soured and her eyes grew cold, like they did the day she put a gun to her head.

It was instant heartache, to sense that what she needed to tell me was something she feared so intensely, like it might grow sharp fangs and eat her alive.

"Tell me," I said. "You can tell me anything."

"I know," said Jaycie. After a huge sigh to catch her breath, she appeared caught, like what was coming next was going to be a doozy. Her pulse was racing. I could hear her heart thumping and smell a variety of emotions leaking into the air around her. "When I said sometimes things happen, what I really meant was I can do things."

"Like what?" I asked.

"Things I shouldn't be able to do," said Jaycie, and her eyes burned with self-hate. "I think, maybe, that's how I came back." She was shaking. What she was digging up was breaking my heart. The wind blew and with it came the stench of the unnatural—scents of rot, death, and brimstone. Something was happening all around us, and it was too late to do anything about it. "I think I might be—"

Then Maynard slammed on the brakes and yelled, "Fuck!"

When the van came to screeching a stop, with several of Maynard's strange artifacts flying throughout the back, we could see the neon light of the gated storage facility a mile up the road, peering over the treetops. However, standing between us and our destination was a man with stark white hair, standing in the center of the road with his arms stretched out wide. There were two cars on either side of the street—one flipped over with bloody streaks across the pavement, creating an impassable roadblock.

As we stared at the man, I clasped the key around my neck. It had been more than ten years since I last wore it, and this seemed like the best place to keep it, for now.

Jaycie reached out, pulled me close and kissed me, then said, "When it happens, run and don't look back."

"Tony!" yelled the man. "Come on out here and bring that beautiful fiancée of yours."

VII

the two-eyed man

Jacinda
Then.

I never met a person who claimed to have enjoyed high school. Being a teenager has to be one of the most difficult times of our lives, Jace. If I remembered my early teens correctly, every day was spent in a haze of confusion, unable to properly gauge and understand personal accountability and responsibility, all while juggling grades, impulses, and trying to master the birds and the bees.

For you, Jace, you crept into high school apprehensively. Amanda was gone, her phone calls and letters more and more sporadic, and without your best friend, you felt unprepared for that next phase of life. You buried yourself in music—listening, writing, and playing every chance you had. You joined every class and club that allowed you to play music and sing, and art classes helped you express that which you couldn't speak.

Try as you might, Jaycie, you were haunted. Your inner sadness bloomed into depression. To admit out loud that you were depressed was almost like admitting defeat—and that was not who you were. You were a fighter. Inside your chest was the heart of a champion that wouldn't quit, no matter what.

The Academy of the Sacred Cross was located in Mercy Point within the confines of an old monastery. The monastery was erected more than a hundred years before and was never any better at stopping a draft than it was the day it was built. It was cold, damp, and at times the echoes within the stone hallways were unbearably loud, especially when you were attempting to carry a conversation or in need of a quiet moment.

Maybe some of the girls enjoyed attending Sacred Cross—perhaps some of them needed it—but you loathed every second. It wasn't just boring and tiresome, you never felt like you fit in with those girls. All of them had filthy rich parents, and that wasn't you. You always saw yourself as the girl next door, a tomboy, musician, horror movie fan, artist, and dreamer. You'd be just as happy watching *Phantasm* with Amanda as you were at strumming your guitar and listening to music— only Amanda was gone, and you were stuck within that monastery like you were on the fast track to becoming a nun yourself.

Then, a few days before you turned sixteen, you had an idea.

It struck you in the middle of algebra as the teacher passed out tests and you caught the girls next to you sharing a cheat sheet. You didn't need to cheat, but that wasn't the point, now was it?

You were expelled that day. Zero tolerance policy.

November 13th, 1996

"Your mother and I have decided to send you to St. Augustine's in Pittsburgh," said your father as they discussed your future. "They cannot accept you until next term, after the new year, but it is a great school."

"No," you said.

The look on his face was priceless.

You and your parents were sitting in the living room in front of a roaring fire. It didn't feel right to be home that time of year. You didn't much like the new house—you had lived there for five years and still thought of it as new. It didn't feel like home, but like a fancy hotel, where nothing was actually yours. Even the couches weren't very comfortable, but your mother thought they looked nice.

Still, it was better than the Academy.

"What do you mean, no?" asked your mother. The way she said it sounded more contemptuous than your own response.

"I don't want to go away to some other school," you said. "I want to go here. Send me to public school."

"I didn't work this hard just to send my only child to public school," said your father. There was something about his words that felt wrong, but you couldn't put a finger on it.

"Sending me away to school feels like a punishment," you explained. "I want to go to a school where I might have a chance to fit in. I didn't belong at the Academy."

"I didn't realize you felt this way," said your father, thawing a little.

"It's not a punishment," said your mother. "It's for your own good." You could almost see her rooting to send you away. Anything to get you out of the house.

Joseph looked at his wife with a momentary glimmer of disbelief.

"Okay," he finally said.

"Okay?" questioned Saoirse.

"I can go to public school?" you questioned, skeptically.

"Okay," he nodded.

"Really?" you asked again, and your father smiled and nodded.

"But if you so much think about cheating, or any element of delinquent behavior, we're sending you to St. Augustine's."

"Of course! Okay!" you said and ran upstairs while your parents dove into an argument. You ran into your room, shut the door, then picked up the phone and dialed a number you had memorized since being expelled. You needed a friend, so you called the only person you knew.

"What up?" the line answered.

"Rick, guess what?" you said.

"I don't know," he replied.

"I'm going to be your new classmate."

"Really? Hey, cool! Now you can come to all my games. You said you'd cheer for me up in the stands, remember?"

"I did, and I will. I promise."

December 1st, 1996

It was a cold Sunday in Grace Falls. You and your mother spent the better half of the weekend getting clothes for your first day of public school that Monday. Saoirse O'Neill hated holiday shopping enough as it was, but the fact that you made her go to a thrift store was an entirely new and demeaning experience for her.

You didn't care how your mother felt, and I couldn't blame you, Jace. This was what you wanted—a chance to make some friends and fit in. You were happy preparing for this new world. Wearing a uniform to school was tedious—you weren't allowed to be yourself. Preparing for Grace Falls High was an exercise in self-identity. You started by laying your new clothes out on your bed, matching them together in various ways to come up with new combinations and outfits. After a while, you started trying them on and laughed at yourself in the mirror as you struck silly poses, imagining all the possible scenarios. Meeting people and making new friends—you wanted to be a normal teenager.

It was the happiest you had been in the longest time.

It was late when you realized the time and quickly prepared yourself for morning. You packed up your backpack and laid out your clothes. You even picked out socks and a necklace your Grammy wore, then brushed your teeth and settled in for bed.

There were too many thoughts and too many ideas swimming through your head. Falling asleep seemed like an impossible task; you felt like a kid on Christmas Eve after snacking on Santa's cookies. After endless attempts and rolling over into every possible angle, you finally gave up, opting to write and draw in your journal, detailing your thoughts—fears, expectations, dreams—about your upcoming first day.

I watched you write in that journal every day for three years without so much as a single sign of trauma. No scribbles of devilish doors or hints of masked soldiers in black. You hid your sadness, your frustration and your depression, and expressed it through your art. A poet needs the pain, and a teenager silently suffering needs the outlet.

There was nothing special about that night. It wasn't even the first time you found yourself unable to put the jumble of thoughts aside, writing in your journal until your yawns carried you back to bed. From where I was behind the Veil, watching you from the far corner of the room, I nearly missed the whole ordeal. As you sat down at your desk and flipped on the lamp, you bolted straight up and went rigid. The chair shot backward with a loud slam, and I swore you were going to scream, Jace, because I nearly screamed right along with you.

In the window, written on the frosty pane, was a message.

"WE FOUND YOU," it said, framed by your terrified reflection casted back.

I don't think you took a single breath for more than a minute.

Once you had gathered your wits, you leapt from your petrified spot and turned the desk lamp off with a snap. Making it disappear was like erasing the message—as if it weren't even there—but the darkness revealed something far worse.

A figure pressed up against the glass, watching you.

I nearly leapt from the Veil as you fell backward onto the chair, but your eyes never left the stranger. He appeared young, but with stark white hair, and two different colored eyes—one dark, and the other as pale as bone.

"Malus," I said, but you couldn't hear me, Jace. By the time I made a move for the window, he disappeared, and I was left knowing I had failed to protect you once again.

You took your time crawling back to the window. When you finally gathered the courage to peek out, you saw him down below, on the sidewalk across the street. He looked directly at you and waved, then turned and walked away. I wanted to follow, to take him down while I had the chance, but I couldn't leave you all alone, Jace. What if it was a trap?

You spent the next few hours drawing what had transpired. You drew him watching you through the window. You called him the man with two eyes—one eye like a man, and the other like a ghost—but I knew him as my enemy.

He was the reason I needed to know what you were, Jace.

He's the man that killed Amanda.

He's the man that took everything from us.

December 4th, 1996

It would be incorrect to say that your life was nothing but tragedy from beginning to end. There were many good moments, and I watched them all. I saw you score that goal in the finals against Mason Township for the win. I witnessed the very first song you ever wrote and recorded on a cheap tape deck that Dylan Jacobs helped you set up in your garage. I watched the thrill you got when you went sledding off the "big beast"—a giant hill behind your house—with Amanda and Morris, and I watched you overcome with emotion when you bought your first album and hit play—what ten-year-old listened to Pink Floyd? I got to experience everything, and in a lot of ways I feel like I have come to understand you that much more because of it. But I still don't know what you are, Jace. I still haven't gotten the information I need. Was I looking in the wrong place?

Maybe it wasn't you? Maybe there was something else—an unseen entity watching over your shoulder, like me?

I started to focus more intently on the tough moments, to experience your pain, hoping it might show me what I needed to know.

What are you, Jace? Who are you?

Your first day at Grace Falls High was unspectacular. It was embarrassing the way the teachers paraded you around each class and forced you to tell your new classmates something interesting about yourself. All the new names and faces were overwhelming, but when the school day ended, you left feeling it was one step in the right direction.

The thing that haunted you the window the night before was like a bad memory, and you did your best to ignore it. After all, Jace, you pretended it was all a bad dream, didn't you?

What was I expecting from you? To investigate? To tell your parents? The police? What good would any of that have done?

Day two came and went in similar fashion.

By day three, you felt accomplished to have survived three whole days at the new school. You quickly realized your time at the Academy had given you an advantage at Grace Falls High. You were well ahead in every class. School itself was a breeze, but like all sixteen-year-old girls, you yearned for more.

You wanted friends. You wanted to meet boys. You wanted to experience life.

On the fourth day, you finally found him.

"Hey! Rick!" you called out, as you dashed through the crowded halls to catch up. It was overwhelming, the number of students one needed to dodge between classes. You weren't used to so many distractions. Rick was taller than most of the boys and easy to spot in the halls wearing his letterman jacket, like a total high school cliché. He didn't hear you until you were right on top of him. "Hey!" You were out of breath. You were nervous and awkward. In front of Rick, you weren't the same Jacinda O'Neill I had come to know.

"Oh, hey, Jacinda," he said. "What's up? Welcome to Grace Falls High."

"Thanks!"

"How was your first few days?" he asked as he gestured for you to follow him.

"They were fine. Nothing noteworthy."

"Right," said Rick, like he was losing interest. "Hey bro!" He spotted a friend in the crowd and high-fived him, for the sake of doing it, I suppose.

"Are we hitting up the party house tonight?" the guy asked discreetly. He was wearing an identical letterman jacket, and he had a crooked nose and a horrible case of cauliflower ear.

"Sure as shit," said Rick.

"What's the party house?" you asked, as the oaf walked off, pretending he didn't see or hear you ask.

"Oh, it's nothing," deflected Rick, as another guy punched him playfully on the arm, and a couple girls giggled shy hellos.

You were getting the feeling that earning Rick's attention was going to be much more difficult than you'd thought over the phone, or at the summer barbecues when he seemed eager to know everything about you.

"Are you sure? I mean, the party house sounds like a good time. It does have party in the title."

"Oh," said Rick, "well, yeah, but it's invite-only. Sorry, Jace."

That didn't take long. The guy was already breaking your heart.

"Well, who sends the invites? Maybe I missed mine in the mail," you said with a smile, and I swear, I almost walked away. You were so desperate for his attention, and it was making me sick. But it didn't matter how hard you tried; his attention was elsewhere.

"Baby!" cried a random blonde just before she launched herself into the air at Rick. Her mini-skirted legs wrapped around him as she shimmied up his torso to give him a kiss worthy of an adult movie. Once they had properly vacated each other's faces, the girl took notice of you and asked, "Who's this?" in the most petulant way possible.

"Tori, this is Jaycie," Rick said. "She's my father's lawyer's daughter. She's new here."

Tori Martin, pre-goth and as *shy* as ever.

"Oh," said Tori. She was a blonde bombshell in knee-highs. She was loud, bombastic, and showed way too much skin—she was everything you weren't, and you took note of that, didn't you, Jace?

You attempted a "Hi," but Tori ignored you.

"Are we going up to your party house tonight?" she asked.

"Your party house?" you asked him. "I thought it was invite-only?"

"Yeah, bitch," said Tori, "and you're not invited."

Wow—this younger Tori was so scared, so territorial, so different than the Tori I knew—same volume, though. She would have torn down anyone she felt was moving in on her man, and she could smell the threat coming off you, Jace.

However, you didn't need to be treated that way. Sure, it hurt, but other things in your life were more dangerous than some girl. You took off and went to your next class, wiping away tears as you went.

In Tori's defense, she changed a lot after dating Rick. I bet if things were different, you'd be fast friends, but that wasn't what fate had in store for you both. You were rivals, and Tori made sure to remind you what she had and you didn't.

By the morning of day five, rumors flew around the halls of Grace Falls High. Rumors that weren't very kind to you.

"She's a man-stealer," someone whispered.

"She's a psycho," said another. "I heard she's a klepto too."

"I heard she's a pathological liar."

"Wasn't that the girl they were talking about? I hear she's into black magic and stuff."

You heard it all. It wasn't like the students were trying to hide it. They brazenly talked about you as you walked the halls—they passed notes and giggled at your expense in the middle of class. Kids could be so mean, Jace, and you were so sick and tired of people being mean to you. You'd made a promise to your father not to do anything that would get you in trouble, so you suffered in silence, alone.

Sometime between sixth and seventh period, as you were walking the halls toward art class, you happened to pass Tori going the opposite way. You never caught what she said, though it sounded like "Raggedy Anne," and you were too busy trying to avoid her when the laughter started at your expense.

You felt embarrassed and sad and alone, but mostly, you felt rage.

I saw it starting to rise, Jace—like heat from hot blacktop—wavy, blurry folds that slithered around the hallway floors, across the walls lined with lockers and dangling from the padded drop-ceiling. I knew something awful was coming, like Death itself was circling in.

You felt the heat, the fire, the anger—you wanted them all to feel your pain, and when you couldn't take it any longer, and needed to un-leash your anger, to teach them all a lesson—the power resting right on the tips of your fingers—someone unexpected reached out to you.

"Hey, Jaycie," said little Whitney, who was no longer very little. "Don't listen to them. They're just being jerks."

"Whitney? Hey!" you said, sounding surprised. "I haven't seen you since—?"

"Since you moved away with all the rich kids? Yeah." Whitney had grown up. She was a freshman and was already taller than you. She had long auburn hair that fell to the small of her back and an aura that proclaimed she didn't give a shit. "Which way are you going?"

"To the art room," you said.

"Cool, I'm going right past there," she replied with a smile. "And don't worry, you'll get through it. Next week it'll be someone else, and they'll forget all about you." The way she said it made it sound like she had experience, but Whitney Berry scared me, Jace. She had a look in her eyes—the same look you had in yours the day you pulled that trigger.

December 25th, 1996

Having an ally at school shielded you from the rumors and the bullies. She helped you tolerate it all—but, let's be real, Jace, Whitney Berry wasn't your friend—at least not by the standard definition of friendship. By your third week, your last before the holiday break, things had already started to wind down. Someone else had become public enemy number one—when they found him and his girlfriend overdosed in the school parking lot that weekend.

The girl didn't make it.

On Christmas Day, you woke up to a big surprise. Your father bought you a red Volkswagen Cabriolet convertible and gave it to you with a big red bow on its hood. Coincidentally, I was the one who wrecked it years later trying to save you. You thanked him profusely, while your mother moped in the kitchen. Apparently, she didn't like the idea of her daughter having independence, but also didn't appreciate a reliant daughter.

As I said before, your mother was a piece of work.

"Why don't you go take it for a spin?" your father suggested. "It'll give your mother time to blow off some steam."

And as much as I hated your father, the man really wanted to love you, he just didn't know how most days.

"Okay," you said, taking the keys from his outstretched hand. You'd learned to ignore you mother's moods. Most times she was mad at you for no apparent reason—just because you were alive, and *she* wasn't. Ten years later and your mother was still mourning Jane.

You drove through the empty streets of Grace Falls. You put the radio on to your favorite station, singing every word to every song. Music had become your life, as you consumed every album, B-side, rarity, and cover from nearly every artist that ever landed a single hit. You were a living encyclopedia of music, Jace, and I was beginning to understand why I always lost at our game. Some people had the aptitude for math or science—but you heard the beauty in every song and developed the kind of musical taste that people three times your age enjoyed—a mature palate of melodic sound without the sideshow or pretension.

Half an hour later, you found yourself pulling up to the Berry household in your old neighborhood. You wanted to share your good fortune with someone, even if deep down, you knew this would turn out to be an unfortunate misstep.

When Mrs. Berry answered, she recognized you straightaway.

"What are you doing out here?" she happily asked.

"I was hoping Whitney might be interested in taking a drive with me?" you said.

Mrs. Berry's face immediately soured as she said, "I'm sorry, Jacinda, but Whitney's grounded." You talked for a minute longer, catching up on small events, before you walked back to your car. You always liked Mr. and Mrs. Berry, even though your father couldn't hear the name without looking bitter.

As your key slid into the ignition, Whitney was knocking on your passenger side window with a thrill in her eyes.

"Let me in," she said excitedly.

You unlocked the doors, whispering, "I thought you were grounded?"

"I am," said Whitney. "Drive, before my mom catches us!"

You drove to Mercy Point and back, then over to the China King for lunch. By then, you were running out of things to do. Whitney refused to go back home, for fear of being doubly grounded, and you complied, because you needed her.

"How are you liking public school now?" Whitney asked as she slurped down a wad of noodles.

"I don't know," you moped, sliding down into the booth. The restaurant was empty, except for the owners, Mr. and Mrs. Lee and their daughter, who was watching *A Christmas Story* on an old black and white TV. "It's not really what I expected."

"What did you expect?" asked Whit. She thought your answer was hilarious, laughing with an exposed mouthful of half-chewed food.

"I guess I expected to fit in?"

"New kids never fit in."

"Why don't you?"

Whitney looked up at you, and suddenly everything wasn't so funny. She swallowed her food and brushed the hair from her face. She even looked up at the ceiling dramatically before answering.

"I've been unpopular for a very long time," she replied.

"Why?"

"Fuck, because I am," she growled. "Why are you suddenly up my ass?"

Yikes, Jace. We could spend all day on her psychosis. You were trying to be a friend, even though you knew it wasn't going to end well.

"Sorry, I was just curious. I thought maybe it was something I could help with."

"Well, you can't help." She already had tears in her eyes. Whitney was broken, ready to shatter at any moment—even in the middle of the China King on Christmas Day. "The kids around here are really fucked up, you know? They never let things go. Never forget. Sometimes I wish I had just kept everything to myself, but I was too young to know better and so fucking dumb."

After spending time with Little Whitney Berry, you knew exactly what she meant. Some kids believed in Santa Claus too long and were teased for still believing it. Believe in monsters under your bed, and be so convinced that something paranormal happened to you, and tell everyone who was willing and unwilling to listen—and you might become a pariah.

I watched you weighing your options behind your eyes. A dilemma I had hoped you weren't foolish enough to mention about your own recent experiences—but you did. You said it, and now you couldn't take it back.

"I believe you. I saw a monster too. He was watching me through my bedroom window."

VIII
showdown

TONY
December 23rd, 2013
Now.

A man stood in the middle of the road, calling out to me. His white hair and long black coat drifted in the wind as he stood between two cars, one of which was flipped upside down and blocking our path. There was blood on the pavement in long streaks ending at the edge of the forest.

"Did you hear me?" asked Jaycie.

We were sitting in Maynard's van, somewhere out on Gossamer Road, heading toward the Store-It—a storage lot facility where Maynard had a "lab," whatever that meant—when this nutjob put himself between us and our destination. There was something familiar about him and his voice, but I couldn't quite place it. I was kneeling on the floor just behind the front seats, and Jaycie was staring back at me. She put her hand on my chin and pulled my face to hers.

"When it happens, run and don't look back." When I didn't answer, she demanded, "Tell me you'll run and won't look back."

"Okay," I said, as a flicker ran across her face. It was the same flicker as before. Her features appeared to move, like they were transforming into someone else before snapping back to their proper place.

"Tony!" yelled the man, now pacing in the center of the road. "You can't run. We will always find you, boy." His tone wasn't angry. It was sensible and fatherly, like he wanted to soothe my fears of walking into the slaughter.

The moment he said "we," I picked up on a few things—blips on an internal radar, just beyond the forest's edge at either side of the road. There were a dozen of them, at least—and the smell was like brimstone and rotting fruit.

Thirteen. There were thirteen of them, just as my Echo had said.

"The motherfucking Thirteen are coming for you. They are vicious. Remember Doctor Celestine's Theology and Mythology classes in college? You'll need to remember. They were once angels, now living as gods on earth. Now they're after you, and that's my fault."

But two of them should be dead, right? Mammon and Summanus? Why weren't there only eleven?

Jaycie had just admitted to us that she was capable of *"things"* she *"shouldn't be able to do."* I was mystified by her words and began to think I might never learn the secrets that led to her death. Secrets with which I seemed connected yet couldn't discern how. Simpler connections had made far greater minds explode—just like the scene in *Scanners* that Amanda and I used to rewind and play over and over while giggling at the cheesy old effects.

"Bring the girl, Tony," said the man. "The three of us should chat."

I turned to Maynard. "Is there another way to the Store-It?"

"Yeah. There are back roads, but I'd have to go all the way around."

"What's your number?" I asked, as my mind sprinted ahead in an attempt to piece together an action plan.

"Here." He grabbed my phone and tapped on the digital keypad.

"Go for the Store-It and wait for my text," I said. "We'll meet you there."

"Are you sure about this?" asked Maynard. "I mean, I could just run him over?"

The forest edge grew right up to the pavement on either side of the narrow country road. It was a claustrophobic stretch of asphalt, one that made a threatening man standing in its center an impossible obstacle, let alone passable with the cars blocking our way.

"Something tells me that would harm your van more than him," I said.

Beside me, Jaycie had begun to tremble. "It's the two-eyed man," she said.

Her words spun me.

I remembered the drawings from her journal—the ones I'd discovered the day she killed herself. A man watching her from a window with two very different colored eyes, and the words "who's watching me?" scrawled across the page. I remembered the terror of seeing it, coming across those drawings after tearing apart our home, after learning the love of my life was crazy. Now I felt guilty for those thoughts, but how was I supposed to know it was real?

The world was a crazy place, with or without monsters.

Jaycie was terrified. Her palms went sweaty, and she was shivering.

Was this the man who killed Amanda?

Like anyone else, I'd spent my whole life relying on sight as the primary source of collecting information, but what could happen when sight defied logic? My other senses screamed—we were trapped the moment we exited the van.

I'd lived through thirty-three years alone before a sudden cramming of various lives and experiences, once scattered through time, converged into my being. Now I had the ability to taste smells and smell sounds, and it was difficult to understand what it all meant. It wasn't like a stoner tripping on acid, it was a crisscrossing patchwork of sensory perfection meant for a superior being honed for this kind of stimulus.

For me, it was like giving a baby a toolbelt and a hard hat and sending him off to work construction. Half the time I didn't know what to do with what I had at my disposal, and even if I did, could I use it to my advantage?

I knew that man wasn't what he appeared to be. He appeared human, but I had no idea what he was, or what the other surrounding *blips* were that made my skin vibrate and my muscles clench.

Though I had a good idea.

"Maynard," I said, making my appeal to him through what could have been misconstrued as uncomfortable eye contact. "I know we haven't seen each other in years, but right now, this is the most serious thing you've ever been a part of. I don't know if that's a man out there—"

"Not a man," said Jaycie, cutting me off.

"—or not, but we're in trouble. Can you do this? Can you meet us there?"

"Yeah," he said. "As fast as can be." There was a change in him. I could sense that he was ascending to the seriousness of the occasion. Somehow, I knew I could count on him.

"Are you ready?" I asked Jaycie. Her eyes looked cloudy, like her mind was far away.

"No," she said. I got the terrible feeling she was answering something, or someone, else.

We got out of the van and closed the doors simultaneously, then paced in front of the vehicle as Maynard shifted into reverse and slowly backed away.

"Careful," said Doshin. "Trust your instincts."

My brain-trust was there, flanking us. I wondered if Jaycie could see them, or if she was watching something else. When we got within twenty feet of the man, Maynard hit the gas and reversed out of there at top speed. There was a sound, like a growl emanating from the trees, but the man just laughed and said, "You look different, my friend."

MALUS

They could not run from us. We had them surrounded. The spark had my prize, and I was demanding her return. All manner of beings avoid confrontation—even gods. Very few of us operated with a lust for tumultuous encounters. The anticipation of seeing my antagonist again, after our encounter within Votan's tomb, sent trills of empowering anger through me.

However, when he stepped out of the automobile, a terrible anger grew from my shock—this man was not the same one I'd fought in Votan's tomb. This spark was different. He was younger and more powerful than even he could realize—a far cry from the wretched thing that had attacked me for the last of Eden's keys.

Then, as if my thought of the Keys had awakened one of their many latent powers, they pulsed, like a magnetic pole nearing its equal.

What did it mean?

When it happened again a moment later, I spotted the spark's shirt dance in response. Then identified the chain links around his neck.

How fortuitous—the spark had returned my missing key.

Never in my long existence had anything come so easy. Nemesis, the traitor, the foul cunt who stole the Key of Capricorn and disappeared into time, had conveniently dropped the key into the hands of my enemy? Who then crossed my path a day later, accompanied by the girl who ran away?

It seemed too easy. Too coincidental. There had to be more to this puzzle.

With just eight days remaining before I opened the gate and took my prize, my plans were back on schedule.

How did you get that key, Tony?

I would enjoy consuming your flesh and learning all your secrets.

"Welcome," I said with a big grin. "Thank you for returning my property."

TONY

My entire body was on alert, a machine gearing up and becoming aware on an even greater, more amplified level. Every subtle shift in the air, every buzz of a nearby insect, every sweet forest scent, was felt and noted—loaded into some primitive, yet higher function of my intelligent mind. My alert, triggered by my need to keep Jaycie safe, felt like a nuclear reactor in my chest.

The same fragile reactor that had exploded and consumed Mammon in fire.

I couldn't let anything happen to Jaycie, even in the face of impossible odds. From the moment she stepped out of that fog and back into my life, all I wanted to do was protect her. There was no way to accurately describe her importance to me. I would live a damned life for her—and in a way, I already had. The sacrifices I'd make in the name of her well-being and happiness were in no way over-exaggerated. Her life for my own was mandatory.

In the middle of this moment—this dangerous moment where our lives were hanging in the balance—the key kept bouncing beneath my shirt. What the hell was it doing? Was it warning me?

"My man, what's up with the key?" asked Montoya. "It's jumping around like my papi doing the jarabe Tapatío."

"That is fascinating," said Chappy.

"It's reacting to something," added Jamaal. "But I don't think it's a warning."

"Curious," said Henry.

"Reacting to him," said Doshin, and he pointed at the man with two eyes.

I saw the white trinket around his neck dance like the key around mine. From the distance I could spot two other items there, all three of them jangling like the jingle bells the kids were playing as they went caroling throughout the town square earlier that morning.

Nothing was ever a coincidence.

Jaycie's eyes glanced toward my chest. She heard it moving, saw the key bouncing around and whispered, "What the hell?"

Yeah, Jace, I'm right there with you—*what the hell?*

"She is not your property," I finally responded, and Jaycie squeezed my hand tight in solidarity. "Never was, and never will be."

"The last six years say otherwise," he said with a snide smile. "I fucked her in ways a spark like you could only dream. What is a filthy spark compared to the cock of a god?"

Anger flared inside me—I wanted to break his nose. I wanted to stomp him out like Marshall stomped out spiders who crossed his path. I wanted this man, this monster, to feel pain and remorse for what he had done—I wanted him to fear for his life, like Amanda just before...

Jaycie whispered, "Don't. If you do, we both die." Only she could have calmed my rage. I missed that. I missed her, and I was beginning to feel like our connection was already slipping away.

"You look like a man to me," I said. "A pathetic man who needs to go around bragging about size because he comes up short." I held up my thumb and forefinger to show the inch I was accusing him of, but his face never shifted.

"Calling me a man is a disgrace," he said. "A man is a pitiful excuse for the sack of flesh it's given. Men are filth. Waste." Then he took one slow exaggerated step forward. His pale gray eye shimmered next to the dark one—the man with two eyes. Despite his platinum hair, he wasn't old. He looked approximately my age, wearing a long black leather coat and a blood-red shirt beneath. "You may see a man when you look upon me, but no—I am no fucking man. I sacked Solomon. I destroyed Hades. I am a slayer of gods. And I killed your friends. You will call me Malus." Then he took a bow, but kept both eyes on us, never once blinking.

"True names even the playing field if spoken aloud," said my Echo. *"That is your best defense and offense against them. Names will come to you, and you won't know why, but be glad they do. I never fully understood the magic of names, but maybe you will."*

When I spoke Mammon's true name, his magic faltered—but how and why his true name came to me was still a mystery. Could I learn Malus's true name too?

When I did, I'd kill him for ruining Jaycie's life and murdering Amanda. Marshall and Anne each deserved retribution as well. My rage was making promises I might not be capable of keeping, but I didn't care. I wanted to tear this monster apart, bit by fucking bit.

MALUS

I could sense his understanding. The brief moment his irises expanded, then contracted, and the slightest change in the rhythm of his heartbeat. He understood who I was and what I'd done.

It was her face, however, that perplexed me. She looked on me familiarly, like the lines between herself and Lilly were blurring, shades of memories bleeding through from one to the other. I had yet to decide whether this was a desirable outcome, if not fortuitous. At the moment, it was surely favorable.

The words of the seer, Frigg, the late Odin's widow, began to swim through my consciousness.

"To gain what you seek, she must first love you, truly. You must make her yearn for you with all her heart. Captivate her mind with all your charm. She must lust for you, her flesh to yours. And she must need you with every ounce of her soul, so that there is no beginning or end to her without you. Once that is obtained, take her to the holy land that was lost and locked away. There you may acquire what you seek by performing the sacramental contract."

I was nearly there. With the walls between realities melting away the resolve within her own mind, it was only a matter of time. Eight days, to be exact.

"Is that supposed to be your name?" he asked. "Malus?"

He spoke to me like a petulant child.

"I know your real name," said the ghost, whispering into my ear. "I knew you before you became this, and you were nothing." I made her vanish and refocused on the spark's attempt to insult me.

I wanted to laugh. I wanted to slice him in half. I wanted to scoff at his weakness and his ill-conceived attempt at bravery. I wanted to rip open his ribs, claw out his heart, and taste it before it had stopped beating. My hatred for Tony was great, but I admired the way he didn't cower before me nor overestimate himself. He knew he was standing before a power well beyond his own. He knew he had very few options, all of which were futile.

"A name is a powerful possession to its owner. Malus is the name I use so that I might be addressed with an understanding of my ways," I replied.

His eyes darted to and from the automobiles, ignoring my explanation. A sign of subversion. There was a slight lean to his body, moving small fractions towards the automobile still resting on its tires. If he had machinations of escaping within such a slow machine, then he was sadly mistaken. Obviously, he had limited understanding of our capabilities.

"Are they dead?" he asked.

"The passengers were consumed," I said, and left it at that. Their spirits were already in my possession—spooled up into a negative ball of ectoplasmic sadness and rage, ready to be unleashed.

The girl grimaced. Her compassion and empathy for others was its own force of will—I could taste it, fueling her defiance. She looked at Tony and said, "There's more of them. In the shadows."

"What do you want?" asked Tony.

"My price is thrice," I said, "the woman, the key, and your life." His heartbeat flinched on the first two, but not when I threatened his life. Was he prepared to die?

"Sounds pretty steep to me. How about I give you this," he said, exhibiting his middle finger, "and she and I drive out of here."

There would be no survival. There was no way out. With a slight gesture, I took away his only hope.

TONY

He mentioned the key. Did he know what it was? I sure as hell didn't. I was chasing the words of a dream-girl, literally—the Jaycie from the other reality. Beyond being a competent window rattler, what else did the key do? Why did Malus need it?

There was the sound of crushing metal and glass. It was swift, and I didn't have to look to know what it was. The car, the one that was still resting on all four tires, was destroyed—smashed from both ends like a bug crushed between two thumbs. I could smell the gasoline leaking onto the ground and could hear the puddle flowing along the pavement toward us.

Jacinda wrapped her arms around me. She was shivering with fear, her teeth chattering from the brisk breeze and the panic, and I could sense a war waging inside her. Like a feverish immune response to an invading virus. When she peered up at me, her head resting against my chest for comfort, I could hear the prophetic words of my doppelganger.

"There will be a time—and it will be different for you than it was for me—that you will have to make a choice. It will be a very difficult

choice. I made the wrong one—I tried to end it before I was ready—but you, if you make the right choice, you will only be faced with another choice, and another, until you either succeed or fail. Tony, you may just find a way."

Was this one of those impossible choices?

"My Thirteen will let her live," offered Malus, reading my fear. "If you give us what is ours to take, I will spare her life."

His words were spoken with an even, emotionless tone. The tone of a liar, one with lots of practice. The stench of his duplicity gave him away. A sour scent that fed my instincts with the notion to distrust even in the face of sincerity. He meant to do her harm.

"No," I responded to his offer. Malus remained unflinching—he knew my answer before I even spoke it.

"There will be a time—and it will be different for you than it was for me—that you will have to make a choice. It will be a very difficult choice. I made the wrong one—I tried to end it before I was ready."

My Echo had tried to end his confrontation with Malus before he was ready. His words were a broken record, repeating his warning, as my brain digested it from every possible angle.

What choice did I have?

"If you run, you could live to fight another day," said Chappy. "He needs her for something. Chances are, you still have time."

How could I just run? How could do that to her? How could I abandon her?

"I don't expect you to listen to me, my man," said Montoya, "but he's been eyeing that key around your neck since the moment he saw it. He needs it. Just as much as he needs Jaycie."

"If you run, you'd be thwarting Malus from obtaining the key," said Henry.

"Protect the key," said Doshin. "Best way to protect woman. While you have key, he does not. It is your only advantage."

"You do this, you have to do it right," said Jamaal. "I've got some ideas."

Jaycie squeezed my hand as if to say she agreed with them. It seemed she really could hear the voices inside my head.

"You can feel them," said Doshin. "Twelve of them. Six on left. Six on right."

The evil that surrounded me was great. I could suddenly smell them all individually as I listened to the information my body was providing.

"Face them on even terms, my man," said Montoya. "Never face enemy combatants on their turf. You choose the place. Face them one at a time, and maybe we stand a chance."

If I stayed, there was no hope—but if I ran, hope stayed alive. The idea of leaving her was complete and utterly petrifying. It was like a sin against myself.

I pulled Jaycie closer and felt her warmth. She'd told me from the beginning what must be done. She tugged at my leather jacket and said, "Run and don't look back."

Then her arms went slack, falling lifelessly to her sides.

Angelic reflexes are mostly instinctual and create responses similar to impulsive animalistic reactions. A strange motion from the trees elicited a warning growl from my own throat. An intoxicating scent urged me to sniff furiously and soak up as much as my nose could gather. Pain and fear made me dangerous, like a pit bull backed into a corner. But when Jaycie's arms went slack, the roar of flames in my chest went to peak level, and I fought back the urge to expel my fear in a blaze of bloody wrath. Something was wrong, and the warmth of our embrace faded. It was all I could do to let go and see what I already knew.

The person in my arms was no longer Jacinda. She was someone else, a woman I'd never met. Her features were similar, but also very different. A whole separate person made of the sum of the same parts, like Mr. Potato Head, only heartbreaking. The constellation of freckles on her face was aligned improperly, and the color of her hair and eyes faded into blonde and blue.

Malus laughed.

"She's mine, Tony," he said, sounding like a doctor informing a patient they had only days to live. A cold, hard bedside manner. He spoke like there was no going back. "She is not who you think she is."

"Who are you?" she asked. Her brow wrinkled as she stepped away.

"Jaycie? Come back to me," I whispered. Her eyes widened, and I watched my favorite constellation of freckles morph back to their proper place, followed by her nose and lips shifting along with the colors of her eyes and hair.

Jaycie returned and trembled, stricken with grief and terror. She jolted frantically, her mouth too slow to catch up to the tremendous thoughts she needed to convey. Thoughts that suddenly overwhelmed her.

"Tony, I forgot so much," she said in a breathy whisper. She shivered while grappling with my hands, gathering my full attention.

"Forgot what?" I asked as involuntary tears streamed down my face.

The smell of gasoline crept closer, and I noted a distance of ten feet from the strength of the scent.

"I'm not what you think I am," she said. "I can make and do terrible things. I made myself forget, but the memories never left. I just hid them away." She turned to face Malus, her posture rigid and defiant.

"Jace, what're you doing?" I asked, my voice choking in my throat, shocked by her courage. I placed a hand on her shoulder to maintain her distance from him and repositioned myself in front of her.

"I can end this," she said as she stepped in front again with the same confident posture I had known to be totally and wholly Jaycie O'Neill. It was the bold charisma, the selflessness, and the thoughtfulness that attracted everyone to her and ultimately held my own heart for ransom. She had raised her hands, twisting them in the air like she was casting a spell or conjuring demons with an archaic form of sign language, when she suddenly fell to her knees with a screech.

"No, you can't," Malus replied. He had a disgusted, disappointed look on his face.

Blood dripped from her lips and leaked from her nose, puddling onto the pavement. I knelt beside her in a panic. What was she attempting to do?

"Are you okay?" I wiped the blood from her face, drawing a streak from lip to ear. Harsh flashes of past memories bounded off the insides of my skull—I was crumbling. I saw her blood on my hands and felt the same panic I did that day. It was happening all over again.

I couldn't accept any more.

"Sir," said Henry, annoyingly. "It would appear Malus has control over the lady."

"I don't know what's wrong with me!" she cried, while the muscles in her body cramped and torqued. Her face contorted, halfway between Jaycie and the other woman, as the two identities dueled for dominance.

"Stop this!" I demanded.

"*You* can stop it. Just give me what I want," replied Malus.

I glared at him while Jaycie cried. I imagined what it would take to cross the next ten yards to his throat, and what might step out of the dark forest if I did.

There was only one viable option.

"Tony," said Jamaal. "Trust us." He was fearful that I might actually cross that ten yards in a blink and go down in a blaze of fury.

"Love," I said, lifting Jaycie's chin to meet my eyes. There was no way to soothe her pain or ease the torment. For the moment, she was all Jaycie, and she hung on my every word, knowing these might be our last. "Be strong for me and don't give up. I promise I'll find you. I won't ever stop." She began to cry, not sorrowful sobs, but gentle tears acknowledging our sacrifice. "I love you and I always will."

"I love you and I always will," she repeated, then was gone. The woman I loved was swallowed by another, willed by Malus and his crooked smile.

MALUS

He said his goodbyes just as Phobos and Deimos combined their wills with mine. Lilly's consciousness solidified, and she was mine once again.

She stood up and shirked Tony like they had never met. Her pace was deliberate as she spanned the distance between us in seconds, wrapped her arms around me, and sealed our reunion with a kiss. Like a shark, I could smell the fragrance of jealousy and anger filling the bitter air around Tony. The rest of my pack shrank around him from all angles. Tightening the noose.

He gave my lover and me a brief look of betrayal, which quickly vanished under the hardened brow of a man who had accepted his fate. It was time for him to make his move.

"Are you ready to die?"

I tracked a streaking flicker of light as it fluttered through the air toward the wrecked automobile. My taste for theatrics had stolen my attention, giving him the smallest of openings to rest his hopes of escape on a single toss. His precision was as immaculate as it was precise, a sign that was all too disturbing to analyze. It would seem he was much more like *us* than human, using his instincts and impulses to guide his way.

A tiny metallic object carrying its own flame flew directly into the gap in the metal surrounding the engine that powered the vehicle. The resulting explosion caught us all off guard. The proximity knocked Lilly to the ground, but I remained tracked on Tony.

Only he wasn't where he was supposed to be.

He had vanished. Blinked out of existence and under the Veil, only to flicker out mid-stride, then right back under as he reached the tree line. He may have been using his instincts, but his skills were weak and lacked stability. It was a clever escape, using the light of the explosion to mask his silhouette and move into the Veil, reappearing just beyond the tightening ring of my Thirteen. It was a bold move, clearly done without intention.

Mere luck.

He was no longer just a mark, a spark, a weak demi-god or halfling. He was now like us. He had power.

"Go," I commanded, and ten shadows chased after the pungent trail of fear Tony left behind as he fled into the dark depths of the forest.

THE CURING
OF BACCHUS

453 B.C.

As the summer sun plummeted below the horizon, the city of Turin celebrated. Music played somewhere in the distance, fanciful and fit for dancing. The fall harvest was beginning, and the final days of summer had left behind a vineyard full of ripened, blood-red grapes. Wine flowed like water, and merriment spread across the city in celebration.

"Where are we going?" said the boy. He was chasing after the girl, whose cheeks were as rosy as the wine within her cup.

"Hush now, Jacobello," said the girl. "You complain like my sister."

"Galiana," whined Jacobello, spilling a portion of his cup as he followed her up the hill. He was tired of chasing and thought they were already far enough away from the celebration.

The music from the city below was dulling into a calming tune, and the moon greeted them, reflecting the sunset's washes of red and pink.

"Don't you want to be alone with me?" asked Galiana. She had gotten ahead of him again, and as she smiled back, he realized there was not a place in all of Turin he would rather be.

Eventually Galiana grew tired of the chase and dragged Jacobello down into the dirt between the rows of grapes, laughing and enjoying the warmth provided by the wine. She giggled as he slipped his hand under her garments and kissed her gently on the lips.

She whispered into his ear something that strengthened his pursuit, their intensity peaking.

"Excuse me."

The voice broke their passion, and Galiana covered her exposed breast.

"I am sorry, forgive me," said the man. He appeared small and feeble, hunched, wearing a dark cloak that covered his entire body. They could not see his face but for a portion of his chin that remained unshaded by the hood. He trembled while sipping on wine from a golden chalice, as if he had consumed too many libations at the festival.

"We are not offended, sir," said Jacobello as he stood to shield Galiana. "May we help you on your way?" His words were kind, but he had ulterior motives to lead the man away. Ulterior motives that grumbled at the man's inopportune arrival.

"No, no, I did not mean to bother you," said the man as he ambled closer. He moved like an old man, suffering through the pain of aging joints. "Please, enjoy a sip and I'll be on my way. It's the finest wine one can buy in the entire city." He held the chalice out and let its aroma entice them. "Go on."

When Jacobello did not immediately take the chalice, the man nudged it closer. Eventually, Jacobello took the cup and drank a greedy gulp, then passed it to Galiana where she sat. She took a dainty, untrusting sip before passing it back to the man, who then took a lusty sip of his own.

"Good, is it not?" said the man.

"Quite good," agreed Jacobello, who turned to the girl and smiled. "Very strong." His smile faded, and he began to sweat, the alcohol warming his blood from head to toe.

"What's wrong?" asked Galiana, as she watched Jacobello's face pale and his limbs begin to shake.

"I'm thirsty," said Jacobello. "I'm so thirsty!"

"What's wrong with him?" asked Galiana, her worry expanding with every gnash of teeth and involuntary spasm.

"He has the thirst, child," said the man. "If you had taken more than a sip, you would have it too. It is a shame. I would have preferred to keep you and eat him."

The man then rose to full height, his mass doubling as he stretched his mighty limbs. He was no longer hunched and crippled but a towering mammoth. He was taller than most men, and as pale as a summer's cloud, with bloodshot eyes and bloodstained lips.

Galiana scampered backward in the dirt at his hideousness. His dark hair fell into his face, partially obscuring the wicked eyes that sent chills up and down her spine.

"Who are you?" she asked.

The man turned to Jacobello. "Go, fetch me more to eat." Jacobello looked upon the man with frightened eyes for the last time, and his fearful gaze dissolved with love and admiration. He left at once to fulfill his master's bidding.

When the man turned back to Galiana, she was so stricken that she remained petrified in the dirt, her fingers digging into the soil like garden tools, softening the earth. He lowered himself upon her and bit her savagely upon her neck. The stream of blood filled his mouth and throat like a fountain of vitality.

"Bacchus, god of wine and blood," said Malus as he plucked a fresh bunch of grapes and tossed one into his mouth, "you have a terrible thirst."

"What do you know of my thirst?" roared Bacchus, pulling away from Galiana to face this man who had intruded upon his feeding. Bacchus rose to his feet as the girl bled into the dirt.

"Your sister cursed you with madness after you defiled her priestesses during Matronalia. Of all the days in a single year, of which there are three-hundred-sixty-five of them, you chose the one that honored Juno to take her most devoted follower," said Malus. "The thirst is strong, Bacchus. Or should I call you Dionysus? I can never remember which was your proper name."

"How may I assist you?" asked Bacchus. Malus knew his affliction, and that knowledge gave Bacchus worry—how did this stranger know of his curse? His addiction? His disease?

"I want to help rid your mind of the madness," said Malus. "To cure your incurable disease."

"What must I do?" asked Bacchus.

"Sign my contract, and we shall discuss the proper terms."

IX
school daze

JACINDA
Then.

Hey, Jace, I'm still here. I'm still watching you. I promised I'd never leave you. I know I broke that promise once before, but I had to. However, if I had to do it over again, would I have run into that forest and left you in the hands of that maniac?

I don't know anymore.

Sometimes I think I'd welcome the end of all this. Maybe there'd be another life for us in whatever came *after*… But I'm not so sure there is an after—and if there is, will it still be there if Malus gets what he wants?

Jace, I've been watching you for so long already, yet there's so much more to learn. I still don't know what you are capable of and how it all started. I don't even know if there are answers waiting for me or just more questions.

Maybe I'm really here because I want to be close to you. To be with you, till the end.

Can I do that? Can I just be with you until the end?

December 31st, 1996

You and Whitney arrived at the party a little after ten. It took theatrics and choreography to pull it off, but Whitney met you a full mile up the road from her house. She was shivering, and her lips were turning purple through the thick red shade of lipstick she was wearing.

"Took you long enough," whined Whitney. Her tiny top and skirt made you feel overdressed.

"If I had known you'd be out here in a bathing suit, I would have hurried!"

"Ha ha," mocked Whitney. "It's time to party!"

Together, you rode off with the music blasting.

"What kind of awful shit is this?" groaned Whitney. You were listening to 80s tunes, like Depeche Mode, Tears for Fears, Howard Jones, and Eddie Money.

"You don't like it?"

This may come as a shock to you, Jace, but most people don't have the kind of love for music you do. Most people listened to the mass-produced top 10 hits on repeat, never searching beyond what was on their radio dial.

Whitney popped your mixed tape out of the player, then channeled to something that had so much bass it made your speakers rattle. "Now we're partying!" she shouted.

The house was located at the end of a private cul-de-sac in Anemone Manor. There were already so many cars that you had to park up the street and walk. When you got to the door you could hear the thumping music inside, like a runaway heartbeat flustering your own pulse.

"This party looks dope!" yelled Whitney. "Aren't you glad I got the invite?"

"Yeah," you said nervously. "Whose party is this?"

"I don't know, one of the guys on the football team."

"And how'd you get the invite?" You'd meant to ask sooner, but it didn't seem all that important until now.

"Oh, Chuck and I fooled around a bit," she said.

"Oh."

"What's the matter?" asked Whitney. You stopped at the bottom of the front porch, and when Whitney turned toward you, she immediately ran back down the stairs. "Stop!"

"Stop what?"

"Stop thinking. You think too much," she said. "You have to learn to be like me."

Phrases like that from a girl who was three years your junior made you uncomfortable. After all, Jace, did you really want to be like her?

"What does that mean?"

"It means, take all that stupid shit you have spinning in your head, all that self-doubt, that insecure bullshit, and shove it behind a door in your mind. Store it all up. Throw it away. Move forward. There's no sense in dealing with your bullshit when there are parties and fun to be had."

You hated to admit it, but Whitney was right. You were having a hard time getting out of your own head. Every time you tried to move forward, something brought you back. You closed her eyes, took a deep breath, and wished all the pain into the furthest corner of your mind. When you opened your eyes, you felt better—you felt free and ready to take on the world.

"Okay," you said with a big mischievous smile. "Let's go."

Once you were inside the house, it was tough to adjust to the rhythm of the chaos. There was smoke, flashing lights, beer and bottles on the floor, and the only thing you could hear was the thumping bass of the speakers in the living room. The house was immense, and room to move was limited. Whitney took your hand and moved toward the kitchen, where each of you grabbed a cup of spiked punch and found a corner to stand in.

"Okay," screamed Whitney. "Now we have to try and look cute so boys will come over and talk to us."

"Is that all? Does it work?"

"Always."

And it did. A few boys came over, and after a few minutes of attempting to talk over the bass, Whitney grabbed your hand and dragged you away from them without so much as a warning.

"What are we doing?" you asked. Isn't that what you were there to do? Talk to boys?

"Those boys were lame!" she shouted.

"What do you mean?"

"They were lame! Unpopular dweebs!"

Whitney dragged you into the next room, and Jace, I was hoping you wouldn't go in there. You immediately spotted Rick and Tori and all the rest of the popular kids in your class. You had eyes for him like I had eyes for you. No matter where he went within that room, you were watching, even when you were trying not to notice.

"This is where we want to be," shouted Whitney.

"Are you sure?"

"Absolutely," she said. "I've hooked up with at least three of those guys." She pointed to a group of them. "By end of tonight, I'll have four. Maybe five," she said with a wink.

You laughed. It was hard to know the difference between jokes and bravado with Whitney. Sometimes it seemed like she was just a big talker, which provided plenty of entertainment value for the both of you, but other times it was like she was trying to bury her darkness with some other kind of darkness. Adding one more layer of experience to cover up the innocence she'd lost. There were moments when she was like a heat-seeking rocket, looking to explode as quickly as possible.

"Hey, I'm gonna score us some," said Whitney, pointing at Rick's general area. You had no idea what she meant, so you shrugged and continued sipping your punch. You scanned the room and noticed a few boys staring at you. They were saying something and laughing, but you couldn't hear them over the music, and it made you overly self-aware and questioning everything about your clothes and how hard you tried to fit in.

"Jace!"

"Rick!" you shouted back. He had moved in when you weren't looking. You felt nervous in his presence, like everything you did had to be perfect to keep his attention. You had too much self-doubt inside you, but you made sure to quickly gather it up, shove it behind that door inside your mind, and lock it tight.

You were too good for him, Jace. Ugh, in moments like this I wish I could stop watching—but I made you a promise. I'd stay right here, just over your shoulder.

"I didn't know you partied," he said.

"Of course, I do!" you replied. "Who doesn't?"

Oh Jace, that's not what he meant.

"Fuck yeah!" he said, then reached into his pocket and pulled out a plastic bag. "Here." He grabbed your hand and dropped something into it. "Free samples."

When you opened your hand, there were two pills resting in your palm. One had a green triangle with a question mark stamped onto it, and the other had a yellow circle with a smiley face. You didn't want to ask what it was—you knew the moment you did, Rick would think you were lame. At the same time, you were struggling with the idea of swallowing a substance you didn't understand.

Peer pressure, Jace. It's awful, isn't it? I once jumped off the top of my high school stadium bleachers, just because everyone was doing it. Thad and Amanda told me not to, but I wanted to belong. I wanted to be seen. I wanted to impress a girl named Monica, who, frankly, was only a fraction of how sweet, interesting, and beautiful you were. It was stupid. I could have been hurt—

Whitney showed up, just in time, and for a second I thought that she might ruin the moment or slap the pills out of your hand with righteous indignation—instead, she plucked the yellow smiley face from your palm and swallowed it with her own smile.

"Thanks, sweetie!" she said to Rick.

"Jesus! Did you just swallow the whole thing?" he yelled, and she smiled and nodded.

"I'm no rookie," she said laughing.

"There's more where that came from," he said with a flirt. "First round's free. After that, we can discuss the price." Then he winked, and it made you feel jealous, if not a tad bit grossed out. This guy you wanted for so long was not who you thought he was, and yet, you'd put him so high up on that pedestal that you started to make exceptions.

"What are you waiting for?" said Whitney, as Rick eyed you up. He didn't think you would do it—it was a test. You were still staring at the pill, unsure if it was the best or worst decision you could make that night. "C'mon! I don't want to start tripping without you!"

"Bottoms up," said Rick, as he placed his hand beneath yours and lifted the pill toward your mouth. You could see the devilish grin on his face and wanted nothing more than to keep that smile for yourself. You swallowed the pill and chased it with a gulp of punch, then immediately felt guilty.

It's okay, Jace. We all make bad decisions.

"Alright!" shouted Rick. "Let's party!"

Every twenty minutes thereafter, the party slowed by a beat. As it slowed, everything you did, everywhere you looked, everything you said, every sensation you had, was amplified and felt like heaven. Consumed with pleasure, you couldn't stop yourself from dancing. At some point you came to realize you were no longer dancing with Whitney. A guy had his arms around you, and he was kissing your neck. Everything about it felt good, too good to care whether or not you wanted it to happen.

"Want to go somewhere?" he whispered into your ear.

"No," you replied. "I just want to dance."

The guy glared at you. He was drunk. Even in your state, Jace, you could see it. He looked like he might fall over at any moment. Then some other guy danced in from behind you. He kissed you on the cheek, and as he began to rub against your back, you caught a flash of his height, his sandy blonde hair, and you smiled.

Rick was dancing with you, his hands were on you, and you wanted nothing more.

You turned and placed your hands on his chest when he said, "Found you."

Those words, Jace, they should have been a warning.

You looked up and saw the two different eyes, gray and brown, and staggered backward into the crowd. As your heart thumped wildly, the chemicals in your blood slowed things down as your fear sped everything up, and you felt like you would die right there.

The world spun and spun and spun until you finally popped.

You threw up, right in the middle of that room.

Someone slipped and fell on it, and you slid backward onto the floor.

"What the fuck!?" screamed Tori. She and a few others slipped and landed in a mound of sweaty drunk teens.

"Oh my God," you moaned as the music shut off and the lights flicked on. Nobody knew it was you, but the embarrassed look on your face was about to reveal your guilt in front of half your class.

Some guy said, "C'mon," as he lifted you off the floor and quickly ushered you from the room. "You don't want them finding out who puked," he whispered.

Once in the kitchen, you swung your arms around to get him off you. You were still high, and freaked out, and now your stomach was sour, and you didn't know how to trust anyone in that state.

"What do you want?" you asked.

"I'm Kurt," he said, holding out his hand. "We've met before, a while back." When you didn't take it, he put it back into his letterman jacket pocket. "Anyway, I didn't want you to add anything more to the list of things Tori Martin already hates you for."

You stared at him, as if you were trying to decide if he was the man with two eyes, only he had two normal eyes—hazel—and you had to get super close to him to see them—then you nearly tripped in the process.

Kurt caught you and said, "Do you need someone to take you home?"

"No, I'm okay."

"Right. Are you sure?"

"I said I'm okay!"

"Sure," he said, backing away. "Sure, you are." Then he left you alone in the kitchen.

Struggling to keep it together, you staggered into the hallway, searching for Whitney. The lights went off and the music came back on—the sudden change nearly made you puke all over again. You used the wall to steady yourself as you walked into the living room, then to the den, and even crawled up the stairs, but you couldn't find Whitney anywhere.

"Are you looking for Whitney Berry?" asked Tori. She was sitting at the top of the stairs as you crawled by.

"Yeah," you said, preparing to be insulted.

"She left with Todd Baker about twenty minutes ago."

"Who's Todd Baker?"

"Senior. Captain of the fucking baseball team?"

"Oh."

"I don't know you, but you don't fucken fit in here. You don't belong with this fucking crowd."

"Thanks," you said angrily. "Neither do you, jerk."

"No, sorry, you misunderstand," she said. "I don't fucking belong here either."

You attempted to leave, to rush down the stairs, but couldn't control your balance. As you teetered, Tori reached out and placed a hand on your arm, steadying you.

"I know you like him," said Tori. "Rick. You look at him like I did when I first fucking met him."

"No, I don't," you lied, but Tori just smiled.

"I said the same fucking thing." She had tears in her eyes. "From one gal to another. Stay away from him."

"Is that a threat?" you asked, and I saw a glimmer of the Tori Martin I knew. The cursed girl who bucked the establishment.

"No. Fuck," said Tori. She laughed and cried at the same time. "It's a warning. Don't end up like me."

"You mean like a total bitch who wants to ruin my life? Leave me alone! You don't deserve someone like Rick."

Wow, Jace. How many ways can I profess how wrong that statement was? She was trying to help, handing you an olive branch—I know you saw Rick much differently back then, but so much could have changed if you had taken her advice.

You slapped Tori's hand away and stormed down the stairs. When you got to the landing, you realized that if you stayed you were going to get sick again. Rather than take on that embarrassment, you walked out the door and down the street, ignoring the cawing crows that watched you leave. Then you drove all the way home. You slept like a rock that night, pushing all the pain aside, locking it behind a door in the furthest corners of your mind.

When school started back up three days later, rumors spread quickly across Grace Falls High School. Whitney had called to give you the news the night before. Tori and Rick split up, and the gossip was that Tori had cheated on him with three different guys. All at the same time, at the New Year's Eve party.

The rumor seemed far-fetched. When you left it was already well after midnight, and Tori was crying by herself at the top of the stairs after spending the whole night dancing. Still, your immediate reaction was that justice had been served. Tori became the new pariah of Grace Falls High School, and soon after she showed up with dyed green hair and a punk attitude.

Somewhere deep inside, you stopped hating Tori and almost admired her courage to be herself. You thought it must have been exhausting pretending to be someone she wasn't.

Oddly enough, it was that kind of thought that pushed you toward Rick. You wanted to feel free again. You wanted to feel good. Eventually you found yourself approaching Rick in the halls, asking for another free sample—and Jace, this finally answered one of my questions.

When did you start using? Now I know.

One free sample turned into two. Each time, Rick handed it over like he was only going to do it just this once. There was a method to his behavior. A slow method that twisted your schoolgirl crush into chemical dependency, and eventually into something more.

Every few days you'd meet Rick out by his car in the parking lot at lunch. You'd sit in his Mustang as he gave you a free sample or two—then one kiss turned into two, and by spring you had an arrangement.

April 4th, 1997

"Did you pass your history test?" You were struggling to come up with things to talk about. The two of you couldn't talk about art—

Rick hated art. You couldn't talk about movies or music—Rick had the exact opposite taste as you—a limited palate of Billboard top hits and lame unimaginative comedies and action flicks. You couldn't even discuss comics or books—Rick hated those too, and this made you miss Amanda that much more.

You met twice a week at his car, where you'd sit there chatting until the kissing started. Rick was dating a girl named Rhonda, but your rendezvous at his car were his own little secret.

"Yeah," said Rick. "I got a seventy-two."

"Wow, just barely."

"What did you get?"

"Ninety-five."

"Bitch," he grumbled. There were acceptable ways to say that word at times, played up for humor, but Rick couldn't be funny if he farted at an open mic night.

"Hey! Am not." You laughed and pushed at his arm, desperate for the attention and to get to all the kissing. Sometimes it took so long to get him to finally relent. Did he have to be high to find you attractive?

"So, listen," said Rick, finally cutting to the chase. "I can keep giving you freebies, but the price is going up."

"The price?" you said with an awkward laugh. You thought he was joking, but Jace, guys like him never joke about the things they want. He was a control freak—nay—a control maniac. He didn't want your money. He wanted your body, and your very soul if he could find a way to manipulate you into giving it to him. "I thought we were just hanging out? Having some fun and stuff."

"We are," he said, almost as if he was placating you, "but I've got a girlfriend, and I can't keep doing this unless it's worth my time."

"What will make it worth your time?" you asked, confused. You were playing right into his plan, Jace. He was a master of a game you didn't even know you were playing.

"I think you know a few ways," he said with a grin.

That day, you did something you didn't really want to do, all for Rick's attention and a small little pill that made the bad feelings go away. The problem was you didn't have enough pills to take away the feelings you had once you were done in that car with Rick.

Yet, up to three times a week, you met him back at his car, and walked away with more guilt.

Then, one night, after attending one of Rick's baseball games, you witnessed something that put it all into perspective for you. Rick hit a walk-off home run, and as the crowd cheered and his teammates high-fived, Rhonda Williams met him by home plate and kissed him publicly. You couldn't help but think that it should have been you down there, and the pain seeped through that locked door inside your mind. That night, you took all the remaining pills you had, along with half a bottle of your mother's prescription, and swallowed it down with the scotch from your dad's liquor cabinet.

Then you locked yourself in your room.

As the minutes ticked and the tears fell, you were torn between your desire to end it all and wanting someone, anyone, to talk to—to bring you out of this misery.

You called Whitney, but her mother answered and said she was grounded again.

Then you called Amanda, but the phone rang and rang. The two of you hadn't talked in years, why would she pick up now?

Who else was there for you?

You noticed a gathering of birds outside your bedroom window. They watched you. Eventually you sat up on the bed and stared at the ceiling as it faded to black at the corners of your vision.

I heard your prayers. The silent ones spoken inside your mind. From behind the Veil, I could hear your thoughts by reaching out and touching them.

"Please," you thought, "please, please, please, I'm tired of being alone. Bring someone into my life that is good and right. Someone who cares for me."

You cried so hard I thought you might die, and Jace, I was ready and willing to step out of my exile and to breathe life back into your lungs if they stopped. I wouldn't let it end now, not like this. Damn the paradox.

Damn it all, I wouldn't let you go, not like this.

The crows continued to come. So many of them that I came to understand they were there for a reason. Were they good? Were they bad? I didn't know, but they gathered all the same, as if to watch you die.

"Don't give up," I whispered. "It will get better."

But would it? You would spend the next ten years struggling, most of that time while you were at my side, facing the world together. Was it mercy to let you go now? Would it have made anything better? And what would become of me?

Was I being selfish to want to love you?

Could I change the past even if I wanted to? Could I influence the future by saving you now?

I wanted nothing more than to take your pain away. I wanted to charge out of the Veil and into your life, grab you by the hand and take you away from it all. Find some corner of the universe just for us, shut everyone and everything out.

"Please," you said out loud. "I want to be happy."

"Then forget it all," I whispered into your ear. "Push it all away. Start new."

I thought I was doing the right thing, but did anyone know that for sure? We always balance the idea of right and wrong by our own morality, but in a world where good people died every day, was "the right" thing truly right? Or was the morally ambiguous nature of reality meant to devour those who fall, for the betterment of all?

"I want to wake up tomorrow and be happy," you said. "I want to be who I was meant to be. I want to find myself. I want to find love. I want to live happy."

And as you cried unknowingly in my arms, the world around you blurred, like heat rising from a hot surface, and the poison in your stomach and veins left you—the demons inside you were locked away in that room inside your mind, padlocked and barricaded—and I never once left your side. I saw you through the darkness and cried with you till the sun came up.

X

run

TONY
December 23rd, 2013
Now.

I was hoping for a diversion, but what I got was an explosion.

I tossed my Zippo, aiming at the puddle of gasoline beneath the car. I had no delusions that it would work, even though Jamaal said it would. In the brain-trust I...*trust*?

Though I wasn't prepared for my toss to be so accurate. Why aim for the puddle when a more desired outcome was four feet higher and five feet to the right? The Zippo fell through a hole in the hood and set off an almost instantaneous explosion, igniting the fuel line and causing a concussive blast just as I made my move. It wasn't luck, but it certainly wasn't the originally intended outcome. The happy accident sent pieces of debris high into the air and scattered the area with puddles of flame.

As I fled, the moving shadows approached from the forest's edge, and my instincts kicked in. I felt like I was separating myself from the world as I broke an invisible viscous plane—like diving into a pool of water. It was a strange immersive feeling, that twisted color and sound. When I passed the incoming shadows, their stench like rotted meat, I felt myself resurface—slipping back into the *real* world.

Then I ran. As fast as I could, I ran. I leapt over briar bushes and ducked under low- hanging limbs, all without relinquishing my pace. I moved faster than a fleeing deer, and small game ducked for cover, away from the oncoming darkness that hunted me. Even they knew what was coming and made damn sure not to be there when it did.

There was a high-pitched wail from somewhere behind, followed by a second shrill on my right flank. The next instant, I was ducking to avoid the clawed swipe of a madwoman. She bore long fangs and fresh blood dripped from her deep crimson lips.

Despite my pace, I found her nipping at my heels, riding the intoxicating high of her recent kill—the blood like nitrous oxide injecting speed into a race car.

She was a vampire. My teenage love of schlocky horror movie nights with Amanda and the gang and a few bags of popcorn told me all I needed to know about her affliction. I wanted to turn around and study her—perform tests, like checking her reflection and finding a patch of sunlight peeking through the overcast skies—

Then the footsteps behind me doubled, then quickly doubled again, all four of them keeping pace, burning off fresh blood from a feeding frenzy.

When I spotted a fallen tree in my path, I decided to use it to my advantage. There were things my new body could do which I had yet to realize. Things like enhanced agility, along with the bending of physical laws—like my Echo strolling around on the ceiling. In many ways, it was all about imagination—what could I do, and how far could I push myself?

"Fuck yeah, my man!" yelled Montoya. "Go for it, bro!"

Great minds…

A dead branch the approximate size of a baseball bat hung from the next tree. I snatched it clean off the trunk and held it at the ready when I made my jump.

The fallen tree had been dead for years and had amassed weeds and other scavenger plant life across its trunk. It laid at an angle more than five feet from the ground. I leapt, placing my foot firmly on its side, then sprung off and corkscrewed my body—the ability to manipulate myself in the air came to me naturally, like I was tapping into some higher function. Nature over nurture.

The first vampire, a young woman with fair blonde hair and a low-cut top, took the bat-sized branch square in the left side of her temple, crushing her skull in on itself and sending her crashing into the middle of a briar thicket. I landed facing my attackers with a wooden nub in my hands. I shoved it through the heart of my next attacker—because what else would I do with a sharp stabby piece of wood and a vampire—a tattooed woman wearing ripped jeans and a t-shirt. She fell dead in my arms, a limp lifeless mass, and I couldn't help but notice how young she was.

She was beautiful, with hopes and dreams, a bright future, and family and friends. It was a waste—a fucking tragedy—these gods, like Summanus and Mammon, used people like toys. They hung back and let their "lackeys" do all the work.

I hated them. I hated them all—Malus and every creature, demon, and asshole—or combination thereof—that followed him.

I discarded the girl along with my sympathies, readying for the next attack. Each moment passed in a hyper-aware state, like everything was speeding up and slowing down at the same time. The other two vampires came from either side and swiped for any part of me they could sink their claws into. I easily dodged their assaults at first, but then an awful scent wafted by on a draft of air, tainted with the stench of malevolence. My senses roared, lit up like NORAD as the doomsday clock struck midnight, urging me to get-the-fuck-out-of-there.

I took off running again, in the same direction as before, anything to put more distance between me and the incoming darkness. I didn't know what it was, but it smelled far more dangerous than the rabid vampire women.

"They are attempting to soften you," said Doshin. "Send slaves first. Make you bleed. Easier kill."

"You can't fight them all," said Montoya. "Keep moving, my man!"

I was going to make Malus pay. I was going to make him suffer.

Running felt like the opposite of that, but my brain-trust was right.

I kept running, building speed and cutting through the thickest parts of the forest. My mind counted and noted everything, from the scents around me to each and every footfall chasing from behind, whether I wanted to or not. My brain was like a high-tech abacus—

"Or maybe a *calculator*?" suggested Jamaal.

Or maybe a calculator—

—in that instant, one set of feet disappeared from the sounds of my pursuers—I had only a heartbeat to counter. One of the vampires threw herself into the air at me. I pivoted and grabbed her by the shirt, taking a slash across the arm to use her momentum against her, and tossed her wailing and screaming into a nearby pine—impaling her on the low hanging branches.

The same part of my brain that identified true names told me she was Bacchae—a maiden of Bacchus, god of wine and ritual madness. One drop of his blood could induce the bakkheia—the changing from human to bloodthirsty animal. The story was always the same: a beautiful young girl catches the god's attention. Mesmerized by the wine-god's allure, he drains her of blood, then offers her a drink of his own tainted blood from his wretched golden chalice. Forever his Bacchae—a psycho vampire zombie.

How I knew all of that crazy particular shit, and where it was being stored inside my head was still a mystery. Another question for a rainier day…

The final Bacchae lunged, hacking into my left thigh to maim me. My leg went instantly numb, and I fell to one knee as the feral woman crept in like a cat circling a wounded rabbit.

Slashing, lunging, she caught me twice with shallow cuts—once across my cheek, and sent me staggering backwards—just as a new set of vibrations from the right captured my full attention—like an incoming earthquake.

I dodged by falling backward at the exact time a set of great twisted bull horns breezed past my vision and skewered the girl in half, breaking her body to pieces like she was nothing but a cheap Lego set. The beast was at least three times my size and was one of the most hideous things I had ever seen breezing past me in a blur. Even his stench smelled of ancient rot.

"Moloch," said Doshin. "Run! Run now!"

"Fuck fuck fuck-fuck-fuck," sang Montoya.

I popped onto my feet and took off at full speed, racing to get as far away from the bull god as I could. One-on-one, without weapons, out in the open with no defense, I was a goner. Killing Mammon had been luck—a combination of pure survival instinct and the god of greed's own hubris. I couldn't expect a repeat performance against such a massive foe of pure physical power. Even Moloch's muscles had muscles.

Moloch's bellow tore through the forest like a mighty horn. I had never heard such a sound. It was otherworldly and made my heart beat twice as fast. The bull god had gored the wrong target and stomped her to pieces, but I was already a mile away—ignoring the pain that sharpened in my wounded leg. The numbing effect had faded, replaced by crippling hot stabs of agony, like a hundred knives jabbing me with every move.

As my pace slowed, the forest began to thin near an overgrown bank next to a small stream. To my left was an overpass for cars up a steep incline with a giant concrete and metal tube running through it, allowing the stream to pass beneath.

I sloshed my way through the ice-cold water, attempting to hide my scent—knowledge gifted from one of the thousands of entities inside my head. The water was waist-high from earlier rain and snow, and I began to feel the flames inside stifle to embers. I passed through the tube and out the other side, then stood at the base of a hill, looking up at the storage facility parking lot. The bright red, light-up sign on top of the building said "Store-It" and could be seen from miles away.

I hobbled over to the nearest entrance and found the door locked with a sophisticated keypad that lit up when it sensed motion.

"My man," asked Montoya, "Do we have to guess the code to get inside? Like a combination lock?"

"We could try," replied Jamaal. "A four-digit code has ten thousand possible combinations."

"Is it phone?" asked Doshin, noting the buttons on the keypad.

"Is there another way inside the building without a puzzle?" asked Chappy.

"No, and doubtful," answered Jamaal, seemingly amused by their lack of knowledge for basic technology.

I grabbed my cell phone from the interior pocket of my brown leather jacket and quickly texted Maynard—my fingers were shaking, but it wasn't from the cold—something was wrong.

"At storage," I typed, then immediately hit send. "Numerical pass?"

As I waited for his response, I scanned the area. They hadn't found me yet, but they would. Soon. It was only a matter of time.

"Pass 1101 – Meet at lot # 1865 BTS – Help coming."

"B-T-S?" questioned Chappy.

"Be there soon," said Jamaal, "It's an acronym. Shorthand for people with slow thumbs." He mimicked the art of phone typing while I entered the passcode for the door.

"The 21st century is an interesting place," said Chappy.

"This is only the beginning," said Jamaal. "The end of the century is a whole *different* place."

The door opened with a small buzz, and I quietly let myself in.

"What help is coming?" asked Henry. "What could Mr. Maynard possibly mean by that phrase?"

Doshin replied with a shrug.

We were only twenty feet inside the door when my leg felt like it was going to fall off. "Are you okay, sir?"

"I feel cold. Weak," I said. It felt like I had the flu. Muscle pains, shortness of breath, and a possible fever.

"Perhaps," suggested Chappy, "the initial feeling of invincibility was merely a finite supply of energy? Perhaps you have overexerted your potential?"

"Or maybe I wasn't nearly as powerful as I thought?" I suggested.

"Or, maybe, you need to recharge?" said Chappy, rhetorically taking a more optimistic approach. "To eat and rest like any normal human being."

"How is your leg?" asked Doshin.

"Hurts like hell," I said, as tremors started in my limbs.

"Mammon appeared to be able to heal himself," said Chappy.

"Yeah," said Jamaal, "you busted him up, and he regenerated in seconds—like Wolverine or Deadpool. Maybe you can do that too? Like the trick you did with your hand after the Red Cap hooked it?"

"Who is Death-pool?" asked Doshin. He sounded intrigued, but Jamaal shook his head as if to say it would take too long to explain.

I heard their suggestions and concerns, but I needed to get further inside. To find a place to hide and rest—a place that wasn't so close to the entrance. Once I had made a few turns down the endless white halls of storage lots with gray metal rollup doors, I realized just how trapped I was—like a roach finding a nice inviting motel and never finding its way back out.

It was dim within the concrete hallways, with long fluorescent tube bulbs on the ceiling every ten to twenty feet. From the outside, you could tell there were at least five floors, but the façade masked the fact that inside was nothing but endless halls full of garage lockers filled with other people's belongings. The floors were solid polished concrete that smelled of cleaning solution and ammonia, and every sound produced an exaggerated echo.

The plummeting temperatures made the metal walls and concrete floors harder—so much so I could almost hear the constricting atoms slowing to a near standstill. Every step seemed to rattle my bones, and I began to stumble, losing my balance and falling into a locker door, creating a huge racket—that in all likelihood alarmed every stalking creature to my whereabouts.

"Rest, sir," said Henry. "That leg is in desperate need of stitching."

"If we had supplies, I could walk you through field stitching," said Montoya. "I had to do it a few times on myself. Hurts like hell, but it's better than losing a limb."

I waved him off and said, "I'll be okay. Give me a few."

But after a few seconds, I only began to feel worse—

—something was terribly wrong.

"Awl righ' guntlemin," said someone new, parting his way through the crowd of brain-trust. "Gef tha' man sum ruum, wull ya?" He was wearing old-timey military fatigues and a kilt, which drew all the attention away from the military helmet on his head with a big red cross. When he got to me, he eyed me up and down before rolling his eyes, then kneeled at my side and began rummaging through a canvas bag. When Jamaal and Doshin didn't immediately back away, he gave them a reason. "Aye! Fuck uff!"

"Who the hell are you?" asked Jamaal.

"Tha meduc," he spat while giving me a quick once over with a stethoscope.

"The medic?" replied Henry.

"Wha tha fuck dae ya thenk I am?" he growled, then removed his helmet to show them, exposing a head full of ginger hair. "I got mae hat with tha rud cruss."

"What'd he say?" whined Montoya.

"He's the medic," translated Henry.

"Dighted buggars," growled the medic. "Ye raff yer heid." Then he laughed like he had said something hilarious and gestured at me and him consecutively. "Fae yer heid, aye?"

"Aye?" I answered, unsure of myself.

"He's a medic? From what planet?" inquired Jamaal.

"He's Scottish," replied Henry with a bemused grin.

The medic looked me up and down, took my pulse for a split second, then moved on like he was searching for something very specific. I stayed slumped onto the floor and felt a cold wave begin to pull me under while the medic did his work. They argued over whether or not the medic was speaking English, and I drifted. My body had healed before, but there was something about the cuts the Bacchae gave me that made me feverish.

Was I poisoned?

Eventually the medic pulled out a syringe and gave me a ginger smile. "Dinnae go cryin' on mae now," he said, just before jabbing the needle directly into my heart—it was an abrasive reaction, one that lit up every nerve ending and put urgency back into my chest.

Seconds later, the color had returned to my face, and I could feel my foot again. My internal heat had yet to kick back in, and my body shivered in the sub-freezing temperatures, but I could move.

"Remarkable," said Chappy, as I checked the wound through the blood-stained tear in my jeans. "I will never find your ability to heal to be anything less than extraordinary." My leg had stopped bleeding, and the raw flesh that spanned the torn gaps was bright pink and new. Healed, just barely, but enough to move—just in the nick of time.

A loud scraping sound echoed through the halls, like blades being raked against metal—like I was being stalked by Freddy himself. There was no way of knowing what floor it originated from, only that it was getting louder, and therefore closer.

"What did you give him?" asked Henry.

The medic shrugged. "Only whut 'e needud," he said, then added, "more luss."

"Which was?" pressed Henry, but the medic winked, packed his bag, and stalked off from where he came, disappearing in a blink.

"Time to move," said Doshin.

"What did he give me?" I asked as I got to my feet, but Henry shrugged.

"The proper question is," replied Henry, "what did you give your-self? Remember, we're in *your head*, sir."

"Now!" growled Doshin.

I hustled down the hall, stifling my footfalls to mask my where-abouts. Sneaking around, my thoughts bounced from Jaycie to Malus, to whatever the hell was in that imaginary syringe, to finding Maynard and surviving the next fifteen minutes. My stomach knotted up—anxiety overwhelmed me. How was I going to save her? How was I going to survive when a stupid henchwoman vampire had carved me up?

"Focus," said Doshin. "Focus on next step. Not two, not three. Only next step."

Whether or not I was capable of following Doshin's advice became moot once the sound of crunching metal and glass shattered my concentration. It had to be the door with the keypad—torn apart and ripped off its hinges, by the sound. A frigid wind swept through the cold halls unchecked, bringing with it the smell of evil. It tasted like rusted metal and rotten egg.

"Why does evil smell so bad?" asked Montoya.

"Should I dignify that question with an obvious answer?" asked Jamaal.

Rather than face off against whatever had broken through the security door, I decided to go up a level. I opened the heavy metal door at the end of the hall and slid into the stairwell lit with emergency lighting. The scraping metal sounded louder by the second-floor landing, so I went up to the third and then the fourth for good measure.

It was a tad warmer on the fourth floor, enough to make me feel less like a living popsicle—my blood a Slurpee—and more like thawing beef. I began to bounce on my toes, trying to pick up my pulse and warm my fingers and toes, as I strode into a long hall of storage units in search of locker #1865.

Maynard's father was a Civil War buff—hence the 1865. Years ago, at the New Year's Eve party, Maynard had mentioned his father's collection—weapons his mother wanted out of the house, deemed with the potential to explode. At this point, I'd take an old rusty musket to swing around, if nothing else.

"934, 936, 938—" counted Montoya. "We aren't anywhere near 1865, my man."

There was a window to my right, along the outermost of three parallel halls. Peering out, I couldn't help but notice the sinister appearance of the darkened sky, like night was coming hours early. The forest just beyond the parking lot seemed alive with shadows—shifting beneath the leafless canopy.

They were there, waiting for me.

CAWWWW!

A red-eyed crow squawked, pulverizing my frazzled nerves like a jackhammer on meth. It buzzed by the window and eyed me up like a succulent grub-worm ready for plucking.

"Crows," I said to myself. "Always crows."

"The Morrigan," said Montoya. "That's the puta that got me. The crow, it's one of her spies. She created the crow-nado."

"The Morrigan?" asked Jamaal. "Irish mythology. The phantom queen. She was a shapeshifter. Goddess of war, fate, and death."

As my brain-trust discussed the finer qualities of airborne spies for ancient Celtic goddesses, my mind was elsewhere.

"Have faith," said Chappy, drifting over my shoulder. "I believe Malus needs her alive. You'll get your chance."

"What if you're wrong?"

"I might be wrong, sure," he replied, "but you had no other option. Let me be clear about something, Tony. Everyone one of us that is now a part of you has lost something. Those Thirteen demons, they each destroyed thousands of lives throughout their reign of tyranny as false gods. If they take her from you again, we are all dedicated to making them pay. Trust you me, we will make them pay."

His words burned. I felt his fire and let it ignite. The flames were roaring back, and my extremities thawed with rage.

"Your priority is keeping that trinket safe," he said, pointing at the key. "They must need the key if they brought out the entirety of their armies after you."

"Armies?" I questioned.

"They're throwing the kitchen sink at you, my man," said Montoya. "Blood-sucking women, crow spies, bull-gods. They're coming in full force. Who knows what else they have in their arsenal."

"We need to find lot 1865," I said. "Before they find us."

"Do you think Maynard can get us out of here?" asked Jamaal.

"I hope so," I replied, then looked over to Doshin and added, "One step at a time."

They knew I was on the fourth floor. It was time to move.

I jogged toward the end of the hall and entered the stairwell, only to hear the slightest vibration of something ascending toward me. It was close.

I jumped back into the fourth floor and staggered backward, trying to think of something, anything. If I had a weapon, maybe I could defend myself. A sword or a gun. Hell, I'd even take a badminton racquet—when I suddenly remembered where I was.

"How strong do you think I am?" I asked.

"Strong enough to impale a full-grown feral woman by tossing her into a tree," said Jamaal, like that feat alone was a unit of measure all by itself.

"That's pretty strong, my man," said Montoya with a nod.

I ran down the center hall, chose a random lot number, and grabbed the roll up door with both hands. "Here goes nothing," I said, and yanked up like I was powerlifting a barbell. The metal lock snapped like cheap plastic.

"Damn!" shouted Montoya and Jamaal, together.

I rifled through the stash of junk, hoping to find something I could use, then ripped open two more units until I found an expensive golf bag.

"Golf clubs?" asked Henry.

"Top of the line," I said, and re-entered the hallway to find both directions blocked with Bacchae. Two to my left—both wearing party dresses—and one to my right in nothing but a bikini top and underwear.

"I guess Bacchus has a type," I said with a smirk.

"Yeah, *scary*," added Jamaal. "Bad luck being beautiful around that jawn."

"You said that word again, my man," said Montoya. "What's it mean again?"

"Anything you want," said Jamaal with a shrug. "In this case, I swapped Bacchus out for jawn. Get it?"

"I jawn it," said Montoya with a nod, feeling proud of himself.

"No, my man, no."

I chuckled as Jamaal shook his head in defeat.

"Chuckling in the face of danger? Are we going mad again, sir?" asked Henry with a smirk.

"Going, Doc?" I said. "I've been mad for some time."

I took a quick practice swing with the biggest, meanest golf club in the bag and wondered how many homers I could have hit if I had my current angelic strength. The thought brought a big ole smile to my face.

"What's so funny?" asked one of the Bacchae. She licked her lips in anticipation.

They were watching me, waiting for me to make the first move.

Maybe they were waiting for reinforcements. I gave her a crooked glare and relaxed, letting the fear wash away with the tide of my adrenaline.

"This." I bounced a golf ball off the floor, took a great big swing, and sent it hissing at her. I was hoping for a distraction—maybe plunk it off her head to briefly lower the odds. Except the ball hit her like a shotgun slug, propelling her body into the air and lodging deep into her chest cavity with a gaping hole. Whether she died or not, I didn't know, but she wasn't getting up.

"Well damn," said Montoya.

I took another golf ball, felt its weight in my hands, and fired a straight overhand toss at the next blood-drooling mistress to my right. It smacked her square in the forehead and put her down for the moment.

Next, I took the bikini-vamp down with a nine-iron after a great big swing that snapped the club in half after it bent around her neck. The impact cracked her spinal cord and left her twitching on the floor.

The last one picked herself up from the ground with an ugly welt between her eyes—you could even see the texture of the golf-ball imprinted onto her skin—and launched for my throat. It was a direct attack. A kill-only mentality. When man fights another man, it's about blunt force and disabling their opponent. When monsters fight, they attack like animals for maximum damage—and I was unprepared. Despite dodging her initial lunge, I somehow ended up on my back, grappling with her wrists as she forced herself onto me. She bit into my shoulder through my leather jacket, sucking greedily with the fervor of a leech. The taste of my blood appeared to send shock waves through her, like my blood was surging with more power than she knew how to handle. Her fangs dug deeper into my shoulder—I felt them hit bone—and put all my force into a punch against her right temple.

One hit wasn't enough, so I kept pounding until I crushed her skull and sent her tumbling into the wall. I sprang back onto my feet, but she beat me there as if we were racing and hissed—her head reshaping, the fragments of her skull putting themselves back together with few pops and a click.

"Oh shit!" shouted Jamaal.

"Don't let her drink your blood," warned Chappy.

"Alright, Captain Obvious," I growled.

She was juiced into a frenzy. The Bacchae slashed at me again, each swipe missing by the slightest margin, until she caught my shirt and flung me into the air. When I hit the ceiling, I stuck there like I had fallen—gravity pulling me up instead of down. It was the same trick my Echo had used in my apartment.

"How'd you do that?" yelled Montoya, looking up at me.

I had no fucking clue how I did it. I just *did*.

I sat up as if I would on the ground, feeling absolutely no different with the gravity switch. The blonde Bacchae raged—I was out of her reach, but she wasn't giving up. She dug her claws into the cinderblock wall and scaled it, desperate for more blood. The throes of the bloodlust took away all her sense and reason; all she knew was that she wanted more, and I had plenty to give.

I tracked down one of the remaining golf clubs, which spilled from the bag across the floor, and willed myself to the ground. I fell from the ceiling and landed on my feet with ease, like I was freakin' Mary Poppins or something. As I grabbed the golf club, she fell onto my back. We spun—me like a mechanical bull—her like a drunken co-ed on a tequila shot dare. I slammed into the wall, grabbed her leg and swung, tossing her onto the floor. She hadn't even gotten the hair out of her face by the time I pounced, wrapping the golf club around her neck and pulled it tight like a noose. Her head slung to one side, and her neck looked like a twist-tie around a plastic bag. She flailed and kicked until I took one last tug and separated her head from her body.

"Holy hell, my man," said Montoya.

"Yeah," I groaned, gasping. "I think I'm going to need a better stomach."

"No time to vomit," said Doshin.

"I think I found 1865," said Jamaal by the window.

"Where?" I asked as I jogged over to him.

"Down there," he said, pointing to a series of large garage-sized containers behind a security fence. Outside.

"Fuck," I growled.

I ran down two flights of stairs before I got a whiff of stale blood. The master of the maidens, Bacchus, was near. Exiting on the second floor, I ran for the far end—if I cut across, then down, I could make a break for it across the parking lot—or so I planned, but I was cut off by the sound of scraping metal.

The Morrigan entered the hall ahead, raking her taloned fingertips against the cinderblock walls and metal doors, like metal nails to a chalkboard. She was shrouded in a black feathered cloak, her pale bare legs stalking deliberately toward me with a gentle pat of bare feet against the cold concrete floor.

The brain-trust shouted various forms of surprise and alarm—and not even one of them registered as I turned away in retreat and ran straight into the outstretched arm of Bacchus. He caught me around the neck, snagged like a fish on a hook, my legs still running in place. His fingers were long and grotesque and could have wrapped around my neck twice. His eyes were red, like an albino, and his pallid skin seemed papery, translucent, and spider-webbed with purple veins. His fangs were four inches long, and his jaw unhinged like a snake, like Mammon as he attempted to bite off my head. In his free hand Bacchus held his golden chalice of blood, balancing it perfectly so as not to spill a single drop, regardless of my frantic struggles.

"Hello, spark," he spoke, breathy and arrogant. His putrid breath splashed me in the face and I gagged just before he lifted me off my feet. I kicked at his chalice—seemed like the smart thing to do—but he maneuvered it away and glared as he began to crush my throat. "Your scent has history. Two distinct journeys, like grafting a new limb upon a familial tree. I know your roots, dear spark."

As he squeezed my neck, I willed the power to punch him square in the nose with a solid left hook. I felt the snapping of bone and cartilage underneath my fist as his unrelenting vice-grip choked the life from me. I punched again, and again, but Bacchus refused to release me, even while I was rearranging his face.

Desperation. While Bacchus had me by the neck, his fangs lingering ever closer, and Morrigan approaching from behind—I was the jam between two evil slices of bread. That desperation manifested itself just as it had with Mammon. From the blackest hole of my memory, like a broken hard drive that clicked and futzed every time I tried to access it—my angel memory, of Heaven and Hell, of places in between, and the secrets that shaped the world—finally found important data. There it was, in my moment of need.

"Detatron," I rasped through a mangled windpipe. It was one of many names he had used, but that was his first—the one given to him at creation. He also went by the name Dionysus, before the Romans took control of ancient Europe.

Bacchus hissed and tossed me aside like an empty beer can. I smashed through the door of a storage unit and bashed my head against a small lockbox resting on a large pile of junk, crushing it open.

"Knowing names will not save you, boy," he hissed in his ancient tongue. "I do not need empyrean magic or devices of divinity to smash you to death."

Bacchus was on top of me in a blur, grasping for my throat with his massive hand, when I slapped his chalice free. The blood spattered across the wall and made him burn with rage, heaving with a brewing tantrum. He punched me over my left eye, and my skull cracked from the impact. I swung back, and he deflected it like an older brother swatting away his younger, weaker sibling, then gripped me by the neck and slammed me down into the concrete, knocking the fight out of me.

I groped the floor with my hands, searching for something, anything to use against Bacchus, as he pummeled me over and over. My hand found the broken lockbox and I rapped it against his head, breaking the lid and sending it skidding across the floor.

Bacchus backed off momentarily, clearing the haze, while a trickle of purplish blood streaked down his forehead. I re-gripped the lockbox in my hand and readied to pelt him again when something from inside it fell and made Montoya scream, "Joder si!"

A gun clanked against the concrete floor, and I snatched it on the first bounce, letting it slide into my hand like a professional. It was a 9mm Glock 17—skills and information offered from one of the many minds inside my head. I flicked the safety off with my thumb in one fluid motion and fired before Bacchus could pounce.

"There are two ways to kill our kind," said my Echo. *"Destroying both eyes will send them back to where they belong. Think of it as a video game respawn straight to jail. Burn them with hell or holy fire—or destroy the heart—that destroys the empyrean spirit and they cease to exist—no afterlife, just gone."*

The bullet entered his body a few inches left of his heart and exited out the back, missing his shoulder blade. It was an incredible shot, considering Bacchus's reflexes. His last second flinch moved his most vital organ away from the trajectory. It was the kind of shot that would have taken any ordinary man down. A mortal wound to anything other than a god.

Bacchus took it and laughed.

"Human weapons," he scoffed, "are pitiful. I will gut you, eat your heart, and refill my chalice, all before you speak my name once more."

I fired again, then a third time, but he kept on laughing.

Fear, pain, and despair took over. My head was literally split open, and I was sure I was about to die. The flames rose inside me, like a can of lighter fluid dropped into a dumpster fire, and something happened that neither Bacchus nor I expected.

I fired the gun once more, equally out of hope and hopelessness, but this time something of myself went with it. The bullet left the chamber engulfed in fire, the same fire that killed Mammon.

The bullet struck Bacchus square between the eyes, igniting an internal fire which began to consume Bacchus from the inside out before he had even stopped laughing. I fired once more, just to make sure, and watched him dissolve into ash right front of me, revealing Morrigan observing from the doorway.

I fired again, only to witness her dissipate into a combination of mist and live crows, which scattered immediately and were gone. My fiery bullet, however, hit one of her red-eyed crows and it burst into flames, plummeting to the ground like a shooting star.

"Now that's what I call *hot lead*," said Jamaal.

white knight, black knight

JACINDA
Then.

For four and a half months, you practiced your music every waking moment, Jace. You sang in the morning, in the shower, in the halls and after school. When you weren't singing, you were playing guitar or writing in your journal, jotting down thoughtful lyrics and writing songs.

I realized then, that fateful night on the brink of an overdose, when you said the words, *"I want to live happy,"* they actually came true.

Did you will yourself into change?

Did you wish it?

Or was it simply a change of perspective?

Jace, you might be asking what the difference was, but the question was simple: did you change out of your own determination? Or did you magically alter your own reality?

You found yourself over those next four months. You found out you were a little bit country, but a whole lot rock n' roll, punk, pop, alternative, new wave, rhythm and blues, hard rock, metal, and industrial. You swam through whole libraries of music, searching for your sound. You learned the lyrics to every hit, and to many songs you believed should have been.

You stopped going to Rick, only occasionally saying hello in the halls on your way to class. You didn't care about rumors, and you didn't care what people thought. Your friendship with Whitney dissolved, mostly because Whitney wanted to use, and you just wanted to create. You wanted to make beauty, and you wanted to be beautiful.

Some guys at school pursued you, but nobody grabbed your attention. You were still interested in Rick, but until he dumped Rhonda, you refused to be the other girl, and good on you, Jace. You were finally seeing your self-worth.

More than anything, you were loving yourself, and the future was bright.

August 29th, 1997

The morning before the Labor Day Fair, you were putting the finishing touches on the songs you were going to perform. You were having a hard time with one of the songs so you decided to take a break.

Sitting on your desk was your journal, opened to a song you were working on. You sat down and read through the lyrics once more, and you were struck with an odd case of déjà vu. The lyrics, as you read them back to yourself, felt like you had heard them before.

You spent the next hour popping CDs into your stereo, reading through liner notes and searching through old journals, when you came across a journal entry from last year.

As you flipped through its pages, you noticed the book was only half full, which was something of a mystery to you. Jace, you never left a journal half full and couldn't remember why you had done so with that one.

The first few pages were a mixture of journal entries and illustrations, even a few lyrical snippets from songs you liked, and songs you wanted to write. Finally, you came across the passage you were looking for.

It wasn't unheard of to write something twice, without realizing it, but what was strange was the sensation it gave you when you did. It made you want to keep reading, flipping through the pages to see what other secrets it kept.

Halfway through you came across a drawing of a naked girl and a creature that was drinking her blood. It was next to a hysterical journal entry from October 31st, 1996, where in your own handwriting you detailed the encounter at the Academy. It had to be fiction, didn't it? Fuck, Jace, even I didn't remember that—did I witness it?

I had been watching you from the beginning, and beyond the one or two redacted dates when you were young—dates I couldn't seem to access, like black holes in time—this was something I missed, right? I was as confused as you were and started to question everything. You never wrote fiction in your journals. They were your truth. They were your lyrics and feelings. No wonder this entry had you rattled.

You flipped through the pages and came across another—a drawing you'd labeled "who is watching me?" It was a sketch of a man staring through your bedroom window, and you couldn't recall anything about it—but I did. I was there for that.

"What the hell?" you said under your breath.

I remembered that one, Jace. Why didn't you? What was happening?

You closed the journal and set it aside, staring at it for a few moments before coming to grips with the idea of solving the mystery another time. You had too much to do today—too much to prepare—and you set out at once to choose your outfit.

That night at the fair, performing in front of a live crowd, taking stage after your old guitar teacher's band, was the most amazing experience you'd ever had. There were people there, classmates, who wanted you to fail—you could tell, you heard the boos and the grumbles as you stepped on stage. But you ignored them and focused on your Grammy's voice inside your head, preaching, "Tomorrow's not a promise. Gotta earn each one," and let go of everything you couldn't control. What you could control, however, was your performance—and Jace, you did not disappoint.

Hearing your set once more, reliving that night, was watching the magic for the first time all over again. You were amazing, and I could feel myself swooning, falling in love like I was seventeen again, experiencing it for the first time.

When you finished, you heard their stunned applause and saw their astonished expressions, and realized then, just maybe, you had real talent.

And best of all?

Rick Jansen was in the audience with Rhonda, and he looked as dumbfounded as any of them.

After you wrapped up your set and un-mic'd your Grammy's acoustic guitar, placed it into its case and gently closed the lid, you thanked Grammy for the wonderful gift and the talents that now seemed more likely than ever to come to fruition.

Your hard work was paying off in many unexpected ways.

"That was baller, Jace!" said Dylan, your former guitar teacher. The guy was like the big, older cousin you'd never had. He gave you a big exuberant high five. You had already outpaced his talents on guitar, but at more than ten years your senior, he treated you like an equal.

"Thanks, Dill," you replied. Coming from another musician, the compliment was great to hear.

"Seriously bro, that was some rad shit. I mean, you chose the perfect songs too! So proud of you, little bro." He was wearing an old black jean jacket with so many studs, spikes, and patches that it soared way past kitsch and into its own form of modern art.

You had the biggest smile on your face. But it all evaporated the moment Rick said, "Jaycie," interrupting, and he shouldered Dylan rudely out of the way.

Word of advice, Jace: look at the way a guy treats others, because that's the way he'll treat you once he's done winning you over.

"Hey, what are you doing here?" you asked. "Nobody's allowed back here except performers." You scolded him, despite being glad he was there.

"Who's going to stop me?" he said with a smirk.

"Yeah, I'm seeing that about you." The words came out of your mouth more pleasant than you intended, and Rick laughed. Thing was, it was a brief moment of pure honesty about him.

"I just wanted to say you rocked it up there," he said, and suddenly that small praise put a giant crack in your defenses.

Oh Jace, you were as hopeless as I was over you.

"Yeah, thanks." You were smiling, even though you tried not to, but no worries—bucket head was about to fuck it up, watch…

"I never heard those songs before. Are they new?" he asked.

"'We Belong Together,' 'Summertime Blues,' and 'Wish You Were Here?'"

"Yeah," he said with a boyish nod.

Told you, Jace. Bucket head.

"No, they've been around for a while." That's when you spotted someone in the crowd. "Hey, let's catch up later," you said and quickly walked away before Rick could answer.

You took the long route through the crowds as you tried to find the right words to say hello to your long-lost best friend. With every step you took, you realized you were running out of time, until you were left with only one option: "Amanda! Hey!"

It was a good reunion, as far as reunions go. It was so good to see her, and you were so proud of how beautiful she was. You kept wondering about all the boys that were knocking down her door and were hoping that the guy sitting next to her was a boyfriend, because you wanted so badly for Amanda to be doing well.

You quickly ran through small talk, as you noticed that the guy next to Amanda was staring at you while trying not to stare—it was confusing. Was he there for Amanda or not?

"Mom and I are visiting my grandmom. Just here for the weekend," said Amanda. "School starts on Tuesday."

"Is he with you?" you asked under your breath.

"Oh, T?" said Amanda.

"You've got a little drool on your chin, Romeo," said someone, and they all started laughing at Tony's expense—well, my expense, right? How meta was this? Me looking at me drooling over you? Good lord, I looked so pathetically awful! Look at those shoes! That shirt! The hair! No wonder you dismissed me.

He, me, was staring and got caught, and you giggled a little on the inside.

"He's my best friend," said Amanda proudly. "He's got a huge crush on me. Let me introduce you."

Whoa there—pause!

Okay, Jace. That I did not know. Did Amanda really think I had a crush on her? Or did she want to believe that? Oh wow, this makes so much sense.

Fuck, Manda! I mean, I did have a crush on you a long time ago, but you dashed those hopes when you started spouting off about how Paul Lucas made your "womanly places sing." That was your direct quote, Manda! Not mine!

Was that something you wanted? Or was it a brag?

The more I thought about Amanda, the more I knew I needed to get to the bottom of all this, Jace. Not just for you, but for her too.

Let's resume…

You recognized some of the others gathered around me. It was Maynard, with Jess, Cyndi…and was that Tori Martin with them? It was a big high school, and you very rarely took note of the cliques and who belonged to where.

"O'Neill, this is my best friend, T, from back home. He's an artist and an athlete like you," said Amanda.

"Oh, cool," you said, your eyes landing fully on me for the first time. "Hey, T. What do you play?"

I seemed nervous, befuddled, like I didn't know how to act natural— because I actually didn't know how to act natural, especially around you. Jace, you were a goddess to me. You were beautiful! Your smile, your style, your eyes! That voice! Ding! Stick a fork in me!

It was nice to meet someone that got nervous around you, wasn't it? It made you feel special, and you decided to flirt with me, if nothing more than to make Rick jealous. He was staring at us like a hawk. You could feel it and saw him look away every time you glanced over.

Damn, Jace. I'm not sure how I feel about this. Were you using me?

When you sat down with me and Amanda, you stopped worrying about Rick. Amanda's presence made you feel at home, while my adoration made you smile. You couldn't speak for Amanda, but if she didn't like me, you thought she was nuts.

Glad I wasn't just a pawn, babe.

Maybe it was perception, but the longer we talked, the more Amanda faded, until it was just you and I going back and forth, bonding over common interests and geeking out over stuff that only we could geek out to.

"Favorite Saturday morning cartoon?" I asked.

"Dungeons and Dragons, obviously!" you replied.

"Yes!" I said with a fist pump, and I remembered thinking you were the coolest. "I always wanted a magic bow like Hank."

"I wanted a unicorn, like Uni," you said with a laugh.

"Hey," interrupted Amanda. "I'm going to say goodbye to Maynard before he leaves." She didn't wait for a response. She got up and left the two of us alone.

You scooted closer to me and noticed how nervous I was at your proximity, and things got awkwardly quiet.

"Do you believe in fate?" I asked, like a total weenie.

"Why do you ask?"

"I don't know," I said, but I was lying. I didn't want to sound like a weirdo. "Sometimes I wonder if opportunities are real, or if they're like, fool's gold or something."

"What do you mean?" you asked. "I'm lost."

Honestly, Jace, me too. I didn't remember this part of the conversation. Tony, dude, what the hell were you trying to say, man?

I smiled and said, "I mean, we live our lives—sometimes bad things happen and sometimes good things happen. Do those things happen for a reason? Did someone write out the story of our lives somewhere? Or can we seize control of our reality? Can we take the opportunities given to us and make a better fate? Or—"

"Or does it even matter? Will we just end up where we end up, no matter what?"

"Exactly."

Exactly.

"I think about that too sometimes," you said. "There's a solar eclipse on Monday." Then you pointed to the crescent moon. "A partial one."

"Really? Is that rare?" I asked.

"A little," you said sweetly. "What's that?"

"Hmm?" I asked, following your eyes to my chest. "This?" I held up the chain around my neck, with a dangling brass skeleton key—the same key I was wearing right now. That's how I got into this mess—stuck here, watching your life from the Veil.

"Is that the key to your heart?" you joked, and damnit Jace, if you only knew what was going to happen. This key was meant for you.

"Yes," I answered with a bashful nod, playing along.

"Where'd you get it?" you asked.

"I found it when I was a kid," I said, and even back then I was omitting things, leaving out the truth because to explain all of it would be too much.

"Oh, and where are you from, exactly?"

"New Jersey," I said, and for some reason I expected you to gag. Nobody likes Jersey, not even the part I was from, with all the open land and country roads. "Small, one-stoplight town."

"I see," you said, as we magnetically drifted closer together. Glad to know I wasn't imagining that. Sometimes I wondered if it was just me moving in, but it's nice to know you wanted it too.

"Did you grow up here?" I asked.

"Yeah," you said with a sigh, and knowing what I know now, I recognized the emotions behind the sigh.

"What's it like? Does your high school suck too?" Because let me tell you something, Jace, mine certainly sucked—but yours sucked more.

"Grace Falls has more ghosts than people," you said. I knew that—learned it the hard way. "Where are you going to college?"

"I don't know yet. What about you?"

"I don't know. Milton State has a good music program. Maybe

I'll go there."

"Where's that?" I asked, gesturing with my hands. I never realized how much I talked with them. I was like a fucking conductor, ushering every word with a wave.

"Locally. It's in Grace Falls. Are you a lefty?" you asked, then clarified, "You use your left hand a lot when you talk." Blasted Italianism—it's the Mediterranean blood—just kiss him—me—already!

I nodded, then asked, "You?"

You nodded too. Both lefties. We were born to be together, Jace.

Our lips were a single inch apart when the crow cawed. His cawing incited the others to caw, creating a mini riot on the railing above us. It was enough of a distraction to break the moment, and it reminded you who was watching. Rick looked away again the moment you checked.

"Sorry," you said as you sat up. "I've gotta go."

Jace, forget about him. Your future was—is—right in front of you.

"Yeah, okay," I said, trying to sound positive. "Will you be back here tomorrow? The fair's open all weekend, right?"

"It is, and maybe," you said with a smile, and you had every intention of coming back.

"Maybe? Just maybe?" I joked, hoping you'd give more assurance.

"I'll look for you." You smiled and nodded.

"Me too," I said, then quickly clarified, "for you. I'll look for you."

You laughed at my dopiness and lit a fire in me that I chased for years. I chased you for years, Jace, all because of that one night.

"Tomorrow's not a promise, Tony. Gotta earn each one," you said, just like your Grammy did. And I tried—I fought for each and every one to find my way back to you. "It was nice to meet you, T."

When you walked away, you felt something you hadn't felt in a very long time. You felt belonging. You felt stimulated. You felt interesting and interested. You wanted to know more about Tony, but when you compared him to Rick in your mind, you were confused. Yet you couldn't stop smiling or thinking about seeing Tony again.

Let's be real, Jace, I don't stack up well against Rick. He was everything I was not—but I was also everything he was not.

"Hey," said Rick. He jumped out at you from behind a pickup truck. You were only twenty feet from your car in the dark parking lot, and there weren't many cars left. His aggressive nature made you uncomfortable, and you should have trusted that instinct. "You think that was funny?"

"Huh? What was funny?" you asked. He'd caught your mind a million miles away.

"You, messing around with that loser," he said. "The ugly faggot you spent the entire night with."

You were immediately offended, not just at the accusation but at the demeaning slur. You sidestepped him when he blocked your path, like he was trying to intimidate you.

"Why do you care?" you asked. "You're with Rhonda."

"Is that what this is about? Rhonda?" he said. "Are you jealous?"

You were, actually. You knew you were, but you didn't want him to know that. However, when you said, "No," it didn't sound honest.

"Am I supposed to believe that?"

"You don't have to believe anything." You brushed him aside and stepped over to your car.

Then the late summer air went cold. As the other cars left, dust hung thick beneath the parking lamps scattered throughout the lot.

"If you really wanted me," you said, while fishing through your pocket for the car key, "you would have already dumped her."

As you placed the key into the lock, Rick's reflection in your driver's side window had two different colored eyes. Even in the darkness you could see them—Rick's blue eyes had been replaced with one pale gray and one brown.

You yelped and dropped the key.

You weren't seeing things, Jace. I saw it too.

Rick retrieved the keys from the ground for you and smiled. "Look what I found," he said, but he didn't give them to you straightaway. He held them, as if waiting for you to take them.

"My keys," you demanded, holding out your palm.

Rick shook his head and handed them over. "Of course."

"Thanks." You finished unlocking the door, then quickly loaded your guitar case and hopped in after it—but Rick was standing in the way.

"Give me a chance, Jane? Maybe we can meet up at my car during lunch again?"

"No," you said, pulling the door closed and forcing him out of the way. It was either that or drag him along with the car. Either way suited you. You didn't like the way the whole situation had transpired and made sure he knew it. "I'm done being second place. And my name's not Jane."

That was weird, and you knew it. Did Rick ever know your sister's name? Heck, did he even know you had a sister? You never spoke of it. You hadn't spoken of it in years, and yet that name came from his mouth without the hint of a faux pas.

Your guard was up, Jace, and rightfully so.

When you pulled off, leaving Rick in a cloud of dust, you felt empowered. You paid no mind to the strange swirls that gathered around Rick as you pulled away, staring at him in your rearview mirror—but I noticed. There were demons in those swirls, Jace.

The evil was closing in on you. It moved through shadow and Veil and followed you home. Were they using Rick to snatch you at the fair? Maybe they were frightened of you? Why didn't they just come out and nab you? What were they waiting for?

"What are you waiting for, assholes?!" I shouted from beyond the Veil.

You slammed on the brakes.

Did you hear me?

Terrified, you peeked into the back seat. You shook it off and shrugged, as if it was just noise coming through the radio, and continued home.

After parking your car in the garage, you entered the house, still on edge.

"Jacinda," said your father. "Come into the kitchen, please."

"What are you still doing up?" you said. You set your guitar case on the floor by the couch and took off your leather jacket, then slung it over the back of the couch. Your father's voice sounded odd—were they going to send you back to private school? Maybe your mother had found a brand-new reason to hate you? Whatever it was, they were up late—it was nearly eleven-thirty, and you couldn't remember the last time you'd seen either of them up past ten.

When you walked into the kitchen, your mother and father were sitting around the table. It was a beautifully arranged kitchen, with only the best appliances and countertops that never got used. There was not a speck of dust, let alone any home-cooked food. What good was the perfect kitchen for a family that didn't cook? The last time it was used was two months ago when you made brownies for yourself.

"Why are you sitting in here? It's late," you said. The light that hung over the kitchen table hurt your eyes. It seemed far too bright for the room, like the bulb was about to burn out.

Splayed out on the table were a bunch of items—a few small bags filled with salt, silver, iron, and other protective ingredients—four talismans covering Christianity, Jewish, Hindu, and Muslim ideologies—as well as crystals, bags of incense, a black candle, and a pair of black fishnets.

Fuck.

"Would you mind telling us where you got these?" asked your mother. She was smoking again, and the ashtray was full of tonight's binge. "Are you into the witchcraft?"

Sorry, Jace. They were mine—except the black candle and the fishnets that were clearly from your Halloween costume circa 1994. We braved a paradox to ward you—and something tells me Malus would have snatched you if we hadn't last year, when you caught him looking through your bedroom window.

I wish I had known this was going to happen…

However, can we please take a step back to analyze your mother's hysteria? First, she called it "the witchcraft" and secondly, what was she doing snooping around your room? I remember hiding those, and let me tell you, we put them into some really well-hidden spots. Fuck, that crystal was under the floor! Nobody knew that stuff was there—for years—until now.

"I don't even know what those are," you said, which was entirely true. You had no idea what they were, except the black candle you bought because it smelled of coconut and vanilla bean—and the fishnets were from your "Winnie Sanderson" costume.

"Why are you lying to us?" cried your mother, while your father sat there stoically. Why wasn't he defending you, Jace? Surely, he knew this was ridiculous.

"I don't understand." She didn't really think you were into witchcraft, did she? And why the fuck did your mom even give a shit, Jace?

"Your mother found these hidden in your room," said your father. He looked shaken.

"In my room?" you growled. "Why were you snooping around in my room? I don't know what these are, so I don't know how I could have hidden them!"

"You're such a filthy liar," said your mother. "You took her from me, and then you tried to cover it up!"

"Who?" you asked.

"Your sister!" she screamed.

Jace, this was blowing up. Something wasn't right.

"I didn't take *anyone* away from you, *mom*," you spat. Your words seemed wrong. They felt incorrect, like a really bad dream come true.

"You did!" said your mother. "You killed her. I don't know how you did it, but you did. You kept crying, *Mommy make her stop! Make her stop!*"

"Saoirse!" scolded your father, "there has to be a perfectly good explanation for all this." Then he turned to you, ignoring your tears. "How did these things get into your room. Your mother found them under your bed." *Lies. She made that up.* "She thought you might be doing drugs."

"I found your pills," she said. "Don't think I don't know what they are." You forgot those were even there, hidden at the back of your desk drawer. You didn't want them anymore; you didn't need them.

"Why'd you think I was doing drugs?" you asked. You looked defeated. You had no valid excuse for the plastic baggie holding a handful of colorful pills.

"You were walking around the house, singing all the time. God only knows you've never been this happy," she said.

Fucking hell, can I slap the shit out of her? Can I? Heaven forbid you actually felt happy without your own fucking mother thinking it was chemical! Then again, how would she know what happiness was without popping a few pills first?

Your father raised his hand to calm his wife, to gather some kind of control over the situation, but it was way past the point of no return. Saoirse was mentally ill, and there wasn't a day that went by where you didn't wonder if you had a touch of it too.

"I stopped taking them," you said.

"Sure, you did," she said sarcastically.

"You're one to talk, Mom!" you shouted. "You sit up in your room all day, smoking, popping pills! That's why you were in my room! You were looking for something to swallow and you found that and more!"

Bullseye! Bingo!

"How dare you!" she screamed. "I didn't raise a cunt, and I sure as hell aren't going to stand here and watch you turn into one now!"

I instantly ignited, flames erupting from my hands, and I swore I was going to torch her right there. And if it wasn't for you leaving the room immediately, I wasn't so sure I could have stopped myself.

Your father appeared shaken, like he didn't know how to wrangle the situation back in. He was a lawyer, used to making structured arguments based on facts, law, and decorum, not this kind of shit-show.

Saoirse was already following you into the next room. Your father caught her by the arm and said, "Don't do something you're going to regret."

Too late, James. That ship has sailed, you feckless ass.

"Fuck off," she said, clearly intoxicated by pill or bottle, or both. "I birthed my biggest regret seventeen years ago."

You heard the insult but kept moving. You were almost to the stairs when your mother rounded the corner and said, "Don't you dare go up there!"

You ignored her—your mother was an ignorant, liquored-up maniac, but she was still your mother, and somehow, you loved her. There was a time when you were young that your mother doted on you, though less than she doted on Jane. She fed you breakfast and read you bedtime stories. But then Jane died.

She blamed you for Jane's death, and that loss chipped away at Saoirse's humanity until she became this: a miserable, awful, wretch. What were you going to do, Jace? Could you stay for another year living under these conditions?

I was right beside you, climbing the stairs as your mother ran to the banister below. She reached out and snagged your ankle—tugging on your old Chuck Taylors.

"Leave me alone!" you screamed as you tried to pull your leg free.

"So long as you are under this roof, I can do whatever I please," she said, then yanked with all her might.

Everything happened in a blink. I would never wish you any pain, Jace, but in a way, this had to happen. The path you were on was that of mutual destruction—you and your mother—on a collision course to something awful.

You tripped headfirst into the stairs.

Stars erupted in front of your eyes, like fireworks. Blood ran down your forehead, mixing with your hair, and the Pandora's box of pain and suffering burst through the locked door inside your mind. You remembered that day—the accident—the confusion, the throbbing head. There was red everywhere—your hair covering your face and the blood. The trauma resurfaced like the Kraken rising from the ocean floor to pull you down into the darkness.

Your father finally pulled your mother away from you, saw the blood on your face, and gasped. Even he knew this would never end well.

You wiped at the warm wetness that ran down your face and pulled away a bloody fist. You were shaking, and I was stuck—I wanted to take you in my arms and usher you out of there, Jace, but you didn't need a white knight. You needed to do this on your own, for you.

The crack in your head let all kinds of terrible things out into the world—your self-doubt, your confusion, your anxiety, and worst of all, your guilt.

Guilt, for someone like you, can manifest in the most terrifying ways.

You made a move to climb the stairs but stopped cold in your tracks.

Memories are fallible. They're biased and easily manipulated. Bury them enough times or wrap them in hyperbole, and you fragment reality into truth and half-truths. When the truth finally revealed itself, it brought you to your knees.

A silhouette stood at the top of the stairs. A small girl with pigtails, looming in the shadows above, wearing a lacy dress that drifted on a light draft. You weren't seeing things, Jace, I saw it too. Was it a coincidence that happened the moment our protections were stripped from your room? Or did *you* bring her here?

There were a handful of protective talismans left about the house, most of them downstairs—which may be why the specter stood on the second-floor landing without moving an inch. Whether or not your parents saw her was only a guess, but she was definitely there.

Jane. It was definitely Jane.

Jace, I could feel your fear. I could smell it. You were in so much pain and torment that the fear nearly stopped your heart. Instead, it limped into an arrhythmia, pulsing irregularly and causing you all kinds of physical discomforts. The room warped, your vision blurred, your joints ached, and you felt nauseated. You were coming apart at the seams—as was everything around you.

The windows rattled. The floorboards torqued. Dust fell from the ceiling, and the lights grew bright, then burst one by one across the room. The television turned on and off, the fireplace roared to life—the gas streams billowing flames ten feet into the room—and the car alarms went off in the garage.

"Bring me back my baby!" screamed your mother.

"That's enough, Saoirse!" yelled your father as he grabbed hold of the banister to keep himself from falling. He looked scared, and he should have been.

"It'll never be enough!" she screamed. "It'll never be enough!"

Your fist shook with so much rage that you stopped fearing the ghost, and then everything stopped. The whole house froze. Your mother, your father, everything stuck in a complete and total suspension of time.

Jace, you did this. It was you. Nobody else. There were no strings being pulled. You willed this into reality. You stopped time. Did you know you could do this? Or did you just accept that you could when you made it happen?

Then you started talking. Did you know I was listening? Or were you talking to your sister?

"I can't do this anymore. There's too much pain in this family. We all need to let go. We all need to forget," you said, and I watched your sister disappear from the top step. "Goodbye, mother. Maybe now, without me, you'll find happiness."

You packed your bags and loaded your things up into your car, as your parents remained petrified. They did not blink, nor twitch, nor breathe—nor did they need to. They were stuck, and when they came to, you were a mile up the road with all your most important things, and a letter was left behind, resting on the stairs next to a small puddle of your blood.

It said:

"Dear Father,

In your own way you loved me, but it was never enough. I needed warmth, and you kept yourself out of reach. I needed you, and you were never there.

Dear Mother,

I won't miss you. Get help. I won't be your excuse to be a miserable, insufferable, drunk addict any longer.

Goodbye,

Jacinda"

THE OMEGA

THE VINDICATION OF THE MORRIGAN

271 B.C.

The ancient land of the druids was a lush green place found deep within the forests of what would come to be known as Britain. The land was rainy and damp and filled with many ancient mysteries. Deep in a forest of oak and evergreen was a craggy old pool of water dug into the side of a steep hill. The way the pool was cut into the earth was unnatural, not a formation of time and chance. A small stream of water tumbled from a rocky wall and collected into a worn basin of stone. Rocks were placed specifically so, pooling the water before it slowly overflowed downhill. It was beautiful, and the forest was filled with the peaceful sounds of wildlife that lingered in the wood. The ancient Druid rituals performed there were lost even to its own people, worn away like the water eroded the rock, forming gentle grooves that ushered its flow.

It was a rainy, miserable evening when Malus arrived. Large raindrops fell from the sky and crashed against the forest canopy, filtering the precipitation down to the occasional soaking drops. The air was so thick with moisture, it was like a soaking mist, gathering into cloudy patches of fog that softly crawled down the hillside into the valley below.

With a hood drawn over his head, protecting his platinum hair from the rain, Malus came upon the pool and stopped to gather a drink. After taking a large gulp of fresh water, a crow landed on a nearby branch and stared at his reflection in the pool.

"I wondered how long it would take you to find me as I traveled through your wood," said Malus, but the red-eyed crow did not speak or caw. It only stared. "Your sisters never did see the best in you—not like I do." The crow fluttered to a different branch but remained transfixed by the stranger in her wood. "I am in need of a goddess. One who has conviction and loyalty.

"Your sisters betrayed you," he continued. "They unified in order to banish you. They turned their most powerful sister into a crow and abandoned you. Babd and Macha, daughters of Emmas, they do not deserve to be your kin. Tell me, Morrigan, crow goddess, phantom queen, goddess of war, would you come with me if I gave you justice?"

The crow bowed, placing its head below its body, and gently fanned its wings.

"Good," said Malus, as Nemesis and Anubis appeared behind him with knives held over Babd and Macha's hearts—one quick thrust away from severing the goddesses from life. "Sign my contract, and you may choose which of your sisters die first."

XII

help

TONY
December 23rd, 2013
Now.

Luck.

I'd never call myself lucky. Jamaal's encyclopedic knowledge defined luck as success or failure brought on by chance, rather than through one's own actions. I couldn't even draw a "chance" card in Monopoly without landing directly in jail and putting Amanda into fits of laughter at my perpetual misfortune. Sure, everyone has a stroke of luck here and there—find a dollar on the ground, catch a break on a test or deadline—but real luck? Real chance? I wouldn't bet money on me.

To quote Marshall one evening after seeing Jaycie's hand in mine, he called me the "luckiest asshole that ever squatted on gold." Never mind the amazing, sweet gift of wordplay Marshall bestowed on me that evening.

"You're a lucky guy," said Anne, moments later.

Sure as a shit, that's true—Jaycie was…is one of a kind.

But lucky? Real luck? Real Chance?

I was never lucky. All my luck was saved and spent when I won the love lottery, stealing the heart of the sweetest, most beautiful woman I had ever laid eyes on.

But today? Today I got real fucking lucky.

I just survived an attack by a vampire god and killed him with a flaming bullet that magically erupted from the end of a handgun my thick hard head found when I crashed through a storage locker and into some stranger's junk.

"Sir, did you know you were capable of that?" asked Henry.

Leave it to the shrink to ask the million-dollar questions.

"Did I know I could shoot flaming god-killing bullets?" I suggested confidently. My throat was still healing, and every word came out in the voice of a raspy Joan Rivers.

"Yes." Henry nodded.

"No fucking way," I said with a shrug. "It just happened."

I felt pieces of my skull lock back into place like an automated puzzle—I was functional, but far from full health. Super-fast healing was great, but that didn't mean it hurt any less. I felt every cut and bruise to its fullest extent. I would have given a pinky for a few extra-strength acetaminophens.

"Awl righ' guntlemin," said the medic, making his way toward me with his flappy kilt and canvas bag at the ready.

"I'm good," I said, waving him off. Despite the sheer amount of blunt-force trauma I'd sustained, it seemed I had found the trick to triage the healing—and all I had to do was recall the feeling I got when the medic's needle pierced my chest.

"Em dunts dinnae luk gud," he said.

"What?"

"Them bumps don't look good," translated Henry.

"Aye," growled the medic. "Thas whit I focken sed, gowk buggar."

"How?" groaned Jamaal. "How did you understand all that?"

"I'm English," said Henry, which seemed to be all the reason he needed.

"I think I have the hang of it, now," I said, as the last bits of my rearranged face sorted itself out. "Thanks."

"Fein, 'ave ut yer way," he said. "Try ta dudge nuxt time, wull ya?" Then he spun on his heel and looked at Henry. "Efee luks shoogly, geeza shoot." And with that he stormed off, back into the far corners of my subconscious.

"Yeah, that guy gives me the creeps, my man," said Montoya after he was gone.

"Really?" I questioned. "That guy? Not the seven-foot-tall vampire god?"

Montoya shrugged. "Kilts are weird. I bet he's not even wearing any underwear."

"What are under wear?" asked Doshin.

The stench of evil was gone, but not indefinitely. I took only a few minutes to rest, counting all one hundred and twenty seconds before filling up my pockets with clips of ammo and uncovering a second gun still inside the broken lockbox. I had weapons—they weren't four-inch fangs, clawed fingers, or twisted three-foot-long bull horns, but they were more than just a couple peashooters.

The storage facility was going to be my tomb if I didn't escape immediately and find unit 1865 as fast as I could. I'd found a reprieve by forcing The Thirteen to regroup. I was no longer an unarmed whelp to be beaten around, but a pair of handguns were no match for the firepower they could throw at me in waves. I had now killed three of them—one by proxy—and my strength could no longer be considered a fluke. This underdog had bark, and they wouldn't continue to make the same mistakes.

My phone went off inside my pocket.

"Still alive? Where r u?"

"Coming," I wrote back.

There was no limit to the lengths they would go to find me and take what they wanted. I reached under my shirt and found the key still there, warm against my skin. Jaycie would be alive so long as I had it—or so I had to believe—and right now, that was all that mattered.

From the door, I could see Maynard's van parked halfway across the lot next to an old beater, where the outdoor storage units were located, but there was no sign of him.

"What are the odds it's a trap?" I asked.

They all answered at once in various forms of affirmative:

"Probably, my man," said Montoya

"Likely," said Henry.

"Undoubtedly," said Chappy.

"Indeed," agreed Doshin.

"Abso-fucking-lutely," said Jamaal.

"So long as we're all on the same page," I replied.

"Tony, my man," said Montoya, "stay low and move fast."

The coast was clear with no immediate threats looming, but after I exited the complex, I felt an immediate wave of evil crashing in on me from all sides. The Bacchae stormed in from the trees and from behind every corner, and there were other things too—things that made strange noises and others that wore cloaks—none of which were worth slowing down for a second look. I shot the nearest one through the head and leapt over the seven-foot security fence as if I were hopping over a baby gate.

"C'mon!" yelled Maynard, stepping out from inside the storage unit with the door rolled up. "Get behind the line!" Along the pavement was a trail of salt that encompassed his van and the beater outside the open unit. Two other men stepped out, but I didn't have time to notice anything more than a priest's collar on the shorter one.

A creature—some ugly ass thing straight out of the Island of Dr. Moreau—jumped the cinderblock wall surrounding the outdoor units, followed by another just like it. They stank of urine and ran like apes with an upright gallop on all fours. I shot one in the chest, the other in the neck, with flaming bullets—just as I crossed the salt line and was hit by a five-ton wrecking ball. Not literally, but it sure as hell felt like it as I ricocheted backward and bounced off the pavement away from the salt line.

"What the mother-fuck?" yelled Jamaal.

It hurt. I felt all my internal organs jostle around inside me when I hit the wall running full speed. I was in one piece and back to my feet with a dribble of blood running from my mouth, ready to fight for my life.

"What just happened?" yelled the chubby guy beside the priest. He was red-faced with a nasally voice, and wore a festive sweater vest. "I thought you said he was clean?"

"He is clean!" yelled Maynard.

"He just slammed into our ward like it was a brick wall! Clearly, he's not clean!" the chubby guy argued, his face darkening three shades.

"Jonah," said the priest, "get me the Sack of Righteousness. Hurry!" The chubby guy sped away like an uncoordinated tween while the priest stared me down curiously behind a pair of spectacles.

"Maynard, what just happened?" I asked, as he turned to the priest.

"He cleared the hag-stone test!" shouted Maynard, as if pleading his case to the silent priest. "He touched iron! He took a ride in my van! You know how warded that is!"

I spun and shot down two Bacchae that had climbed over the security fence. There was no way to know how many more there were, but I could smell them—I could hear them. They were everywhere. When I looked back, the priest was staring at me like he had just solved the most unsolvable mathematics problem of all time, as the chubby guy came back with a burlap sack.

"Tony," said the priest. "Put this on. Hurry!"

He tossed the burlap sack at me, and I didn't question it. By the time I had slipped it over my head, he had brushed aside a portion of the salt, then invited me over. When I stepped up to the salt, I leaned my foot out like I was testing the pool water temperature. Nothing happened, so I leapt inside the line, and he quickly reconnected it.

"Don't worry," said Maynard, "they can't get inside."

"Thanks," I said, and despite my own experiences with the salt barrier, I had my suspicions. Could the Thirteen be stopped by rock salt? Then I looked at the priest and held out my hand. "Thanks, Father."

He looked down at my offering and smiled, then backed away and said, "No, not yet. Come inside."

"Where's Jacinda?" asked Maynard.

I shook my head and followed him to the door. "He took her."

"I'm sorry," said Maynard as the first Bacchae hit the salt barrier and spun away like it had just waltzed into a human-sized bug zapper. There was even a smell, like the garbage bin outside a Sizzler steakhouse. "We'll get her back."

Maynard grabbed the rope tie to the garage door and pulled it down along the rollers as the others stepped inside—there were three strange symbols spray-painted onto the back of it.

"What are those?" I asked.

"Aegishjalmur, Metatron's Cube, and Hulinhjálmur," he said, pointing them out from left to right. Then we ducked inside, and he slammed the rolling door shut and locked it in place.

"What do they do?"

"The Helm of Awe drives away enemies. The cube wards off demons and protects us. The last one makes us invisible to U-Nats, like my tattoo."

"Do they work?"

"They do. We'll be okay."

The fluorescent bulbs came on with a flicker, and I was staring at Maynard plus two—the old priest and the chubby guy with the annoying face.

I looked down at the burlap sack I was wearing and saw a big red Y drawn onto it. I looked up at them and shrugged. "Why?"

Maynard chuckled, but the other two didn't appreciated the joke.

"Would you mind placing the firearms aside, Mr. Oscuro?" said the priest. He was sitting on an old kitchen chair, while the other two leaned against the work bench. He had a kind face, a thick white mustache, and a bald head with hair growing along the sides.

The other guy, the chubby one, looked like he was always in a foul mood. He was in his forties, with black sneakers, khakis, and an ugly holiday sweater-vest over an even uglier novelty tie with reindeer—like he had come straight from a holiday party. His poofy curls made his head look like broccoli—the guy had a massive noggin.

"Yeah, sure," I said.

Obviously, I wasn't giving them the best impression standing there, eyeing them up with a gun in both hands. I placed the pair of guns on the workbench beside Maynard, then scanned the room. That's when I realized the immensity of it—not the size of the room, but the overall collection of items. On my left were several huge bags of salt, piled five feet high on a pallet, in front of a pile of old Civil War memorabilia that looked haphazardly stashed aside. Moving around the room, I saw a small set of firearms with ammo, various medieval weapons, a few computers and surveillance equipment, along with a small lab. On the near side was a corkboard with hundreds of newspaper articles and pictures as well as various supplies like food, rope, and more. Most impressive were two symbols on the wall—one spray-painted symbol I'd seen before—notably on the welcome sign into Grace Falls just off the highway ramp into town—and the other was on a black flag. It was a white shield with a twinkling star at its center.

"Wow, some place you have here," I said.

"I recognize that symbol," said Jamaal pointing to the flag. "Historically."

"Oh yeah?" asked Montoya.

"It's a long story," he said. "A long, long story."

"I want you to know," said the priest, "the symbol on your back wards us against any evil you wish to incur upon us."

"Evil? Why would I do that?" I asked. When I looked over my

shoulder, I could just make out what looked like a grouping of blue circles that formed an eye resting at the center of an open palm painted onto my back.

"You tell us," he demanded.

"And the Y?" I asked.

"When we tossed you the sack, you were given a choice. Pythagoras's Y symbolizes two paths that come together as one. By accepting our invitation, you accepted our terms and we allowed you into our—" said the priest as he searched for the right word.

"Unit?" suggested the chubby guy.

Maynard snickered.

"Into our unit," finished the priest with a shrug, having run out of words.

"Okay, and you are?" I asked.

"The Patronus Lux," said Jamaal, pointing to his own head. "Eidetic memory."

I didn't need Google with Jamaal around.

"We are one chapter of the Patronus Lux," the priest said, pointing to the star symbol on the black flag. "The other glyph was derived from local symbolism. It is a native Shawnee symbol rooted in Maynard's heritage, representing the Children of the Mkateewa."

Tori's words rang inside my head once more. *"We are the Children of the Mkateewa. We're cursed."*

"And what are the Patronus Lux?" I asked.

"The protectors of light," said the priest. "I am Father John Monaco. This is Jonah Johnson. And you know Maynard. We have been investigating various phenomena in and around Grace Falls for the last few years."

"What about Doctor Celestine?" I asked. "Wasn't he part of this group?"

They looked at each other, then Father Monaco said, "David Celestine has decided he would not like to be part of our investigative—"

"Unit," said Jonah.

"Unit," finished the priest.

"Why?" I asked.

"This isn't twenty questions, man!" Jonah yelled. "You need to start answering some."

"What do you want to know?" I asked.

"What are you? What were those things?" asked Jonah. He was fidgety and nervous, and seemed to be on the verge of a nervous breakdown. His face was almost as red as his sweater vest.

"Are you okay?" I asked.

Father Monaco placed a comforting hand on Jonah's shoulder.

"He's okay," said the priest. "Jonah was once on the bad end of a gremlin curse. He went through a lot before we rescued him."

"What is a gremlin curse?" I asked. "Did you eat after midnight or something?"

"What?" replied Jonah, then his eyes narrowed. "Oh, ha-ha-ha. Funny guy." Maynard turned away so as not to be seen laughing. "I just get very nervous around high stakes. I saw some pretty messed-up things." The look in his eyes, I recognized the trauma—like permanent shellshock.

"Let's start at the top," said Maynard. "What happened with Jacinda?"

For the next several minutes, I recounted everything. From the stand-off with Malus to all the information I knew about who and what I am. I even stood on the ceiling to prove it. Jonah nearly fainted but seemed to accept that I was one of the good guys. I told them about the voices in my head, and about a crime I committed against…*Heaven?*—a crime in which I had no recollection. I even threw in the added mystery of the flaming bullets but didn't expect answers.

"Divine Devices," said Father Monaco.

"What are those?" I asked.

"Really?" said Maynard. His eyes lit up.

"I have to admit, I may be a priest, but I am not the expert here. Our friend David Celestine is, but for now, I will tell you everything I know."

"Please, I know so little," I said. My entire body hummed with anticipation. Any information, even vague, was more than what I had.

"Heaven and Hell. God. The Devil. That's all been written. What came next has not." Father Monaco got up and stretched his legs. "Something happened. Unrest of sorts. Rogue angels were rounded up and cast into the Pit. Some escaped and fell to earth. You see, a long time ago, there was a pact made between Heaven and Hell, sealed by emissaries from either side in the Judaean Desert."

"You're talking about the Temptation of Christ," said Maynard.

"I am, but David and I have discussed this thoroughly. He claims it was a prearranged meeting. The son of God on one side, the devil on the other. They made a deal, a treaty if you will, based on long-standing assumed principles. Humans have Free Will, and Earth was off limits to direct intervention. Humans could be tempted or soothed to either side, but no direct mediation was permitted with the world of man."

"Why?" asked Jonah.

"I'm sure there were reasons, just as I am sure they are beyond our context to understand," said Father Monaco. "When those rogue angels fell, cast out of heaven—their wings removed, halos shattered—they were free—free to live as they wanted. Some lived as immortal beings, passing the centuries peacefully. Others became kings, gods, seeking worship and adulation."

"What kind of gods?" asked Maynard.

"Wouldn't we have heard of them?" asked Jonah.

"We have," I answered. "Zeus. Odin. Ra. Mythology from all over the globe."

"Shit," blurted Maynard. "Mythological gods were fallen angels? But wouldn't that mean—"

"David believes so, yes," said Father Monaco, waving off whatever Maynard wanted to say. They had a history with these things, I could tell. "I tend to agree after knowing him all these years. Some Fallen were as evil and duplicitous as demons. They thrived under the Judean Accords, knowing they couldn't be touched by Heaven or Hell. Some became vicious, awful creatures, their inward identity spilling into their outward appearance. Other Fallen wished to do penance while here, hoping to be accepted home once again. They were sometimes referred to as *cruciati*."

"What does that mean?" asked Jonah.

"Tortured," I answered, via brain-trust.

"Is that what you think Tony is?" asked Maynard. "A Fallen seeking redemption? A cruciati?"

"I believe so, yes," said the priest. "He committed a crime against Heaven, and from what he's told us, it seems connected to the girl. Jacinda."

"What were those Divine Devices you were talking about?" asked Jonah.

"Right. Old age. Makes me forget," said Father Monaco, scratching his bald head. "We've all heard stories of Divine Devices. The Spear of Destiny. Excalibur. The Golden Fleece. Odin's Eye. Mjölnir. Weapons, items, things imbued with godly powers."

"You're saying I created my own legendary weapons?" Despite all the shit I'd been through to get them, the comic book geek inside me was already squeeing.

The priest shrugged. "Certainly not the strangest thing that's happened today. You've fallen—your spirit burns with hellfire. It looked like you were shooting hellfire to me."

"And Jacinda, what about her?" asked Maynard.

"I'm afraid I have no clue," said the priest.

"You said she changed right in front of you?" asked Maynard, reminding me of a moment I wished to forget.

I started playing nervously with my thumbs. Thinking of her made me feel an intense, sickening sadness, while my eyes watered uncontrollably. "She did. She became a whole new person."

"Shapeshifter?" suggested Jonah.

"Nah," grumbled Maynard, "I tested him *and* Jacinda every which way I knew. She said she could do things…"

"A witch?" said Jonah.

"No," Maynard and I grumbled simultaneously. Why was everyone so adamant that she was a witch? No wonder Salem had a problem—it was the slanderous go-to for any woman mixed up in the supernatural.

"Maybe a jinn?" said Jonah.

"Jinn? You mean a genie?"

Jonah nodded.

"No, I don't think so. Maybe?"

"Zombie?" squeaked Jonah, like he was running out of ideas. "You said she was dead, right?"

"No," I growled.

"How many zombies do you know that change shape?" groaned Maynard.

"I don't know, Maynard," sassed Jonah. "I've never met a zombie. Have you?"

"Boys," scolded the priest.

After a short pause, Jonah asked, "Changeling?"

"Why would the Fae get involved in this?" asked Maynard, like he knew better.

"I did fight off an invasion of Red Caps yesterday," I said, and realized I had accidentally omitted everything that happened between Summanus strangling me through a bathroom mirror, the group of people who rescued me in those strange masks, all the way till when I found my dead girlfriend roaming the Grace Falls Cemetery. "A goddess named Hekate came after me on Highway 13 right outside of town." Maybe I'd omitted those details for a reason—Amanda was dead, and I didn't have the heart to tell Maynard…yet.

They stared at me for a moment before exchanging silent looks—again—and Maynard eventually shrugged in frustration, like I had trampled on everything he thought he knew.

"The pile-up on 13 yesterday?" asked Maynard. "Were you responsible for that?"

"Responsible? Eh," I said, "more like carelessly caused after being attacked by a psycho masked goddess on the way into town."

"We've been investigating these events and creatures for years now," he replied, "and in the last day you've gone as deep into this shit as anyone ever has and lived to tell the tale."

Maybe he thought that was an impressive feat—something to be proud of. All I knew was that it filled me with a terrible sadness that sent me spiraling. I got up from my chair and walked around the room.

"How do I get her back?" I was crying before I realized it.

I had underestimated what seeing her again would do to me. Having lived that fantasy—getting her back for just one day—I'd miscalculated how losing her again might crush me. It felt like an unnecessary life lesson—a wish to get back something that was lost, only to lose it again. And what about Amanda? What about Marshall and Anne?

"I'm sorry," said Father Monaco, "but we don't have the resources to go up against something this immense. This kind of evil is out of our league. Even if we pulled the Philadelphia, New York, and Chicago chapters, we'd still be in way over our collective heads."

"I haven't heard from Thaddeus in a few days," said Maynard, and the name struck like a dagger. "Do you think everything's okay?"

"Thaddeus? Does he do what you do? In Philly? Does he wear a mask with a jagged smiley face?"

Maynard said, "Yeah, how'd you know that?" in a way that creeped everyone out.

"*Friends are the only thing worth fighting for,*" the man in the mask had said—Borrower—it was Thaddeus. I knew it was him. Deep down, I knew it.

Oh, fuck me.

An eighty-pound bag of rock salt hit the wall and busted open from the end of my fist.

"Chris Withers?" I choked. "Was he with them too?"

Their eyes were as wide as Jonah's jaw was dropped.

"How do you know all this?" asked the priest, but the look on his face said he knew the answer before he even asked.

"I was attacked. They rescued me. Called themselves Nightmares."

"That's Knightmares, with a K," said Maynard.

"What happened?" asked the priest.

I gave them a sad look as I sat down on top of the pallet of salt bags. "Dead. Anubis killed them. They sacrificed themselves to save me."

"Anubis?" said Maynard. "Egyptian god of the dead? They couldn't fight something like that. It had to be a slaughter…"

"Why?" asked Jonah. He was wrapped with a terrible fear that shook his entire body. "Why'd they sacrifice themselves for you? Why are you so important?"

"I don't know," I said as I rubbed my eyes. Jonah was right—I was nothing. Just a guy with random powers. I was much closer to Steve Buscemi than I was to a mythological god—they could call upon minions, create crow-nados, and were armed to the teeth with power and weapons. How infinitesimally small was I next to a god? Who was I to stand up to *them*? What exactly were the stakes here? What the hell was Jaycie, and what was so damn important about the key? "I've gotten everyone I ever love, killed."

I was just one against Thirteen—what chance did I have?

"We're all screwed," whined Jonah. "We're all so screwed!"

I was all set to explain what happened in detail, to come Clorox clean, when Father Monaco said, "We will honor them later." Maynard sniffled back the emotion then nodded, as Jonah bent over to stop himself from hyperventilating. Monaco, however, seemed unfazed. "This isn't the first time we've lost friends. And it won't be the last."

I sucked up the pain and bottled it for Malus. I had only one objective—to destroy him and protect Jacinda. Anything and everything else was secondary.

"Tell me what you know about Malus and The Thirteen?" I asked.

"I'm sorry," said the priest as gestured toward Jonah—then he and Maynard began preparing a bag of weapons and checking the surveillance equipment. "I know nothing about them. Thirteen mythological gods coming together for a common cause? Sounds unrealistic."

"My man, *that* sounds unrealistic to you?" whined Montoya. My brain-trust had been quiet throughout the entire discussion, soaking in the information.

"You mean other than mythological gods being real?" I asked.

"Imagine the hubris," said the priest, "the arrogance it takes for one to assume the position of a god over mankind? Now, imagine those same beings working together for a common goal? Even the individual pantheons had horrible disagreements. Affairs. Fights. Plotting. Revenge."

"There's something moving out there," said Jonah, looking at the screen. It was connected to a laptop that was loaded with heat-signature software filtering the video.

"Is it a U-Nat? Can you tell what it is?" asked Maynard.

"Negatory-nada," sang Jonah.

"What about my scar? And this?" I asked, removing the key from beneath my shirt. I could sense Monaco's nervousness and fear. "Malus wanted this too."

Maynard peered over his shoulder. "We've seen some weird stuff, but that's some crazy shit."

"I have no knowledge of the scar on your face, nor what it means," said the priest. "I've only ever met one of your kind, and he did not often share the secrets of the next world." He gave me a weak smile as an apology. "As for the key, show me."

I took the key and brought it up to my wrist, then slid it into the Sharpie keyhole. There was a humming like low bass, and the nearby jugs of chemicals swayed—their contents vibrating.

Father Monaco walked over to me, perplexed, and pulled the key free of my wrist.

"Where did you get it?" he asked. He held it in his hands for a moment before giving it back to me, feeling its weight as if he expected something different.

I placed the key back under my thermal before answering. "I found it when I was a kid."

"Sir, why are you lying to them?" asked Henry. Just because we shared the same head didn't mean the brain-trust had the right to question what I did and did not share. I ignored him and the others.

"Keys of power are written throughout many religions, including Catholicism, Judaism, Zoroastrianism, and more. These holy keys unlock gates to other realms." Monaco turned to his men. "We need to get him to the university."

"What?" said Jonah. "I thought he was on his own?"

"I believe this might just be the most important task our particular group has ever been a part of," said Father Monaco.

"How so?" asked Maynard. He wasn't arguing, just curious to hear their leader's perspective.

"We have an angel with no memory, hunted by thirteen mythological gods. They took a girl who came back from the dead, and they want that key," he said. "Gentlemen, we could be witnessing the end of days."

"What?" said Jonah with a serious case of the blinks. "The apocalypse?"

"Not the zombie-apocalypse, right? I mean, I was already assured it was only a regular apocalypse," said Maynard.

"What?" asked Jonah, but even the priest knew Maynard was joking around.

"The Book of Revelation didn't say anything about a girl, a key, and thirteen assholes," said Maynard. "I mean, I could double-check."

"It does not," said the priest. "But this is not our apocalypse."

"How so?" asked Jonah.

"The Book of Revelations sets forth the end of mankind. Or, rather, the end of a fourth of the population, leading to devastating effects on our world," explained the priest.

"And this apocalypse?" asked Jonah. His hand was twitching when he asked.

"The end of everything. Creation as we know it. Time. Balance. The physical and unphysical world. The entire third dimension. A cataclysm."

There was a long moment of silence, until Jamaal sang, "well, fuuuuuh-uuuuuck."

Over the next half-hour, we prepared our escape. The surveillance system continued to pick up moving shadows, which left Maynard, Jonah, and the priest confused.

"Why isn't the Hulinhjálmur working?" asked Maynard. "They should have scattered to the wind by now."

"Maybe it doesn't work?" I suggested as I removed the Sack of Righteousness. "I mean, if it's supposed to affect things like me, I can still see you."

"Did you hear me escape this morning at my parents' house?" he asked.

I shrugged.

"Did you hear the ignition on my van?"

I shook my head.

"Exactly."

"Fair point, I guess," I said, "but we did hear the fan belt squeal."

"Ah, shit," he groaned. "Nothing's perfect."

I looked over at the monitor and saw a Bacchae flash past with fresh blood dripping from her mouth. "How fast can your van go?" I asked.

"Why?" asked Maynard.

"How else are we going to outrun them?" I'd seen what the Bacchae could do with a mouth full of fresh blood. Fifty miles per hour from a thirty-year-old van wasn't going to cut it.

Jonah laughed like it was the funniest thing he had ever heard.

"Who said anything about outrunning them?" said Maynard, as he and Jonah moved the workbench aside. Beneath it was a metal sewer cover with the same intricate Hulinhjálmur design spray-painted onto it.

"You're kidding," I said.

"Nope," he replied with a double eyebrow raise and a grin stuffed with extra cheese.

The tunnel was a drainage system that Maynard and the others burrowed into, with string lights attached to a car battery to illuminate the path. After a hundred yards, the drainage system continued toward an industrial park, but we took a detour.

"Who knows if the construction crews found the caves when they built this place," said Maynard as we stepped through a crumbled opening in the concrete wall into a natural cave beyond. Both sides of the opening had additional protection symbols spray-painted around it. "But they left them alone. We only found it by chance when we mapped our escape route."

Maynard had a shotgun resting against his shoulder and carried a duffel bag, like the vagrant John Rambo in *First Blood*. Jonah, on the other hand, was as rigid as a plank of wood. He was carrying two duffel bags, one in each hand, but that wasn't the odd part. One of those small chemical tanks with the sprayer wand that people used to kill weeds was strapped to his back.

"Have you ever had to use it?" I asked, referring to the escape route.

"Once. Twice," he replied without details.

String lights were daisy-chained leading to the right, but the caves to the left smelled the foulest. It smelled old, stale air that tasted like dust with a garnish of evil. The cave's ceiling hung low, and the uneven floor forced us to duck our heads as it rose and dove every few feet. Eventually the string lights stopped, and the priest lit a modern battery-operated lantern for the remainder of the journey. The deeper we traveled into the unending darkness, the more I began to question the spread of the caves.

"Ever explore this place?" I asked.

"Not on your life," said Jonah.

"Some old places should remain unfound," said Father Monaco, though part of me didn't believe him.

If I ever wanted to know what it was like to be an earthworm, this was the opportunity I never wanted. We traveled within a narrow tube burrowed into the rock—whether it was natural or created by some man or beast, it was beyond my willingness to imagine. The tunnel wound its way on the path to nowhere, sometimes diving, other times corkscrewing up or down, eventually straightening before it flattened. Every so often we would converge with a separate tunnel, and I was left wondering what lay beyond—and why it bothered me so much.

"She ever talk about me?" asked Maynard. Only when he turned and looked at me did I realize I was the target of his question.

"Who?" I asked. By my calculation, we were connected by no less than three "shes" and all three were or had been, at one point, dead.

"Amanda," said Maynard. "She ever talk about me?"

It seemed an odd place to have this discussion—underground, chased by any number of ghouly things that wanted a slice of this Sicilian.

"She called you Morris," I said. "She told me how the two of you used to explore the forest behind your houses. That you were her sidekick."

He chuckled and shook his head, as if to say "that's so Amanda." We turned a corner and began traveling up before he spoke again, finally saying, "This one time, she and I explored all the way out to the highway."

The highway seemed like an uninspired thing to discuss without context—so I smiled and said a polite, "that's cool." I didn't want to think about Amanda. Everything had been happening so fast, I hadn't even had the chance to mourn my friends. To my knowledge, Maynard was still unaware of Amanda's death, and it didn't seem the appropriate time to tell him.

"It wasn't that far," he said, "but about a half mile back, there was this climb. We used to call it The Tower—and the only way past it was to climb or go around the crevice, an unknown distance either way. We were just six? Maybe seven years old? We could have gotten hurt, seriously hurt, but Amanda wouldn't listen to reason. She kept push-ing—'C'mon!' she said, 'are you waiting for someone else to see what's on the other side of the Tower?'"

"She had a way of getting me to do things I wouldn't have done on my own," I said, smiling. "The very first day we met, she helped me stand up to a bully."

"Sounds like her." He nodded. "I never wanted to let her down."

Father Monaco and Jonah both marched ahead, pretending not to hear our conversation. Jonah was trembling so badly, there was a good chance he couldn't hear us over the chattering of his own teeth.

"When she left, she never called, she never wrote. She disappeared from my life," he said, and I swallowed a jagged imaginary pill—I knew what that was like. "It was like I never existed. Like I never mattered.

"A few years ago I went back to the Tower. It's funny how big and surreal things seem as a kid, and how so small and insignificant they actually are as an adult. It was probably only ten feet high, but back then, they were the walls of Jericho. That day, when we climbed the Tower, we were kings—because, you know, even back then Amanda was before her time, threatening the patriarchy. If only kings could rule a kingdom, then she was also a king, because that's who she was."

I never thought about who else may have been affected by her death and pondered whether or not I should tell him. Would it make any difference if I told him now or later? Some things were best left discussed at times when they could be properly absorbed—like over a few glasses of whiskey.

"I miss her," he continued. "I miss Amanda. I miss Tori. Hell, I have to admit, I even missed Jaycie when I heard about her." He paused, as if he was searching for the right words. "I know what you're going through."

Before I could respond, Father Monaco said, "She was one of my flock."

"What?" I asked.

"Jacinda O'Neill and her family attended my mass," he replied, "...for a time."

"Yeah," said Jonah, "I met them once or twice." The way Jonah said it carried subtext that even made the Father look over at him inquisitively. I knew what it was like to grow up in a small town where everyone was connected—but this seemed strange to me, like conspiracy—like a corkboard of unlike pictures needing to be connected by a length of yarn.

"We all lost people," said the Father, and the words to continue the conversation escaped me.

We continued in silence, our footfalls softly echoing through the stale air, when I stepped through a curtain of roots hanging from the ceiling. We were close to the surface.

"How much further?" I asked. I felt uneasy moving so slowly when the creatures after me could move as fast, if not faster than I could, at full speed.

"Just a little," said Jonah, looking back at me. When he stopped dead in his tracks and gazed right through me, that uneasy feeling I had since entering the tunnels turned to dread. "What is that?"

The four of us spun around as two creatures stalked into the light of Father Monaco's lantern. Their skin was leathered and gray, like mummies wearing tattered rags. They were like zombies, with arms as thin as bone, and sections of flesh dangling from ligaments and dried sinew. They also had wings—terrible, scaly, deformed wings. Several rows of feathers were missing, exposing flaps of sick skin coated in infected pus. Their faces, however, sagged from the skulls, with shriveled eyes and sharpened teeth dribbling black bile.

They looked like dead angels.

"Mother fucking zombie-apocalypse," groaned Maynard. "I knew it."

"Jonah," said Father Monaco.

Jonah quickly dropped his bags and used the spraying wand to coat the floors, walls, and ceiling, then backed away.

I raised my guns and asked, "What is that?"

"Zombie angels? Zangels?" said Maynard.

"No," I groaned, "the stuff in the sprayer."

"Oh," he said, shaking his head. "Salt and holy water."

"A holy saline solution," corrected Jonah.

We backed away and watched as the Zangels approached the spray-on barrier, then stopped.

"We're not actually going to call them Zangels, are we?" asked Jamaal.

"Yeah, what about Zemons?" suggested Montoya. "Part demon, part zombie."

"Zangels it is," said Jamaal, spiting Montoya's awful suggestion.

"How'd they find us?" asked Jonah.

Father Monaco looked at me and said, "That witch, in the alley, did she touch you?"

I was starting to feel like I could have elaborated a little more on the details of my story. My omissions were coming back to bite me on the ass.

"Yeah," I nodded shamefully.

"He's been marked!" said Jonah, backing away like I was some kind of leper.

"Fudge," said Maynard as he dropped his bag and readied his shot-gun. Jonah and the priest began rifling through one of their duffel bags. "Why didn't you tell us you were marked?"

"Dude, I know *nothing* about *any* of this!" I argued back. "How do we remove it?"

"I don't know, man," said Maynard. He was getting itchy as the Zangels tested the boundary, probing it like a physical membrane, searching for gaps.

Father Monaco found several items inside the bag and said, "We don't have time to do this the slow way."

"What's the difference between the slow and fast way?" I asked as he pulled a vial of oil out of a protective sleeve and flicked open a book of matches with the other hand.

"Pain," he said with an apologetic smile. "Hurry, before we're surrounded!"

When someone tells you that something's going to be painful, it's typical to want to scoff. Everyone's pain threshold is different, and most people tend to think getting blood drawn is torture. But when a priest tells you that removing a "mark" is going to be painful, it's within your best interest to listen.

Father Monaco asked me to hold out both hands, palm up, as he poured a small dab of oil into each. Then he dabbed a spot on my forehead between my eyes.

"Ready?" he asked as he stuffed a wadded rag into my mouth to bite down on.

I muffled, "Yes," and he quickly lit a match. Then he took a deep breath and placed it a few inches over the small puddle of oil in my left palm.

"You're left-handed, correct?" he asked.

"I am," I mumbled, and he swiped the flame against the oil.

It lit gently like a candle flame, and I felt its warmth run up my forearm, into my elbow, then the shoulder. It was pleasant at first, but by the time it got to my neck, a panic set in.

"Don't fight it," said the priest, as he began to say a prayer under his breath.

"Hey," said Maynard. "Looks like we've got another visitor."

A third Zangel appeared, this one with horns, and somewhere I thought I heard Montoya say "See?" through gritted teeth. "Zemon."

As the uncomfortable warmth split and spread up into my head and down into my body and right arm, I could almost hear the witch cackling into my ear. Then the oil in my right palm lit, followed by my forehead, and I dropped to my knees as flames shot and crackled like Fourth of July sparklers.

For a moment, I blacked out. The pain was like pouring peroxide on an open wound that covered every external and internal inch of me.

When the intensity hit its peak, the burn rising to crescendo, I bit down hard enough to break my jaw in two. It felt like cracks were forming along my insides—like branches of lightning, fractals of pain that splintered and shattered my very being. Searing heat spread along the jagged edges—and wings—I felt their absence—phantom limbs that spread wide and bristled.

Then, less than thirty seconds after it started, the pain subsided, and the cackle in my ear was gone. I was sweating, hyperventilating, and my muscles ached after they unclenched.

"Did it work?" I whined as the priest removed the rag from my mouth. I sounded worse than I thought I was, and my knees failed me when I attempted to stand.

"Let us pray," said Father Monaco.

Jonah had already repacked everything and was ready to go when I finally stood up. Maynard had his shotgun trained on the creatures behind us. "That holy saline solution crap is drying," he warned.

"Are you ready?" asked the priest.

"Yes," I said, and we began to evacuate, at twice the pace as before.

We jogged through the tunnel toward a dim light as a strange sound echoed off the rocky chamber behind us—were they howling? Communicating? Jonah was the first through, pushing aside the plant life that had grown over the mouth of the cave. Next went Father Monaco, followed by Maynard, then me—but try as I might, I couldn't get my body to move.

"Take my hand," said Maynard. With his help, I broke through whatever had prevented me from escaping the caves. As I stepped out into the forest, I could sense the sacred native land around us. It was a burial ground—ancient and full of positive wards against evil. I felt confident that nothing chasing us would be able to exit the cave from there—heck, even I couldn't push myself through alone.

Jogging up the hill behind the cave, we found an old dirt road that cut through the forest, with private land postings plastered on all the surrounding trees. There, parked in the center of the road was a VW Bug that looked older than Maynard's van. Its panels were painted in different colors, harvested from other Volkswagens.

"There she is," said Jonah affectionately.

"You brought the Bug?" asked Maynard.

"Yeah," said Jonah, oblivious.

"How are we all going to fit?" asked Father Monaco as something big howled off in the distance.

XIII

carina

JACINDA
Then.

The truth was coming out, Jace. Little by little, I was learning. The big questions still remained—like what you were, and how you got that way—but I was beginning to understand you better than ever.

I didn't want you to run away from home, but I also would never have stopped you. To say living there was an untenable situation was an understatement. Your mom was like Cruella De Vil, and you were the Dalmatian she never wanted. She would have destroyed you and the amazing person you were.

Still, where would you go from here, Jace?

Now I know why you never showed up at the Labor Day Fair the following day.

August 30th, 1997

You left in the middle of the night. Your parents lied. They told the police there was no warning, just a letter you left on the kitchen table where your father read the paper every morning before work. Your mother nearly collapsed after reading it. Your departure positively impacted your mother's road to recovery, a wake-up call to someone who had sleepwalked through the last dozen years of life.

The first hundred miles felt like an adventure. Sure, you had been to Ireland a few times with your family, and gone on a few other vacations here and there, but this was the first time you were doing it all on your own. You took your guitar and most of your clothes, along with most of your life savings and a few other items, and hit the road. Everything you needed was in your little red car as you cruised down the interstate, heading west.

The second hundred miles became a terrifying mess of nerves and second-guessing. You began to question what you were doing and even had the notion of turning around, which you very nearly did after passing a bulletin board that said, "Going the Wrong Way?" The sign advertised a financial planning business, but the giant red message planted the seed of doubt. All you had to do was remember why you left, and things were suddenly put back into perspective.

It wasn't just your mother and father, and their crazy accusations—accusations that were partially true—but it was also Rick, the drugs, and the last decade of your life since your Grammy died. You could do things that you shouldn't have been able to do—things that terrified you. And then there were the scribbles you found in your journal, the memories you had forgotten, and the questions that came and went like the tide, filling your head with anxiety to the point of panic.

So, you drove, and you denied yourself any attempts at looking back.

By 7 a.m., your pager began to buzz—your parents were calling, followed by Rick, on and off in a pattern, until they finally gave up sometime after 9—then it started again around 10:30. Rick called your pager so many times that you actually thought about pulling over and calling back. Maybe he actually cared? Then you opened your car window and chucked the pager out as you drove sixty-five miles an hour. You watched it bounce twice from your rearview mirror.

The worst of it, you thought, was now behind you.

By nightfall, you were already an hour past Indianapolis, so you decided to pull over and take a break. You found a rest stop at a restaurant named Mavericks—it was a large bar where truckers and travelers could stop in for a quick drink and a hot meal. It was the kind of place where you might go unnoticed. You were almost seventeen, but you weren't interested in a drink, just some food before you continued on your way.

The bar was a puke stain or two away from being a complete and total dump. A few bar stools were broken, the pool tables scratched and worn. It wasn't so bad for a roadside bar in the middle of nowhere-Indiana. It was almost cozy, and you could count the number of customers with the fingers on one hand.

Nobody was there to take your order as you hopped onto a stool at the bar. There were shouts coming from the kitchen. Someone was arguing about taking the trash out to the dumpster. You could hear them over a country song playing on the radio that was popular before you were born. A hot meal and some time to put your thoughts down on paper was all that mattered to you after a long day on the road.

You had your journal and a pen, so you flipped through to a clean page and began jotting down thoughts. I half expected you to begin with the ghostly reappearance of Jane at the top of the steps, but instead you wrote something that caught me off guard.

"What's wrong with my memories?" you wrote.

I had seen these kinds of notes before in your journals. Questions to yourself, sometimes reminders. Seeing you write one left me chilled—I was witnessing a symptom, but still had no clues to the origin of this disease.

Behind the Veil, I could hear loud thoughts, sense strong emotions—but one thing I could not do was truly get inside your head. Everything was by proxy, and nuance was lost in translation. It was an empathic connection but not your own voice. It was interpretive.

I often wondered how you were able to move on from the dark moments. Some people have selective memory, focusing on the good or bad in any given situation. But you had fragmented memory—whole moments and details that seemed to disappear. Perhaps that was how you survived...

"What'll ya have to drink, hon?" the bartender asked, startling you. You jumped and quickly closed your journal to hide what you had written, as if you had jotted down something dangerous.

The bartender had dark hair, a Mediterranean complexion and bright gray eyes—the contrast was striking. She didn't look like someone who worked in a hole-in-the-wall pub at a highway rest-stop, and her appearance disarmed you. She was wearing all white with a black bartending apron but seemed too beautiful and young to be working there. This was the place where a grizzled lifetime bartender slung beers and un-measured glasses of whiskey to truck drivers who went days without hot showers.

"Oh," you said once your thoughts reconnected, "I'm fine. I'm actually not old enough to drink."

"Really?" the bartender asked. She might have said it sarcastically, but you couldn't tell the difference.

"I'm traveling," you said.

"I see that," she replied. "So, whadd'll-ya have? It's on the house. Nobody'll say nuffin'."

You thought for a moment about what you'd like, or what you were supposed to like, having only ever drank cheap party beer, bad punch, and expensive wine, when you realized how familiar the woman appeared. You couldn't pinpoint where from, or how, but you were positive. Without a doubt, you knew that face.

"Have we met before?" you asked.

I know I recognized her, Jace.

Carina, the EMT from a decade ago, right after the accident. She checked you for a concussion, then checked out. She wore a key around her neck, just like mine, and I knew there was something fishy going on from the moment I saw her.

A thought crossed my mind—she looked like someone from an old hazy memory, but I quickly punted—I didn't even want to think it.

"Maybe? You come by here often?" she asked. "I've been bartending here for a few years now. Pays the bills, ya know? Name's Carina." As Carina leaned over the bar and extended her hand, a silver chain holding a brass key tumbled out of her shirt and dangled in front of you. It made you think of me—the boy you'd met just yesterday, who wore a similar key and chain.

"Mo," you replied as you shook Carina's hand. Moira was your Grammy's name. It seemed fitting for you to adopt a new name for this new life you were embarking upon. Carina gave you a pleasant smile and returned to toweling off a few beer steins.

"That key," you said, "it reminds me of someone. He had one just like it."

"Your boyfriend?"

"No, just a friend," you replied with a sigh. You were supposed to meet me at the Labor Day Fair earlier that day, and you were imagining my disappointment.

"A woman who sighs like that is never just friends with a fella," said Carina, giving you a sisterly glance.

"It's complicated," you replied.

"Always is with love." Carina chuckled. "I was in love once. True love. That once-in-a- lifetime kind of love. He was a powerful man, very busy, and didn't have enough time for me. I became bitter and left. I thought he loved someone else. I've regretted it ever since and went through a long phase of self-destructive behavior. Then, one day I met a girl a lot like you, and she helped put me on the right path. I may never have *his* love again, but I won't stop trying to find it."

"Do you know where he is? Can you go after him?" you asked, entranced by Carina's vulnerability.

"I know where he lives, but I'm not welcome back. I did some horrible things," Carina said, the sass in her voice mysteriously gone. "What about you? Tell me your story?"

"Wow, I don't know where to begin," you said, flustered by the question.

"Start anywhere. I'm listening," said Carina.

"There's a guy I really like," you said, "He's the guy all the other girls want. Sometimes he shows interest, and other times I feel like he's using me. Like I'm his backup plan." You paused, thinking about Rick, until you realized there was more to tell. "Then, recently this other guy came along. He was so different than the first guy. He was good. Sweet. Fun. He wasn't as cute as the other guy, but he had such heart, and it made him so beautiful to me. He made me laugh, not because he was the funniest guy ever, but he was fun and gentle, and playful. I felt like I've known him my entire life." Carina started pouring your drink, and you continued. "Yet, as much as I enjoyed my time with him, I couldn't stop thinking about the other guy. Am I being stupid?"

Yes, pretty much.

Carina smiled sadly, then said, "Sometimes the heart wants what it wants." Then she set a beer down in front of you. "If you know what you want, why did you run away?"

You were caught off guard by Carina's intuition. "There's a lot going on."

"Always is."

"Yeah, but what happened to me is different."

"How so?"

"Things have happened that are…" you said, searching for the right word, "…terrible? Awful? Insane?"

"Sounds like you need to forget all that and move on. Live your life. Put the past behind you."

"How do I do that?" you asked.

"You close your eyes and will it upon yourself. You tell the world and all your demons to forget about you. To go away and leave you alone."

You took a healthy sip of beer as you thought about that. There was something about what she said that made sense in the most unusual way. You were aware that you weren't normal, and that strange, sometimes spectacular things happened around you—but could you really make everything that ever haunted you—the past, your demons—go away?

"Sometimes I wish I didn't exist."

"Honey, let me tell you something, if you ever meet a man who makes you wish you didn't exist, you're associating with the wrong man."

"Yeah," you replied. Carina might not have understood what you were going through, but she was trying.

Then again, something told me she knew exactly what was happening. After all, she was like me—an angel. She wasn't there to hurt you, but I didn't understand her purpose either.

From behind the Veil, I could get within five feet of the other key before they both began to pulse. I watched the other key's equal sway in rhythm to my own while it dangled from Carina's neck. She grabbed hold of it before you noticed and pretended she was playing with it.

"And, let me tell you another thing. If you ever, ever, come across a man who genuinely loves and cherishes you in the way you want to be treated, don't ever let him go. You may not get another chance," she said.

"I can't. Not yet. I have to figure myself out first."

"And you think you'll figure yourself out by hanging around this group of losers?" Carina gestured around the room. There was a guy falling asleep in his plate of food, and another guy who was so drunk that he was drinking out of an empty glass.

"No," you said. "But I can't go home. It's too—complicated."

"Then find your own way," she said. "Figure yourself out, but never lose sight of what you want in life. Go get it. Don't end up like me, trying to make up for things I wish I didn't do."

"Thanks," you said, taking another sip.

"And when you're ready, find your way back to him," she said, lingering on you with an intense but caring stare. The kind of look a mother would give a daughter.

"Okay, but maybe Rick isn't right for me," you replied. Carina's stare was beginning to give you chills as she reached out and took your hand.

"Not that boy, the other one," she said as she pulled at the chain around her neck. "The one you're reminded of when you saw this key." Suddenly Carina's eyes fluttered, and she sniffed at the air.

"How did you—?"

"He'll protect you from the beast," said Carina, her tone frigid like an icy wind. "From the man with two eyes, the pale man who wants what only you have. Your love, your true love, will be the only thing that saves you." The words left her mouth in a fearful rush of compassion, and a chill ran up my back.

What did Carina know, Jace? Who was she really?

You were shocked, like you were locked inside your own body, unable to move. Was it in your head? Or was it done to you on purpose? Were you drugged?

"Make them forget. Make yourself forget. Then when you're ready, find your love."

Carina let go of your hand and immediately paced to the other side of the bar as your mind went fuzzy. You watched the woman take off her apron and hang it on a hook beside the kitchen door. Then she left through the back exit.

As soon as the door closed behind her, your mind slid back into focus, and with it came a surge of questions. You leapt from your barstool and chased Carina through the back door. Who was she? What was happening? Why did she know all these things?

You were only a few seconds behind the bartender, and you stepped out into a small area behind the building, with foul-smelling dumpsters and glowing rat eyes darting through the darkness.

A shooting pain gripped your stomach, a cramp that almost crippled your ability to move. Through the pain, you searched everywhere, even around the far side of the building, but Carina was gone. She had completely vanished into the night.

You fled back inside the bar as the cramping subsided, but a creeping fear settled into the base of your neck. Something was coming, as quick as a storm.

"Excuse me," you said, grabbing the male bartender, who carried a tray full of dirty dishes. "Where did the other bartender go? Carina? I have a few questions for her."

"Carina?" he muttered. "There's nobody here named Carina. I'm the only bartender working tonight."

"Are you sure?" you asked. You were feeling panicked. "Tan skin, wearing white?"

"Nope, sorry," he said and continued into the kitchen.

You made your way back to the bar, sat down, and grabbed your beer—as you lifted it to your lips, paying no mind to the contents within, I whispered, "No," into your ear.

The remaining beer within your glass was bubbling and solidifying into a thick sludge that appeared to move on its own. There was a buzz on the air, like a thousand fluorescent bulbs, and you knew it was danger. Somehow, some way, the crazy had found you again. You ran from crazy, and it hunted you down several hundred miles from home.

I felt for you, Jace, as you dropped your glass and ran from the bar. When you got to your little red car, you hopped inside and floored the gas, hitting the on-ramp at seventy miles per hour. You didn't let up until you were twenty miles away, obsessing over Carina and her words of wisdom.

"Put the past behind you," the woman had said. *"You close your eyes and you will it upon yourself. You tell the world and all your demons to forget about you. To go away and leave you alone."*

You were completely alone in the world, left to deal with things you had no capacity to understand. "Go away," you said, "and leave me alone."

How many people had ever faced down the darkness all alone?

How long could one person see the world through your eyes and remain intact? Your life was filled with misery, with confusion, and the idea of true unconditional love was lost on you, an idealistic fantasy. The fact that you were still fighting, still pushing forward, was something of a miracle. Like anybody else, you deserved a normal life. Maybe not everyone got a perfect or even blessed chance at life, but you at least deserved normal.

Your tragic life was filled with struggles nobody should have to face. You were at the crux of a power struggle. The target of evil.

I stood by and watched you struggle.

I stood by and watched you *suffer*.

Was there anything I could do?

Was there any way for me to help you?

December 24th, 1997

Las Vegas during Christmas was so much different than you expected. The weather was warm, the sun was shining, and the loneliness was like strangulation. Your apartment was small, just a mere four hundred square feet, but it was large enough for a small kitchen, bathroom, and bed. You practiced your guitar nightly, even if your sessions were sometimes cut short by your neighbor banging on the wall, and you worked hard every day just to survive.

If your parents could see you, would they be proud of you? Or would they pity you and your struggle?

That small apartment was your fortress—it was home, and it was cheap, but even though you had a roof over your head, you weren't happy. Something major was missing. This wasn't what you meant when you said you wanted to figure yourself out.

Las Vegas was a cruel city. Working double shifts at a hotel casino bar just to make ends meet showed you how easily the real world consumed people into lifetimes of despair. You spent the rest of your time attempting to find gigs, on and off the Vegas strip, wherever you could find them. You even played for free just to get your foot through doors.

You were thirteen hours into a double shift when you finally peeled your sticky apron off, stashed it in the washing machine at the back of the breakroom, and clocked out. You said goodnight to a few co-workers and wished them happy holidays, then left with purpose. There was one thing you had been saving money for the past few weeks, and this was your last chance to get it before it was too late.

All you wanted, all you needed, was a Christmas tree. Something to make the holidays seem meaningful. Something to take away the aching loneliness.

You may not have been able to afford a nice perfect pine or fir, but you were determined to bring back something small and sweet you could hang a few decorations from, to keep your spirits alive.

You were a fighter, Jace. This was you taking another jab at life. It was this kind of fight that always struck me as special. Even in the most trying of times, you were always pushing and fighting for something better—so why did you give up on me? Would I ever learn the answers to all my questions?

There was a local department store a few blocks from your apartment where a vendor sold trees in the parking lot. The sun was down, and he was nearly sold out when you finally swung by. He had already shut down for the day, but after you pleaded with him, he agreed to sell you one of his leftover trees.

His inventory had been picked through, leaving only a handful that were decent, and of those you couldn't afford a single one.

You cried for a moment, then settled for something closer to pathetic—a tree only Charlie Brown and you could love.

You lugged it back to your apartment by yourself and used an old rusty Christmas tree holder you'd found by the dumpsters a few days prior. You filled the basin with fresh water, then hung a few bulbs you bought in a dollar store and placed a beat-up old angel on top. When you were done, you backed away and turned out the lights.

The fluorescent streetlamp filtered into the room through your window and made the tinsel twinkle. You admired your first Christmas tree with a great big smile from your bed, which slowly changed into a frown and was followed by tears. You grabbed the bottle of cheap booze you bought from work, then drank until there was nothing left.

I cried with you. There was nothing more heartbreaking than watching you despair. I laid down next to you and held you, and even though you couldn't feel it, I was there. I wouldn't leave you, no matter what.

An hour passed, quiet and still, as you stared at your tree in a drunken haze.

Your alarm clock, the one you took from your bedroom at home, ticked therapeutically, counting the seconds as you drifted—too tired to sleep, too drunk to move.

And then, the clock stopped.

I watched as the madness began, Jace.

It started slow, as all evil things do.

The streetlamp shining through your window blinked. Then it blinked once more and went dead.

Shadows moved through the room. Strange shadows that existed without light, as if they absorbed all the luminance. Un-seeable evil, without form, meddled like gremlins conspiring to mischief. A wisp of black vapor blew into your ears and removed your ability to hear.

I shot up from the bed next to you and was checking back and forth from reality to the Veil when I was suddenly pushed aside and restrained—caught within the Veil like someone had locked an impenetrable screen door. I was being forced to watch.

I tried everything, Jace—but the more I fought, the stronger and more confined the Veil became, like I was trapped in quicksand.

The fire alarm buzzed. Loud sirens blared from the hallway, waking the neighbors. Many of them ran from their rooms in complete hysteria, bolting for the exits in such haste that they forgot to close the doors behind them. Car alarms went off outside, filling the block with noise, masking the world from the horrors set to begin inside.

Ice formed along the windows with crackling speed, and the carpet captured frozen moisture like frost on frozen grass. You clung to the warmth of the blankets, pulling them up over your shoulder, when the sensation of a wet tongue glided and froze across the back of your exposed neck.

You sat up in a startle as a cramping pain gripped your stomach, like something was trying to claw its way out of you. You rolled over, clutching at your midsection, and flung yourself off the bed onto the crunchy frozen carpet, a sensation that drew your mind away from the pain. You scanned the dark room and grabbed the alarm clock, shook it, and held it up to your ear.

You couldn't hear the ticking and smacked it against your hand a few times until you realized you couldn't hear anything. Not a sound. Nothing.

A panic manifested as you tapped at your ears and dug a finger gently inside, as if searching for an obstruction, when something moved inside the room.

You screamed for help. Your yell vibrated through your entire body, but you heard no scream. You screamed again, louder, but there was nothing. You tried to stand but slipped and fell on the icy floor after feeling something coarse caress your arm.

Sprawling for the door, you lost traction on your bare feet, so you crawled instead, until something grabbed at your ankle. You yelped and rolled to the nearest wall and sat up against it, facing the rest of the room, searching for the intruder.

There was nothing inside the tiny apartment, but you felt a presence. It touched you. It was there, it was going to get you, and there was nothing I could do to prevent it, Jace!

You scuttled to your knees, dove for the kitchen counter, and grabbed hold of a large kitchen knife. With the knife in your hands, you held it out like a warning, daring your intruder to test the sharpness of the blade.

You banged the knife against the wall but heard nothing.

You stomped your feet and banged your elbows and continued to hear nothing but silence.

A claustrophobic feeling swept over you like locusts devouring a field. You were shivering in the cold and felt surrounded—like there was no way out.

Out of the darkness from beneath your bed, something crawled across the ground. It skittered this way and that—a tiny little shadow, like a bug, moving toward your bare feet. The skin on your legs began to crawl as if you were covered in a thousand spiders, and you realized it wasn't just a feeling.

Thousands of spiders covered you, nasty ones, large and small, with red eyes and pincers and hairy long legs, all of them creeping and crawling up your shivering body. You smacked at them and thrashed violently on the ground. Some crawled across your face while others wiggled up your nose. Some even got into your mouth, but the majority wanted your eyes. You squeezed your eyes shut as tightly as you could until everything went dark—

—even when you finally opened them.

As fast as the attack had started, the spiders were gone, but so was your vision.

Was this a dream? Was it a nightmare? How did all those spiders get inside the apartment? Maybe you were allergic to the alcohol?

You decided you were sleeping, the only possible explanation, and tried to wake up, but something wasn't right.

"Wake up," you said to yourself, your words unheard by your own ears. "C'mon, just wake up!" you shouted, but nothing happened. You rubbed your eyes again and again, and when nothing changed, you screamed. You took the knife in your hand and cut your forearm, purposely. Hot pain burned through your arm, but you didn't wake up from the nightmare. You cut yourself again, and still nothing changed.

You were vulnerable. You were alone. You were blind and deaf. Fucking hell, what could I do!? I ignited, my body fully engulfed in hellfire when the heat was stolen, extinguished and absorbed by the restraining darkness. I was helpless and so were you, Jace. Was this the end?

You took the knife and held it out in front of you. You needed help, and your panic was crippling you.

A sudden rush of cold air blew across your bare feet and jolted your other senses, electrified with terrified urgency. You were caught, completely exposed with no way to defend yourself except through blind slashing from your kitchen knife.

Then something moved. You felt it.

"Who's there!?" you screamed, but only silence registered in your dead ears. There was another brush of air, quickly followed by the feeling of chain wrapping around your arm at the wrist and fastening tight. You tried to break your arm free but couldn't. Three more chains tied your three remaining limbs, then pulled—stretching you to four corners.

You screamed and began to lose control.

"Leave me alone!" you bawled at the top of your lungs and felt a wave of angry power roll through you like the rumbling of thunder. The chains broke apart and you landed on the ground with a loud thud. Your ears burned, eyes stung and watered, but sight and sound had finally been restored.

The fire alarms were blaring as if they were screaming directly into your ears. You were confused and scared with two bloody cuts on your arm. You calmed, like the worst of it was over, and the chill inside the room seemed to lift.

The calm spread from a few manic seconds into a solid peaceful minute when something slimy touched your bare foot. It felt like a tongue or some other slimy appendage, but there was nothing there. You could see your feet in front of you and touched them with your bare hand, but there was nothing there. You felt it again, and you were trying to pull your feet in closer when it grabbed you tightly around the ankle and dragged you across the floor toward the bed.

Your hands grappled for something, anything to hold on and stop from being dragged away. But there was nothing to hold onto, nothing to prevent you from sliding helplessly across the icy wet floor. You latched onto the bedpost in a last-ditch effort as *whatever it was* pulled you underneath the bed.

You screamed and flailed, trying to kick free of your invisible assailant, and I fought back with you. *Jace, I won't let it end this way!*

Your fingernails bent and strained against the force, dug deep into the wooden post. The floor below dissolved and warped and dangled you on the edge of a cold black pit. Several sets of icy hands pawed at your bare legs, pulling you down into the black madness below. Tears streamed freely, the salty taste of them dripping into your own mouth as you screamed and choked at the terror.

"Help me!" you screamed, terrified further than you had ever been before, pushed to the very edge of your limits. "Please!" You wept. "Please! Somebody!?"

I screamed along with you. I roared like something tearing its way out of hell, and I nearly broke free when a hand was offered to you. Someone had found you. One of the other tenants? Had they stayed behind? Did they hear your screams for help?

You took the hand, and it pulled you free from harm.

Once away from the bed, you collapsed. You were exhausted, nerves shattered, and struggled on the icy floor to pull yourself onto your knees. The person in front of you remained in shadow—and I couldn't see from my angle.

"Thank you," you said. "I don't know what's happening, but thank you." You were confused and crying. How could you explain what had happened to anyone? You hid your face, too embarrassed to look the rescuer in the eyes after they had stumbled in on the madness.

"What's going on?" asked the rescuer. Her voice sounded young. Way too young.

"Who are you?" you asked, rubbing the tears from your eyes. None of the neighbors had kids.

She had long blonde pigtails, and she wore a lacy dress.

"The monster is here," said the girl. "You can't hide from him."

"Who are you?" you asked, as a new fear took over. You backed away from her, but you knew who she was.

"I'm your sister, and you killed me," she said angrily. "Why did you kill me?"

A memory plucked like a guitar string—silent at first, then loud and high-pitched, reverberating over and over until it connected. That door inside your head swung wide open again. You could see the whole picture.

This was your sister. Live and in the flesh, and she was not very happy with you.

"I didn't mean to!" you cried. "I couldn't control it!"

"We know what you are!" she growled.

"I'm sorry," you cried. "I'm so sorry!"

"We found you again," she said, her voice like a wild animal. The voice over-enunciated each syllable, prolonging the creeping shiver it sent up your spine. There were beings in the room with Jane. Things you couldn't quite see, but you could feel them. They were powerful, dangerous, the epitome of evil.

You shut your eyes, shook your head, and said, "No."

I punched and clawed and kicked and was almost free when something grabbed you by the throat.

"No, you won't have me," you cried. "I want to disappear. I want to be left alone, and I want it all to go away. I want it all to go away and I want to be left alone!"

"We have you now," said a chilling voice.

"I want to forget and be forgotten! I want to forget and be forgotten! I want to forget and be forgotten!"

Then the world bent, like heat rising from a hot dark surface.

You were focused on the ticking of your alarm clock from the comfort of your warm bed. You watched it flip from 11:59 p.m. to midnight. You said, "Merry Christmas," then shut your eyes and fell asleep.

Merry Christmas, Jace.

I love you.

XIV
celestine

TONY

I used to love mythology when I was a kid. I loved learning about when the gods ruled the world with their petty arguments, revenge plots, and monsters. Amanda introduced me to *Clash of the Titans* and *Jason and the Argonauts*, with the stop-motion effects of Ray Harryhausen. I became obsessed and immediately checked out all the Greek mythology books from my school library the next day.

Years later, I took a few mythology courses with Doctor Celestine, learning about Greek, Egyptian, Norse, and even a bit of Chinese myth. Unfortunately, after I bombed the midterm and achieved a string of embarrassing D's, I wasn't as enthusiastic about the legendary stories. Celestine had managed to ruin something I enjoyed.

"You're just jealous," Jaycie had said to me one night as we reminisced.

"Of what?" I scoffed as we were snuggled up together waiting for the drive-in movie to start. I don't remember the movie, but I remembered her, and our conversation—the way she smelled and even what she was wearing.

"I got straight A's, and you barely held down a C minus in Celestine's classes," she recited with accurate detail. Leave it to Jaycie to remember my grades as well as her own.

"That's only because Celestine hated me," I replied, half joking.

"Face it, T, I'm better than you at everything."

She wasn't wrong. She was the better half of us.

"What's your favorite myth?" I asked.

"Narcissus." She beamed.

"What? Really?" I asked. It seemed a bit of a downer to me, given the tragic ending.

"Yeah, think of it? It's so poetic!" she explained passionately. It was that passion that really got my heart pounding for her. "Guy is bored and lonely and hates everyone and everything, and suddenly looks down into a pool of water and sees his own reflection. Bam! Falls in love with it and ends up dying because he can't look away from his own beauty."

"Yeah, what's not to love," I said sarcastically, prompting her to punch me on the arm.

"Stop teasing me! It's a great story."

"Uh huh."

"See, that's why you nearly failed his class," she said, then quietly grabbed a handful of popcorn and waited for me to digest her accusation long enough for me to ask—

"—why?"

"Because you miss the point!" she said with a beaming smile. "Mythology is fascinating, not because there are heroes and monsters, but because the stories are allegorical connections of a more primitive mind attempting to make sense of a complicated world. Their fables have become our words, our culture."

"Spoken like Celestine," I grumbled, then received a fistful of popcorn to the face.

Jaycie was right, like always—but even she couldn't have guessed the truth. Perseus and Theseus. Thor and Odin. Isis and Osiris. These stories were more than just myth—they were real.

December 23rd, 2013
Now.

The ride over to Milton State University was a tight fit—clown car tight. We loaded into Jonah's late 70's VW Beetle with its backfiring engine and drove down a dirt road through the forest. Eventually the road connected with a barely paved back road that fed into another, and ultimately came out of a well-hidden service road that led to a stretch of Route 42, about ten minutes north of the university's athletics complex.

"Turn in here," I said, as we pulled up the windy wooded lane that led to the locker room parking lot. It was nice to see that the university had never put up those extra lights and security cameras they promised. We passed the exact spot where Rick Jansen had jumped me from the woods, and the memory felt like a million years ago.

We parked in the empty lot, and I helped them unload their things as the parking lot lamps switched on. It was only 4:30p.m., but it was dark, and the early winter cold felt like mid-January with its blustery winds.

Father Monaco told me that Doctor David Celestine, my old professor, had answers. It was a cold, overcast Saturday, and the university was shut down for the holidays—but that didn't mean it was completely abandoned. There were always students who opted to stay on campus, and staff who came and went as they pleased.

I led them along a paved path lit by ornamental English lamps from the athletics complex, past the stadiums, and up to the academics building, where most teachers had office hours during the week. Father Monaco promised Doctor Celestine would be there, and his confidence made me curious—didn't he have somewhere else to be on a Saturday, two days before Christmas?

We snuck into the academics building, our weapons loaded into Maynard and Jonah's bags, and tiptoed down a dark hall. A single light shone through a crack beneath an office door.

"As usual," said Father Monaco, pointing to the office light. "Jonah, come with me. The rest of you wait here."

"Why? Why are we waiting here?" I asked Maynard, as Father Monaco and Jonah approached the door.

"Celestine's a private kind of guy," Maynard explained. "He doesn't like a lot of attention." The priest and Jonah knocked on Celestine's office door, then walked in. There was a loud shout, followed by calming voices before the door closed behind them. "Also, he's kind of pissed at us."

"What for?" I asked.

"We lost someone, a while back."

"Who?"

"A good friend," said Maynard. "A guy named Dylan Jacobs."

A few moments later, Jonah walked out of the office and approached us like had just been scolded by a parent.

"Only Tony can go in," said Jonah. "Maynard and I need to stay out here."

"Why?" asked Maynard. "He knows me."

"He's being," said Jonah, who paused for the right word, "eccentric."

"Go on," said Maynard. "Get your answers before he changes his mind."

I nodded, then calmly walked to the door at the end of the hall and peeked inside. Doctor Celestine looked exactly as he had twelve years ago when I took his class. Thin, crew-cut silver hair, a day's worth of stubble, and a pair of black-rimmed glasses. His hand gestures alone were enough to illustrate his fiery passion—and irritation. He was the kind of professor who locked his door once class started and wouldn't admit anyone late, then stood in front rambling for an hour and a half straight without questions or pauses. And God forbid you had to use the lavatory—hold it or miss out on crucial information pertinent to weekly tests.

Celestine's office was a lot like Doctor Hammond's—clean, organized, precise—but with an added wacky flair. Where Dr. Hammond hung psych degrees and certifications on his wall, Doctor Celestine hung African masks and classical illustrations depicting Homer's *Odyssey* and Dante's *Inferno*.

Father Monaco and Celestine were locked in a semi-heated debate and never noticed when I stepped into the doorway.

"He could still be out there, John," said Celestine. "We abandoned him."

"We did not abandon him," said the priest calmly. "We look for signs every day."

"Ahem," I said. I actually said *ahem*—it wasn't a throat clear.

Celestine's eyes glanced on me for only a moment when he jumped, literally, out of his chair. He stood with his back to the window, as if trying to make himself as flat as possible.

"I thought you said he was like me?" said Celestine. His voice was shaken—scared.

"Isn't he?" said the priest, confused. He stood up to calm his friend by gently patting his hands up and down gently on an imaginary animal—why the heck do we do that? It looks ridiculous, yet we've all done it. "Calm down, he's a friend. A fallen angel, like you."

Whoa whoa whoa, Celestine was an angel? Made sense, I suppose—and after hearing it I could sense it—feel it—smell it on him. He was different, and that knowledge opened a whole new door for me. I had context, and it was suddenly very easy to tell human from non-human.

"He's a killer," said Celestine.

A what!?

"Go easy, sir," said Henry. "This man exhibits a vast array of paranoias."

"I don't mean you any harm," I said. "I'm just looking for answers."

"You won't get them from me," sneered Celestine.

"I think you'll want to hear his story, David," said the priest.

"Ask Gabriel, he's your prince," growled the doctor.

"What do you mean?" I asked, stepping further into the room.

"You don't know?" When I shook my head, he said, "How do you not know this? What are you after?"

"Information," I replied.

He thought for a moment before he leaned over his desk and stared, as if trying to ascertain my truthfulness. "The scar on your face is the brand of the crescent moon. It scarred when you fell. That brand belongs to Gabriel. You're one of his, and don't worry, it'll heal—eventually."

"One of Gabriel's what?" I asked.

"Host," he answered curtly, as if annoyed by my lack of understanding. "Wait a minute. Anthony Oscuro?" I nodded. "I remember you! Spark so small, you sat in my class for almost a full semester before I even noticed."

"I tend to fly under the radar," I said, jokingly.

"How'd your spark get so big?"

"Sounds like a personal question," joked Montoya, and Jamaal started laughing.

"You were shattered," he said suddenly. "That's why you don't remember. Still putting the pieces together?"

"Apparently," I replied as I sat down next to Father Monaco, who sat down with me in solidarity. Suddenly the three of us were having a conversation—sort of.

"I bet you can't even slip behind the Veil," he scoffed arrogantly.

"The Veil?" questioned Chappy. "The upside-down place? When we escaped Malus and disappeared."

"Yeah," added Montoya. "When the color got all weird, like we were eating shrooms with hippies."

"I don't even know what that is," I responded. "The Veil?"

"A pocket world," said Henry. "One that overlaps our own."

"Of course you don't," said Celestine snidely, as he folded his hands in front of him.

"If only we knew how," groaned Jamaal. "And this asshat doesn't seem to be sharing those secrets any time soon."

"You're a cruciati," he said, wagging a finger at me. "I gave up trying to earn my way back a very long time ago." Then he scrutinized my face like I was part of a perp lineup. "But what Order are you?"

"Whatever we are, you're out of order," joked Jamaal. It was hard not to laugh with a comedian inside your head.

"How do I find that out?" I asked, but I hadn't the faintest what he was referring to.

"There are seven Demonic Orders and seven Angelic Orders. The Demonic Orders are simple—Pride, Gluttony, Wrath, Envy, Greed, Sloth, and Lust."

"The seven deadly sins?" I questioned.

"Indeed," replied Celestine. He pulled a book from the nearby shelf—it had his name on the sleeve and a black and white photo of his face on the back. He opened it and flipped through the pages until he found what he was looking for, then handed it over. Each page had an illustration as well as a description depicting the Angelic Orders. "The seven Angelic Orders are as follows. The Archangels, like your Prince, Gabriel—they are the highest order, and arguably the most powerful. Then there are the Seraphim, Virtues, Dominions, Thrones, and Cherubim. Unfortunately, there's no way to test what Order you belong to, but we may be able to understand your role within the Host."

I was following along as Celestine pointed to various aspects of each.

"No matter the Order, each angel has a duty to provide the Host. There are Seven Empyrean Authorities. Messengers are the first, like me—angels who spread the divine word. Then there are Harvesters, or Psychopomps—they harvest the souls of the dead and escort them to their final destinations. Next are Guardians—those who guard over individuals, both the important and the meek.

"The next two classes were carefully created for aggression—the Warrior and Destroyer. Similar in concept, different in scope—Warriors were meant for battle, whereas Destroyers carried out the Maker's wrath. Sodom and Gomorrah were prime examples of what a Destroyer could do.

"Virtues were unique. Each were given a specialty, such as performing specific miracles or helping old ladies cross the street," he said, tongue-in-cheek, I thought. "The final Authority is the Sentry—they are the guardians of the gates between realms. They are the first line of defense."

Father Monaco and I exchanged a quick knowing glance—I was going to mention the key until something caught my eye as I flipped through the pages of Celestine's book. Right after the description of the Cherubim was a small entry, with less than half the total information of any other Order.

"You said there were seven Orders," I said. "You named six. Tell me about this one."

The illustration was of an angel with four wings, a flaming spear in one hand and a radiant sword in the other, protecting a large gate looming behind him. Dangling around his neck was a key half the size of his sword.

"Powers?" he said with a laugh. "I only mentioned Archangels because even the most unholy know about them." Then he stood up and chuckled some more. "Powers are rare. Only a dozen or so were ever created. They were borne from the hearts of stars, like nuclear weapons of the Host. Only one has ever Fallen, and of those that existed, most are dead, missing, or worse."

The priest shrugged, as if to say, *maybe we found one.*

"No," scoffed Celestine. "Impossible."

Gesturing to the illustration, I said, "He's got a key," as I pulled my own out from under my shirt, "similar to mine."

The reaction was as instantaneous as it was excitable. Celestine fell to the top corner of the ceiling, as if the key was going to eat him. He looked to the door, poised to flee.

"Be calm, David," said Father Monaco. "You once helped us recover cursed artifacts from the Dream Lands. Your bravery has always been admired. Tell us, what is it?"

"If you understood the item you possess as I do, you would be equally terrified, old friend," he said. "That key was entrusted to Tammuz, two million years ago. I was the messenger who delivered it to him." He gasped, then said, "It is the Key of Capricorn. The first of four."

"What does it unlock?" asked Father Monaco.

"Together with the other three, it opens the gates of Eden where Yggdrasil grows," he said.

"The World Tree," clarified the priest. "Does it perform any other tasks?"

"All gate keys are powerful. Unknown," said Celestine. "Why do *you* have it?" Spit flew from his mouth as he spoke—he was coming undone.

"I don't know," I said, "but my fiancée shot and killed herself six years ago. While I still don't know why, she showed up yesterday, alive. Earlier today the Thirteen took her, and now they're after me—and they want this."

"The Thirteen?" he scoffed. "I am old enough to know the original Thirteen, but what you speak of is blasphemous. What you speak of is dangerous—demons, gods, Fallen, it doesn't matter what they are, but they're after you and you came here?" he shouted. "Are you mad?"

"Who are they?" I asked.

"You brought them here? To a university? There are students! Maintenance! You've damned us all!"

"Who are they?" I asked again, growing impatient as Father Monaco shifted uncomfortably in his chair.

"Easy, Tony," said Chappy. "What good is it for someone to gain the whole world, yet forfeit their soul? Mark 8:36."

"He's not worth it, my man," said Montoya.

"He's a creep. Hit him," said Jamaal. "I bet it'll loosen his lips."

"Of all the dumb things you could have done—" started Celestine.

"Who are they and why do they want it?!" I screamed and leapt out of my chair. "Why'd they take her?!" Steam rose from my hands, head, and shoulders, and I would have hit him to get the information I needed.

"Your fiancée is fucking damned!" he shouted as my fist met his face.

I had launched myself into the air at him and connected with his jaw. I felt it break apart in six places—and as I brought my fist against his face a second time, the bones had healed and rebroke all over again.

"Okay, yup, he deserved that," said Montoya, nodding.

"That's enough now, son," said Chappy into my ear. My rage immediately died, and I was staring at the bloodied face of Doctor Celestine.

I fell to the floor and set him down in his office chair as Father Monaco stared at me with confused anger, and yet compassion.

"I understand what your fiancée must have meant to you, but we do not strike our allies," the priest said firmly. "I apologize, David. I never meant for this to get violent."

I nodded. "I'm sorry."

Rage was still present—fire, brimstone, wrath—maybe I was more demon than angel.

"I'm starting to believe that whoever you are," said the priest, "that your true self was hidden from you for a reason."

"I apologize as well," said Celestine. "I did not mean to insult your fiancée. When a demon or Fallen finds interest in a human woman, they typically mate with them." He held his hands up as if to claim he spoke in peace. "To sire progeny."

"What happens to these impregnated women?" I asked.

"Usually, they die," he explained. "The half-breed inside is too much for them. Depending on the parent—let's say, perhaps a horned demon? The infant might claw its way out of the womb. It's a horrible death, really. However, not all the victims are women. Have you ever heard of a succubus? Demon women who seek out lonely men to impregnate themselves. If the men were to wake during the process, it might cause them to lose their minds."

Father Monaco waved his hands as if to stop Celestine from rambling.

"Too much information," groaned Jamaal. "I would have hit him again for that visual."

Celestine saw the pain in my face, and said, "they would destroy Empyrea, Heaven and Hell, just to get that key. Without knowing your fiancée, I could not accurately depict what they're after."

"You knew her," I said. "She was a student too."

"Who?" he asked as he wiped away the blood with a tissue from his desk.

"Jacinda O'Neill," I said, and his face turned cold.

"You should have mentioned that the moment you walked in," said Celestine. He looked dire. Shaken, as if the importance of that information was more valuable than me, the key, and the whole damn world combined.

"Are you going to help?" I asked, as he stood up from his desk and opened a few drawers as if he were looking for something.

He removed his cell phone, then looked at me and said, "Absolutely not. I'm getting as far from here as humanly possible. Do you know what she is?"

"What is she?" asked Father Monaco.

"The Omega," he said. He grabbed his bag from beneath his desk and began rummaging through his drawers like he was beginning to pack.

"What does that even mean?" asked Montoya.

"Omega," said Jamaal, "It's the twenty-fourth and last letter of the Greek alphabet. To some it means—"

"The end," I finished, then to Celestine I asked, "Where are you going?" When I stood up, Celestine held a blade angled at my right eye. He'd pulled it from one of his drawers when my guard was down and moved with such speed, I hardly saw him. He really was a divine messenger…

"David, there's no need for this," said Father Monaco, standing from his own chair. I may have hit Celestine, but even the priest knew this was another threat level entirely.

"I assure you, there is. There are Thirteen of the deadliest maniacs closing in on this place. They will get what they're after, and when they do, I want to be on the winning team."

"Does that include me? Jonah? Maynard? What about Dylan?" asked the priest.

Celestine winced. "You don't get it. That girl. The keys. Eden. This isn't just the end. This is the end of everything. Either the collapse of the Third Dimension or the Omens breach their way into our reality."

"You're not making any sense," said the priest. "Help us understand." Father Monaco had reached the same apocalyptic conjecture as Celestine, and yet we'd come to him for answers. All we received for our troubles were paranoid warnings from a paranoid creep.

Meanwhile, I remained perfectly still. The knife blade dangled an inch from my eye, and I could taste Celestine's desperation and fear. He was an angel, and he was capable of taking out at least one eye before I could blink.

"Careful," warned Doshin. I got the feeling this wasn't the first time my samurai friend had been in such a pickle. He was calm, so I was calm too.

"All of us, the whole world cannot equal their vast power," said Celestine. "And there aren't enough benevolent Fallen left to stand up to them."

"Summanus and Mammon are dead. I killed them," I said. "And I killed Bacchus a few hours ago." The look on Celestine's face was like my third-grade teacher listening to why I didn't finish my homework, only this time I was telling the truth. "Three of the Thirteen are dead."

"You're lying," he said.

"I can be a real asshole when someone eats all the peanut butter, but I'm no liar."

Then he looked at Father Monaco and said, "Oh come on—"

But before he could finish his thought, I had already slapped the blade from his hand and aimed one of my handguns into his left eye, ready to pull the trigger if he twitched.

The silence between us was as tense as a Pentagon war room, and the only thing keeping me from pulling the trigger and proving his assumptions was my respect for Monaco. I don't know how these two were friends, or why Monaco trusted someone who was as duplicitous as Celestine appeared to be. Jaycie may have enjoyed the doctor as a professor, and maybe he was once an honest angel, but he sucked as a human.

Amidst the standoff, a howl came from somewhere outside the building. A bloodcurdling sound that cut through the walls and rattled eardrums. We were out of time.

"They're here," said Father Monaco.

I nodded. "We're leaving," I said to Celestine, then to the priest, "Check the windows."

Father Monaco ran from the office, leaving me alone with Celestine.

"How'd you know I was a killer?" I asked curiously as I stopped inside his office door. That was one of the first things he'd said to me when I walked in. What he meant could be parsed a hundred different ways. Killer of gods? Killer of Thirteen? Killer of man? What did he mean?

"I could smell it all over you," said Celestine as another howl ripped through the night. Still miles away, but closer than the previous one. "You were a poor student with an aversion to detail. Your inability to extrapolate information that wasn't stated directly on the page was abhorrent. I see maturity has only blinded you further, Mr. Oscuro, and that blindness will certainly get Ms. O'Neill killed, if she hasn't already been ensnared by the necromancer." He was smiling, and I wanted nothing more than to wipe the grin off his face.

"Fuck off, Dolios," I said, using his real name. It had only come to me a moment before. The look on his face was priceless for a split second before he disappeared the next. Vanished like an illusion.

"What the fuck, my man?" said Montoya.

"True names even the playing field if spoken aloud," my Echo had

said. *"That is your best defense and offense against them. Names will come to you, and you won't know why, but be glad they do. I never fully understood the magic of names, but maybe you will."*

Was Celestine ever there? Was this another kind of magic?

I ran from Celestine's office back to the building's receptionist desk, where Maynard, Jonah and Father Monaco were peering out the windows. It was dark, but the campus was well lit with lamps every twenty feet along sidewalks and outside buildings.

"Where's David?" asked Monaco.

"Somewhere. He left." I shrugged, then asked, "I thought we got rid of the mark?"

"We did," replied Monaco. "By the sound of it, they have other ways to track you."

The howl. Wolves could smell their prey from nearly two miles away.

"This isn't good," said Jonah as he spotted people walking by, ignoring the howl like it was just a harmless wild animal.

"There's people out there," said Maynard, as he gripped his shotgun tight. "Why are they here? It's fucking winter break! Go home!"

I ran over to the receptionist desk—during normal office hours there was always a student worker earning minimum wage taking phone calls for faculty. I leapt over the desk and woke the computer up by moving the mouse back and forth a few times.

"What are you doing?" asked Maynard.

"When I went to school here, they had an emergency system that sent texts, emails, and robo-calls out to every single student, faculty member, maintenance worker and security guard. It would warn them of inclement weather, closures, even violence," I explained. "If we can get that message out, put the school on lockdown, and lead the danger across campus, away from the dorms, we can save lives."

I didn't even have to argue with them. These men may not have been trained professionals, but they knew why they were there—to protect innocents from evil.

"Leave that to me," said Jonah, reacting without another word. "I work in the computer industry."

"I thought you did data entry?" asked Maynard.

"I can handle this," promised Jonah.

"Spoken like a man who knows true failure," said Jamaal.

"Okay," said Father Monaco. "But I'm of no use to you out there. I'm slow and old—my soldier days are long behind me. Jonah and I will stay here and get the emergency system deployed. Then we'll go for the car once the evil has passed. Meet you both on the other side."

Montoya groaned. "Bad choice of words, my man."

"Sounds like a plan," said Maynard.

"Where shall we meet?" the priest asked me.

I thought about campus, the way the layout was structured, and the best possible opportunity to lure the evil away. There was only one building in mind—the only building I ever got lost in. "The Performing Arts building, Deschain Hall," I said, as I grabbed a brochure from the desk and unfolded it to a map of campus. The Performing Arts building was about eight or nine hundred yards away, and only another fifty yards from Main Street. It also happened to be the furthest building from the dorms and several buildings away from the Quad—the only possible busy place this time on a Saturday evening, even if it was winter break. "We're here. We need to lead them there." I circled the buildings on the map, then drew a line to mark our path, followed by a dot where I expected them to meet us with the car. "You follow?"

"Yes," said the priest.

"Are you up for this?" I asked Maynard.

"Are you? I've been doing this for years," he said with a smirk. "Amanda would be so fucking jealous right now."

"Best not to tell him, sir," said Henry. "Not now."

"See you guys on the other side," I said, nodding to the priest and Jonah. "Of campus, I mean."

"Look after him, Tony," said Father Monaco.

"I will," I said. Then Maynard opened the door, and we charged out into the night.

MALUS
Five minutes ago.

I sensed his grace before he streaked across the open field and into the shadows. He was a messenger, gifted with speed, but he stank of mankind and duplicity. I did not aim to trust him but decided to listen to his plea.

"Lord," he said, "I am Doctor David Celestine, and I am at your mercy."

"Indeed, you are," I said, as he fell to one knee. A show of respect.

"You are looking for the Key of Capricorn. I saw it. It is in the hands of a former student of mine," he said. "I lied to him. I said I didn't know who he was. He is the Raptor. He is five kilometers south, on the grounds of Milton State University. That is, a modern place of higher education and learning."

"We know exactly where the key is," I lied. "Or we would not be here."

We knew he was near. We had trackers spread across several miles, closing the noose.

With or without the mark, we were always going to find him. The mighty Fenrir could have tracked the spark across the entire world if we needed him to, and my assassins had already been deployed. We would not make the same mistakes as the others had.

Bacchus was foolish, arrogant, and clumsy. He died not by the hand of the spark, but of his own hubris. When Morrigan cowardly returned with the news of Bacchus's demise, the ring had already notified me of the voided contract. Her failure would be her last—she was warned and punished with the collective suffering of every tormented soul my ring carried. Special souls for the spark's audience, disturbed and agitated—ready to cripple and gut his bleeding heart.

"I remember you," said the girl. She was trapped somewhere between Jacinda and my Lilly—half of each, but full of neither. She was as a half-wit, confused and speaking nonsense.

"As I remember you," sniveled Celestine, still kneeling. "You were one of my best students, Ms. O'Neill."

"Who?" she asked, then turned away and stared off into the starry night sky.

"Is she the Omega?" he asked.

"Why does it matter?" I responded. "You'll be dead anyway."

"No," he pleaded. "You remember me? You tortured me, remember? You're the reason I fell. I gave up my secrets to you and broke my halo, and they will not allow me back."

"And?"

"And I can be useful! I hear you have a need to restore your fearful number."

"My contracts are only offered to the most feared, most powerful Fallen. That is not you, weak, pathetic Dolios."

"I can be your eyes. I can spy on the Raptor. I can bring you information. Any information you desire."

"Perhaps you are right," I said, as I stepped closer to him, placed my hands on either side of his ancient face, and lifted him to his feet. There he stood, smiling, eager to please. "I would like to you go, then hurry back and report to me what it's like in Hell."

Then I took my thumbs and destroyed both his eyes.

THE INTIMIDATION OF ANUBIS

939 A.D.

There are few forces stronger than the inevitable call of death. From birth, there is only one promise: that death will reap which the Earth has sown. Gods of Death were plentiful, but few were truly worthy of the title.

It was the dead of night, and the moon was so big and bright it looked as if one could reach out and pluck it from the heavens. As he crested the dune, the wind picked up and cast stinging sand into his face—but that did not prevent Malus from stalking toward the Pyramid of Amenemhat III—also known as the Black Pyramid.

Time had already begun to wither the stone structure. The sands were an unforgiving presence to the great walls and foundation—a testament to the power of human hands when pushed to revere their gods.

The pyramid was abandoned. Civilization had moved on. There was not a single living soul for miles. Even the creatures that used the night as their time to hunt and feed avoided this place. There was a hum, a gentle strumming of evil, like a dull throb behind his eyes.

How strange, he thought, to be so like and unlike humans at the same time. He was an anomaly, and he was aware of it.

The man with the platinum hair, Malus, seemed to glow under the moonlight. He stood at the entrance to the pyramid and lit a cigarette. His lighter sparked a burst of orange light that devilishly lit his face and revealed the disparate coloring of his eyes. He wore dark blue jeans, heavy leather boots with comfortable rubber soles, and a black duster made of wool and cotton. It was the most comfortable he had ever been. Modern clothing, he thought, was the best invention of man. It softened humans, but it was better than the days of togas and vestments.

The desert under the full moon was a frigid landscape, and Malus was prepared for it to get colder. He nudged his ring, and several hundred slaves clawed from their resting place beneath the sands and stood. Some were just bones, while others had the spectral presence of ectoplasmic light. Malus did not command them to move, nor to speak, just to stand and await orders. It was a show of power. An affront to the judge and protector of the Egyptian dead.

It took only seconds before Malus's brazen message was answered. A rival army of the dead crawled its way to the top of a powdery dune and stared down at its enemy, as silent as a gentle breeze. A being of significant height strode out of the desert, its head deformed into the guise of a desert jackal, and began swinging a sling. The creature wore old fabrics and sandals adorned with gold and carried a staff in his free hand with a curved sharp blade, like a scythe.

The god was ready to fight.

"Fool," threatened Anubis. "The dead shall remain, but you must flee at once. I will cut out your organs and place them in canopic jars, then discard them from one end of the Nile to the other. You will be undead, cursed to roam this realm with no brain, no stomach, and no balls. A dumb, hungry, impotent wanderer."

"An admirable threat," laughed Malus, and he meant it. "I applaud you for equal parts banality and originality. Instead, I have an offer." When no response came, Malus reiterated. "It will only take a moment. A moment for an immortal is still merely a moment."

"Speak," said Anubis, but the subtext in his tone was that of tethered anger.

"I offer you an opportunity. Sign my contract, and you shall have dominion over all spirits of the deceased, across this entire planet, for all time. Sign it, and there will be no more squabbles over the rights of the dead. You, and only you, Lord Anubis, will have last rights."

Anubis pondered the Pale Traveler's offer. His yellow eyes flared in the darkness as he allowed himself to fantasize over the possibility, until finally he shrugged and said, "You offer what you have no dominion to give."

"Oh, but I can. Join with me and it will be yours—all the rot and decay you desire." Then Malus shifted his weight and his tone, a smile drifting across his face. "But stand against me, and I'll destroy you."

Anubis chuckled humorlessly, then turned to his dead army. They were shadows under the moonlight, shades of once living, breathing, loving beings that were trapped and bound to serve.

"Drag him to me," said Anubis, but the dead did not move. "Attack my enemy." And still they did not move, not even a twitch. He raised his staff and demanded their attention, and yet again, they did nothing.

"The dead—all dead—answer to only me," said Malus.

"Impossible," the god scoffed as a thousand dead eyes turned on him. His own risen dead snarled, awaiting commands from another.

"There is only one thing capable of commanding the harvested dead I reaped myself over the many centuries across this desert," said Anubis.

"Indeed, there is. And it is mine."

Fear alone dropped Anubis to one knee. He accepted Malus's contract while surrounded by the dead that once called him, and only him, master.

XV

fortune

Jacinda
Then.

What can I say, Jace? You were doing it. You struggled at first, but when you finally got your footing, things started coming together.

By late spring, you had signed up to get your GED, and you passed the test with ease. Then you made the phone call you were dreading.

Your father answered on the third ring, and when you said, "Hi Dad," it took him a few moments to remember he had a kid, like you had completely disappeared. After a short talk about where you were and what you had accomplished, your father offered to help you get into college. His assistant filled out the paperwork, and you were off applying to schools.

Within a month, you received responses.

They weren't the glowing acceptances you were hoping for, but being realistic, with a GED instead of a diploma, you weren't expecting much. You managed to get accepted to a few decent schools. Besides, when your father got his boss involved, Mr. Jansen used his connections. It was one of the few times you had ever appreciated your father's business ties. *All that hard work, Dad,* you thought, *finally paid off for someone other than Mom.*

I was so proud of you, Jace. The darkness was gone, as if the demons had forgotten all about you. You were living your life, even if it wasn't exactly how you planned it.

A year and a half flew by before you knew it, but something was still missing. Something that you yearned for deep down without ever being able to put your finger on what it was. Or maybe you didn't want to know, because identifying the void would make you want it more.

February 14th, 2000

"Stop being a stick in the mud!" Kelly scolded.

It was one of those overcast days that rarely appeared in Los Angeles. Thick gray clouds desaturated the color of everything and left you in a foul mood. Luckily, it was still Los Angeles, and the temperature was mild, even for late winter. It was one of the many things you had come to love about the west coast. Everything was sunny, for the most part, and Vitamin D was never in short supply—even if you were susceptible to sunburn.

"I'm so not being a stick in the mud! I just don't believe in that sort of stuff," you whined.

Even the gray skies couldn't take the luster out of your color— that brilliant red hair always burned as bright as your emerald green eyes. There was a spark in you, Jace. That big bright spark was back, like the weight of the world wasn't resting on your shoulders. But there was still something missing. The void was getting bigger, and you feared it could drag you under at any time.

"Mo, you're bringing down the fun factor a teeny bit, doll," sassed Cheryl.

You had officially changed your name. Moira was Grammy's name, but it was also your middle name. If Robbie Maynard Morris could do it, so could you.

"I don't see the point! Tarot reading? Fortune telling? Why?" you shrugged, sticking up for yourself. You were happy, and bantering with your friends was the highlight of your day. The three of you were sitting at an outdoor picnic table following a boring lecture during your literature class. You had grabbed a coffee, intending to head home to study. Then Kelly started going on and on about the "reading" her cousin got last week. You were always so fascinated by spooky stuff, but you'd grown to bear a distaste for it these days—and even if you couldn't remember all the fucked-up things you experienced, they still happened, and your subconscious was still aware of the evil.

"It's Valentine's Day!" scoffed Kelly. You and Cheryl both blinked at her, awaiting further explanation. "We can get our palms read or something. They can tell us if we should expect great love coming into our lives! Duh, I thought it was obvious!"

Kelly was a silly girl with enormous energy—more than anyone her size should have, according to you. Kelly was tall, with cheekbones any aspiring model would kill for, but she often wore ponytails and comfy fleece sweats, and you didn't think that would impress many college boys. She had long brown hair and dark blue eyes, and a rosy color naturally filled her cheeks.

"Oh. I just thought it'd be fun. I didn't even equate it to this bastard-son of a holiday," said Cheryl. She was a thicker gal, with dark brown caramel skin and eyes. Her hair was short, and she wore thick, red-framed glasses that showcased her unique style.

"Ouch, what crawled inside your ass and died," Kelly asked, feeling rejected from the romantic possibilities she was hoping for.

"My ex," said Cheryl bluntly.

"That must be uncomfortable. Do you need a proctologist?" you quipped with a straight face, causing both girls to laugh. "I didn't think you were into that kind of *stuff.*" The two girls laughed even harder, especially Cheryl, whose laughter always felt like sunshine.

"I knew, from the day I met you, that you were the kind of girl I wanted to be around," said Cheryl. "It's the hair! All kinds of feisty."

For the first time in years, you felt like you belonged. These two girls, who belonged to different college cliques of their own, came together with you and formed something special. Something unique to your world. There were times when you worried this would last only as long as all three of you were in each other's classes, but lately you were beginning to think you were forming a real friendship.

"Well, I'm looking forward to meeting my Prince Charming," Kelly quickly added before you went too far off subject.

"Girl, you wanna meet Prince Charming, you'll need wear something a little more exciting than fleece," Cheryl sassed.

"I'm just too lazy in the morning! I clean up well, though," Kelly said, then looked at you with an intense stare. "What about you, Mo? You know all about my last relationship with Derrick."

"The asshole," added Cheryl.

"And we know all about the horrible men Cheryl's dated," continued Kelly.

"Amen to that," responded Cheryl.

"But what about you? We know hardly anything about you," probed Kelly. It was true, you didn't share much about yourself. You were slightly embarrassed by your past and confused about it at the same time.

You thought about the question for several seconds, opening your mouth to speak and closing it multiple times, not knowing what information to provide. Should you tell them all about Rick? The fact that you lost your virginity in a Ford Mustang parked in the Grace Falls High School parking lot? What about the addiction that led to Rick using you? Your awful family life?

Maybe it was best they didn't know, but Jace, you needed friends. You needed to share, to trust.

"I dated a little," you said. "Well, just one guy."

"Just one?" asked Cheryl, a little shocked.

"He must've been something special," said Kelly.

"He was popular. Gorgeous. Muscles. Stony blue eyes," you said, and I was already groaning that I even suggested you share.

"That's it?" asked Kelly. "How long were you with him?"

"Now tell us how he hurt you," commented Cheryl, waiting for the other shoe to drop.

"Not very long," you admitted. "We weren't together, actually."

"Was he…endowed?" asked Cheryl, holding back an infectious giggle. "I mean, why would you get so hung up on one guy unless he was—hung up?"

"Definitely not," you said with a laugh, and I laughed too, fist-pumping in celebration. Your outburst made Cheryl laugh as well, but only seemed to depress Kelly, who had an incurable case of hopeless romanticism—and if you were being honest, you were jealous of that. You wanted to feel that way too about love, but you couldn't summon up those feelings, even if you wanted to. It was like that part of you was dead—had died on the vine before it could be plucked and harvested.

"There wasn't anyone else? No one at all?" asked Kelly. She looked as if she might cry.

"Yeah, there was another guy," you admitted, and I sat down next to you as if I were part of the group. I wanted to hear all about this, Jace.

"So, what about this other guy?" Cheryl asked. Your love life made her own sound so exciting and wonderful, all things it certainly was not.

"Things weren't right," you explained. "Bad timing. Distance."

"Cop-out," said Cheryl bluntly.

"What?" you asked. You'd given a perfectly valid explanation, or at least one that was perfectly valid to you. It was true, our timing was awful, and the distance would have been an issue—except I was already living in Grace Falls at this time, though you didn't know that.

"It's a cop-out. You were too afraid to break it off with the first guy to be with the second guy. Am I right? Or am I right?" said Cheryl, her voice devoid of all its usual sassiness and replaced by something closer to annoyance.

"You're…right," you said, a bit unsure about simplifying such a complicated situation. You could have kissed me that night at the fair, and who knows what would have come of that, but you still had Rick on your mind, even while you were getting cozy with me. Remember that feeling, Jace, when we kissed?

Ugh, you didn't remember that. My past was still your future.

You took a long swig of your lukewarm coffee as a stall tactic while

Kelly and Cheryl waited on you to elaborate.

"Did you love him?" Kelly asked, leaning forward with delicious anticipation, not being able to contain herself through the longest sip of coffee anyone had ever taken in the history of caffeinated beverages.

"No," you sighed. "We never even kissed."

"Do you still think about him?" Kelly pressed. She was hyper for intriguing love stories.

"I don't know." You smiled, then quickly wiped it away with another drink. You thought of me from time to time; I knew that much. Just not as much as I would have liked, Jace.

"Oh my," said Cheryl.

"Yeah, I saw that too," said Kelly.

"Saw what?" you asked incredulously. You felt a strange mix of annoyance and excitement, and you seemed to enjoy talking about it for the first time ever.

"Saw you smile just thinking about him." Cheryl pointed at your mouth.

"No, I didn't," you defended yourself.

"Yes, you did," said Kelly, laughing.

"For real, you did," Cheryl laughed and clapped her hands, applauding all the fun they were having putting their mysterious friend, Moira, on the spot.

"Okay, okay. I want you to do this one favor for us," said Kelly. "I want you, right now, to think of his name."

As soon as Kelly said the word "name," you instantly smiled. A reflex you couldn't resist.

"See!" Kelly laughed. "You can't even picture his name without smiling."

"So what?" You laughed too, trying to brush it off.

"So what? So what?" Cheryl teased.

"Call him! You're single. You're available. Reconnect with him!" Kelly suggested.

"I can't," you said, deflating your friends. "I don't have his number. He could be anywhere. It's been a long time."

"All the more reason to go to the fortune teller and get our fortunes read," Kelly demanded, excitement creeping into her voice again like a cheerleader pepping up a crowd. Kelly's positivity was beginning to win you over, making you truly think about going.

"Okay, fine!" you grumbled with a smile. Kelly screamed in victory while Cheryl laughed and shook her head.

With that, the three of you left with coffees in hand and walked to the bus stop. The fortune teller was only a fifteen-minute ride away, a place Kelly had seen several times before but never had anyone willing to go with her.

The neon sign outside said *Madame LeStrange*. A piece of paper taped to the window below offered a "Free Palm Reading with every Tarot Fortune Read." The neon sign blinked on and off with a buzz and reminded you of the shadier strip club portions of Las Vegas. A young couple left as you and your friends approached the door. They happily clasped each other's hands and smiled into each other's eyes like a stock photo stuffed into a retail picture frame. It was a good omen watching the two of them, and you began to let your mind swim through the possibilities.

Not that you believed in any of this hokum, Jace. It was all absurd to you. Amanda once made you play around with a Ouija board, and after a few terrifying moments, you realized Amanda was messing with you, despite her denials. These supernatural things—tarot, Ouija, palm reading, astrology—they were for entertainment value only, but something inside you was still warning against poking around in the unknown. Heck, I thought I had learned the same lesson when Cyn tried to commune with Tori a month after she died. Seemed like a whole lot of bogus bullshit, but now I was swimming in the unnatural.

This, you told yourself, was just some innocent fun, and it had been so long since you felt the warm butterflies of your hopeless romantic heart fluttering in your chest. The returning sensation made you feel alive.

Of course, that sensation was immediately followed by doubt.

"Are you sure about this?" you asked. What if they told you something you didn't want to hear? Whether you believed in it or not didn't matter.

"Come on, girlfriend. Ain't nothing to be worried about!" said Cheryl.

"Don't worry," said Kelly, placing a hand on your back. "What're they gonna say? That you're doomed? Cursed to be alone the rest of your life?"

You sighed while the other girls joked around about what their fortunes might reveal. Deep down inside, that was exactly what you feared—that you might be cursed. It was bad enough there were portions of your life you couldn't clearly remember. Hazy memories, like they were quickly erased with an old, dried eraser, leaving portions behind that couldn't be scrubbed out of the cracks. The idea of someone potentially knowing more about you than you did was discomforting.

The *what ifs* were terrifying.

"How much is it?" you asked, grabbing the clip from your pocket with your money and ID. You didn't have much to spare but had come all that way and didn't want to be the buzzkill who couldn't afford it.

"Just ten bucks," said Kelly as Cheryl peeked over your shoulder.

"Who are they?" asked Cheryl. She was looking at the picture clipped along with the money you had: a twenty and two fives that had to last for another two weeks. The picture was the one of you, Grammy, and Jane—

—but then you answered…

"Oh, that's my Grammy and me," you said.

"Who's the blonde girl?" asked Cheryl.

"I don't know," you said. You weren't lying. You really didn't know. "She must have been a family friend."

"No brothers or sisters?" she asked.

"Nope, I'm an only child," you replied.

Oh, Jace. I didn't realize the magnitude of what had happened that Christmas Eve, but it was suddenly crashing down around me like an anvil of truth on top of my unassuming Wile E. Coyote head. You told the darkness to forget about you, and willed yourself to forget about them—but did you really forget your sister right out of existence? How was that possible?

It made some sense—why nobody remembered Jane back in Grace Falls.

The inside of Madame LeStrange's boutique smelled of flowers and incense, with an extra scent of something buttery. The walls were draped with heavy woven earth-toned cloth that hung from the ceiling in crossing patterns. At the center of the room was your average ordinary crystal ball held in place by a copper stand. It sat on top of a round table, which was covered by a purple tablecloth that hung all the way to the floor.

"Welcome," said an older woman, approaching them from behind a beaded curtain. The woman was in her late sixties with frizzy brown hair streaked with silver. She was oddly accessorized with silver bracelets, necklaces, a scarf, and a long navy-blue dress made of thick natural fibers.

"I am Madame LeStrange, and I will be your host on a journey into the beyond. Please, sit," she said, as she ushered the girls around her table. Her voice sounded eastern European, like the caricatured film version of a Transylvanian in a vampire movie.

You were the last to walk over, and as you passed Madame LeStrange, she gave you an odd look. When you were all seated, Madame LeStrange asked for each of your names.

"Kelly."

"Hello, Kelly," said the Madame with a smile and nod.

"Cheryl."

"Hello, Cheryl," said the Madame, again with a smile and nod.

When it was your turn, the Madame refused to look you in the eyes.

"Moira," you said.

"Young lady, if you would like your fortune read, you must not lie to me. Tell me your name," Madame demanded.

"What?" said Kelly. "Moira is her name, isn't it?"

"Moira is my middle name," you said apprehensively. "My first name is Jacinda." You said it almost fearfully, looking at Madame LeStrange like she was a scolding grandmother.

"Thank you, Jacinda. Hello," Madame said coldly with a bizarre glare. It was an accusatory glare, like you had done something wrong, something beyond lying about your name. "Let us begin. My dear, Kelly. What brings you here to Madame LeStrange?"

Fifteen minutes passed, and when the silence finally caught up to you, you pulled your eyes away from the window and saw the three women staring at you with anticipation.

"I'm good. No thanks," you said, waving your hands in front of you, politely denying the reading.

"C'mon, Moira!" Kelly urged.

"Or should we say, Jacinda?" Cheryl laughed. "You'll have to explain that later."

"I don't know," you said defensively.

"Please?" Madame said with a genuine hint of concern.

You gave the woman your hands, palms up, which Madame LeStrange cradled with her own. The Madame took a long look at them, studying the creases.

"You are special. This is true," Madame said. "Your path is unclear. There are many obstacles." She continued to study your palms, then shook her head, as if something didn't make any sense. "You will meet an early end, yet your life will continue. This is the first time I have seen this."

"I don't understand," said Kelly. She hung on every word out of Madame Lestrange's mouth, as if she were the only one taking it seriously.

"That doesn't sound good," Cheryl added sarcastically, with a hint of genuine worry.

You didn't know how to respond. This was exactly what you were afraid of. You had no idea what any of it meant, and you cursed yourself for going along with the fortune-telling escapade in the first place.

You were still waiting for the revelation and hoped that wasn't it. How disappointing, to know your palms had such bad news written on them.

"What does that mean, exactly?" you asked.

Madame LeStrange gave you a shrug, and comically said, "Come with me. We give you special reading for special circumstance." Your friends stood up to follow, but the Madame gave them a stern look. "Just for her. Friends must stay here."

You followed her apprehensively, part of you wondering why you were even going along with this, and into the back room. You disappeared behind several sets of beaded curtains and into another section of the house altogether.

Behind the curtains was a long hallway, decorated with various portraits in large gaudy frames that hung from the walls. The pictures were aged and yellowed, displaying a proud family heritage that dated back to the gypsies of eastern Europe. Many of them wore furs and strange hats and stood beside covered wagons. At the end of the hallway was a small stuffy kitchen with a table in the middle. It was a dark kitchen, with only a trickle of overcast light filtering in from an uncovered window above the sink. There were knick-knacks on shelves next to old cookbooks, and a pair of nesting dolls with grotesque faces.

"Please, sit," said Madame LeStrange. When you were seated, the Madame left and walked into the next room, where she spoke in her native tongue. She then re-emerged, followed by an elderly woman who looked no younger than ninety, if she wasn't older. Her hair was thinning and stood at odd angles, and she was aided by a squeaky walker she could hardly push. When she sat down next to you, her eyes seemed to brighten with compassion, looking at you through two different colors—the left was the brightest gray eye you had ever seen, while the other was dark and cloudy.

The old woman inspected you up and down, then turned to the Madame and said a few things in her own language before giving you a toothless smile.

"This is my grandmother," said Madame LeStrange, which sent a trill down your back. The math was simple—the woman was more than a century old. "She wants me to tell you that you are very beautiful, and that her name is Mona, but you can call her Grandmother since she is old enough to be everyone's grandmother." The old woman chuckled as she translated her grandmother's joke.

"Thank you," you responded with a smile, which prompted the old woman to speak.

"She says," translated the Madame, "that the most beautiful, as in nature, are the creatures to be most feared." As she relayed the old woman's words, the old woman patted you politely on your hands, as if to console you and your affliction.

"Oh," was all you could say.

This was interesting, Jace. I wasn't sure how this was going to go down, but I was as curious as you were.

"There is something I sense in you, my child," said Madame LeStrange. "Reading your palm only proved what I could sense from your aura. It would be irresponsible of me to let you leave here today without doing my best to place you on a proper path."

You saw the expression on her face and realized how serious she was. You may not have been a believer, but you were too curious and too lost in your own life not to listen.

"What did you sense in me?"

"I'm not sure. My grandmother has a better gift than I," said the Madame. "She has purer blood."

"What do you mean? What kind of purer blood?" you asked hesitantly.

"My grandmother is the daughter of a special stranger," Madame LeStrange said, and her grandmother followed every word with a smile, as if she understood everything that was being said. "When I was just a little girl, Grandmother told me stories about her father. He only visited her at night, when the moon was full. He taught her many things, including the art of *seeing*."

"Seeing?" You needed clarification.

"We all see with our eyes, but some of us can see beyond what eyes can see. Some of us see the strings of fate," the Madame explained.

"Who was her father?" you asked innocently. Madame LeStrange spoke to her grandmother in their tongue, who quickly replied with an added shrug.

"He was neither Angel nor Demon, but something in between. She did not know his name, she only knew to fear him," the Madame explained. "Her gift to see was in her blood. It was passed down to my mother and to me, within our blood line. However, my ability is weak compared to Grandmother's. She will be our guide."

Madame LeStrange grabbed a wooden bowl from a shelf in the room and set it in front of her grandmother, who couldn't stop smiling at you. Next, she handed her two black pouches, one of which Grandmother emptied into the bowl. Several flat pieces of bone with runic symbols carved into them clattered around inside. From within the next pouch, Grandmother carefully removed a handful of strange medical-like instruments that gleamed in the gloomy light.

Grandmother took your hand and held it over the bowl, then looked at you apologetically and said, "Hurt." With that, she sliced across your thumb, spilling several drops of your blood into the bowl. You winced, but weren't hurt, just a little miffed over the brief warning. The Madame handed you a towel to wrap over your thumb as Grandmother continued.

"Spit," Grandmother said and tilted the bowl towards you. You obliged as the Madame handed her grandmother a stack of strange tall cards that were yellowed and blunted around the edges, along with a plain iron ring as fat as a small donut.

Grandmother displayed the cards in front of you face up, which ranged from simple illustrations of cups and swords to more intricate depictions of demons, a pair of lovers, and more.

"I don't know if I believe in tarot," you said with embarrassment as they were set to begin. Reading palms was one thing. Finding someone's destiny in a stack of silly cards was another.

I agreed with you, Jace, but somehow this felt different.

"That's okay, my dear. This is not tarot, and it does not matter what you believe. The cards believe in you," said Madame LeStrange. "Divination of this kind is not about getting answers, but rather illuminating the truth about one's Higher Self. Imagine understanding who you are, and your inner purpose. If you had those answers, would it not be easier to choose between paths?"

You nodded and returned your attention to Grandmother, who continued sharing her toothless smile, then floated her hands above the cards in a circular motion.

"Each card in this deck has meaning. In order for them to illuminate your truth, you must blow on them gently," said Madame LeStrange. You did so, much to Grandmother's delight, who laughed playfully like it was the start of a game. Grandmother took the cards and flipped them over face down in a single swipe, like a casino dealer trick, then placed her hands on the table and waited patiently. "Now, you must cut the deck five times." The Madame watched as you pulled the deck apart at various depths five times. Grandmother took the top card from each cut and placed them face down in the form of a cross. Without hesitation, Grandmother took hold of what looked to be a fancy pair of pliers and yanked her thumbnail out in one quick jolt. You jumped. You were appalled, but the pain didn't seem to faze her. She flicked the nail into the bowl and added a pinch of salt.

"Do not worry. Grandmother has nine more fingernails," joked the Madame, and Grandmother laughed along with her. "The thumbnail represents the dealer's hand, declaring Grandmother as your guide. The salt represents purity, which ensures the reading has not been tampered by demon nor evil sprite. The runes will determine the order of the cards. Your spit speaks their truths. Your blood will illuminate that which lies inside you."

Then Grandmother held out her forefinger to you—a gesture for one last selection. She drew a card at random and placed it perpendicularly over the center card, crossing it. "The last card is drawn by your guide, a neutral force."

With the Madame's words spoken, Grandmother took the bowl and closed her eyes while shaking it four times, mixing its contents. When she opened her eyes, she made a delighted gasp and pulled five runes from the bowl, then waited for the Madame to explain.

"The cross is divided into elemental stations. The card above for air. The left for water. The right for earth. The beneath for fire. The center for body, or in other words, you. Each rune has a blank and an inscribed side with a number and elemental sign scrawled into it. Those that remain face down are left inside the bowl. Those that show their face are placed on the table next to their matched element. You will notice, only five runes have shown their face, and all five correspond to one of the five stations. This determines order."

"What if more than five runes are showing? What if there's more than one for each sign?" you asked.

Madame LeStrange smiled. "There are never more than five faces showing, and never more than one elemental of each kind. The spirits won't allow it." You nodded, not knowing how to respond to something that seemed to go against statistical probability, but Jace, somehow, we both knew it was true. Then the Madame continued. "When the five runes have been placed, order receives importance. The lowest numbered card being drawn first and of least importance. The higher card being drawn last, of most importance." You noticed that the rune with the most markings fell on top of the card dedicated to the body. Even without pulling the card, you knew this was an ominous sign.

"Okay," you said, allowing them to begin. The first card to be revealed was the water card. Grandmother reached over and removed the rune, then flipped it over gently and removed her hand from its face. Immediately Grandmother spoke, relaying her message to her granddaughter.

"Thirteen snakes," Madame LeStrange began. The card depicted a woman surrounded by serpents which had begun to wrap around her body, constricting the life from her. "The water card in the formation tells us your dilemma, as water is often seen as an obstacle to be crossed. Thirteen snakes tell us something is coming from all angles, and it is close. This is a dangerous card. The snakes represent evil, or negativity. It would be wise to keep an eye over your shoulder in the future."

You felt a tingle of fear rise up your spine, and the room suddenly felt cold. The idea of the Thirteen Snakes made you nervous, but it was frighteningly accurate. You kept thinking to your past, to the strange cracks in your memory, and couldn't help but feel they were important. Did this card portray something to do with those lost memories?

Abso-freaking-lutely.

Grandmother waited for your thoughts to come back to you before she turned over the next card in order of the runes. This was the fourth most important card, and you were hanging on every word and gesture.

As the card was flipped, Grandmother instantly went into her assessment and began to explain the significance.

"Seven of Roses," Madame LeStrange noted. The card was simple, just a hand holding seven roses, three of which were wilted, while the other four were blooming beautifully. "The air card in the formation tells us what you need. Like air is essential for life, so is this card. Seven of Roses stands for a decision to be made considering love. Three of the seven roses have wilted, and if you wait much longer, the rest will die along with them. This tells us you need to decide what to do about the one you love."

"But I don't love anybody," you said.

Ouch. You will, one day.

"Perhaps a missed connection is waiting for you?" she suggested. "His heart holds true, but his hope is dying."

That was true, Jace.

You instantly thought of Rick—was he your missed connection? But the longer you thought about it, the more you thought of someone else. Still, how could you rekindle either of those relationships? After all this time? What if they had completely moved on? How would you know where to find them?

Grandmother waited for you to be ready, then flipped over the third most important card.

"Star-Crossed Lovers," said Madame LeStrange. The card was marked by a star in the sky with two lovers staring up at it, parted by the sea. "The fire card in the formation tells us what your heart burns for, your one true passion, just as the fire that burns inside us all. The Star-Crossed Lovers tells us you and your love have been forced apart, but there is hope. For whatever you feel in your heart, his heart falls under the same star. Whenever it would seem that all hope is lost, this card is a reminder that you have lost nothing. Paired with the previous card, this card suggests that your true love exists, and he is waiting for you."

Ahem. True.

Confused, you had to remind yourself that this was all a bunch of nonsense. You weren't in love. Who in their right mind would be out there waiting for you? For a few moments you caught yourself believing it, believing in the hocus pocus, and struggled to reel yourself in.

"Are you okay?" asked Madame LeStrange. After zoning out for a moment, you gave them both a quick nod.

The fourth card was then flipped, the second most important card.

Grandmother began to speak with piqued urgency.

"Dance of Death and Devil," said Madame LeStrange with a shaky voice. The card depicted a hooded skeletal figure dancing with a horned devil, laughing while the damned screamed on their hands and knees all around them. The way Grandmother spoke, along with the card itself, took all the remaining warmth out of the room. "The earth card in the formation tells us where you are going. As paths are laid upon the earth, so shall yours be revealed. Dance of Death and Devil is not a curse when paired with earth, nor is it a portent of things to come. It is merely a warning. Be wary of the path you choose, for it could lead to dark places. Strife, pain, and survival may be your destiny. A wrong turn may bring death, and worse."

"What's worse than death?" you asked weakly.

"Plenty," said Madame LeStrange with a tear in her eye. You couldn't tell if that tear was meant for you or for someone who was once part of the Madame's life. Heartbreak was something of which you needed no reminder.

Grandmother reached out and patted Madame LeStrange's hand, then rubbed your shoulder, attempting to comfort you both. The last two cards were both in the center, one lying on top of the other, like a mini cross within the cross formation of cards.

You sighed, then nodded to Grandmother, who then flipped the first card over, but held her hand over the top, waiting for the Madame to explain. "The center cards in the cross formation represent the body—that is, these cards reveal truths about you. The top card represents the mind, while the bottom card represents the spirit."

Grandmother removed her hand, revealing the top card. It was a man in a cloak at night, carrying a key across the desert with his eyes on the stars to navigate, traveling toward a far-off golden land in the distance. "Ah, the Traveler's Mystery. When this card is played at the center, it represents secrets, and the search to reveal their truths. Your journey has taken you far from the answers you seek. Returning is the key to illumination—but beware! Of all we have learned, this journey, though fruitful, travels with Death and Devil."

Of everything that had been revealed, it was this card that intrigued you most. You knew there were things that didn't add up—things that kept you up at night, wondering. You had proven to yourself that you didn't need anybody, including your parents, and maybe it was time to find out what skeletons were hidden in your own closet.

"Ready?" Grandmother asked, her broken English struggling to leave her throat. You were still lost in your own evaluation of the cards. You took a deep breath, then nodded, and Grandmother hovered her hand over the final card, keeping her eyes locked with yours, preparing you for the last and most important reveal.

She flipped the card, then gasped. Grandmother jumped from her chair. She slammed her frail body against the nearby counter, and dishes and kitchen utensils fell to the floor, a few of them breaking. She panted and sweated with an urgency that scared you so much, you sprang to your feet and sent your chair flying backward.

Grandmother shook nervously as Madame LeStrange rushed to comfort her, and they spoke in their native language so fast and furiously that you had no idea when each word ended and a new one began.

Trust me, Jace, you didn't want to know what they were saying.

"What's wrong?" you asked, but neither of them listened. "What's wrong?!" you yelled, gathering their frantic attention.

"Grandmother says she has never seen this before," said Madame LeStrange.

"Is it that bad?" you asked, peering down at the card on the table. It was nothing but a strange-looking tree growing in the middle of a desert. The inscription read "The World."

"We do not know what it means. The runes professed the fifth card to be revealed, the most important card in the ceremony, paired with the body card from the center of the formation. This combination is—" said Madame LeStrange, "—is unusual."

"What does the card mean?" you asked. "Tell me. Please!" It suddenly occurred to you that you were invested in the ceremony. You believed. The supernatural allure had swallowed you up, and it wasn't about to let go.

"This card, from the center of the formation, gives us insight to your spiritual self. It tells us who you are. The World in this spot has no meaning, and yet means all. Usually, when played in other spots, this card could mean a life decision that could influence the world. But here, it is played from that spot. That one spot changes all meaning," said Madame LeStrange, and you could hear the worry in her voice.

"What does that mean for me?" you asked. Grandmother walked up to you, not with fear like you expected, but rather with sadness and sympathy. She placed her hand again on your shoulder for comfort, then took the metal ring from the table, dipped it into the bowl where the leftover runes remained with your blood, the spit, and her own fingernail, then handed it to you.

"Look," said Grandmother, gesturing for you to peer through the ring and into a mirror that hung beside the sink. You slowly brought it to your eye and looked.

What you saw felt like a hallucination. Without looking through the ring, you appeared to yourself in the mirror as a normal 19-year-old. Your red hair was slightly out of place, but it had been seen publicly in worse states, or maybe you were just being extra self-conscious, like usual. Your green eyes were worn down from all the late-night studying after work, but overall, you appeared in good health. Yet, when you peered through the ring, you gasped.

"Oh my God," you sobbed.

"When that card is played from the formation set for the body," said Madame LeStrange calmly, "it means something much more. It means... you *are* the world."

Jace, I've asked so many times; what are you? What is "the Omega?"

You lowered the ring from your eye before I could see what you saw and gave Madame LeStrange a puzzled look. "I don't understand," you said. When you placed the ring back to your eye, the magic was gone. You felt astonishment mixed with fear, and the great big question mark that hung over your head, set its full weight upon your shoulders.

"We don't understand either. This has never happened," the Madame replied. "The ring shows you what you need to see, the truth of sight from the final card."

Grandmother tugged at your arm and held the deck of cards out to you once again.

"A gift. Take one," said Madame LeStrange with a sympathetic smile. "Grandmother knows what it is like to be alone in this world with so much evil." Grandmother nodded sadly, then smiled at you, asking you to choose. "Do not fear, take one."

You pulled another card and took a long, puzzled look at it. "What does it mean?" Your card was simply a crescent moon in the night sky. Grandmother smiled a wide toothless grin.

"Ahhh, the Crescent Moon," said Madame LeStrange with relief. "In rare moments, Grandmother can bestow a final card to someone who truly needs it. This card reveals nothing about you but is a sign of things to come. The Crescent Moon is the symbol of Gabriel, the mighty Archangel. When you see the Crescent Moon, take heart. Everything will be alright."

You let out a small sob. Your emotions were flying in all directions. "How do I know any of this is real?" you asked from behind your tears.

Grandmother then handed you the entire stack of cards. "Look," she said. When you took the cards and flipped them over, their faces were blank. There were no inscriptions, no words or pictograms. They were just old pieces of uniformly cut cardstock. "Good luck," she said, squeezing the proper words out of her aged throat.

"Thank you," you replied, and you meant it in ways you couldn't profess. The enormity of what you had experienced was enough to make you woozy. Was it real? Was it fake? Was it all a game, Jace? You had no answers and neither did I, and yet we both felt compelled to believe it all.

For as long as you could remember, you'd felt lost and alone. Alone in a crowded room full of people. Lost in a world you had no place within. You were an anomaly, and nothing proved that to be any truer than Grandmother's reading. There were so many questions forming, bubbling up from the cracks in your memory. Questions that nobody could answer. Questions that could only be answered by living.

When you stepped outside of Madame LeStrange's shop with Kelly and Cheryl berating you with questions about what you had experienced in the back room, you should have felt worse. You should have felt like the world was crumbling down around you. Instead, you felt stronger than you had been in a very long time. You were willing to take chances. Willing to make a bold move.

And it started by going home.

Now I knew why you thought I was the moon.

274

XVI
trapped

TONY
December 23rd, 2013
Now.

As soon as we left the faculty building, Jonah and Father Monaco began warding every window and door with salt, iron, and various symbols they had sketched into hardcover notepads. They called it Apotropaic magic, which was just a fancy name for telling evil shit to "ward off."

I took Maynard's duffel as we sprinted out the doors and across campus, once it became clear that it was weighing him down—and one thing was certain, we needed speed. We were about halfway to Hallows Hall, the science building where I once took biostatistics and chemistry, when the alarm sounded in an array of obnoxious buzzing, wailing, and flashing lights.

"THIS IS AN EMERGENCY," said the automated female voice over the outdoor loudspeaker system. "PLEASE REMAIN INDOORS UNTIL FURTHER NOTICE." The flashing lights were everywhere—atop lampposts, buildings, doors, and in hallways. The alarm repeated multiple times as Maynard and I hustled across the open courtyard. We were the bait, luring the creeping darkness away so that Father Monaco and Jonah could grab the VW Bug and get us out of there.

Maybe there were other, more efficient ways of preventing death to innocent people caught up in the crossfire, but in the moment, nothing came to mind.

It dawned on me as we fled, the fateful path I was now entwined in—The Thirteen would never give up. They would never allow me time or shelter. This would be my life for the foreseeable future. What lengths would I need to go to disappear? And how would that ever get me closer to getting Jaycie back?

As my mind wandered, Maynard yelled, "Wait up!"

I could outrun Olympians with ease and was only now coming to realize the breadth of my potential. Slowing down for Maynard felt like a powerwalk as his lungs and legs labored to keep pace.

The scent of blood was on the air, sweet like iron, and I knew it was already too late for someone, caught outdoors as the evil swept in. Would they have died if we hadn't come? Was it my fault? Celestine called me a killer, and maybe he was right.

"Do you really think we're a killer, my man?" asked Montoya. "Sometimes you do what needs to be done in the line of duty."

Henry replied, "The angel, Celestine, would have sold out his own friends. He considered us a killer? That leads me to believe our crime may have been something rather awful."

"Semantics," said Jamaal. "Are we capable of that? Sure, we took down a few evil gods and some of those vamps, but are we a killer?"

"And what have we killed?" added Chappy. "Was he speaking from the perspective of a man? Or an angel? Context is key."

"He lives as a man," said Doshin. "But considers himself more."

"Killer of his own kind? Which *kind* does he mean?" asked Montoya. "I've killed enemy combatants. They were human. Does that make me a killer?"

"Precisely what I was attempting to say," said Chappy. "The term *killer* usually references one's own kind. A man may squash a hundred bugs, but is he considered a killer?"

"You think he means we killed other angels?" asked Jamaal.

"Mmm hmmm," said Chappy.

He may have been right, but as we followed the path from Hallows Hall to Milton Hall, past the Dunwich Observatory, toward the covered bridge, and through Visitor's Center Courtyard, the chance that we might make it all the way to Deschain Hall without any obstacles quickly dropped to zero percent.

"Shit," said Maynard between gasps of air. He spotted them too, stalking toward us from the mouth of the covered bridge. He was winded, and we needed to find cover. "What are those things?"

Bearing down on us were two—Zangels? Zemons?

"Zemons, definitely Zemons, my man," said Montoya.

These two were different than the others, like variations of the same twisted creature. One had great leathery wings, while the other was as wide as a professional wrestler.

I tossed Maynard's duffel like I was launching a discus, then sprinted out ahead of him. The duffel slammed into the furthest Zemon, knocking it off its feet as I leapt into the air and Superman- punched the jaw right off the nearest with a sick thud-tearing noise that sent it rolling several yards away. As the other Zemon stood up, I broke its leg with a swift kick to the inside of its knee, then took a knife I swiped from Maynard's storage unit and buried it deep into its heart—

—only it didn't die.

It launched itself at me and used its leathery wings, like two long arms, to backhand me across the courtyard. When I came to a stop, the other Zemon grabbed me by the top of the head and tried to twist it off like a bottle cap. Pain rocketed up and down my spine as I grappled with its wrists and put my knife through its forearm—then with a simple twist, the arm broke clean off.

It roared and swatted me away, crushing my collarbone in the process. Before I stopped rolling across the ground, the other Zemon had its hands on me—like I was being passed off in a professional wrestling tag-team match. It yanked me up from my knees and screeched, preparing to chew my throat out as its jaw widened, when a shotgun blast took its head clean off.

Maynard was huffing and puffing from three feet away, clutching the smoking shotgun.

"How'd you know to blow off its head?" I asked.

"I—didn't," he explained as he gasped for air. "Nothing—lives—without a head."

"Fair point," I replied, then removed my knife from the severed arm and discarded the limb over my shoulder like a banana peel. Afterward, I hobbled over to the injured, armless Zemon, drew my gun, and blew its head off as it wound up, preparing to pounce—its body fell limp into a heap.

"Are you okay?" he asked. There was pain in my neck, shoulder, forearm, and knee. It was excruciating, but if the last few hours had taught me anything, it was that I had the ability to heal everything from gashes to cuts, to broken bones and poison—I just needed to learn how to jump-start the process when my body wasn't reacting fast enough. The medic, in all his kilty glory, taught me that. I felt bones stitch together with audible pops and groans as I forced it with a little concentration. It was so loud, Maynard heard it over the automated warning message blaring through the loudspeakers. "Guess so. Fucking hell, man! You sure can take a beating."

"That's what she said," I joked with a big grin.

"Jesus, man, don't make me laugh," he said, as another howl boomed in the distance. This one was the closest yet. "We can't stay out here."

He was right. Our way forward was blocked—who knew what creatures were waiting for us on the other side of the covered bridge. We couldn't turn back—I could feel the evil surrounding our position.

"Inside," I said, gesturing to Hallows Hall. "We lure them in, then sneak out the other side."

"Or they trap us inside with no way out?" he suggested, just as a herd of creepy things stalked out of the surrounding shadows at the edge of the courtyard. They passed beneath the flashing lamps in every direction. They moved slow, methodical, but even with my enhanced vision it was hard to tell what they were from so far away.

"Shit," I fumed—a sentiment shared by the brain-trust. "I don't think we have a choice."

"He's slowing us down," said Montoya. "My man, we should have done this alone."

I nodded to him as I retrieved the duffel bag, then Maynard and I retreated laterally into Hallows Hall.

Hallows Hall was a science building, covering everything from chemistry to physics to biology. I'd taken Mr. Thomas's physics class on the second floor. The building had a brick façade, and it contained four floors of lecture halls and labs, classrooms, and storage closets. There were three main entrances and a maintenance exit with a small dock in the back for supplies. I knew this building, and I knew every exit and service entry, even the maintenance door that exited out of an unmarked closet.

Once through the metal security doors, I moved further inside, enacting a plan that was revealing itself to me on survival instinct, when Maynard asked, "Shouldn't we barricade the door?"

"No time," I said. "Once they're through those doors, we'll be on our way out the far side."

Maynard was sucking wind like a stuttering jet engine, so I gave him twenty seconds to catch his breath and hoped it was enough time to make a clean getaway. If I was still human, the me before my transformation, could I have survived this long?

Was I actually any good at this? Or had a lifetime of bad luck finally caught up to me, allowing me one narrow escape after another until even my bad luck ran out?

I was standing beneath a large, framed painting of an old man. The nameplate said *Goodman Hallows*—one of the University's rich donors, whom the hall was named after once he disappeared twenty-five years ago.

Jamaal said, "Hallows. Must be the family of that sick fuck that murdered everyone after they built his estate. From Maynard's story."

"Looks like a sick fuck," said Montoya.

"There are some who suggest that madness manifests itself physically," said Henry. "That you might see traces of madness by the structure of one's face, their build, their body language."

"Do you believe in that?" asked Chappy.

"I do not know," said Henry, pensively. "I am, however, revisiting the idea after our encounters with Mammon, Bacchus, and the others." He looked up at the Hallows portrait, then back to us. "Imagine a celestial creature falling from grace—the psychosis and the madness, the power, isolation, and frustration—and imagine how awful that must be. Imagine what that might look like if it were allowed to manifest itself physically."

"Ugly," said Doshin. "The inner self, reflected out."

"Precisely."

Food for thought. What would I look like if my inner self was reflected outward? Would I appreciate what I saw? Or would it scare me like the hideousness of the Thirteen?

"You good?" I asked, as I heard Maynard's pulse slow into an even beat.

"Yeah." He lifted the shotgun back onto his shoulder, and we moved further into the building.

We had already wasted too much time.

Racing through the halls, we worked our way to the far side and out the unmarked closet door, just as I remembered. The rusty deadbolt snapped off easily with a little pressure. We were twenty feet away and home-free—not a U-Nat in sight—when we heard the scream.

"Help me! Somebody, help me!" A girl's voice, coming from back inside the building.

It sounded familiar.

Maynard turned back, then said, "Keep going!" before he charged inside with his shotgun raised. He was already inside before I realized he wasn't following me. I slid to a stop, then heard the scream for a second time, from somewhere on the third floor—my mind triangulated the refraction with the source and vibration from the windows.

As far as split decisions go, we made the right one for the right reasons. Neither of us could live with ourselves if someone got hurt. I leapt onto the side of the building and ran up to the third floor, then crashed through the window in a shower of glass and sped into the hall.

In my limited experience, fear puts out a rather distinct scent amongst people—like sour citrus and, of all the things, rotting ginkgo berries. That hallway on the third floor smelled about as generic as any university hallway across the country—like aging paper and cleaning supplies—not a trace of fear. While I tracked down the call for help, Maynard slammed through the stairwell door at the near end and nearly shot me.

"Fuck man, how'd you get up here so fast?" he asked, retracting his aim.

"Took the express," I deadpanned.

"Are we too late?" he asked, and I couldn't shake the feeling he was right—we were too late, just not in the way he was thinking.

I peeked inside the first two classrooms and shrugged. There wasn't anyone there.

"Over here! Help!" the girl cried out from somewhere behind us.

Maynard spun and charged down the hall, around the next corner, as I peeked out the nearby window. We were being swarmed upon—shadows shifting within shadows—and there wasn't going to be an easy way out, not now.

I chased Maynard down the hall and found him searching from room to room.

"Hey man, I don't think there's anyone here but us," I said as my suspicion grew.

"What do you mean? You heard her," he replied.

Every sense and impulse told me we were alone. I'd heard the cry for help, but I also knew we were dealing with creatures that did things beyond our understanding. Having lived this life for as long as he had, Maynard should know that as well as anyone.

"I think it was a trap to keep us here."

"What?" said Maynard. There was something about his frustration that made me question his demeanor. "Someone cried out for help and you're just looking to save your own ass?"

"Where did that come from?" I asked. "We don't have time to argue. We need to leave."

"Go, I'll find her. Save yourself," he grumbled.

"No, I'm not going to leave you to die."

"Some replacement you are." He began to walk away, his urgency wholly aimed at finding the *girl* who called for help—a *girl* I was confident didn't exist.

"What's that supposed to mean?" I asked.

Maynard had his back to me and took a deep breath before spinning around like he was juicing for a confrontation. "Amanda was my best friend too. Then she moved away and forgot all about me. I never knew why until I met you. You replaced me."

It seemed like an odd time for this level of pain to be spilling out. "Where is this coming from? Why now?" I asked.

"Why not now?"

"Because we're being hunted by freaking monsters, man!" I growled.

"Something's up, my man," said Montoya.

"Indeed," added Henry. "This is not typical. His anger would have betrayed him much sooner if he truly felt this way."

"Listen," said Doshin, as if hearing something the rest of us could not.

Maynard looked at me strangely, then rubbed his eye with his free hand. "You're right. I don't know what came over me." Then he lowered the shotgun from his shoulder and leveled it at my chest. The hole it could blow right through me would challenge even my healing. "Are you the reason she stopped calling?"

"No! I haven't talked to her in years!"

"You're lying," he growled. "Why are you lying?"

How did he know I was lying? Up until yesterday, I hadn't heard from Amanda since high school. There was something erratic about Maynard's behavior. It didn't feel like him. It didn't smell like him either.

"Is she dead?" he asked.

I was caught. "Yes."

"Did you kill her?" he growled, as tears formed under his eyes.

"No," I said, yet somehow that felt like a lie.

"You're unfairly blaming yourself," said Chappy.

"Amanda's dead and your old girlfriend comes back? Is that supposed to be a coincidence?" Maynard's hands were shaking.

"That's not what happened."

"You could have brought Tori back, but you chose the weird girl. The strange girl who made Amanda move away."

"I didn't bring anyone back," I argued.

"You know I was there? I saw stuff, man. Creepy shit happened. Unexplained shit surrounded Jaycie. And when your girlfriend killed that kid from our class, I was there for Amanda as she cried her eyes out. Then she moved away, found you, and that was it."

As he ranted—describing a history that sounded like delusional ravings—something new caught my attention. It was there all along, it just took me till now to understand what I was seeing—a shadowy figure at Maynard's back, playing him like a puppet. "Hey, be calm. Something's got a hold of you," I said. This was the last thing either of us needed. We'd wasted too much time.

"Oh, fuck off! I've had about enough of you," he said, as a sound from the hall made his skin go as pale as the rising moon. "Tori?"

"Tori's dead, Maynard," I reminded him.

"No," he grumbled and rubbed his watery eyes again with his free hand. "She's alive."

He ran into the hallway chasing after a ghost. I followed around the bend and into a storage room with metal shelving loaded with supplies and chemicals. The room was long and narrow and looked like a spare laboratory. The windows along the outer wall faced the Dunwich Observatory—the direction we were headed to rendezvous with Jonah and the Father. The four tables at the front were equipped with gas jets for Bunsen burners, and a chalkboard on wheels was parked beside them.

Maynard was standing in the center of the room, motionless, when I entered. I set his duffel bag down by the entrance and walked into the cold room. The only illumination came from the flashing security lights and the low-hanging moon. From the window, I could see shadows everywhere. We were surrounded, but it did not appear that any of them were entering Hallows Hall after us.

They were waiting.

"I'm starting to think," said Jamaal, "that the thing we have to worry about most is already in the building with us."

"Maynard," I said, but he didn't move. The shotgun was on the floor next to him.

When I got within three feet, he wavered and said, "I miss you." Before I could ask who, Maynard fell backward, a self-inflicted wound blooming with blood to the left of his navel. I caught him before his head hit the ground, his hands still clutching at the knife.

Maynard was right. We weren't alone.

I lowered him to the floor, then stared up at the thing that whispered dark thoughts into his ear.

"Hey bitches," said Tori. "Miss me?"

MALUS

After every corrupt and immoral thing I had ever done, I always asked myself if it was worth the damage darkening my soul. I can say, with every wicked intention my heart has served, that the inner peace of getting back what was mine was the only thing worth a damn in this broke fucking world.

I saw for the first time traces of fear amongst the gods—those who thrived and feasted upon mankind, at the very top of the food chain, were suddenly making mortal decisions. Great ancients like Dagon summoned his brides, and Hekate beckoned her Fae offspring to join us. Even Loki assembled his remaining children to serve as fodder against our antagonist. I thought it strange how Loki professed to love his children but would throw them into the pits if it would save his own hide. Hypocrisy was a Fallen's greatest sin and likely our most precious weapon.

Anthony Oscuro was now a pestilence. The filthy fuck of a spark had managed to accomplish something none of us had ever seen. A modern weapon made to propel a leaden ball of *hellfire*? He did not need to battle at close range with blade, fang, or talon; he could kill from several paces away with precision more accurate than a bolt. Neither did he need to destroy our eyes or heart to vanquish us—he could burn us to ash with only the pull of a trigger. Not that striking us with a bullet was an effortless accomplishment, but he was one of us, after all, *apparently*, and his gift for precision would be as perfect as ours.

Still, there were other issues that consumed me. Phobos and Deimos begun their reconstruction of the glamour, spinning their psychic silk around the girl's mind like an insect cocooning their prey. But the girl was fighting—stuck somewhere between both Lilly and Jacinda.

"Let me go!" she screamed. Her eyes held a petulant fury.

"She wants to get away almost as much as I," said the ghost.

"Shut up," I threatened them both.

I ignored the girl and continued dragging her by the wrist down a paved stone path. We exited through a covered bridge and toward a building across the courtyard, surrounded by our dark armies.

Tony's scent was still heavy on the air, although he had passed through several moments ago. The girl yelped when she took notice of the familiar grounds and buildings, which jolted a new-found spirit to escape. She pulled against me as I tugged, her feet skidding across the path behind me.

"What are you going to do to me?" she asked while gasping for air. Her intense struggle had pillaged her energy.

"Will you do to her what you did to me?" whispered the ghost into my ear.

"Do not worry. You will no longer be yourself when I get what I want," I said with a smile. I hung my gaze upon her for a lingering moment to bask in the horror taking shape as the truth took her hostage.

"Why are you doing this? I didn't do anything to you!" she yelled.

I stopped in my tracks, then lunged at her—my rage boiling at the ignorance of the accusation.

"You didn't do anything!" I growled, my forefinger pointed between her eyes. "Do not mistake this as an affront to *you* and *your* existence. You did nothing, and yet you are everything. This world took *my every-thing*! Whatever I need to fuck this world and get what I want, I take. I am owed! There are two very precious gifts hidden inside your soul, and they do not belong to you."

My rage caused her to shrink beneath me like a cowering kitten.

Reaffirming my grip on her wrist, I continued to drag her unwilling husk toward the large brick building. Before the hour was up, I would be in possession of all four keys of Eden and be rid of the only creature standing in my way.

I was lost in my thoughts when the girls' constant struggles ceased—both the girl *and* the ghost. In the next moment she paced beside me as one, her hand gently wrapped around my own, our fingers interwoven. "Where are we off to tonight?" asked Lilly.

"I decided to take you out for an evening stroll, my dear. I thought, perhaps, we might meet up with a few friends a short distance away," I said smiling, playing up the ruse. The glamour was reestablished, her mind lost somewhere between dream and wakefulness. What she saw was not what was, but a fantasy created in part by my imagination with her own mind filling in the details. It was held together by the psychic magicks of Phobos and Deimos—their tendrils sinking deeper and deeper into her mind.

"*To gain what you seek, she must first love you, truly. You must make her yearn for you with all her heart. Captivate her mind with all your charm. She must lust for you, her flesh to yours. And she must need you with every ounce of her soul, so that there is no beginning or end to her without you. Once that is obtained, take her to the holy land that was lost and locked away. There you may acquire what you seek by performing the sacramental contract.*" Those were Frigg's words, words spoken by the famed Seer, and the whole reason for the glamour. The girl could never love me, there were no delusions otherwise, but if her reality were altered, her active mind replaced, and she were tricked into loving and trusting me?

Such ruses were common amongst our kind. Zeus, king of the Greek Pantheon, had used similar tricks to court the women of his desires. Though even the almighty god of sky and thunder would have had a difficult and dangerous time bewitching the mind of a woman with so much potential. Such were the lengths I traveled...

Without my ring, none of it was possible.

"What a lovely night," she responded happily, tossing herself into my arms for a gentle kiss. It was an intensely tortured experience, to kiss something that my innermost desires and self-hatred begged to rip apart—there was a time when I yearned for such connections, but that sentiment was gone now. I needed the resolve of Atlas—with the world upon his shoulders, he never once faltered under its weight. I would not falter and give in to my temptations.

In the midst of my own masked revulsion, her lips passionately pressed against mine, I felt her flesh drain of its tender warmth and grow icy cold and rigid. She punched and clawed at my chest, then squirmed away under my iron grip. When she finally liberated herself from my clutches, she instantly vomited and rolled away on the cold damp ground like she was searching for fresh air to breathe.

"Leave me alone!" she whined between sobs. Jacinda was back in control, quivering in disgust. "Help me! Please! Help me!"

"Let us go!" screamed Lilly's ghost. "We hate you! We hate you!"

Their screams forced me to react—not that anyone could do anything to help them, but the fewer human casualties, the better. There was a balance to preserve. If any of us were caught slaughtering too many humans at one time, in one area, there was sure to be a cleansing. A group of angels would be dispatched to take apart the incursion. This was the way things were. The uneasy peace between us. The events of this world were largely left alone, off limits to Heaven's touch. A loophole in the Free Will debate that allowed us free reign, so long as we did not grossly misbehave.

I slammed my hand over Jacinda's gaping mouth hole and channeled all my strength into my ring, forcing my powers of the dead into her, and saturated her will. It was a waste of energy in an attempt to overwhelm her soul. Resistance to me was fruitless. My will was inevitable, but I needed her sedately locked away inside the glamour. The gathering of evil within the courtyard was sure to be too much for a human mind to witness. It was like peeking into Hell itself.

After flooding her system, there was an immediate change, forcing her into a catatonic, compliant state, following my every command. Our remaining approach toward the building was quiet, as Lilly's consciousness pressed her will upon Jacinda's—one mind subduing the other—a war for dominance.

Surrounding the building, beasts and dark denizens of shadow realms descended, of all twisted unnatural shapes and sizes. My disciples, the dead angels I'd slaughtered more than four millennia ago, with their leathered skin and wings, brought me the information I desired, speaking in a lost holy language from before recorded time began.

Tony was trapped inside with no way out. Cornered like an animal. The key was all but mine. He had managed to escape our clutches three times, each by destroying a member of our feared number. Summanus, Mammon, and Bacchus, all gone from this world, forever—all because some fucking spark picked a fight he had no chance to win.

It was like David versus Goliath, if one wanted to believe a false allegory. David's sling struck the mighty giant warrior, Goliath, in the leg with an errant toss. An accident, a fortuitous shot, which crippled Goliath just long enough for David to lop off his head. It was chance. There were greater chances of being struck by lightning.

I inspected my gathered army, one the greatest, most terrifying hordes ever assembled, second only to the Siege of Solomon. The hellish creatures stalked impatiently, begging to be unleashed upon their prey. Among them was my newest contract, Kukulkan, the snake god, and his Gorgon daughters slithering in the darkness. Kukulkan was a thirty-foot anthropomorphic black snake, with two arms, a Mayan headdress, a flitting tongue, twisting horns, and fiery yellow eyes. The god had contracted his spirit to my ring for nothing more than the rights to one-hundred virgin brides. It was all I could do to avoid laughing in his serpentine face.

Beyond them, the Black Priests, the unholy followers of Thanantos, wearing their black robes and masks. Then the Brides of Dagon with their pregnant bellies and pallid skin, and the Sisters of Venus, the devout immortal witches who served the will of Astoreth. And in the front, the mutant sons of Moloch—a twisted tale of genetic failures and brute strength—beside them, The Black Ka, an order of undead Egyptian warriors, conscripted into Anubis's army moments after their deaths, for fear their hearts would weigh more than a feather.

These with Loki's surviving children, Hel and Fenrir, constituted an army that could rival even the most powerful Angelic Host. I smirked at their loyalty and began to devise a plan to bring the key to me.

"Send in your children, but keep them subdued on the floors below," I barked. "The dead will bring the spark to them, broken."

THE OMEGA

XVII

malum memorias

JACINDA
Then.

I've been watching you for nearly twenty years, Jace, searching for information. What started as a refuge became an obsession—to find all the answers to Jacinda O'Neill's riddles. They were there, but hidden, like a subtext in need of decoding.

You were a haunted, tortured soul, and I learned your darkness a day too late.

After examining your youth, I came upon a crossroad—should I venture forward into the times when our lives intertwined? Or was my perspective of those events enough to know the truth?

Eventually, I decided the truth would set us free.

There had to be more I did not know. So, I journeyed forward, self-preservation be damned.

April 13th, 2000

The first day back in Grace Falls, you spent the evening riding around town, talking to booking agents at local bars and clubs. The next day you drove to Mercy Point and did the same. You drove to and from every surrounding town, shaking hands and getting your name in front of everyone willing to listen. Your second trip to Down the Hatch, a large bar near the Grace Falls town square, happened to be the night a local act cancelled, and since you were already there, you struck a quick handshake deal and grabbed your guitar from the back seat of your small red car.

Anything to get a gig. Anything to not be home with your mother.

Your first and second set went off without a hitch, and as you grabbed a water from the bar before finishing up, you were approached with several offers to buy you a drink.

"Sorry guys, I don't drink," you said.

Truth or not, it was a good excuse, Jace.

"Since when?" asked a familiar voice.

"Since I decided not to do anything that was bad for me," you said purposely, knowing exactly who the voice belonged to. You had only been home for a few days, and he had already found you.

"What? No hug for an old friend?" asked Rick.

"Were we ever friends?" you asked through narrowed eyes.

"Ouch," laughed Rick, sloshing around his beer. "That was harsh, Jace."

It was harsh, Jace. Good job!

"What are you doing here?" you asked. Your mind was already filling up with ridiculous notions of Madame LeStrange's Star-Crossed Lovers card. Was Rick really there for you?

"Oh, I come here all the time," he said, but that was a lie. I knew people who went to that bar, and he wouldn't be caught dead inside.

"That's cool," you said, grabbing your water and taking a long sip to soothe your throat.

Rick was in the middle of his own quick sip when someone bumped into him on their way to the rest room. "Watch it, shithead!" he spat.

"Fuck off," groaned Sid.

I knew I liked you for a reason, Sid. We had the same disdain for assholes.

"Faggot," said Rick. "This place has too many asshole punks."

"Yeah," you responded sarcastically, rolling your eyes. Rick spoke like he thought everyone appreciated the perspective of an alpha male piece of shit. "You may have had one too many tonight, Jansen."

"Nah, I have a high tolerance," he bragged, as his mouth nearly missed the bottle going in for another sip.

"Riiight." You were beginning to feel this reunion was quickly going nowhere and decided to cut it short before it got any more awkward. Maybe Madame LeStrange was wrong? Maybe this wasn't your path after all? "Hey, it was good to see you."

"Yeah," said Rick as you turned away, but he quickly grabbed you by the arm and spun you back around. "What are you doing tomorrow night?"

I missed you by thirty minutes. I was there when you left through the side exit, but I couldn't get to you—fate stepped in, and his name was Sid.

A few minutes after I left, frustrated and confused, Rick stumbled out of the bar and handed the dish washer a fifty, then said, "Tell your buddy I'll hook him up next time."

The dish washer said, "Thanks," and quickly pocketed the cash. "Hey, why'd you need me to cancel my buddy's band anyway?"

"Does it matter?" asked Rick, as he walked off to his car parked at the other end of the block behind the bar.

And the rest was history.

I thought I knew the story from there.

Girl meets guy. Guy is a good looking, steroid-raging control freak. Girl falls for guy because they have a history. Girl meets Guy #2 and friend-zones him while suffering through a tumultuous relationship with Guy #1. Meanwhile, Guy #2 is always on her mind.

But I was wrong.

You were happy at first. I could see it on your face, as much as it killed me, and even though I was only a watcher, it made me burn with jealousy. For his part, Rick anticipated everything. He bought you flowers, said sweet nothings, and romanced you with the kind of time and affection you had always desired. Was he honest? That was debatable, but Rick was a man who had endless resources and a reputation that got him anywhere he wanted to go.

Lucky for me, money has never and will never buy happiness.

I watched the two of you grow as close as couples can be—the romantic dinners and the laughter, day trips and lazy nights spent at his apartment overlooking the river—

—and I also watched you fight like cats and dogs.

Your first ever argument came the evening of your one-month anniversary, when Rick decided the guy at the next table was paying too much attention to you. He threatened him, then fed the poor guy a piece of his fist.

You may have left him that night if it wasn't for how convinced you were that fate had brought you together—that Rick Jansen was the only person in the world who could truly love you. Before too long, your occasional fights became more frequent. Your disagreements erupted over the silliest things and escalated more quickly than the plague through Europe.

When Rick fought, he fought dirty. He took no prisoners. Every shot he took was meant to break your spirit. I heard Rick call you a slut, bitch, slime, and worse, and that was when he wasn't taking the time to be creative in the way he eroded your confidence. Rick's form of love was control. He methodically broke you down with his words until you were left questioning how anyone could ever love you. And when you fought back with legitimate points, expressing your feelings and desperately attempting to make things better between you both, he made sure to twist everything you said back around on you. It was gaslighting at its finest.

Rick's mental abuse quickly took its toll.

He broke you down emotionally until you fell so low you began to feel numb. You needed him just to feel something, anything, that wasn't emptiness. Eventually the only times you ever felt loved was when you were fighting, because it was always followed by making up. The rollercoaster of extreme highs and lows made you need the lows just to feel the intensity of the highs. You were addicted to him.

And like any abuser, he found other ways to control you.

Before spring's end, Rick had you shooting up with him just to connect. You didn't want to, but Rick made sure to remind you that you were a user, and users used. Heroin was different, and you knew it was different, but he made it so easy to say yes and so disappointing to say no.

You started living according to his approval.

Rick Jansen turned you inside out, Jace. You were together for only a few months and you were already fading away. Somewhere inside your mind, you knew this wasn't right. You were losing your identity one high at a time.

When classes started in late August, you started skipping them. You turned in papers late. You struggled to maintain a schedule. The only thing you managed to do was pick up your guitar and sing, which was when the realization struck that maybe, just maybe, you were in the wrong relationship.

There was never any doubt that Rick loved you. He loved you with all he had to offer. But his dangerous love nearly destroyed you. He was the hero of his own story, and I was the villain, whether I wanted to be or not.

When I showed up, you changed. You stopped using. You spent more nights at your own place with Anne, and you started getting your life straight. To see my influence on you from this perspective was astonishing, and it made me miss you that much more.

But you did not love me.

You were so, very much in love with Rick.

March 5th, 2001

It was almost seven by the time Rick showed up with three thunderous knocks on your door. You'd made plans with him that night instead of going to Mercy Point with Anne, Tony, and the gang. Rick didn't like karaoke, so when the opportunity arose to go laugh and have a good time, you usually took it, even if that meant leaving your boyfriend behind. However, that night, you decided to stay home with him to stop a fight. Rick had lost his cool after seeing you and me together. I was carrying your guitar case from the locker room, and if you hadn't defused the situation, it was going to explode.

When you answered the door, Rick barreled in, still wearing the same sweats he wore to practice. He was sweating and mumbling to himself. You had never seen him act that way, and it worried you.

"He's going to get me," he said.

"Who's going to get you?" Your question seemed to snap Rick back to reality with a crisp jolt. "What's that on your hands?"

His hands were covered in red, like he had spilled paint all over them, and there were tiny little spatters of it across his sweatshirt.

"Nothing," he said, rushing toward the bathroom sink.

He frantically began scrubbing his hands, and you wrapped your arm around him. "What's wrong baby? Talk to me."

"Whatever you do, don't listen to what they say. I didn't do it."

"What who says?" You had never seen Rick so lost and vulnerable. The idea that such a mountain could be so fragile made you worry even more.

"That fucker, Tony. He's going to set me up." Rick finished washing his hands. Most of the red swirled down the drain, but there was still some on his shirt.

"What happened?" you demanded, as Rick frantically sidestepped you and stalked out of your bathroom and into the living room. You'd spent the last hour making a romantic dinner that was deliciously laid out on the coffee table for you both to enjoy. The sight of it caught Rick's eye as he quickly sized you up.

"What's this supposed to be?" he asked.

"I wanted to do something special," you said. In truth, you wanted to bury the sins of that afternoon behind you. Make him forget all about your indiscretion with me.

I was a sin to you, Jace. A weakness.

I should have been your strength. This hurt me more than you will ever know, Jace.

"Because you feel guilty?" he asked. He was dead on, if not a bit biased. You weren't feeling guilty as much as you felt the need to put it behind you, and quickly.

"Can we just drop what happened this afternoon? You're my boyfriend,

Rick. Tony's my friend. He's my pal. There is nothing between us."

"He looks at you like some lost puppy," said Rick angrily. "How would you like it if I had some girl following me around like that?"

"You have. You still do," you said.

He was cheating on you, Jace. It was so obvious. He cheated on every girl because he could. And the other woman didn't care about the girlfriend, just like you didn't care about Rhonda at first.

"You're just fucking jealous," he shot back.

"You're jealous of Tony!" You couldn't believe you were already descending into a fight. Not after you gave up your night out to be with him and made all that food. You'd created an Italian dish with a vodka sauce and a salad with all the fixings. How could he not see that you were making a huge effort for him?

"Listen to me," said Rick, as he closed in on you. For the first time, he put his hand on you in a way that made you feel threatened. His grip on your chin, angling your face into his eyes as he spoke, was as painful as you had ever felt with the man you loved. "That faggot called the cops on me."

"What?" you asked. You were afraid, and confused, and you hated it when he spoke like that. He demeaned people all the time, and you were sick of it.

"Bill called me! He said the cops are looking for me!" Then his face narrowed into a devious, conspiratorial glare. "I need you to do something for me." He let go of your chin, then put his hands angrily through his hair. "When the cops come looking for me, I want you to tell them I was with you all night."

"What did you do?" you asked, suddenly realizing it was blood on his shirt. You were horrified and backed away. "Did you hurt him?"

"Guys do guy things, Jace. He took it too far."

"Too far? That's blood on your hands and shirt."

"Jace! They're going to arrest me because he said I did something I didn't do!"

"Did you hurt him?" You were feeling sick.

Your question enraged Rick. He grabbed a piece of paper and

snatched a pen, then sat down and started writing. After he had been writing for more than ten seconds, you approached him and asked, "What are you doing?"

Rick ignored you, until finally he stopped and let you read.

"Sign it," he said.

"But I didn't write it," you shot back. It was a sworn letter to the cops, saying Rick was with you all night. Leaving aside the obvious lie, you weren't comfortable with this. You were afraid of what he did to me and what he might do to you.

"That doesn't matter. Sign it," he demanded.

"No, I can't!"

Suddenly Rick was on you, grabbing you painfully by the back of the neck and forcing you toward the letter.

"If you can't sign it, then I can't be with you," he threatened. "This is your fault. You brought him into our lives. You made this happen, and you're going to get me out of it."

That was the first day in your relationship that you felt like a prisoner. Rick became obsessed with me. So much so that you were left with only one choice—to stop being my friend or risk losing the love of your life.

A few days later, you waited for me outside the door to my room. You needed to see me—the damage—with your own eyes. When I told you to fuck off, I meant it. I was so hurt, and so angry with the part you played, I didn't ever want to see you again. I didn't know you were forced into signing that letter.

Seeing my face black and blue, with stitches and a swollen, broken nose—it cut you deep. You felt like an accomplice, and you were. You hated yourself. You hated what you had become, and you swore you couldn't fall any further—you refused to allow it.

That day, you finally woke up from that deep sleep and decided to make a change. A change that you could control. Little by little, attempting to bring small portions of your life back from the dead.

And therein lay the ultimate problem. You still thought you could keep Rick and your soul. But soon enough you'd learn you couldn't have them both.

September 1st, 2001

Rick started a fight with some random bystander after losing to me at the speed pitch booth, and you decided you'd had enough. The Labor Day Fair was once one of your favorite things and was now just another bad memory. As people swarmed to either join or stop the fight, you told Anne you needed a break and walked away before anyone noticed you leaving.

You walked down past the food stands into the woods to the forest trail, where you followed it until you came upon a waterfall. It was the third and smallest of three in Grace Falls, about a mile from the old Jansen Mill. You watched as the gentle rumbles soothed your breaking heart. The air was filled with a cooling mist that gently clung to your hair and skin and left tiny droplets on your eyelashes.

As the sky darkened, you were left all alone with your thoughts, until you heard the footfalls of someone coming up from behind you.

"So, you just ditch me now?" asked Rick.

"I needed some quiet." The words barely left your throat, as if your body was resonating with the silence.

"I need you there supporting me," he said.

"What was I supposed to be supporting?" you asked. "Chauvinism? How big a man you are?"

"You're such a cunt, you know that?" he said. It was the first time he had ever used that word for you—in your presence, at least—even though he had used it often in reference to women. It was one thing for someone to use that word in a cheeky way, like the Brits did, but it was another to use it as a derogatory descriptor.

"You always do this," you replied with a humorless laugh.

"Do what? What am I doing?" he asked, laughing as if he was amused by the accusation.

"You're such a jerk!" you yelled.

"Oh, naughty word alert," said Rick, mocking you. "Why don't you grow a pair and give me a real insult."

"You're such a prick! A fucking piece of shit!"

I would have high-fived you, Jace, if I could have.

"There you go," he said. "Are you happy now?" He said it as if it was you who had stormed over to him and started arguing.

"Why do you do that?" you asked. "Why do you turn it around on me every time?"

"You're the one who's—"

"—being a bitch?" you finished for him. "Yeah, you've said that before. Plenty of times. I have it memorized." You pointed to yourself to illustrate exactly how often he's accused you.

"You're such a fucking drama queen," he groaned.

"Me? Are you serious? You're the one who put on a show for everyone, like you're some king of a stupid speed pitch at some stupid fair in the middle of nowhere!"

"Are you psycho? That prick—"

"Don't you dare call him a prick, and don't you dare call me a psycho." You were steamed, and it was about time. So much so that the misty vapor around you appeared to be doing just that—steaming.

"You're a joke, Jaycie," he said, then repeated it so loud, it could have been heard from the other side of the falls. "I don't know what's gotten into you, but I'm beginning to wonder if it wasn't a little faggot," he said, using a hand gesture to mimic penetration.

You stormed from your spot by the fence overlooking the falls and got right into his face. "I have never cheated on you. Never. I have been loyal to you despite everything!"

"Right, like you're so innocent," he shouted.

"I'm not the one who destroyed the trust in this relationship!" you defended yourself, as your voice cracked, and the tears fell.

"How can I trust you when you're sticking up for that asshole? He's a punk! Now more than ever! Did you see the way he was dressed? He thinks he's hot shit! Guys like him need to be put in their place. He's below me. He's below you!" Rick growled with betrayed rage. Then under his breath, he said, "Can't believe that dickhead threw ninety-six."

Actually, it was ninety-eight, but who's counting?

"What did he ever do to you? He was my friend, so you put him in the hospital? What if it wasn't just the hospital? What if you had killed him? You almost killed him! I'm sticking up for him because nobody else will! He's a good kid," you responded, as you pleaded for some kind of sense and perspective.

"After everything we've been through, you're going to choose him over me?" said Rick, his voice calm but angry.

"Rick, I love you. I love you so much. But sometimes I actually hate you. I hate the way you make me feel. I hate the things I've done with you. I hate the person I've become with you. All I want is for you to stop trying to prove to the world you're king of the jungle and just start being a good man," you pleaded.

"Jaycie, I'm just having fun! It's guy stuff. Guys pick on other guys. Guys are aggressive. They mark their territory, let the rest know who's boss. I think you take it too personally. You say you love me, but do you really love me? Or are you just in love with all the free stuff I give you?"

"Fuck you!" you shouted.

"You know what's really sad?" he said, closing the distance between you with two big aggressive steps. "When you get high, you always talk about the monsters. *Oh, the monsters want me, Rick! Oh, the monsters are coming to get me, Rick! Protect me, Rick!* You just say that to get more junk to shoot up. You're a fucking junkie cunt."

The words hurt, but there were two problems with what he said. "Let's be real, you have no interest in protecting me. And if you haven't noticed, I haven't used in months. I don't need to anymore."

"Once a junkie, always a junkie, Jace."

"Wow," you said with disappointment.

"Wow what?"

"Just wow," you said, and I could hear you stifle a sob. "Rick, maybe you should leave."

"What?"

"I want you to go."

There was silence.

"Fine. Fuck you, junkie cunt." Rick slammed his fist against a nearby tree, and it made a sick, crunching sound. He grabbed a huge rock and tossed it as hard as he could across the falls, screaming the entire time. Then he grunted and said, "I'm outta here."

"Yeah, you do that," you said under your breath as he stormed off.

After you took a few minutes to cool off, you realized there was only one person you wanted to spend the rest of the night with, and that was me.

When you caught up to me, wandering aimlessly through the fair, you weren't sure how I was going to react. We hadn't spoken a word to each other in months, and you were ashamed of that—you were ashamed you'd sided with Rick over someone who had your best interest at heart. As you approached me, you went with the first thing that came to mind—the caveman approach. Just drag me along and I was sure to follow, right?

Sure enough, it worked, and soon we were stuck atop the Ferris Wheel with our feet dangling a few hundred feet in the air. You didn't mean to feel the way you did, looking at me. You didn't mean to blush when I complimented you. You didn't even mean the jokes you made or the sexual innuendo, or the compliments—

—Except you actually meant them all.

And when I spilled my guts out to you, and said all you ever wanted someone to say, filling you up with such hope, love, fear, and confusion, you responded in the only way you could.

"Thank you," you said. "Thank you for the kind words, I really appreciate it. Nobody has ever said anything like that to me before."

You meant it. You meant it all, and yet it didn't come out the way you intended.

The fact was, you hated yourself. You loathed yourself. When you looked in the mirror you saw a recovering addict who had barely kicked her worst habit—the man who helped her learn to hate herself.

You weren't who you wanted to be. You weren't who I saw when I looked at you and opened my heart to you. Even if I did believe those words, you knew they weren't true.

And so, you fought against yourself. So many thoughts, so many feelings, so much confusion, and no resolution. You were lost and couldn't bear to confront my disappointment.

A few moments later the Ferris Wheel started moving again and our car stopped at the bottom, where the attendant unhooked the car and let us out. We walked away from the Ferris Wheel in silence, and when we got to the first intersection, we stopped.

…But this wasn't how I remembered that night. It went very different according to my memory. I didn't understand what was going on, but I kept watching, seeing this reality for the first time. Had I changed the past? Did I mess everything up?

"Do you want to keep hanging—?" you suggested, pointing off toward the food trucks, as if inviting me along. I was broken, Jace. We both could see it.

"No, I think I'm going to go home," I said. "I'll see you."

You saw the pain in my face, the defeated posture, and couldn't even pluck up the courage to stop me and apologize. You watched me walk away into the crowd until the pit in your stomached clenched and you sobbed to yourself, sinking to your knees, whispering, "It's not fair." You didn't mean to hurt me. You didn't mean to deny me so coldly. You didn't mean to accumulate another regret.

As you looked into the crowd to see where I had gone, there was no trace of me—just the crowd and the big, bright, crescent moon above…

"It's not fair," you sobbed. "I'm sorry, please understand. This isn't what I want. I'm not who you think I am. I'm not perfect." You sobbed so hard you choked, and people were starting to stare, when—

—when we were suddenly back on the Ferris Wheel.

What just happened, Jace? Did you do this? Did you just redo the whole moment?

The entire world reset five minutes, like a skip on a record player, only the second time through it played out differently, just like I remembered.

"Don't give up on me," you said into my ear. "I don't know how, but you get inside me. You can see me. Who I really am—not who everyone else sees. You see the real me. It's like you've known me forever. Nobody has ever—nobody has ever—" you cried. "What's wrong with me?"

"Nothing's wrong with you, Jaycie," I whispered to comfort you.

Several minutes passed, and your sobs died away.

"I don't want to let go," you said weakly.

"Then don't," I replied.

"Eventually," you coughed, clearing your throat, "I'll have to."

"I know."

"I'm sorry."

"What for?" I asked.

"For not being who you need me to be," you explained.

And just like that, I finally understood. You weren't who I thought you were. You were human. You had flaws. You had struggles. You had personal demons. And you weren't ready to be the woman I saw in you. But you wanted to be. You knew you could be. You knew you were her deep down inside.

When the night ended, and you kissed me goodbye, I walked away feeling like a new man. You on the other hand, left with hope for something new and positive.

As you drove home, you couldn't shake the dopey smile that kept curling the corners of your mouth. You kept thinking about me, about holding me, about the way I looked into your eyes like there was something secret hidden behind them. It gave you goosebumps and made your pulse race.

Did it all really happen?

Was the do-over real?

I invaded your thoughts like soldiers storming an occupied beach, with your heart and brain defending their territory to keep me at bay— but I just kept on coming, wave after wave of onslaught. You fought as hard as you could. You couldn't let me in; you didn't want to make this more confusing than it already was.

It was for my own safety. If Rick ever found out…

And Rick. What exactly were you feeling about him?

Even though I could take care of myself, you couldn't let another assault happen, not over you. That was something you could control. You couldn't bear to see me hurt again.

But what about my heart? You felt something, Jace. You wanted me back.

You had never been so confused.

After living in Grace Falls for most of your life, you had perfected a shortcut down from the fairgrounds. It took you off the beaten path and down a small one-lane country road that brought you closer to your apartment and past an old Shawnee burial ground. Only those who'd lived in Grace Falls for as long as you knew about the shortcut.

The night was still. There was no wind and no clouds obscuring the moon. The cricket chirps silenced, and the sound of your car seemed to echo into the night.

It was all so very eerie, like you were standing on the edge of a moment, feeling the momentum of your night coming to a complete stop.

Around the next bend, you saw Rick's Mustang pulled off to the side of the road beneath a thick canopy of trees and weeds. During the day, you loved driving through this stretch, where the sunlight trickled through in thin shafts—but at night, especially on this night, it appeared ominous.

Rick had left the fair nearly two hours ago. You started running through the possibilities. Did he pull over to take a leak? Not likely for two hours. Did his car break down? Rick had top-of-the-line driver's assistance and should have been towed ninety minutes ago.

After your fight, you'd debated if you should pull over. You were still in the middle of nowhere, and if things escalated, you preferred a public place. You knew how angry he could get. Rick's fury was legendary, but you never gave it much thought until it was aimed at you.

Was he okay? What was he doing? Was he waiting for you?

Of all your positive traits, the most mesmerizing was your compassion. As you slowly pulled up toward Rick's car, your conscience got the better of you. You pulled over behind him and put the car in park but kept the headlights on. You could see him sitting behind the steering wheel—the back of his head lit, his eyes illuminated in the rearview mirror.

At first, you thought he might get out of his car, so you sat there—until it became clear that he was not moving. You carefully exited your own car and paced cautiously over to his, where you stopped parallel with the back seat, leaning to get a better look at him.

CAWWWWW!

The trees above his car were loaded with a dozen crows. It was odd, you thought, how often you saw crows—but before you could think about it any further, your mind came back to the creeping, eerie sensation of your boyfriend parked along the side of a small country road in the middle of nowhere.

Rick, for his part, was perfectly still. You couldn't even tell if he was breathing.

"Rick?" You stepped up to the window. Your headlights, reflecting off his rearview mirror, lit his face. He looked distraught, and you swore you could see the tacky remains of tears just under his eyes. "Are you okay?" It felt weird to ask those words. There were two shades of Rick—partly irritable and angry. Those were the range of his emotions. You'd never once witnessed him sad, not even while watching a particularly sad movie. He often made fun of you for such things. Seeing him in that state was like seeing a turtle without its shell.

You were just about to repeat your question when he finally spoke.

"How was it?" he asked, never breaking eye contact from the forest ahead. His hands were still tightly gripped around the steering wheel at ten and two.

"How was what?"

"How was the fair?"

"Good," you admitted. This wasn't the way you imagined your next meeting with him. You wanted to sit down and think before you confronted him. Staying with Rick meant hurting me. Leaving for me meant hurting Rick. You never wanted to hurt anyone.

"Because I wasn't there?" he asked.

"Have you been waiting here for me this whole time?"

"I couldn't go home. I almost turned around and went back. I couldn't stand the thought of you being there without me," he said. It was about as honest and forthright as Rick had ever been with you. His eyes were still fixated in front of him, entranced.

"I understand, but I'm still mad at you. I didn't want you there," you said, and there was a long pause. "Maybe we both should both go home and get some rest. We can talk tomorrow."

"Okay," he said calmly.

As you turned to leave, a sharp pain rose within your wrist. Something clamped down and pinned you there, igniting a paralyzing pain into your shoulder. Rick's massive hand had slammed against the door, purposely twisting your arm. His whole body shook as he put all his strength into the vice-grip.

Your eyes widened. It was the first time Rick had ever physically hurt you, and yet it didn't shock you one bit. In the back of your mind, since the day he attacked me, there was an subconscious fear that your boyfriend would someday be the end of you, that you were forever doomed to be his.

"Ow! Stop! You're hurting me!" you protested, but he only stared at you with cold hardened eyes—then he grabbed you by the hair and twisted. The pain shot up your neck as you felt the pressure forcing it into an angle it wasn't meant to go.

"I don't know what I would do if I found you with that punk. It might just make me a little crazy. I might even kill somebody. Stay away from him," he whispered. "You're mine, and you'll always be mine. You don't seem to understand how much I love you." Without releasing your hair, he started up the Mustang and revved it once before pounding his foot on the gas. He released you only after the car had dragged you a few feet, as he peeled out, spraying dirt and grass all over you.

Was it murder to kill a dead man before he actually died? I could have gutted him and not thought twice about it.

Rick had driven home the seriousness of his intentions and left you with few options. It took twenty minutes before you managed to pull yourself together. You drove home in tears, and you only stopped crying when the tears stopped coming.

XVIII

dream warriors

TONY
December 23rd, 2013
Now.

"Hey bitches," said Tori. "Miss me?"

Maynard was stabbed and fell. I caught his head before he hit the floor, then looked up at the friend I lost thirteen years ago. She looked exactly as she had that night—in a red mini skirt, fishnets, knee high-boots, and a black button-up, with her magenta hair pulled up into dueling buns on the top of her head.

"Aww, look at you two," she said. "A couple of fucking losers."

My eyes and heart saw Tori Martin, but my other senses relayed a different story. She smelled moldy and hummed softly—like a vibration.

"Tori," said Maynard, "stabbed me."

"I know, buddy," I said, as I dragged him back to the nearest wall and propped him up, "but that's not Tori."

"Fuck you," she growled. "Who else would I fucken be?"

"Can you heal him?" asked Chappy. "It is written that angels can perform miracles."

"I don't know," I responded.

"Don't I look like fucken Tori?" she growled, answering me.

"Tori Martin died a long time ago," I said as I looked Maynard in the eyes. "This is going to hurt. Put immediate pressure on the wound right after." When he nodded, I pulled. The blood erupted from the gash, and Maynard clamped his hand onto the wound.

"Of course, I'm dead, asshole," said Tori. "Because of you."

"Don't let her get to you, my man," said Montoya. "You know the truth."

"I may need to cauterize the wound," I said.

"Aw fuck," groaned Maynard.

"I don't think they fucken believe me!" shouted Tori. Her vibrations sped up in synch with her frustration, and she nearly flickered out of phase.

"Maybe he needs more convincing," said another voice, and I quickly picked up five more hums from within the room. I couldn't see them, but I could feel their presence, like someone was watching me.

"I'm dead because of you," said Tori. "Dead! I got into that car because I wanted to apologize. Why did I do that? You killed me. You killed me! You!"

The room froze with a snap. Windowpanes audibly contracted and frosted over, followed by every other surface—the shelves, the walls, the floor, even the air. From the frozen foggy vapor moved wispy shapes—entities that brooded beyond sight.

"No," I said, standing up to her. "I didn't kill you."

"Sit down, punk," said another voice, as a fist erupted across my chin.

Then everything went black.

Somewhere Else...

"What in the jawn is going on?" said Jamaal, and my eyes snapped open.

The saturated color of my surroundings told me all I needed to know. As I sat up in the thick underbrush, I was struck with sensory overload. I was in the dream world once again, and it smelled like smoke and rain.

The familiar forest was thicker than usual, with heavy brier covering the floor with razor- sharp thorns. It was summer, hot and humid, and the greenery of the forest was fully in bloom—and burning.

"Where the fuck are we, my man?" asked Montoya as the wind kicked, like a storm was about to strike.

We awoke in my usual spot at the bottom of the hill beside the gully. Water flowed through it like a rushing river, feeding the growing plant life. The once still, dead winter of the dream was now full of movement—a chaotic scene of embers and soot raining down on lush plant life. The ground rumbled, and the trees moaned.

"Jacinda's dream world," I said. It was the truth—this was her dream world—despite it being the first time the thought ever crossed my mind. The warehouse and the mill, the demon door, the Mistress. This was happening inside her head, inside her subconscious, somehow.

"Sir," asked Henry, "are you suggesting we are in someone else's mind? Not yours?"

They were all there with me. All five of them, for the first time.

"Yeah," I said, "I think so." I reached out to place my hand onto Doshin's shoulder as he stared up the hill at the flames burning in the treetops. I had interacted with them hundreds of times as if they were actually there and had watched as my hand passed through their incorporeal, ghostlike bodies. Only this time, my hand hit solidly against Doshin's shoulder—causing both of us quite a startle. He was real. Live flesh and blood. As real as I was inside the dreamscape.

"That's interesting," said Chappy, shaking Henry's hand. "I can feel this!"

Montoya tried to give Jamaal a hug, but the big guy just hoisted him aside with a snappy "get that outta here." It must have been a great feeling for them, to have their independent lives back, not just tethered to the whims of my own personal nightmare.

I was in such a state of heightened awareness, getting caught up in my brain-trust enjoying their new leases on life, that I never stopped to examine myself. I was no longer spattered in blood, my leather jacket was once again in perfect condition, and I could feel the surge of energy inside me, like the flames had an unending supply of fuel ready to burn at a whim.

Flashes of movement caught the corners of my peripheral vision. They were all around us, running toward the top of the hill, toward the clearing. Flashes of color—the nymphs—mobilizing. Something was happening, and I wasn't paying attention.

"Oh no," I said. "Come on!"

I leapt over the gully and sprinted up the other side while the others remained in varying degrees of confusion—Jamaal at the onset of a full-on panic attack.

"How do you expect a three-hundred fifty-pound man to run up that hill?" yelled Jamaal as he neared the edge of the gully like he was creeping toward a cliff.

"Give it a try, my man," said Montoya, waving him on.

"I can't do this! You don't understand!" whined Jamaal. "I'm scared of everything. I once had crippling anxiety over retrieving the mail. Didn't leave my apartment for weeks because I was so convinced the letters were out to get me."

"Do it! Or we're going to leave you behind for the Thirteen," said Montoya.

Jamaal paled three shades, then leapt over the gully like an antelope. "Fuck! What the fuck! That was fucking awesome!"

"Doesn't look like you'll have a problem, my man," said Montoya with a wink and smile.

"This is unreal!" yelled Jamaal, motoring up the side of the hill like he was galloping through an open field.

"Very real," corrected Doshin, prancing up beside me like a silent assassin.

"You guys don't understand!" shouted Jamaal. "I'm cured!"

As the brain-trust followed, the scent of blood and death grew pungent. Whatever was happening, we were needed. We arrived at the top of the hill to the devastation.

At our feet were fallen bodies from prior battles, some ripped apart and others gnawed upon. They were piled three deep in some places, with blood soaking the soil. Some were small women, the naked nymphs of the forest with their brightly colored eyes, while others were angular beasts with fangs, claws, and grayish-black skin.

"Goblins," I said aloud, ripping a spear free from one of the many carcasses.

"Goblins?" asked Henry.

"What is a goblin?" asked Doshin.

Chappy shrugged. "Ugly."

"A goblin is a 14th century mischievous critter from European folklore," said Jamaal.

"Does that look like a critter to you, my man?" asked Montoya, pointing at the dead thing. It was mostly hairless, like a mangy dog, and its skin was the color of used motor oil—splotchy and black. It had pointed ears, wiry limbs, and vicious teeth.

Montoya was kicking at the body when Henry asked, "What's going on, sir?"

"What is this place?" asked Chappy. "Does it have meaning to you? To Jacinda?"

"I think it means everything," I said, as we climbed over the bodies toward the clearing.

The clearing was a smoky mess, shrouding the warehouse and the mill behind a thick curtain of gray. The trees along the far edge were burning under an overcast sky, set ablaze by great medieval war machines. The ground shifted and rolled like thunder as the war machines trampled over the stalks of amber grass in the distance, dragged along by beasts of the ancient world.

Waves of goblins marched through the trees with jagged spears. There were Gemini—slimy dark men with two heads, two torsos, and four arms, wielding swords and axes—marching within their ranks. Black wolves howled in the distance, as tall as a man on all fours. They had sharp yellow fangs and drooled acidic saliva down their snarling snouts. Red-hooded Obsidian Witches stood throughout, casting black magic on their ranks for protection and bloodlust empowerments, while setting fire to the trees with cursed powder that ignited on impact.

The horde escorted three great medieval war machines, surrounded with black armor and fitted with large spinning saw blades, mowing down trees to let the machines pass. Spiked grinders—two large rollers, one atop the other, spinning inward to mash and grind any living thing—crushed everything within its path.

The center machine was tallest, bearing a woman in white at the very top. The maiden wore a white dress and sat upon a throne of rusted metal as the largest and most vicious of the goblins guarded her on either side. Her flowing blonde hair waved wildly in the wind as the storm intensified with flashes of lightning and epic thunder. From the distance, I couldn't tell if her screams were commands, fears, or threats, but the horde kept marching and snarling like something from the Evil Dead.

We stood at the edge of the forest, several hundred yards away, and watched the battle, stupefied by its existence, rather than joining. The dark horde army were going to tear right through the forest like wet tissue paper, and a small contingent of goblins were already thrashing battering rams against the warehouse doors. It was an unstoppable wave compared to the forest's natural defenses.

I was stunned at first, watching the horrific beauty of it—evil marching across a stormy landscape, like the battle at Helm's Deep in Lord of the Rings—when I heard a shriek.

"Help me!"

It was Jacinda. The horrible symmetry, the terrible coincidence, wasn't lost on me. Like in my nightmares, she called out to me.

She needed me.

Across the battlefield, a small contingent of nymphs were fighting their way through a wave of goblins, when the battering rams broke through the warehouse doors with splintering efficiency.

Until you experience a loved one in trouble, there's no way to describe the rushing combination of fear, rage, and urgency. In my mind, it felt like I was standing still for several minutes, while in reality, I broke off into a run before the next second ticked.

"Shit," said Montoya, watching me go.

As I charged, I felt the weight of the spear in my hands, contemplated my options, and decided to go at them with all I had.

I rushed their lines with the speed of a Messenger streaking across the heavens and struck with the power of a Destroyer across their lines.

After skewering a full row of goblins with a single spear thrust, like a goblin kabob, I stole the club of the nearest monster and used it to bash the closest Gemini across one of its heads, knocking the beast back into the third row. I whipped the spear around and flattened the whole flank before it could react and moved toward the interior lines. A goblin with a thick stripe of white hair attacked, but I caught his wrist and snapped if off with a twist, disarming him—literally. I held his sword in my hand, felt its weight with a single twirl, and embedded it into the skull of an incoming black wolf.

I was fighting like a dream—as if I was a fully realized version of myself. As if I had all the ability and powers of an angel at my disposal without the learning curve or doubt—without the imposter syndrome and the fear of losing everything.

I felt…*free.*

Maybe, just maybe, I was a Powers after all…

There was a hoot—like someone whipping by on an amusement park, demonstrating their enjoyment with a high-pitched shout. That's when the nearest war machine launched itself into the air like it had been hit by an anti-tank missile. Pieces of metal and splintered wood showered the area; some of the debris shredded a series of Gemini and left a whole pack of black wolves shrieking and cowering away.

"I love this fucking place!" shouted Jamaal as he removed himself from the debris. He had rammed into the horde like a cannonball, taking out everything in his path.

"Heads up!" yelled Montoya as he came in hot, landing at my side with a swipe of a stolen axe, chopping down goblins like a lumberjack.

Doshin was slaying anything that moved, charging up the center like a man possessed, as Chappy and Henry rushed over to help the Nymphs. They were more passive than the others, focusing on defense—they took down the battering rams, then solidified the doors as we faced the horde.

The shrill call of a battle-cry echoed from within the forest, followed by a series of bolts impaling a wave of goblins grappling all around me. Out of the wood came a few dozen nymphs followed by Dryads: male nymphs that lived within the eldest trees of the forest until such time as their services were needed. They were much taller than the nymphs, the tallest of which was slightly larger than me, and they wore petrified-wooden armor and cleverly-crafted weapons from an age before man walked the earth. They hacked into the beasts with a rabid fury, desperately defending their land.

From behind the Dryads came Fauns and Pixies. The Fauns carried spiked clubs and rushed their enemies with their heads down, ready to gore them with their horns. The Pixies were tiny creatures, perhaps only a foot tall, who flew about on wings like those of dragonflies, wielding poisonous thorns tied to the end of twigs.

It was like fucking Disney on acid.

I put the nearest goblin into a headlock and said, "See that?" and pointed off toward the rushing forest creatures. "Fantasia's come to kick your ass!" Then I snapped its neck and moved on, cutting down enemy after enemy and leaving a pile of corpses behind, forcing the enemy to climb over the pile just to engage me.

Before long, I was surrounded, buried deep into a crater of the dead horde, my enemies spilling over and on top of me, when I heard the call.

"Heads up, mutha fuckas!"

Jamaal slammed into the ground next to me, sending shock waves that liquefied goblin brains and throttled Gemini and Obsidian Witches alike.

"I kind of like this," I said. "Fighting by your side."

"This jawn is lit!" nodded Jamaal. "My haptic rig has nothing on this!"

"My man," said Montoya, rushing over. "What are you doing? You're letting Doshin have all the fun."

We stormed out of the crater to find Doshin with a flaming sword, chopping down enemies in ferocious numbers. He fought like he was dancing—graceful moves that led from one to the next, effortlessly.

It almost felt like a romp…

Then the trees swayed and new creatures emerged onto the battlefield, as if they had been waiting just out of sight. We watched giants—actual *fe fi foing* giants—stalk toward us shoving whole trees aside, uprooting them, as Doshin stepped to our side.

"Oni," said Doshin. "Be ready."

They were hideous things with huge fangs sprouting from enormous mouths. They had wild greasy hair with misaligned horns growing from random spots across their giant heads. And when the nearest of them approached, we scattered, just in time to avoid its massive club thundering the ground between us.

I fought my way through the endless attacks of goblins as the oni tore through our ranks. The storm overhead intensified and spat hail as large as walnuts into our lines, threatening our retreat, but the forest creatures didn't give a single inch against the greater numbers. They even took down an oni all by themselves as more entered the battle from the forest. As the horde neared Jacinda's warehouse, briar sprung up, snaring them like coiling razor wire. Then the trees began to fight back, swinging their low branches at unsuspecting enemies, clobbering them with bone-crushing blows.

It seemed the tide of battle was evening when several Gemini from the rear lugged five large cauldrons of steaming, scalding hot liquid to the front line. Before I could cut them off, the horde purposely sacrificed themselves by throwing their bodies in front of my sword, and the cauldrons were dumped along the front line. Searing hot iron splashed and flowed like molten rivers into the trees and across whole ranks of Dryads and forest folk, partially solidifying into a thick seeping sludge and sparking several small fires amongst the dry brush. Several Pixies dropped dead from the gas alone—dissolving into golden dust before blowing away.

Iron was poison to supernatural beings, especially to the creatures of the wood. The whole army retreated back behind the iron line at once, leaving Jamaal, Montoya, Doshin and me to fight alone as Henry and Chappy pulled our troops back.

The goblin army was advancing when a half-baked plan dinged inside my brain, somewhere between splitting the skull of a goblin and ripping the neck out of an obsidian witch. Skidding to a halt, I stood on top of the rapidly cooling metal and reached a bare hand to the sky. I could feel it there, the swirling energy waiting for me to call to it, and with a burst of light and the crack of the air, a bolt of pure electricity struck my outstretched hand and channeled into the iron. The resulting explosion of thunder, lightning, and quaking earth devastated the evil horde.

Oni melted, and Gemini burned. Goblins disintegrated and witches disappeared.

Burned, electrocuted bodies fell sizzling by the hundreds, shocking the advancing army into hysterical retreat.

"What the fuck was that, my man?" yelled Montoya. He and Jamaal hit the dirt for cover.

"You could have warned us first," said Jamaal as he wiped his face clean of all the dirt after taking a face-plant to avoid the blast.

Doshin reappeared from beneath a few dead enemies after using them as a shield.

Several packs of black wolves fled, howling, followed closely behind by Gemini and goblins. Before the great war machines could be turned, I leapt onto the nearest one, then onto the larger machine and climbed toward the maiden's throne.

"Relentless," said Chappy, as he and Henry caught up to them.

"My man's a machine," said Montoya. "He doesn't stop."

"It's her," said Doshin, pointing toward the warehouse behind them, where a red-headed woman was watching from a window above. "He would do anything to save her."

"He would. Let's hope that doesn't include self-sacrifice, or something really stupid," said Jamaal.

"C'mon," said Montoya, "there's more evil stuff to kill."

The maiden's head was bowed, and her grimy blonde hair clung to her face, obscuring her identity. The goblin guard launched into attack and I snatched them both by the neck, then forced hellfire into their black souls and burned the torment from their pained existence.

I advanced on the woman, unable to decide if she was their leader or just hitching a fancy ride. She didn't look like she belonged with them. With a bold move I made to gently lift her chin—when she looked right at me. She lashed at me but was caught by the chains shackled to her wrists and ankles—chains connected to the throne. The metal dug into the sore wounds beneath the shackles while she bit at me like she was possessed. At first the blonde hair and blue eyes threw me, like a stranger, but I recognized her.

"Lilly," I said. She was the other woman—the alter-ego fighting for supremacy inside Jacinda's mind—the other face that appeared after rearranging Jaycie's own. There was a clue here to the nature of this game, but I had no context. Why was Lilly here?

"Get away from me!" she screamed. She spoke in a language I could hardly understand through the heavy accent. "Go to hell where you belong! Go to hell where you belong!"

"Thanks," I said with a heavy dose of snark. "I'd rather not."

I had no sooner finished speaking when a goblin wrangled me around the ankle. In the brief moment I spent examining Lilly for clues, goblins had begun scaling the sides of the war machine. They came in overwhelming numbers, suggesting Lilly was more important than their own lives.

I kicked at the goblin's grasp, then planted a boot to its nose, smashing it like a ripe pimple as the machine nearly toppled through the turn. They were careless in their retreat, putting the machine on two wheels as they went.

The second war machine broke apart like a pile of dominos as Jamaal slammed into its side, gleefully throwing his weight around.

"I'd love to stay and chat," I said to Lilly, "but I have to go see about a girl." Then I leapt over a wave of goblins and landed inside the shady realm of the forest. As soon as I breached its hedge, a wall of brier rose from the ground forming a thick defense, sealing them off.

From the moment I landed, there were eyes on me. As I moved casually through the forest, none of them dared to speak. Were they scared? Respectful? I couldn't tell which. The last time I was there, they'd tried to attack me and sent me on a quest to unbury the key. After a quick probe of my chest, I could feel the hard metal key beneath my shirt and continued on, hoping that would be enough to buy my safe passage.

When I reached the warehouse, my eyes fell upon a group of lined

Satyrs: armored half-man half-horse creatures with spears and shields. They were the last line of defense against the impending evil, should it breach the forest guard. They stared blankly toward the retreating enemy as I passed them, like the Queen's Guard outside Buckingham Palace.

I met up with Henry and Chappy near the sliding warehouse door as the others arrived, fresh from battle.

"That was awesome!" yelled Jamaal.

"We make a great team, my man," said Montoya, shaking Jamaal's hand. "And you, my man, are wicked with a sword."

Doshin smiled and bowed.

"I have to admit," said Chappy, "I felt more alive than I had when I was only twenty. Ah, to be young again."

"It was indeed exhilarating," said Henry. "If this is a dream, let it never end." It was a turn of phrase, but it stung. Henry didn't mean it, and I still had somewhere to be.

"Where are you going, my man?" asked Montoya.

"To see a girl," I replied.

"Want us to come with?" asked Jamaal, but I had already walked over to the barn door.

"Let him go. He needs to do this part alone," said Chappy.

When I slid aside the barn door to the warehouse, I knew exactly where to go.

Through the warehouse and up the stairs, toward the devil door, marching—when something caught my attention. A scent? Maybe a taste? Or was it the sound, like scratching? Down the adjacent hall was something that did not feel right. A strange pressure tightened around me, like a constrictor squeezing my torso and throat. I followed it, curious to see where it led, cautious of the traps that were loaded into every twist and turn of the old building. It felt like I was being called, or perhaps I was being lured? Like this dream world of Jaycie's was subconsciously attempting to summon me toward a different destination.

Since Jaycie had reappeared, the dream world of hers felt open-ended—unlike my previous visits and the repetitive nature of their torment, like a macabre amusement park ride that never strayed from the tracks.

There were clues here, answers that could help solve riddles—What was this place? What was Jaycie really? Who and what was I, and who was the Two-Eyed Man, Malus? I was on the verge of an important discovery.

At the end of the hall, I rounded the corner and found a single door—the mirrored version of the Devil Door along a narrow passage—the plain wooden door seethed as if it had its own pulse, slowly straining the integrity of the wood, then shrinking like an exhale and starting all over again. The space beneath the door was lit, like a bright light beyond, and there was movement inside—a shadow pacing back and forth.

The door itself was ordinary, but it did feature something that sent eerie shades of tingles through my cheeks and shoulders. Carved, as if by knife, was the word "FORGOTTEN" on a broad horizontal plank.

"Jaycie?" I called out and reached for the knob.

The door opened softly without my touch. There was not a squeak of the scarcely used hinge, as it slid open wide to reveal an empty room. The room was windowless, bare, dark—the light blotted out the moment the door began to open—yet my senses betrayed me. The room felt full, as if stuffed to the brim with vacancy. The walls were unpainted, showing the wooden planks in their natural state, and a bed with an old, scuffed frame sat in a corner. The only thing of note within the entire room was lying on the bare mattress—I saw the black-marbled cover to one of Jaycie's treasured notebooks.

I stepped inside the room and sat down on the bed, then picked up the rogue notebook. It was exactly like all the others, the ones that were filled from beginning to end with all the things she had written and sketched—ideas jotted out across every inch of space in ink, pencil, and pastel of all colors. Every cover of every notebook that filled Jaycie's shelves was always marked with dates—when she started, and when she finished filling its pages. This one, however, repeated only the word from the door. "FORGOTTEN," it said in big, bold red marker.

Why was one of her precious notebooks here, inside this world she had created?

Holding the notebook in my hands, I paused, debating whether or not to open it. I felt that guilt all over again, like I was intruding on her privacy, but decided to peek inside anyway.

There was a short letter to herself on the first page, written in her own handwriting.

"Dearest Jacinda Moira O'Neill,

This is a record of forgotten things, and some things better left forgotten. You will find within these pages no answers, only answers left to find. I kept these memories here for you, a purge of once-kept memories. Leave them here or take them with, but do not take what is better left.

Fair warning,

Jacinda Moira O'Neill"

The words were confusing, more like a riddle than an explanation for the notebook and why it was left in this empty, *forgotten* room. Curiosity got the better of me, and so I proceeded to flip the page, but found a mishmash of gibberish and symbols on the next. I flipped to another, and another, but saw only the same confusing hodge-podge of letters and numbers which held no coherent meaning to me. Backwards or forwards, it was random, except for one disturbing image I came across—like a child's drawing of dark soldiers in white masks with deranged smiley faces drawn in red—and even curiouser, a child's drawing of a group of men protecting a little red-headed girl from the masked soldiers—

—and the men looked a lot like me and my brain-trust.

What was this room?

Time was ticking, and I felt a nagging sensation that I was needed elsewhere. Like I was forgetting something important by wasting time inside this room. Snapping the notebook shut, I left it behind on the bed where I found it. I had left through the FORGOTTEN door, closing it gently behind me, when I caught a whiff of strawberry and lavender. Her scent was the only warning I had before she began to speak.

"A lot has changed since you were here last," she said. She was no longer helplessly waiting inside the back room but wandering through the building. I felt like I had been caught, and looked back at the FORGOTTEN door, but it was gone. Vanished, as if it was never even there to begin with.

"It's only been a day," I explained. Even now, it felt odd seeing her, like it was a blessing—something that shouldn't be taken for granted. She was wearing the same green dress with yellow embroidered flowers she always wore in the dream—the same dress she wore when I'd found her in the cemetery.

Nothing was a coincidence.

"Time here is different," she stated, then looked on me as if she hadn't seen me in several years. "I missed you." Tears welled up in her eyes and she wavered slightly on her feet, overwhelmed by her emotions.

I grabbed hold of her and said, "It's okay, I'm here now."

There was something different about this version of Jacinda. She seemed less like herself, and more dreamlike—almost as if this was a representation of her—a figurehead that could summon and command the fantastic creatures to defend her. She slunk into my arms and grasped onto my jacket, holding me as tightly against her body as possible. The world she had created felt as real as any other.

I felt at home there in her arms. I almost wished to stay within the dream forever, to never leave her again, as I felt the guilt clawing away at me. I'd left her with the devil, and getting her back was the only thing that could forgive that sin.

"Where have you been?" she asked, burying her face into my neck.

"I had to find my *heart*, didn't I?" I said and removed the key from beneath my shirt.

"You found it." She lifted her head and smiled. "I knew you would."

"I did. Right where I left it," I added, but the return smile I gave her quickly faded, and she knew something was wrong.

"Why do I feel like something bad happened?" she asked. She had this special voice—a caring sweet voice when she needed to pry hidden truths out of me. Such a simple ploy, but she could get me to confess to the stupidest of things. Like my hatred for John Travolta, or eating all the red Skittles.

"Because something bad did happen," I said, turning away.

"Tell me," she demanded as she reached out and took my hand in hers.

"When I found the key, you were there," I said, as if she knew nothing from her counterpart in the real world. "I hadn't seen you in years, and we spent the day together."

"That doesn't sound so bad to me," she said with a grin, as if she'd read between the lines and knew all the things we did. She always put my frustrations at ease by putting my feelings into immediate perspective.

"Malus took you from me. I've been running ever since. Trying to keep him from getting this," I said, gesturing to the key. I sighed as I placed it back underneath my shirt and felt another surge of guilt.

"You made the right decision," she said.

"Did I?" I was frustrated and shook angrily, like I couldn't hold the burden inside me without it bursting. "I should have stayed and fought for you. I should have done something. Anything. Whatever I could to protect you."

"No," she stopped me, making sure I was listening to her. She demanded my full attention. "What you did was the right decision. What you're doing is protecting me!"

"How?" I asked. If I had any reason to disbelieve that this Jacinda was entirely her, she shattered all those doubts. As time progressed, she transformed from a dream phantom into this warm, loving person—

—it was as if her reappearance in my life had made her strong, forcing the cold winter forest into a blooming summer. Was Jacinda coming back to life affecting this place?

"If Malus, the man with two eyes, gets his hands on that key, the entire reason for all this would be over. You would never have another chance to save me. He would slip away somewhere unreachable until my will lost its battle here. Then I'd be his. All his," she said, meeting my passion with her own. "That's what this is. This is my subconsciousness' last refuge to stay alive. This is my willpower fighting a war against a spell that's slowly consuming who I am and replacing it with someone else. By running, you learned from your mistakes!"

"What do you mean?" What mistakes had I made?

"This isn't the first time you've been here to rescue me," she said, choking on her words. "There was another you, one who tried to do the right things but ended up making all the wrong choices. He went to hell and back to make it right. He bested the Fates and stole his own Thread of Destiny from their loom, all to confront Malus one last time. And when that failed, he did the only thing he could to keep hope alive. He broke all the rules and bent his own Destiny. He came to you. He died to warn you. He did it to set you on the path to make better decisions than he did. A smart man knows how to run and fight for another day. His sacrifice was for us!"

"What decision did he make?" I knew she was referring to my Echo. "How can I make better decisions when I don't know how he failed?"

Jacinda took a long, lingering look at me. "His reality unfolded very different from yours. Like you, he was born of loss. However, he was caught in the darkness before he was ready. A remnant of another time. Reality is already different. If you are looking for a specific decision that created a chain of events that failed, there was none, but that Tony lost himself in his journey to find me. What good is saving me if you cannot save yourself?

"The other you became obsessed with accumulating power and eventually found his way onto a dark path. He became a shadow of himself, lost in the occult and black magic. That Tony lost his way and his humanity in the process. He sought revenge for my death, only I was still alive, a secret even I didn't know."

"That's exactly what I'm afraid of," I said. "How can I expect to succeed if I've already failed?" There was anger and contempt in my voice, not for her, but for the damned situation we were cursed with. "I'm afraid I'm turning into a monster." It was the first time I had admitted the depth of what I was feeling. My transformation from a depressed husk into a powerful entity on the verge of a mental breakdown, housing thousands of individual minds, pains and passions—and the loss of people I loved—Marshall, Amanda, Anne—was taking its toll on me. The pain and the torment inside me was ripped wide open, and the power of the flames was pushing me closer to the edge.

"No, not you. Tony, you could never be a monster," she said sweetly, placing her hand on my cheek. "There's too much love in you. Too much heart. On your darkest days, lost in jealousy, you were never less than a prince. You're the best man I've ever met." She paused and took a deep breath. "You won't fail. You may be the same man, but you're different than him. The power inside you is unlike anything he ever had. You're stronger, and you have something more to live for."

"What's that?" I asked with tears running down my face. Jacinda began to cry too at the sight of them, our empathy for each other tying us even tighter together.

"Because you know I'm alive."

I couldn't speak. There were no words to express what I felt. How could I be so self-defeating when the love of my life was in the clutches of my enemy? She was sacrificing herself, fighting a war inside her own subconscious just to stay alive—for me.

"Who are your friends?" she asked, changing the subject.

I stared at her for a moment before I realized what she had asked. "They are pieces of me. Different versions of my spirit. We were reunited when the Thirteen killed them all."

"I don't know what any of that means," she said with a laugh.

"It sounds bat-shit crazy, huh?"

"Totally guano, but no more crazy than being inside this place."

"Yeah, crazy."

There was silence between us as she caressed my hand with her thumb, when I remembered where I was—where I really was. I had to wake up. I had to get back to Maynard.

"Jace, you need to wake up," I said, and she looked at me like she didn't understand. "You need to wake up and you need to escape. You need to run and get away from Malus."

"How?" she cried.

"I don't know. Find a way. Find a way back to me," I said.

"Can't you stay?"

"No, I'm in trouble." I stepped away. Being close to her was like falling into a trap—a pleasant embrace that numbed my pain. But I needed it. I needed that pain. That pain was going to get us through this—it was going to keep me going until I had her back in my arms again. "I have to get out of here."

"Why?"

"Because if I don't, it's over. I'm surrounded, Jace. Maynard and I are going to die, and Malus will get the key if I don't wake up."

"Go. Go! You stay alive, and you keep that key safe," she said. Her green eyes blazed. "Tomorrow's not a promise."

"Love you, always," I said, then kissed her. I held her close, the two of us together in the dark void of her dreamscape, trying to wake up to the real world. "Wake up. Wake up, Jaycie. Wake up."

THE ENTICING
OF DAGON

883 A.D.

There was an island in the Gulf of Aden, near the Adriatic Sea, that no longer exists. It was not a large island, nor was it lush with life. It was small, with only one significant structure upon its rocky, desolate surface—a temple built to honor the fish god, Dagon.

The temple had four outer walls that eventually intersected into a spire, at the top of which was the symbol of Dagon. Cast out of metal, it had rusted in the salty surf. The symbol was an eye created by two intersecting curves, surrounding a full circle. The structure resembled a church, and if one did not recognize the symbol before entering, they would never forget it once leaving.

Inside the temple was a room with a rotten floor of decaying filth, and flies as thick as fog obscured the horrible sights beyond. There was an altar at the back, built of coral, bone and brine, with an apparatus that stood beside a hole in the floor that opened to the sea below. The apparatus was built with shackles that spread apart arms and legs. It was used for sacrifice and other infernal rituals that would rot a man's heart if witnessed.

Malus's heartbeat was vital and strong, and he had participated in many atrocities, all of which would see him burned for eternity in the fires of perdition should he be cast into the pit. His heart was tempered in madness and cast no warmth, for it had seen all manner of disturbed, depraved, and diabolical behavior. However, when he stepped through the door of that temple and saw the fish god in the throes of passion, and *feeding*, Malus resisted the breadth of his own revulsion for the betterment of his plan.

"Mighty Dagon," said Malus, tugging the fish god's attention away from his frenzy.

"Who are you?" asked the god. He was a massive creature, with skin like a shark—smooth to the eye but rough to the touch—and eight barbed tentacles where his legs should have been. His jaw was square and solid like stone, and his eyes were empty black pools, like that of a gill breather. "Why have you interrupted me?" His voice was not angry, nor was it bored. It was strong and assertive, unafraid and plotting.

"I am a friend."

"A lie."

"A new friendship then. One of respect," Malus offered.

"I do not respect you, stranger. You entered my temple. Tell me, do you have a temple built to honor you?"

"No," answered Malus.

Dagon smiled and slithered his way closer to Malus. The flies parted for him, avoiding his touch.

"What do you want? Speak quickly."

"When the world was young, you were one of the many who fought for control, to be amongst the first gods," said Malus. His statement appeared to rankle Dagon—the god's tentacles curled and flapped in response. "Your enemy, the one god who took your rightful place as a Titan, is my prisoner. Join me, help me achieve my ends, and I will gladly give you Chronos."

"Lust is sweet," said Dagon, peering over his slimy shoulder toward his helpless victim. "Revenge is sweeter."

"Sign my contract, and you will have it."

XIX

extraordinary girl

JACINDA
December 31st, 2000
Then.

I have to admit, Jace, this was becoming tough to watch.

Just because the hauntings stopped, and you didn't remember them, didn't mean you were any less haunted. The gaps in your memory remained, and you only wanted to survive the psycho boyfriend you couldn't decide to love or hate. The man of your dreams became your nightmare, yet you still loved him. You believed you deserved him. You believed you weren't worthy of something more—something better.

You only saw me twice over the course of the next five months—the first time was the day after the Labor Day Fair, when you watched from across the street of the Grace Falls Diner as I patiently waited for you. You cried all day—not just for standing me up and breaking my heart— but because you were hurting too.

The second time you saw me was from across the campus quad,

just before the holiday break. I was with Tori Martin, and it upset you so much that you immediately began to despise me. Tori represented a time when you felt most alone in the world, and it repulsed you to see me with someone you disliked so much. That repulsion only furthered the thought that you cared more than you should for me, and in turn that made you feel guilty, in the worst masochistic feedback loop ever constructed within the confines of your struggling psyche.

The day you saw us together, laughing, you died a little inside. It was the day hope took its final bow before retiring, and you fell back into your darkness. Rick was there to provide you every escape from reality that you desired. You shot poison into your veins when Anne wasn't around and spent time at Rick's place escaping life.

My presence brought peace. Without me, you were adrift.

You sleepwalked through Christmas, and when New Year's Eve rolled around, Rick informed you he was throwing a party. He said it was something he and the "boys cooked up" but never informed you.

"Where is it?" you asked with the kind of narrow-eyed glare that showed both inquisition and surprise. Rick was a lot of things, but he was rarely romantic, and the mystery roused your interest for the first time in months.

Maybe you could look past the fear, the ever-present threat from the night of the fair, and just be a normal couple again. That's what you wanted, wasn't it? To be with Rick? To be a normal couple again?

Maybe you were starting to feel something for the first time since the Ferris wheel, the first time since that encounter with the man who confused and excited you. An encounter with someone who genuinely liked you, and challenged you, and brought out the best in you. But that was gone now, right? After all, you'd found your Star-Crossed Lover, right, Jace?

Or maybe you needed another hit—needed to get high just enough to feel numb.

"It's a secret," said Rick while flipping back and forth between MTV's *Road Rules* and a rerun of *Baywatch*. He was wearing the same sweatpants for the third day in a row, and you were suddenly aware of the smell in his apartment—like a crack pipe mixed with moldy pizza.

You had been there for two days and were just now noticing how messy his place was and how much that stench bothered you.

"Why is it a secret?" you asked.

Rick smiled. It was that smile I hated most.

"Because I want to surprise you," he lied.

"What should I wear?" you asked—still dangling from his hook.

"Something nice," he said as his eyes flitted back and forth between you and Pamela Anderson running on the TV. "Something sexy."

The concept of a secret location got your imagination humming. Rick had means beyond anyone you had ever known. You imagined a big party boat in the city, or escaping town and jet-setting off to New York, Philadelphia, or Chicago for a night to remember. After all, Rick had taken half the baseball team to Vegas—even though you were too busy with midterms.

You even dressed for the occasion—a burgundy dress with a matching shade of lipstick and earrings. You spent more than an hour on your hair. You joked that it was the first time you had ever been fancy enough to call what you were wearing an *ensemble*, giggling to yourself at the thought.

Rick loaded you into his Mustang, and you never even gave a thought that you might be overdressed—even considering what he was wearing. A grimy ball-cap, jeans, and a sports coat that looked old and worn. They were "distressed" and bought off the rack for double the cost of your dress.

You grabbed a snack, expecting a long drive, but when you arrived at the old Jansen Family Mill up by the falls, about a five-minute ride from your old house on Cross Road, the disappointment was hard to conceal.

"What are we doing here?" you asked as Rick pulled up to the old warehouse. You could hear the rumbling of the falls nearby. There were already more than thirty cars parked at the mill, and the lights inside were strobing.

"This is the party," said Rick.

"I thought we were doing something special?"

"We are," said Rick. He noted your disappointment and kissed your forehead to placate you. He took your hands in his. "This is a big night."

"What do you mean?"

"You're always talking about commitment and how I need to open up to you," he began. It was true; you always felt like Rick was hiding something. You were curious, and at times it bothered you, but you had been so miserable for so long that pondering the potential infidelities of your boyfriend had long since evaded your mind. "This place has been the party house since high school. The boys and I from the team come here to hang out every week. And we decided to throw a big party."

"Oh," you said. It seemed so obvious that he didn't need to explain it any further. There were rumors about the party house in high school, but you'd never been considered cool enough to attend. Now, here you were with the coolest guy in high school, about to party up the New Year in a dump—except you were in college, and you didn't know how to feel about this revelation.

The warehouse and mill had been the site of a gruesome series of murders back in the 80s. That local mythology made it an attractive place for a bunch of hard-partying college students. Besides, nobody would bother them up there. It was private property. Jansen family only.

Once inside, you began to drown your dismay in as much alcohol as you could consume, as quickly as you could consume it. The music was loud, there were three times as many people as there were cars outside, and more people were showing up every minute. The mill was dirty and cold, but there was a dance floor, space heaters, a DJ, and strobe lights. There was a whole bar, several kegs, and even food—and nobody seemed to care that they were in a rust bucket awaiting next week's tetanus shot.

As the minutes ticked and the party roared into the night, strangers passed you drinks, which you quickly consumed on your destination to obliteration. You didn't want to feel that night, and unfortunately, you got your wish.

The air was heavy with menace. Even from this side of the Veil I could feel it, like this was an important moment in time. You could feel it too, Jace, couldn't you? Like a bad omen nipping at your heels all day?

When you began to feel woozy, it came on all at once like a swarm of ants crawling from your stomach outward into every limb and digit. Then you felt weightless, as if you were falling for an eternity, when someone caught and carried you away.

You remembered ascending a series of metal stairs on someone's shoulders—people laughed, and you were too dizzy to understand why—and you remembered an unending hallway that stretched into infinity. Then you remembered the face, the red demon—it smiled hideously, and you wanted to scream but for some reason you couldn't move—and the demon door threatened to devour you. When the door yawned open, the world went red, and you fell helplessly into that terrible warm void.

When the door closed behind you, something happened to me. I'm not proud of it, Jace. Seeing that door—the real Devil Door—not the dream version—did something to me. I was suddenly back there watching you pull that trigger on the other side, and I froze. This door, that gun, that moment—it's what I feared most. I'd faced monsters—I'd faced true darkness, but this? This was my failure, my darkness, my trigger. I froze and I cried, and I was caught in that moment all over again. Forever stuck at that fixed point in time watching you taking your own life—your stranger-eyes pushing me away, and a gun to your head—I was petrified—terrified of what laid beyond that door. I fell to pieces. I crumbled, shaking and sweating, a full panic attack that crippled me.

Fuck time.

Fuck the rules.

Fuck paradoxes.

Fuck me and my fucking failure to keep you safe!

I am a fucking failure!

Nobody deserves what happened to you.

Nobody.

Why wasn't I strong enough for you? If I had been, I would have stopped it. I would have destroyed myself to prevent it. Why couldn't it have been me?

Why couldn't it have been me?

Your dress was ripped. You could feel the slit along the side riding extra high, all the way up to your ribs, and a wet sensation between your legs. As consciousness returned, slowly, as if those warm ants were gently receding, leaving behind pins and needles across your body, you became aware of others nearby.

You wiped at something sticky across your face and tried to open your eyes, but everything hurt. Your brain, slow to register, began to clarify the voices around you into words and phrases.

"Want another go? She'll be out for a while," said someone with a laugh.

I was grieving. I was too appalled by what I found when I finally got past my own bullshit trauma that I was rendered useless to you. I messed up, and I am so sorry, Jace. I was too late to stop it. Too destroyed by the state I found you in to step out of my fucking hiding place and slaughter them all.

I cried. I cried so hard I thought you might hear me.

A sharp ache sprung at the base of your skull. It wasn't an injury; it was a warning. It wasn't anything supernatural—it was a human warning of violation.

"Nah, bro," said another, as the sound of a belt being fastened clinked and echoed. "I'm out. Someone let Rick know his broad is fine as hell."

The fluffy cloud you were lying on became coarse and springy, like an old couch, and the room stank of stale beer, vomit, and sex. The haze in your head had not lifted, and your thoughts were still jumbled, but the sadness and the embarrassment were already there. As your motor functions returned, you could hear soft moans and grunts from the other side of the room. What was happening around you? Where were you?

You had to get help. You had to tell Rick. You had to tell him and let him handle the situation. He had to do something about this. You could hear the thumping bass and knew you were somewhere inside the warehouse. Rick wasn't that far away, and you could get yourself ready and make a run for it. They were athletes, but so were you. You could outrun them.

"Oh, I know it," said Rick. Hands clapped together, like a high-five, and there was more laughter. Rick was there, but he wasn't doing anything?

Rick was there.

Rick was there!

"She's a great bang. Only reason I keep her around."

He was complicit.

Rage rose up between your sadness and embarrassment.

I wanted to know why our lives went down the path it did, and as much as I had learned, it was this moment that carried the most significance. Now I knew why you ended your life here.

Some people desire control over others. Others seek only to control themselves. To Rick, control was everything. He had to control every aspect, every notion of his life and those within it. His entire being was predicated on influence and subverting his will onto others. It was an obsession. You thought he was merely fighting with his own demons, but there was a darkness inside him that you never noticed until your eye opened just a crack and focused on the man who was your boyfriend, standing with his buddies in various stages of undress.

What you saw was evil. A demon just below the skin. A terrible monster that was going to ruin you—and actually, had just succeeded. It was true darkness, true evil, and it cast its shadow across the wall. Maybe it was a dog, a wolf, or a jackal, whatever the shape it did not matter. It was evil. Its influence infected Rick right down to his rotten soul, and you had let it go on for much too long.

The secret door inside your mind burst open, and every horror and wicked thing you had ever witnessed came stampeding out of you like a horde of angry demons.

And then you were standing.

The three men in front of you looked as if they were going to laugh. They didn't feel shame. They didn't feel sorrow or guilt. They looked at you like you were a joke. You were the punchline of their misdeeds, and it took some kind of awful entitlement to look at a woman who was just raped and laugh—which was exactly what they did.

There were seven of them in the room, along with two other unconscious women. You were in some kind of clubhouse, with Red Devil pennants on the wall. Old kegs, beer bottles, and pizza boxes sat on top of a card table. This was a place where rotten men went to be themselves. It was their own room of horrors, but not one they kept inside their minds, locking away their demons like you. This place was in the real world, and they had brought you unwillingly into their nest of misconduct and malefaction.

The seven of them looked at you and laughed.

They looked at you and laughed, Jace.

I was too shocked, and too destroyed to move, but you weren't.

You didn't look angry. You looked bewildered. Your dress was torn and stained with body fluids. Your hair was a tangled mess, and your eye makeup had already smeared across your face. But your eyes told the story—they were wide, and your irises swirled around your pupils like the fury of a hurricane.

"Have a good nap?" joked one of the guys.

Rick laughed too but cut it short. Maybe he could sense your rage, or maybe he recognized it just before the snap.

"I'm sorry," you said. A tiny fissure, nothing more than a stress fracture, opened inside you. A fault along your armor of sanity.

"You should be sorry," said the other guy. "I wasn't done with you." He took a step toward you, and you instinctively took a step back. Noticing the look on his face, you knew he meant you trouble. You knew that look all too well.

Rick stepped forward and moved his buddy aside. "This is just a misunderstanding," said Rick. "Nothing bad happened."

"I'm sorry," you said again.

"You should be sorry," said Rick, sensing an opportunity to subvert his control over you. His voice was cold and precise. "After all I've done. After all I've given you, you'd think you'd be a bit more appreciative. I gave you happy pills, skag, all for free. I treated you to fancy dinners, got you gigs in Mercy Point. I have given you everything and more. Other women have thrown themselves at my feet for just a touch of what I have given you. So, ask yourself, what do I deserve in return for all my kindness?"

His hand snatched a fist full of your hair and yanked, forcing your neck into an excruciating angle. The pain sent spasms to all your limbs and brought instant tears to your eyes. Your hair was being ripped from your scalp, and Rick's physical strength was too much for you to fight back.

You felt claustrophobic, like a black hole, as if the world was collapsing around you. Rick threw you back into the couch. You put your hands up, bracing yourself against the fall, but the impact forced your head into the table beside it. Warm sticky blood ran down your forehead for the third time in your life and dripped from brow to cheek. He grabbed you by the hair and whipped you to the ground, and your feet slammed against the coffee table on the way down, splintering one of the legs. Your head took another blow, one so violent your vision dimmed like a mid-summer's brown-out.

"Hey, come on now, Rick," said one of the guys. "We don't need to beat on her." It was as if the rape wasn't as awful as the violence. As if being unconscious during an assault made it all just fine. Was their morality so askew? Did they think this was okay?

The room spun blurry, motion from stillness, tilting and shifting, dizzy equilibrium. Rick leaned over and slapped you across the face, snapping clarity from your daze. Your cheek swelled, numbed and puffy and red. Your skin felt like it had been ripped raw from your face, burning and stinging in equal severity, just as the mood changed within the room. A shift in pressure, like an ocean dive; the air felt heavy and thick and bitterly electric.

A thousand-mile stare settled into your eyes. It was like you weren't even there. When your mind focused, you were staring at yourself in an old cheval mirror. You didn't see the torn dress or the humiliation. You saw self-hate. Rick interpreted your lack of fight as a reason to continue, like you had given up. His smile darkened, and with his left-hand corralling both your arms at the wrists, you merely said "Stop," devoid of emotion.

The cheval mirror cracked liked thunder.

The word froze on the air, icy and sharp. Rick's arm went dead, and he could no longer move it any closer to you. Soon the dead petrifying feeling had moved throughout his whole body. Rick couldn't even blink.

"I'm sorry," you said once again, and Rick stared at you with bewilderment. "I'm sorry for what I am going to do to all of you."

The crack inside you split wide open, a gaping hole in your soul. With nothing more than a thought, you willed Rick into the air and over the couch. He landed on top of an old keg and tumbled into a few of his pals by one of the other unconscious girls. By the time Rick found the strength to stand, you were on your feet, simply staring off into nothing. Your eyes were wide and wild, and your mouth was slightly gaped open, hyperventilating.

"How did you do that" he asked, more baffled than frightened. His hand was bloody and his shirt was torn. Woozy from the impact, he stumbled a bit and wasn't sure what to do next. Should he cut his losses and leave, or make you pay for ruining his shirt? To a man like Rick, the shirt was worth more than some slut who didn't appreciate him. He could find five girls in the next half hour who would do anything to pleasure him, but he wanted to hurt you for hurting him.

The twisted mind of a sociopath was something to ponder.

You had been pushed too far. You snapped. Would a simple act of vengeance be enough? Every sorrow and every painful event bled from your soul. Every haunting, every fear, everything that ever kept you down. You needed to make the world bleed for hurting you, and it started right now.

"If you want me, come and take me," you said to the two who had joked over your unconscious body. Your voice was trancelike; your mind instinctively mapped out what would happen, weighing and measuring every move, a one-sided game of chess.

"What kind of crazy is this?" said one of them. He was the more aggressive of the two.

"We're just having a little fun," said the other, rationalizing his involvement like his fun was greater than your livelihood.

As you approached, the first reached out as if to stop your advance. His arm snapped in three places, in three opposite directions, and he screamed in pain.

Rick retrieved something from beneath a loose floorboard, then charged back into view. There was fury in his movements as he paced toward you. He was going to make you suffer. He was going to make you scream. With each step, he thought about what he was going to tell the cops when they came for him. How it was self-defense. How you had cut him. They were going to believe him, even if he had to bribe them. Yes, he was going to make you scream. It was written all over his face as he lifted the gun to your head.

Only it was Rick's friends doing all the screaming.

With each vengeful step Rick took, you made the walls behind him ignite, like a match to cardboard. When he noticed the fire, he ran. The walls burst into flames, then three of the rapists ignited too—but not before you snapped each of their bones from largest to smallest. Their screams were drowned by the crackling flames—but they did not die. No, you kept them alive until the fire hit bone.

The unconscious girls were gone. They weren't there, as if they had been transported away safely. One of the rapists looked for them, maybe his girlfriend, and when he couldn't find her, he turned back and became engulfed in flames.

The whole mill was burning, forcing Rick to jump from a window, down into the tall weeds below, where you were waiting for him under the stars.

"Are you doing this?" he asked, his breath escaping in a panic.

"After all I've done. After all I've given you, you'd think you'd be a bit more appreciative," you said, mocking Rick with his own words.

Then he lifted his gun and shot you. He shot you all nine times, emptied the clip, but not a single bullet reached your skin. Each and every bullet went scurrying around you as if the metal were afraid to touch you.

"What are you?" he asked, trembling. His knees were failing him. He shrank before you, almost kneeling as you loomed over him.

"A monster," you replied. Somewhere inside, you believed it. But now, you wouldn't deny yourself those inhuman urges.

"Get away from me!" he yelled, waving his hands in front of him and sprinting through the tall weeds, tripping over something in the grass. There were screams, and a flood of people were exiting the mill, racing for their cars. There were fender benders and dented car doors as the night sky blossomed with orange and red light. The fire grew, its tendrils snaking high into the night sky.

With one last sweaty look back, Rick turned and ran, while you calmly reached out your hand and pulled the entire building apart. All the walls and the roof remained intact, pulled apart like an exploded diagram, then tossed aside into a fiery heap. Rick was lost in the fray, distracted by the screams, spinning like a rat inside a maze. With every stride, something smashed at his heels, nipping him with sprayed debris. Cars were thrown at him, fiery timbers, and then even trees, levitated and tossed around like Matchbox cars. Random people were caught in the crossfire, maimed and crushed and torn apart in your deadly cat-and-mouse game, all while you slowly stalked Rick like a serial killer, causing absolute chaos.

Crows circled and cawed overhead. A split in the earth opened, and a deep chasm formed. Dozens of people cascaded to their doom, swallowed by your wrath. Rick slid to a halt and turned, attempting to escape another way, but found himself facing you, who had somehow appeared just behind him. The fear in his eyes mirrored the fear you felt when the demons terrorized you, but that was too little vindication to you. You took only an ounce of pleasure from his fear. It just wasn't enough. The world had pushed you too far, and you wanted it to suffer along with you.

I couldn't blame you, Jace. What you had experienced in your life was beyond anything anyone had ever dealt with. Emotional torture, knowing you were the cause of so much pain, and so much pain being inflicted on you by people you should have been able to trust. Every day you struggled. Every day you lived in fear—the unknown of what you were and the evil that stalked you was more than a sane mind could bear to lock away.

A splash of molten rock sprayed into the air behind Rick, splattering the ground with a hiss. The earth crumbled as a massive earthquake ripped through the countryside. Ocean water filled the streets of cities hundreds of miles away, while a tsunami formed a few miles off the coast. The entire country was sinking into the ocean. Gas lines exploded, volcanic ash erupted, and glass shattered from high-rises. Small towns were swallowed by the earth, and skyscrapers toppled to the ground, entombing whole city blocks under heaps of glass and steel. Millions of people died in seconds, wiped out in the spreading carnage, while two people stood at its epicenter, in the calm eye of the storm.

"What the fuck are you!?" Rick spat defiantly.

"I am the cataclysm. I am destruction," you said. The words and the voice sounded foreign to you, like someone else's words spoken from your own mouth.

Rick screamed as an intense pain built up inside and out.

It is said that the human body is comprised of ninety-nine percent empty space. A factoid of which you were entirely aware, and you had always wondered if it was true. It started in Rick's hands—each finger breaking, compacting, like an empty tube of toothpaste being rolled up from the edges. Next, the soft external parts—the eyes, ears, nose, and genitals—crushed and compacted into only a small fraction of their overall space. Next came the tongue, the windpipe, the chest, the lungs, and stomach—all condensed and crammed. This was followed by every remaining bone being pulverized and sucked up into the body, where the mound of human DNA was then folded in half—then in half again, and again, and again, and again—until it was finally one one-hundredths of its overall mass.

Rick was then pulled apart, atom by atom, right in front of you, dissipating into a mist of particles that floated away on the building wind. His death was unlike any other. It was the most painful death for anyone who ever lived, his pain lasting to the very second his body disintegrated into its most basic fundamental parts.

When Rick was pulled apart, I expected you to be done with it—to put things back. To put everything back as if it never happened. I expected you to calm and let it go, to set it aside like a bad dream.

Instead, more destruction came.

You were spinning out of control, and the world was going to suffer because of it.

The Earth was dying, and you were its destroyer.

Shock waves rumbled across the other side of the planet, and three billion people died instantly. The Earth spun off its axis, and its magnetic poles spun with it. It was doomsday. The planet as I knew it was coming apart, just as you were.

Angels circled through the air overhead like vultures scavenging for rotted meat, but they did nothing but watch, like me.

Why was I watching, Jace? Why was I letting you destroy it all? Was this what was supposed to happen? Could I ever make this right for failing you?

I was done watching, paradox be damned.

I appeared in front of you, out of the Veil and into reality, like an apparition as the sky ignited. Your eyes stared right through me, like I didn't exist. An impossible man standing in an impossible place. Like an unimportant stranger, an ant before a goddess. It had been years since I had stepped out of the Veil and into the real world. The air was toxic, and life was over, except for us. The destructive smells, tastes, and sounds invaded my senses. I had watched for so long, I had almost forgotten what it was like to speak, and to interact. Did I look at all like myself? Like who I used to be? Would you even recognize me?

"My love, you can't do this," I pleaded with you. The words left my throat like splintering wood. A thousand tiny daggers jabbing the soft fleshy lining.

"Why not? Who are you?" you asked, your eyes focusing on me for the first time.

"You know who I am," I said.

"You look like him. You talk like him. But you're someone else," you said.

Out of the stillness came a great rush of air. The wind blew in my face so fierce I thought it might take my skin with it, but the wind had no effect on you. Your hair remained perfectly still, as did your clothes, like the gale force was avoiding you. You were, by all accounts, an anomaly like me—but so much more.

"Look into my eyes," I said. "You'll know it's me."

It took only a moment, a moment that lasted an eternity, with a giant earth-crushing ocean wave closing in to swallow us up, when you stepped closer and peered into my eyes. I strained against the wind, standing on the edge of the volcanic abyss, and willed my eyes open against the tempest. Your coldness turned to recognition, but guilt and embarrassment filled the void where your rage had vacated. We had only moments before the end, so I told you the only thing I knew to say.

"Let go," I said.

"I can feel your pain," you responded, "and all you've gone through to be here."

"You are all that matters."

"How can you go on?"

"I go on, because of you," I said. "Let go."

"I can't. Everything in my life is so messed up," you cried.

"Jaycie, let go. Everything will be okay, I promise," I said, but I was lying. The evil would find you, and it would succeed in taking you from me. Things weren't going to be okay. I was going to lose you and any chance I had at making it right. For so long I had convinced myself that there was nothing I could do, that I was in way over my head. Just one against Thirteen, weak and powerless. How fucking selfish was I? I didn't belong here, and whatever it was I did to cause this mess—my crime—my real crime was the mess that ruined your life. There was a planet full of people involved. Innocent people. None of them more innocent and thrown into the horrors of life than you. I loved you with all that I was, and I was letting you down by wallowing away and watching, because that was the truth hidden behind the excuse. I wasn't just here to learn more about you—I was hiding from fate.

"How can you promise that?" you asked, wanting desperately to believe me.

"Because I won't ever abandon you." My words came out with such conviction it broke your will and closed the rift inside you. You began to cry, and I placed my hands on either side of your face, holding your attention on me. "I can't explain to you why things happen the way they do. I can't say the rest of your journey won't be hard, but you need to fight. You are a fighter. That brilliant, golden, Jaycie O'Neill heart is not only beautiful, but it fights! Fight it! Let go."

"How? How can I let go when I will always remember? The pain will always be there," you pleaded. So long as you remembered what had happened, the hauntings, and the terror of who you were and what was after you, the pain would never go away, and you could never move on.

"You start by trusting that there will be good," I said, but the end was still coming. "This is my fault. You were never meant to have this life. I have fought so hard and so long—I failed you."

"I don't understand," you cried.

We had only seconds. We were running out of time.

"Forget. Make yourself forget," I said, and you understood. I was buying us time. "Forget about the pain, the fear and the guilt. Forget about me. Forget! Make us all forget and start over."

I understood the implications of what I had just asked you to do. I was putting a Band-aid onto a larger problem. With a thought, you could put things back the way they were, except you could make everyone forget what you had done and what you were. You could even forget yourself, living your life without ever knowing, blissfully ignorant, and most importantly, safe. I was willing to sacrifice us, our relationship, for your future. I was giving you away for something better, Jace. You would move on from me, and you would find some kind of happiness away from the madness. If I had to watch over you from the Veil for the rest of your life, I would. A guardian angel, protecting you from harm. Anything for you.

"Okay," you said. The precious moments were down to their last few ticks as the Earth was nothing more than floating rock and empty space. "I'll forget," you said, then looked deeply into my familiar eyes. "Everything but you."

The call went into the 9-1-1 operator at 1:06 a.m. on New Year's Day.

"The Jansen Mill is on fire!" said the girl, screaming.

Cars slammed into each other, and several people were injured as they all rushed away from the scene. Rick was running for his life. The terror that drove him was immeasurable, even though he couldn't remember what it was.

He got into his car and slammed on the gas, leaving you behind. He nearly ran over his teammate as he pulled out at top speed—the guy bouncing off his hood—as he sped down the dirt road through the overgrown lot and out onto Cross Road. Rick never came to a stop. He took the turn at close to sixty miles per hour, then shifted his Mustang into its next gear and slammed his foot onto the gas.

His headlights flickered, and as he played with the switch, his eyes casually glancing up into the rearview, he saw two green eyes staring back—he never saw the car pull out in front of him and plowed right through Tori Martin, on her way to apologize to her sister and friends.

You woke up on the couch inside the mill. It smelled of mildew and funk. Your head pounded—a throbbing ache that paced to the rhythm of your heartbeat. You couldn't remember how you got there. You couldn't remember much from the night, except the need to get as far away from Rick Jansen as possible.

You made your way outside just in time to hitch a ride with a girl who was heading back to campus. Everyone was so upset and confused, but nobody seemed to know why.

"What happened?" you asked.

"The mill was on fire or something," she said as they drove down Cross Road. They were only a mile or two up the road when they saw the flashers. A series of cars, most of them from the party, were lined up in a queue, unable to pass.

When someone approached the car window, the driver rolled it down.

"Big accident up the road," the guy said. "We're going to have to turn around."

"Okay," said the driver as she rolled the window up and performed a three-point turn.

Even though you didn't find out till morning, you knew it was Rick. You just had a feeling. You could even picture his scream before he slammed into the other car.

You broke up with him the next day while he was still in the hospital for observation. He had a stiff neck, some whiplash, and a sore knee, but he deserved so much more—even though you couldn't remember why.

When you said you were done with him, Rick fought with you to stay—but you turned and walked away, knowing he could never follow. It was over once and for all.

As for me, I now knew what needed to be done.

It was all my fault, and it was time I owned up to ruining your life.

XX
psychopomp

TONY
December 23rd, 2013
Now.

"Wake up, Jaycie! Wake up!"

I was pulled away and shoved into the dark, alone—screaming one last desperate plea to Jaycie to follow me back into the real world.

The dream didn't fade. There was no wash to black. It was a rude yank. Torn away without a chance to say a proper goodbye—expelled from the deepest parts of my subconscious. It was so jarring that I only realized my eyes were closed when I clenched them after my jaw popped—the fractured bones shifting back into place.

My jaw was healing—three broken sections of bone and two teeth knocked out of place. Then came the sudden recollection of being clobbered—nay, sucker-punched—by the Invisible Man.

Reality arrived a moment later with a splitting, brain-freeze headache—like the kind you get after gobbling down ice cream too fast. Daggers jabbed behind my eyes, and I felt the urge to rub them.

"Wake up," said Maynard.

My eyes snapped open, and the urgency of the situation loaded like a sleeping hard drive spinning back to life.

The air in the room wasn't just cold, it was fucking arctic—suffocating—it was so frigid, sucking the dense vapor into my lungs was like breathing liquid. It was so cold that breaking the frozen bond between my cheeks and eyelids took extra effort. Once open, my eyes stung like I had diced a dozen onions.

The classroom air had solidified into a thick mist, with particles of floating ice settling on the ground in a thin, fresh, powdery sheet of snow. The windows along the far side of the room were frosted over, filtering the light from the moon and courtyard lamps, creating a haze that thickened along the ground.

I remained perfectly still. There was something in the room other than Maynard and me. Something dangerous.

We were in a classroom of sorts, only two dozen feet from the door, but encircled by—*anger*? My body registered five entities in the room that radiated anger with the intensity of a nuclear reactor. Were they ghosts? And the building, Hallows Hall, was surrounded by an army of unnatural things, like something out of a siege battle in a medieval movie.

It was a bad situation—and I'd like to thank the Academy for awarding me the Biggest Understatement of the Year Award.

The air tasted like an electrical fire and plastic—the combination reeked of danger and pulsed like bass from a nightclub. Goosebumps rose and fell on my skin, involuntarily communicating what I already knew—

—Some righteously fucked up shit was going down.

"Tony?" asked Maynard. I couldn't see him with my face still slobbering all over the floor, but he was nearby. I wanted to remain perfectly still until I understood the danger and calibrated its location.

I groaned, "I'm good," and rolled onto my knees.

Maynard sat in a pool of his own blood. "I thought you were a goner," he chuckled, as a wisp of icy vapor shifted.

"Yeah, well, I couldn't leave you here by yourself," I said, as the last misaligned tooth slid back into place.

"Wow, a true gentleman," he joked.

"Are you with me?"

He nodded. "Yeah, I wasn't seeing things clearly." Tori appeared to have the ability to infect Maynard's mind and extract his worst impulses and doubts.

"Are you okay?"

"I'm cold," he said. "How much blood does a person have, anyway?"

"One and a half gallons," I responded via Jamaal, but decided it was best to leave out the latter half of his response. Maynard didn't need to know how close he was to dying. "Bite down, it's about to get hot in here." I held the sleeve of my leather jacket to his mouth. He apprehensively bit down as I ignited my free hand and clamped it over the wound.

For his part, Maynard didn't scream nearly as much as I thought he would, but the bleeding had finally stopped.

"Fuck," he groaned when it was over. "That always looks so fun in the movies."

"Trust me," I said, "It was more fun from where I was standing."

"I bet," he said with a chuckle.

"I'll get you out of here."

"Will you though?" said Tori. "Everything you touch, you break." She was leaning against a nearby shelf, still dressed in her New Year's Eve outfit—the clothes she died in. I had mixed emotions seeing her—especially after Maynard ended up on the sharp end of a knife. "Come on, big boy, you might want to stand up for this."

Maynard and I exchanged a nod—he was in pain, but he wasn't bleeding anymore. I handed him one of my guns. He took it and said, "Will this work on her?"

"Maybe." I shrugged.

"Thanks for the honesty," he quipped.

"You betcha," I replied, then stood up. My hand rested on the other gun in my belt as I swiveled to face Tori, like it was high noon at the O.K. Corral.

"T, you always were such a spaz," she said.

"I don't know Tor, you're the one who just knifed a friend," I said.

"The dead have no friends," she replied. Then she evaporated into particles of nothing and disappeared.

As I stepped into the center of the room, the plan was to bring the danger with me. The closer it was to me, the further it was from Maynard. This wasn't his fight, and I wasn't going to lose him too—not on my watch.

"What do you want?" I asked. It was a total cliché, but wasn't that the question? Every movie ever made had that banal line tattooed into the script. Figured I'd get straight to the point, right? Time was ticking.

Malus had brought her, and I was sure the other angry blips within the room were going to be similar surprises. This was a mind game, and a dangerous one. I felt like I was already hanging on by a thread—my thoughts and doubts like poison, turning even my better judgments against me. I was second-guessing myself and trying hard not to think about the fact that if we survived this, there were hundreds of other horrors waiting to gnaw my bones clean.

"Retribution," said Tori from the ether.

"Retribution?" I asked. "For what?" I had nothing to do with Tori's death. It was an accident—Rick's Mustang plowed into her on Cross Road in the early hours of New Year's Eve more than ten years ago.

A cold draft blew across the room, and with it came the fresh stench of rage.

"Because you killed us all," said another voice. I'd know that voice anywhere. "Your friendship was always a chore."

"Amanda," I said. There was a silhouette in the corner, and I moved toward it slow and steady, as if not to startle it.

"We're dead because of you!" she shouted, and the whole room trembled.

"Amanda's dead?" cried Maynard. "You killed Amanda?"

He wasn't all there. Maynard was in shock, and his heart was pounding at twice the normal speed. I could hear it halfway across the room.

"I didn't kill you," I responded, but it felt like a lie. "I didn't kill either of you."

Another drift in the frozen vapor—the mist curled—and Amanda disappeared, then rematerialized to my right between two rows of metal shelves. She was still only a shadow, but I wanted to see her. I wanted to beg Amanda for her forgiveness. The years of guilt resurfaced along with the new, and my heart was too heavy to continue.

Stepping into that row between shelves set off new waves of goosebumps, but I ignored them. I ignored them so I could see her.

"What about me?" asked a shadow from the next row. It was Anne. Her southern drawl gave her away. "The monster came after you, and I was in the way."

"I didn't know," I said. The guilt was almost too much. How was I supposed to know I was marked? How was I supposed to know that the Thirteen would find me? That they would kill everyone to get to me?

"You didn't just kill me," she said. "You killed your best friend too."

"No," I said. I shook my head as my pulse pounded. I was halfway to Amanda, and I wanted the guilt to stop.

"Hey buddy," said Marshall from the opposite row. "We should get out, like old times." He was confused. I could sense it. And his body wavered, like he couldn't maintain consistency. "Where am I? I don't understand where I am." He was disembodied thoughts and memories. A formless spirit projected into the room. The sadness it brought crushed me.

That's why they were here. Malus wanted to destroy me. He didn't just want me dead, he wanted my complete annihilation.

"Don't forget about me, asshole!" said Brad. I got the feeling he was standing right beside me, but there was nothing there. "I was smoking a bowl, then some fuckwit slit my throat."

"Sorry isn't good enough," said Amanda. "I was engaged! I was happy!"

"And you took that away from us," said Anne. "You were the rotten egg. It was always you. Like a cancer, you destroyed everything around you. Even Jaycie."

"I'm sorry," I said. "To all of you." The silhouette was only a few feet away as I edged closer, but it was only when I got within arm's reach that I started to take notice of what was on the shelves—Jamaal and Montoya both said, "Wait," but I was already reaching out.

When I grabbed at the silhouette, my hand passed through it—did

I really think I could touch a ghost? Its hands, however—two massive hands—snatched me by the leather collar.

The silhouette wasn't Amanda, and I realized too late I had been tricked into making a huge mistake.

The shadow grew, its volume and density doubling, and towered over me.

"You stole everything from me," said Rick—a massive angry shadow. "Burn."

That's when the chemicals—a mixture of glycerin, potassium permanganate, and sugar—burst from the shelves, coating me from head to toe. I pulled away, but the ghostly grip was too much, locking me in place.

When I started to smoke, Rick said, "Goodbye," then the smoke exploded into fire.

I yanked and pulled, but Rick's grip on me was unmovable—I slipped out of my jacket and rolled away to staunch the fire, but it was chemical. The fire kept burning until it had consumed all the reacting agents. Fucking hell, it hurt—and as the last flame flickered out and my body began to heal the searing damage, a ghostly fist smashed my jaw.

I slammed into the far wall and bashed my head. It left a streak of blood as I melted to the floor, too damaged to move. A quick self-diagnosis noted the third-degree burns on my arms, neck, and back—as well as two cracked ribs and a skull fracture at the back of my head.

"T," said Tori, "you're looking weak."

"Is that why you're here?" I asked. "To heckle me?"

Tori stomped out of the vapor and leaned against the wall next to me. Then she peered out the window and smiled. "No, I'm here to keep you busy."

The ghost wasn't transparent like I would have imagined. It was dull and drained of color, desaturated of its very essence. Fully realized yet blurred around the edges. Tori herself was a twisted, angry apparition. Her eyes black with rage, her appearance a distorted amalgam of reality and fiction—like a doped-up maniac.

"Why?" I asked. "I never hurt you."

Tori looked away from me. "I died because of you."

"No, you died because Rick was a drunk asshole," I said. "You stabbed Maynard. He was one of your best friends."

"Shut up!" she screamed. "Shut up!"

"You can hate me, Tor," I said. "But Maynard? He loved you."

"Is that true?" she asked. Her spirit flitted next to Maynard before he could respond.

"I died inside the day you left," said Maynard. His finger on the trigger, the gun resting in his lap should he need it.

"No," growled Tori. "No, no! You can't!"

"I was right under your nose," said Maynard, "but you had eyes for everyone else."

"Shut up," she growled, "shut the fuck up!" Her frustration made the lingering ice floating on the air rattle like a bag of sand vibrating on a subwoofer. Tori sobbed once, then was gone, but it was far from over.

"Hey buddy," said Marshall. "I think something is wrong."

The fog shimmered, and I thought about grabbing Maynard and making a run for it, but could I outrun a pack of ghosts?

I wouldn't have gotten very far…

"I know, bud," I said, trying to comfort Marshall. "I'm sorry you're dead."

"Do you want to know what it's like to die?" asked Anne. She charged out of the fog—a semi-transparent entity of pulsing, negative charged ectoplasm—and rammed all ten of her fingers into my skull. They penetrated the skin and bone like it was nothing but soft butter, taking me to my knees.

My teeth chattered and my eyes fluttered as if I was having a seizure.

"I want you to feel it," she said. "I want you to feel all the pain that monster inflicted upon me. I want you to feel how my body was flayed, drained and pulverized, all while keeping me alive!"

I screamed.

It was awful. I felt it all. Mammon had found a way to keep her conscious, her heart beating, as it destroyed her. When she pulled her fingers from my head, the pain subsided, but the tears wouldn't stop.

"I'm sorry, Anne," I whispered. "I wanted nothing more than for you and Marshall to be happy.”

"Then why did you pull us into this?" she asked.

"Because I love you," I said. "You're all the family I had."

The pulsing negative charge around her dampened—and her face slackened, like the fight had gone out of her.

"Where am I?" asked Marshall. "I don't understand where I am."

He approached me, confused. He was a lost soul in need of guidance.

"I'm sorry," I said. "I failed you."

"Failed me?" said Marshall. "I failed you. How does a guy fix his best friend when the love of his life was taken from him so horribly?"

As Marshall's words hit me, eliciting a whole new set of emotions, a bass hum vibrated through the room like a foghorn. The seething inside the room was grew fouler with every passing second.

"You're still an asshole," said Brad, shoving Marshall away into the vapor.

"You're still short," I said, and Brad's face contorted like he wanted to laugh. If there was one thing Brad couldn't resist, it was a good comeback. His blackened rage-filled eyes softened and relented.

"I was doing good, T," he said through tears. "I had a baby girl, man. Now she doesn't have a father."

Marshall was nearby, listening.

"I wish I could have seen it," I said. "You as a father."

"In life I was short, but as a dad I came up big," he joked, and Marshall placed a comforting hand on his shoulder. I tried to do the same, but my hand passed through him.

"I understand why you hate me," I said. "You were all important to me. You meant something. I wish I could have prevented it. I wish I could change it."

As the anger within Brad and Anne subsided, their rage was absorbed by another.

"What exactly did I mean to you, punk?"

The negative energy flowed toward Rick like he was a black hole. His anger and rage could have blotted out entire area codes as he stepped forward and materialized.

He was more of a monster in death than he was alive—he appeared at almost twice his original size, anger rippling inward and outward from his body into the room like he was breathing it. Veins bulged and twitched beneath his skin like live snakes, and his fists were the size of basketballs.

Seeing his face drained all my sadness, and I was filled with a rage equal to his own. I raised my gun to his head and squeezed the trigger. I wanted to end it—to emasculate and cripple him—our rivalry resurfacing on boil. A flaming bullet struck him in the right eye, passing through the ectoplasm and slamming into the far wall. A small flame burned within the hole and quickly disappeared, smothered by the cold.

"Not this time," he said, shaking his head, then his clenched fist and hit me. Stunned, he hit me twice more, a left then a right that sent the gun sliding across the frozen tiled floor.

It was Rick who'd knocked me out cold when I first entered the room. The strength of the dead was powerful, and I was reeling in my first real title fight. It was a grudge match I couldn't afford to lose.

"This seems a little unfair," I said after spitting a wad of blood. "You can hit me, but I can't touch you?"

"You stole my girlfriend and broke my heart," he said, "I'm going to tear you apart, then break yours."

MALUS

Hubris.

I should have seen it coming.

Our gathered armies were unstoppable—but I should have known. Nothing was ever this easy. Our gathering was not an Empyrean Crime— the angels would not stop us, not when we were hunting their own criminal—the Raptor. And the Demons? They were content to witness chaos.

With the two sides content to let Earthly affairs play out, it was hubris that kept me from seeing the signs. As the spirits tortured the spark—familiar souls I'd collected and tortured to amplify their anger and rage, like an agitated snow globe—I never once saw it coming.

Saturn's Clock, the God of Time's infinitely precise timepiece, did not strike but a single solitary second as I witnessed the entire event unfold. One second was all it took to change the course of events. In one single second, two great slabs of rock, dirt, and cement crumpled inward like two colliding ocean waves and crushed the entirety of Moloch's mutant sons, as well as the newest of my Thirteen, Kukulkan, and most of his Gorgon daughters. In a blink, we had lost half our army, and we were moments away from losing more.

"You stay alive, and you keep that key safe," she had mumbled a moment before the catastrophe.

Jacinda stood beside me, awake, arms outstretched and hands clenched, like she had just clapped them together—the rock, dirt and cement slabs pulled from the ground and reacted to her gestures, crushing her enemies. Before she could do any more damage, I struck her across the face with my open hand. She sprang back to her feet with the vacant look of complete control in her brilliant green eyes, and her hair gently flowed like wildfire in the cold evening breeze.

She aimed her wrath, and when she attempted to strike me down, to tear me apart atom by atom, nothing happened.

Her face contorted, unsure and frustrated. She could not understand why she was incapable of ending her suffering by destroying the creature who'd caused all the pain she endured. She tried again and again until I slapped her once more across her face, busting her soft lip with my ring.

"You cannot kill that which owns your soul," I explained, "You cannot harm me."

How she was capable, once more, of digging her way out from beneath the glamour was beyond the limits of my frustration. Not only had she destroyed my glamour, but she had torn the psychic silk of Phobos and Deimos to shreds.

I was bordering on a psychotic break when she looked at me and smiled.

She smiled like she had deciphered an unsolvable riddle, and a diabolical idea formed. I could see its inception as she glanced along the ground, then up at the trees and the surrounding buildings.

An angry growl, followed by a demonic charge, and Jacinda was being swarmed upon by angry hordes—focusing their rage on the creature responsible for the instant annihilation of half our army.

"What do you plan to do?" I asked. Phobos and Deimos were at my sides, casting spells from behind the Veil to bring her back under our influence—but nothing worked. "You're surrounded."

"You've had me surrounded my entire life," she said. Her mastery over her own abilities was weak—and yet she still could have destroyed us all. Her emotions and physical strength had no actual bearing on what she could accomplish, and yet they were the conduit through which she could manipulate them. When her neck tightened and her muscles flinched, I dodged away in time to avoid being impaled by an uprooted tree.

Then she ran—the tree bowling down our numbers as she fled in its wake toward the building, using it as a shield—projecting it forward like a Psychokinetic.

Astoreth attempted to stop Jacinda's advance by putting herself in the way of the girl's escape and was thrown aside—the tree was rendered harder than the goddess's own legendary skin. Then Loki made a move to stop the girl, his hammer raised for a maiming throw.

I made a gesture, and Loki resigned his pursuit.

Jacinda slipped into the building, and the crunch of metal and glass suggested she had barricaded the door from the inside.

"Why did you stop me?" asked Loki. "You let her get away!"

There was something going on inside Jacinda's head that I could never reach. And if I couldn't reach it, I was left with only one option— my original intention all along.

I had to kill her beloved. Her essence would dissolve under the realization that hope was lost. Without Tony, she would relinquish all fight.

"Send in your children," I ordered Loki. "Kill the spark."

TONY

I was losing.

I was losing to the biggest piece of shit on the face of the planet. The Ghost Prick, a.k.a. Rick Jansen, was landing rope after rope. He hit like a bucket of bricks, but every retaliation hit nothing but air—my fists passed through him like an apparition. I was a punching bag, and there was very little I could do about it.

"I wanted to fuck you up," said Rick with a sly grin, "from the moment I saw you."

"In the locker room, wearing nothing but a towel?" I said. "Aw Rick, I knew I got you off, but I didn't know how much till now."

He followed that up with a right hook, and my bloody spit spattered the wall.

"You're a nothing! A punk. A poor faggot. A loser!"

"What shitty things to say from a shit human being," I responded before he shoved his fist into my gut. Even when I tried to dodge his attacks, Rick flitted into position. He could land a punch starting from the other side of the room.

"I was born into royalty. This town—this state—worships my family," he said.

"Must be nice," I mocked. Even in death, the guy was still bragging about the riches he couldn't bring with him.

"I took whatever I wanted. I took the best, the prettiest, and I made them do whatever I wanted."

I shrugged. "Until Jaycie left you."

He swung and finally missed as I stepped back onto something hard. There was a streak in the ice along the ground, leading from Maynard's smirk to my boot. My friend was too weak to move but sent me a little surprise to even the score. Under my foot was a pair of brass knuckles, and knowing Maynard, they were anything but ordinary.

Rick wound up as I threaded the weapon through the fingers on my left hand and swung—the impact was jolting, like I had rammed a piece of metal into a live outlet. Rick fell backwards as I shook the pain from my wrist.

Maynard said, "I call 'em *blessed-knuckles*."

"Handy," I said with a nod. "Does it work on all ghosts? Or just assholes?" The metal knuckles had four different symbols carved into them—one for each knuckle.

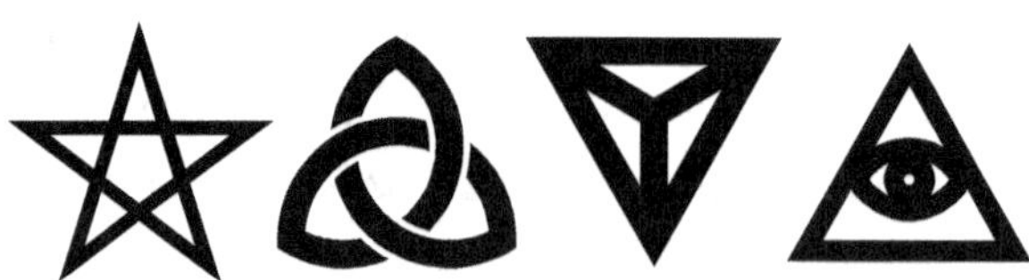

"Lucky shot," said Rick as he grabbed the bloody knife from the floor—the knife Tori had used to stab Maynard. "I'm going to carve you up like a turkey."

"Cliché," I said. "You're a walking cliché—and a turkey. Rich kid who thought he was hot shit. I can't believe people bought into your bullshit."

"Your dead girlfriend bought into it," he said, and his words immediately wedged themselves under my skin. "I used to make her beg for it. She worshipped me from her knees—"

His jaw opened, like he was attempting to add more fuel onto my fire, when I slammed the blessed-knuckled fist into his chin. I swung and I swung until I was standing over him and he was twitching on the ground. The consistency of his form had become soupy, the ectoplasm a malformed mound of the man I once knew—his face stretched like old newspaper funnies copied in silly putty. In my rage, I had punched right through him and cracked the marble tile floor below.

When I realized what I had done, that there was no way to kill a ghost, I backed off. And the maniac started laughing.

He sat up, and a blink later, he was back to normal. He didn't need to heal—there was no deterioration—he wasn't even hurt.

"My turn," he growled, and with the force of a freight train, he threw me into the air. When I hit the ceiling, I stuck like a wet wad of paper, hoping to gather my spun senses before he continued his attack—

—only the dead could also manipulate gravity.

He floated in mid-air, wrapped his big paws around my neck, then forced me through the ceiling. Piping ruptured under the pressure and impaled my side in a bloody Alien-inspired burst. When Rick finally let go, my head blacking out, my weight slowly ripped the pipe from my side and when I came free, I slammed into the floor with a thud.

Was I really going down like this?

"Stoppit," said a meek voice.

"Who the fuck are you?" growled Rick.

I used the distraction to heal.

"Nobody," said Amanda. Her blackened eyes and twisted form stared up at the hulking ghost—innocent and small, unassuming. "But

I once wasted a Breacher when I was six." Then she kicked him square in the ghost-balls—ghost-on-ghost violence was an even playing field. As Rick doubled over, she gave him the kind of Ryu uppercut worthy of our teenaged StreetFighter tournaments.

When Rick landed on his back, Amanda smiled at Maynard, then me.

"Morris, T," she said. "I see you both grew up to be a couple of troublemakers." It felt like she was scolding us, until she smiled. "I like it!"

When Manda turned back to Rick, he was gone.

"Where'd he go?" asked Maynard.

With Rick gone, Amanda turned to me and smiled—like everything was forgiven. The darkness in her eyes paled and she looked human. For the moment, I allowed myself to watch her. Amanda may have been a ghost, but seeing her, grown up, for the first time in sixteen years, left me at a loss for words. She was tall, thin, with long blonde hair, and she was healthy—a fully functioning adult. She was the complete opposite of who I had become. The more I thought about her, and about the fact that I was looking at her ghost, I became hotter and hotter with rage. Her life was cut short, unfairly, and I wanted justice.

There was a pulse, and the air shifted within the room. When Amanda blotted out, I knew the danger was far from over. "No! Leave them alone!"

"Manda?" I called out to her, but it was already too late. The mist in the room violently swirled and gathered at the center.

"What's happening?" asked Maynard. "Manda?" His voice was weaker than before. I wasn't sure how much time he had left.

What formed out of the cold dense vapor was as much Rick as it was a monster. He was seven feet tall and twice as jacked as he was in life—his head marked by a giant gunshot—a hole straight through his brains and out the other side. The vibrations in the room hurt, like my bones were tuning forks. Maynard grimaced and my healing slowed, as if the ghostly hum was crippling my power.

"No more games," said Rick. "No more distractions."

"Have you been juicing?" I asked, noting his increased mass.

"Only after I squash you," he replied.

With my left fist still threaded into the blessed-knuckles, I let the flames roar and ignite my right. Then I charged in and slammed him with a left hook followed by a right. I unloaded every martial art to back-alley brawler combination my entire expanded brain-trust had to offer—until I was gassed. My internal flames reduced to a smolder. The damage I inflicted was minimal.

Rick followed that up with an onslaught I couldn't defend against, hitting me with telekinetic powers that blasted me from all sides, like Luke fending off Vader in *Empire.*

I had cracked ribs, a broken jaw, and a crushed windpipe—my body was healing as fast as it could, but not fast enough. From my knees I launched a desperate, half-hearted swing, but Rick caught my arm and broke it, like he was breaking a broomstick over his knee—then he wrapped his hand around my throat and lifted me over his head.

With the bloody knife appearing in his free hand, he said, "I know what you are. Take the eyes, go to Hell. But take the heart…" He took the knife and made it dance back and forth playfully. "…and I end you. I go on, and you become a bad memory."

I couldn't even give a clever retort. There was no breath in my lungs to say what needed to be said—to call the maniac a lunatic psycho—to say I never thought I'd ever smell his shitty breath again…

I was hoping to buy time.

I was hoping for a miracle—

—when one ran into the room.

Rick's knife reared back and paused for the briefest second, before he thrust it toward my chest. When the hilt struck, I thought dying was going to be a lot more painful—

—only I wasn't dying.

There was no knife—at least, not anymore.

Jacinda stood inside the doorway but didn't scream. Though from the look in her eyes, she wanted to. Her presence shook the room up like an unbalanced washing machine as all the passive spirits reacted in a swirl.

"Jace?" said Anne. "Is that you?"

"Stay back!" roared Rick, and every ghost in the room was silenced. He was more powerful than them, and they immediately scattered. Rick dropped me, and I landed in a wadded mess as he turned to face her.

"I'm not afraid of you," said Jaycie. Her eyes darted from Rick to me and back again.

"Yes, you are," said Rick as his trademark grin reappeared. "You were always afraid. Afraid of losing me. Afraid of what you were without me. Afraid of what I could do to you. You were always afraid, Jace. I owned you. I had complete control over you."

He never took a step toward her, but he moved closer. He was a transparent phantom that phased in and out of reality, closing the gap between them. The closer he got to her, the more massive he appeared, dwarfing her under his spectral shadow. His manifestation flickered from corporeal to transparent and back again, as if absorbing more rage—then at last, he went fully solid. He no longer looked like a fucking hologram, but like a real, live monster within the room.

Jaycie looked over to me again, then down to Maynard on the floor. He was looking like death, and I could hear his heartbeat slowing.

As my body reassembled from its heap on the floor, I watched as Jaycie's face softened from shock to disappointment, then to something that resembled pity. She stepped forward and passed through Rick, despite his attempts to grab and throttle her. With each swipe, he came up empty. She took me by the hand and helped me to my feet, then threaded her fingers through mine.

"Are you okay?" she asked, and I nodded. Instantaneously I felt stronger, and my broken bones and bruises disappeared. Her touch gave me strength.

Rick seethed at our united front. The room brooded along with him. His icy vengeance grew as the frosty vapor sharpened, like needles into our bare skin. "You're mine!" shouted Rick, his power cracking the windows and rattling the floor beneath our feet.

Jaycie said, "Nobody owns me. Nobody controls me." Then she smiled, as if she saw something nobody else could see. "Go to Hell, Rick."

Rick's next step saw the lower half of his leg melt into a puddle of ectoplasmic goo that dissolved him further with every motion. He fought against it, as if he were trying to pull himself out of quicksand.

But as the temperature in the room warmed, he kept on melting.

"No, not yet," growled Rick. He was panicking—the rage and the aggression dissolved into whining threats and begs. "I'll kill you! Don't do this to me! Please! You're mine! I'll kill you both! I'll—" Then he liquefied into nothing.

Jaycie turned and found me already watching her in disbelief. I didn't have the chance to ask her anything—no how, why, who, and what in the hell just happened—when she kissed me.

"I missed you," she said, as a chill ran up our backs.

We had an audience, and they were slowly emerging from the remaining frost.

"Is it really you?" asked Anne. She was nearby, watching.

Jaycie let go and turned to her. When she'd entered the room and dissolved Rick, the negative energy evaporated, like Rick was the poison that infected them all.

Jaycie and Anne locked eyes, and I watched Jaycie put out her hand. When Anne touched it with her own, a gentle light bloomed as Jaycie said, "Goodbye."

One by one they disappeared, each blinking into reality before dissolving away—

Brad nodded, then said, "Look out for my daughter," before disappearing.

Marshall said, "Love you, boo." Then he laughed at seeing us together again.

Tori looked at Maynard and me and smiled apologetically. "I miss you fucken fools." Then she went to Jaycie and said, "I never hated you. I didn't want what happened to me to happen to you." Jaycie appeared guilty, and I could smell the sorrow.

Then, there was one.

Amanda stepped forward and into the growing light. She looked older, wiser, and took note of our hands, still intertwined.

"It was inevitable, I suppose," she said with a humorless smile. "I sure can pick 'em. My three best friends." She looked at all of us and smiled. "And two of them became lovers."

"I wish things had been different," I said to her.

"You brought us together," said Jaycie.

Amanda nodded. "Live for each other."

"We will," said Jaycie.

Then Amanda drifted over to Maynard and said, "Morris, make sure these two get out alive, would ya?" Her voice as delicate as ever, noting the wound at his side.

Maynard laughed. "Anything for you, Manda."

Then the room grew bright, as bright as a star and warm. After, when the light relinquished, they were all gone, and the frozen temperatures dissipated from the room.

Jaycie put her head on my shoulder, and for a moment we both let the peace settle—until someone cleared their throat.

"Little help here," said Maynard. "I'm dying."

We both went to his side, and Jaycie, without a warning or any kind of explanation, touched his cheek and brought the color back into his skin.

"How do you feel?" she asked.

"Whoa," he replied. His heart rate went normal between beats. "I always knew."

"That I was a witch?" she replied with a smile.

"That you were something," he said, "something more."

"What did you do?" I asked, but what I really meant was *how did you do it?* Jaycie looked at me with expressive eyes, as if to say it was a long story.

"Can you move?" she asked him.

"Yeah," he said, as he stood without the need for help.

The bloody puddle beneath him was gone, and when he checked the wound, he kept poking at the skin, expecting it to tear apart. We were ready to ask any number of qualified questions when a loud howl vibrated through the halls.

"What was that?" asked Jaycie.

"Out of the frying pan and into the fire," said Chappy.

"Trouble." I could smell mildewed fur somewhere inside the building.

"My man, you got beat up by a ghost," said Montoya. "How're you gonna fight whatever that is?"

"He's got a point," said Jaycie with a smirk, responding to Montoya. I shook my head—Jaycie was full of surprises.

"We have to go," I warned, as I collected my leather jacket, my guns, and slipped the blessed-knuckles into my inner coat pocket. Maynard went to grab his duffel bag, but I caught his hand. "Leave it. Grab a weapon or two. We have to travel light."

"Why?" asked Jaycie.

"Because we're going to make a run for it."

XXI

killer

JACINDA
May 3rd, 2002
Then.

I know what I said, Jace. And I was serious.

"Forget about the pain, the fear and the guilt. Forget about me. Forget! Make us all forget and start over."

But you didn't listen. You had to keep me in it.

"Okay, everything but you," you said, and you ended up changing nothing! You only pushed your inevitable end further down the road.

It was all my fault, and it was time I owned up to ruining your life.

"We found you," said the creepy little girl, and you took off running into the darkness.

It was moments like this. Moments like this one, right now, that I needed to change—to prevent them from ever happening to you again. It was up to me, and I was going to end it.

Five minutes ago, you were so lost in your own thoughts, you almost forgot your way home. The walk to your apartment started off pleasant—the air was fresh and helped to cleanse your mind of the strange guilt that tickled up your spine when you heard Tori Martin had died. You tried to understand the guilt, but couldn't grasp why you felt so—*responsible*?

And the worst part? The mention of Tori's death had ruined a fun evening of games with friends before your last few finals. You'd needed some fun to unwind and destress, but now you were even more stressed and more tense than you were before.

You really disliked Tori. Your paths had crossed bitterly as you both fought for Rick's attention back in high school. You both eventually learned that Rick was the worst thing that could have happened to either of you, and the irony wasn't lost on you, Jace.

You had more in common than you'd like to admit—like there were threads of destiny connecting you both.

Campus evenings were often filled with students taking walks and attending night classes. So, it was something of a surprise when you exited Residents Row and crossed the bridge from the Observatory toward the off-campus housing and found the next stretch of your walk home was as vacant as a ghost town.

Any and all student life was nowhere to be found, and the last stretch home, your favorite across the campus gardens and the covered bridge, appeared ominous in a way that gave you chills. A crow squawked and flew away nervously from a nearby tree, but it was when you had stepped between sidewalk lamps—where one bubble of light ended and the next strayed off in the distance—that you heard the tip-tapping of small feet.

The lights, without dimming, appeared to cast less light—like the darkness thickened into an obstructive force. The tiny feet grew louder until they stopped right behind you with an abrupt clap of hard wooden heels on pavement.

"We found you," said a little girl's voice. And then, suddenly, your internal crisis was suspended. You weren't thinking about Tori Martin or Rick's car crash on New Year's Eve. You weren't thinking of how I had omitted that information, and why.

You were thinking of survival.

You ran through the gardens, trampling through shrubs and over newly planted spring flowers. You stumbled out the other side, right into the path of a little girl skipping into the failing light of a nearby lamp.

"Hi, little sis," said the girl. "You got big!"

"Who are you?" you cried out.

"Silly. I'm your sister, Jane. Remember? You killed me. Did you forget all about me?" she said in a disturbingly delightful way.

"No," you said. "My sister Jane is—" you started to say it, the words were there before you tried to speak them, but several strange things happened when they formed in your mouth. You simultaneously had no recollection of a sister and yet remembered her. You only vaguely knew your sister existed, as if you had forgotten all about her, but there was a giant void in your mind where the memory of your sister should be.

You forgot, Jace, don't you remember? You made yourself forget and remember so many times that memories were covering up memories.

"Dead! Dead! Dead! Dead!" Jane screamed, twisting and contorting, her joints dislocated, allowing her head, arms, and legs to move in unnatural ways.

You backed away from the creature, your legs unresponsive to your intense desire to flee. When the thing finished its transformation, it stalked toward you like a hunter on all fours, preparing to strike. When it launched itself, you fell back into the garden mulch and held your hands up to defend yourself, your tears and screams choked by your panic.

There was no impact. There were no teeth around your neck or bloody mauling at the mutated hands of your long dead and forgotten sister—instead, you opened your eyes.

It was gone.

You forced yourself to move on, sticking only to the lit areas along the sidewalk. You didn't dare step into the darkness beyond, which seemed to swim with foul evil things. You left the evil behind in the campus gardens beyond the Observatory bridge, but you struggled to keep yourself from looking over your shoulder every few steps as you briskly marched away.

If you had kept your eyes focused on the path ahead, you may have avoided what came next.

You slammed face first into something blocking your way. From the touch, it was a person wearing fleece, but you couldn't see who it was beyond the drawn hood. Your nerves were too shot, too shattered to react in any other way but to scream.

"Hush now," he said as he stepped into the light of the nearest lamp. You could see the bridge of his nose, the sharp edge of his chin.

He reached for you and caught you by the collar, ripping it as you spun away and ran. You were so close to home. The last stretch was through a small wooded area, over the pedestrian bridge, then out the other side and across the courtyard, where the front door to your apartment complex was waiting—a bright light in the distance.

Stumbling at first, your body found rhythm, your muscles pumping together, picking up speed as you passed through the trees, when something slammed into you and took you right off your feet. When you hit the ground, your attacker rolled on top, holding you down. Even with your assailant's great strength, you were able to squirm away, making you a difficult target to collect. In seconds you were off again, this time into the deep black nothing, crossing the pedestrian bridge and running down the stairs. You ran as hard as you could toward a tiny glow of light a hundred yards away.

The footfalls behind you were deep and heavy. Your pursuer was frustrated with your quickness, the way you darted away like a wild rabbit escaping the jaws of a hungry wolf, and growled to show his resentment. You tried to scream, to call for help, but didn't have the extra wind in your lungs as they burned for air while you pushed yourself faster. Nearing the sidewalk lamps, the light began to fade, like the shadows had rushed ahead to swallow the light.

You were within fifty yards of the building. Just a little further and you'd barricade yourself behind the door and lock out all the madness. You reached into your purse, losing speed in the process, and fumbled with your keys. You tussled with every object, trying to grasp the keys beneath, but you always snagged the wrong item—your lip balm, your cell phone, even a wad of tissues. You had only a few more yards before the door when your hand locked onto both the keys and cell phone, but then he caught you—this time by the hair.

He yanked you violently into the bushes beside the entrance, and you hit the ground hard enough to make you woozy. You kicked and screamed as he climbed on top, then punched you in the stomach, knocking the wind from your lungs. With that punch, you lost your ability to fight back. He grabbed each of your wrists and straddled you above the waist, rendering you helpless. Then he leaned forward into the dimmest of light available and exposed his identity.

"I told you, you'll always be mine," said Rick with wild eyes. He looked wrong. He looked evil. "The sooner you realize that, the better."

The slow rhythmic pattering of little feet approached as Rick wrangled you into submission. "Why'd you run away?" asked Jane.

"Leave me alone!" you screamed. Then, with the depth of your singing voice, you screamed with all you had. "Help me!"

As the light dimmed, so did your voice, muffling on the still air.

Rick tore at your shirt, the maniacal smile on his face rippling in violent delight as you cried hysterically—the way one does when there's nothing to do but accept fate, and imagine they were somewhere, or someone else—someone with superhuman strength or the power to control the situation you could not prevent.

Nobody was coming to help you. No divine intervention. No Angels. Nothing.

The evil was there for a reason. The creatures were there to break you, then to take you. There were entities in the shadows, not beyond the Veil like me, but in a half-life, able to flee and keep their distance while implementing their will through possession and suggestion. Rick was their puppet—I saw the demons in his eyes.

You cried. You wanted to scream, but it all seemed hopeless.

You were the woman I loved, and I wouldn't let anything happen to you—never again.

"You're mine, Jace," said Rick. "We love you more than anyone. If you won't come with us, we will take you." His raspy voice was deeper, like there was something inside him generating the words that passed through his lips.

"Oh, little sister," said Jane. "Your *guard* has lost you."

Not true. She had me, and I had come to this day with a purpose.

"No," I said. "They haven't."

I dropped out of the Veil, silent like a shadow. The scent and taste of evil was all around me. Bitter and pungent, like brimstone and souring citrus fruit, as well as the vibration of surprise.

The little girl turned and distorted—her neck and her arms torqued into strange positions. She moved in strange patterns, like she was out of tune with reality. Her movements and scent defined her—she was a ghost, a caged soul, and I had already experienced their tortured anguish.

Rick turned to me and in a flash—when his eyes connected with mine, so he knew who it was that ended him—I put a bullet of pure hellfire into his brain to the tune of your screams. His body fell limp as his blood painted the building's facade, forming a perfect spray and angle—a trajectory in line with suicide. I took my gun, removed its divinity, and placed it in his hand.

Then I retreated behind the Veil.

The darkness lifted, and the twisted shape of your sister disappeared. You remained tangled in the bushes, panting and breaking apart in the hysterical aftermath. I whispered to you through the threshold, an inaudible whisper you couldn't hear but understood all the same.

"Call Tony," I said.

You picked up your phone from the ground beside you and called me, as I stepped back and let him come to your rescue—I was now that Tony's Echo.

This was always how it happened. I was always there, ending Rick's miserable life. I was a murderer, but it felt like retribution.

I listened to your phone call. Your terrible cries, pleading for me.

That Tony would forever be your knight in shining armor, but how could I ever live up to that? I was only a piece of him now—a tiny piece that voluntarily lost himself behind the Veil, witnessing the madness as a watcher. I experienced the horrors of your life, and it was only a matter of time before the horrors caught up. No matter what I did, no matter how hard I tried to save you, you were always doomed.

Still, for love, could I do any less for you than try?

"What have you done?" asked Sid.

He was looking right at me, even though I wasn't in tune with his reality. He walked over, grabbed me by the collar before I could react, like a mother escorting her son away from a fight, and ripped me from the Veil.

"What the fuck?" I groaned.

"No, what the fuck?" he shot back, gesturing toward the scene. We were too far away for you to hear, but Sid pulled me around the corner, his eyes blazing and angry.

I would have asked how, but suddenly it all made sense. The way he showed up in our lives? The things he said to me? The things he knew? Somehow, he was in on this—but was he on my side?

"What are you?" I asked.

"You need to run."

"What?"

"You heard me, asshole," said Sid. "What you just did goes against everything we've fought so hard to control."

"I killed a rapist. It was justice," I said.

"Who gives you the right to determine what is and isn't justice? It isn't your place!" he growled. "You committed an Empyrean Crime. Two of them just now! Three total! You are putting the entirety of existence in jeopardy!"

"He was a rapist!"

"That's not how this works! You don't get to be the executioner! You don't get to rewrite Fate!"

"Why not?" I growled, then, as if on cue—

Something happened. Maybe it was a trick of the eye, but the way Sid responded, I knew it was more than just a vision. In front of my eyes an image of the same scene slid into place, like superimposing one photo onto another until they aligned perfectly—but something wasn't right. The brick façade of the apartment building, the tree, the hedge, the street, and Deschain Hall in the background, silhouetted by streetlamps under the night sky appeared the same, but it was different. It was overrun. Strange ghostly shapes lurked, and twisted, cancerous creatures roamed.

"That's why. Temporal Paradoxes—a bad one," said Sid. "It's one thing to overlap your own timeline—but you changed it. You killed someone. Paradoxes like this break down the walls between worlds. They widen the Breach. You don't get it. This is so much bigger than you."

"What the hell…"

"Every time we topple the Cosmic Scales' balance, another world falls," he said.

When the flashing disappeared, I was left unsure of what I had witnessed. Then I heard the three knocks, like someone politely rapping on my chamber door—to quote-eth Poe. I couldn't tell where it came from, but make no mistake, it was ominous in nature.

"It was for her," I said quietly, then growled, "For her, I'd burn the world down." I pulled away from his grip and put my hands up to show my bafflement. "Do you know what she is?"

"Why do you think I'm here? I've been watching over her since she was just a kid."

"So have I, and I haven't seen you."

"Like always, you have tunnel vision, man! You only ever see Jaycie. You never see the bigger picture. Sometimes you have to sacrifice for the greater good!"

"What would you know of sacrifice?"

Sid slugged me in the jaw and said, "You have no idea."

We stood there, angrily staring at one another, when the younger me came sprinting through the darkness toward the building.

"You need to go. Run. They'll be hunting you."

"The Thirteen?" I asked.

He smiled humorously and gave me the famous Sid chuckle. "No, you dimwit. Heaven." Then he turned, took his cellphone, and began dialing for an ambulance. "We tried to keep you two apart, but it was inevitable."

"Why?" Why? Why would anyone conspire against us? What reason could anyone have to prevent Jaycie and me from being together?

"Because we knew this would happen. You're a predictable creature, in *every form*," he said, glaring with disappointment. "Get the fuck outta here. I don't want to lose a friend tonight." Then the phone connected, and Sid turned away to relay the information to the dispatcher.

I took his warning and opened a new temporal gate as a flock of crows began cawing.

It was time I visited the end.

But what good had I accomplished? I'd only achieved something that had already happened. If I couldn't learn what you are—if I couldn't change the outcome—then what was the whole fucking point?

December 30th, 2007

It was a good crowd. The kind of crowd you always enjoyed playing in front of, Jace. You had come a long way and built a name for yourself around Mercy Point. You even played a few gigs in Philadelphia and had a few leads for a record deal. Your set was finished, and you were in need of a quick fifteen-minute break.

You and I had been together for almost seven years, and you couldn't have been happier. We were good together. The bright future you envisioned for yourself seemed possible—inevitable. You and I were secretly engaged, and you wore the key around your neck faithfully, rarely removing it and always keeping it clean and shiny like the day it was given to you. It was a symbol of our love, the binding gift that was just as honorable as any ring, but discreet. It was nobody's business what we were—married, engaged—only that we were together.

Being discreet was for the best where your mother and father were concerned. They'd never liked me, and you never understood why. They never gave a reason, and they never would. Once your mother died of an apparent overdose, your father's opinion wasn't the kind of thing either of us needed to deal with, when we both knew exactly what we wanted—success, followed by a house, a kid, and growing old together.

The life.

Someone to hold our hand when we die.

My dad loved you. Thought of you as a daughter.

We were happy. But happiness, if I learned anything, was relative and fleeting, Jace.

You chugged a shot, followed by a full liter of water before going on stage. Upon wrapping your first set, you always took a restroom break. It was a running joke that you could hold your water like one of the boys, and in most cases could outdrink everyone but Marshall. He was by far the champ, having downed a full bottle of tequila the last time you tried. You and Marsh went head to head, shot for shot at the Fourth of July bash at his place. I had to carry you home and hold back your hair as you puked out massive quantities of alcohol, and I did it all with a smile. You were the happiest, funniest drunk I had ever seen, singing and dancing to old show tunes and bopping everyone on the nose and giggling.

Still, Marshall proclaimed you the winner of the Largest Bladder Award, because he took three pee breaks during the whole escapade.

"Need anything?" I asked, meeting you offstage with a kiss. You were hot, a little sweaty, and I had a look in my eyes—like excitement— like I was seeing you for the first time all over again.

I had just told Marshall and Anne I was buying the ring tomorrow morning. He'd bought us shots and was as happy as I had ever seen him. Two of his best friends, engaged. He almost spilled the beans when he congratulated you, and at the last second swerved and added, "for the best rendition of 'Running Up That Hill' I've ever heard."

It was a good save. It really was a great cover.

A girl from the front row got up and walked by, passing us on her way to the ladies' room. Her bright gray eyes caught your attention, and in some way, you felt you knew her.

"Nah, I'm good," you said. "Just a bottle of water."

"You got it, gal of mine."

"Hey," said a random guy. He leaned in between us, blocking me out. "Can I buy you a drink?"

Had he not seen us kiss just a second ago?

"No—" you started to say, but I reacted before you could finish.

When I jumped in and shoved the guy away, I said, "Her drinks will be bought by me, and me only, pal."

He was tall and blue-eyed with a man-bun, and covered in tattoos. He was everything I wasn't, and I don't know what came over me. I felt threatened. I had baggage, and in the end, maybe Rick had won—there was always a glimmer of unreality to you being with me. Like you were a handful of dry sand slipping away until there was nothing left. That this guy, this kind of man, was always better than me.

"Cool down," said Marsh, reacting instantly.

"Yeah, listen to your token, pal," said the idiot. "I'm talking to the lady, not you."

When I raised my fist, Marshall hooked my arm and spoke directly into my ear—

"Look at your girl," he said. "Look at her and remember what happened the last time."

You were already crying. "I'll be back," you said as you left.

"Don't you dare lose that woman's trust ever again," he whispered. "Annnnnd! Oh, hell no." Marshall moved me aside and I swear I could see heat rising off his head. "No punk in a man-bun is gonna call me 'token' and not taste his own teeth. You don't wanna mess with a Philly boy! We fight dirty. I'll gnaw your balls off if you give me the chance."

"Try it," said Man-bun.

"Hey look!" shouted Marsh, "that guy's fly is down!"

It wasn't, but Marsh made everyone around believe it. A few girls started laughing.

"No, it's not!" shouted Man-bun as he double- and triple-checked his fly.

"Yes it is!" said Marshall. "He said he was going to whip it out, right here in this bar."

"That's enough, hon," calmed Anne as she gave him a big hug from behind. Man-bun scooted away as soon as everyone started looking.

"Sorry, babe, I was on a roll."

Seeing the whole escapade transpire from this angle made me realize just how bad I looked.

Guilt.

I felt guilty making a scene and embarrassing you.

Trauma.

I'd never gotten over all we went through. All these years later, Rick still cast a shadow over me. I wanted you to have my ring because I wanted to marry you—but maybe, I also wanted there to be a physical symbol staking my claim. You were always up in front of the crowd, adored by anyone and everyone who ever heard you perform. It was hard to sit back and watch man after man take their swings at you—and I was lucky. They were all whiffs. All strikeouts.

But this wasn't about me, Jace.

We had come so far, and this was it. The end. The last seventy-two hours.

You quickly paced toward the ladies' room at the end of the hall. The bar was an upscale place, with fancy lighting that kept the entire ambiance at a dim glow. Maybe you were dehydrated, it was warm inside, but you began to feel dizzy as you neared the restroom door, like your body was trying to warn you.

You were frustrated, and maybe that was weighing you down. Seeing me like that, made you feel like I didn't trust you. As if you hadn't turned down men before.

But I trusted you—make no mistake about that. I didn't trust them and what they might do.

As you entered the restroom, you found the girl with the bright gray eyes washing her hands. You gave her a sideways glance as you walked toward the stalls—when your eyes met in the mirror. The connection made you dizzy, and you grabbed for the nearest stall door to keep from falling. It was like someone had trounced over your grave.

"Easy," said the girl, who rushed over to help.

"I know you," you said.

"Do you?" asked the girl. It was more of an accusation than a question.

"Carina," you said weakly. The image and the name fluttered to the surface. Memories and feelings associated with the name and her image played upon your mind like a tap dancer stomping out a fire.

"You remember," she said.

"Pieces." You rubbed your temples, a headache descending behind your eyes and between your ears. "What's wrong with my memories?" It was semi-rhetorical, a question you hoped Carina could answer, but not one you expected her to answer.

"Your memories have been erased, or perhaps better defined, they've been forgotten. Anything forgotten can be remembered," said Carina. "Sometimes, though, they should be forgotten, and eventually, need to be remembered."

"How do you know what's happening to me? Aren't you a bartender?" you asked. You were unsure of trusting this woman—unsure why she was there, a decade after your last meeting.

"One day still to come, I won't be as you see me now," said Carina, who was dampening a wad of paper towels to cool your burning fever. "I was lost, and you showed me the way. You changed the course of my existence, and I have since been indebted to you."

"I don't understand. What do you mean by one day still to come," you asked as Carina glanced curiously at the chain around your neck. You felt the pulse under your shirt, the key dancing to some unknown force. "Why is this happening now? Did you do this to me?"

"No, I didn't." Carina backed away and leaned against the door to one of the stalls. "I triggered a memory that made your total recollection come a few hours early. Nothing more. In a way, I am giving you a gift." You shook your head, displaying your complete and total confusion. "A few hours from now, the man with two eyes, as you know him—Malus—will attempt a bold plan to capture you. One that involves several moving pieces and the potential death of you and your love."

"Why? How do you expect me to believe any of this?" you asked. You were irritable, and the pulsing and throbbing behind your temples was extreme. With every pulse came clarity, old memories resurfacing.

A car crash when you were only six came crushing back into place where it belonged. You remembered Jane's death, and the pretty young EMT who helped calm you down. The same woman who stood before you now.

"Because I am an angel," said Carina. "I fell from grace more than twenty thousand human years ago. Ancient tribes and civilizations worshiped me—some called me Invidia, but most know me as Nemesis. I masquerade as a human, hoping to earn my way back home. I do not expect you to believe me without proof." She stepped forward as a blade of pure fire extended from her hand, crackling and blazing with intense heat. You couldn't believe your own eyes. Somewhere in your mind you had the image of winged men, circling the sky above as the earth crumbled under the crushing weight of your own pain and despair. The forthcoming memory terrified you more than the sight of the flaming sword inside the bathroom of a Mercy Point bar and restaurant.

When the air returned to your lungs, all you could manage to say was an exasperated "Whoa," followed by a long silence. After a short time, Carina decided she had been exposed enough, and she retracted her sword as easily as she made it appear.

"What do you want from me?" you asked. "The last time I saw you, you told me about your lost love. You told me that the man with two eyes wants what I have, and that my *true love* will be the only thing that saves me. Then you told me to make myself forget."

"Time is linear," said Carina. "Time should not be toyed with. Time has rules, but those rules can be bent." Then she pulled at a chain around her neck and exposed a brass key. Seeing it, you reached down underneath your own shirt and did the same, then studied them closely. It was the same key I wore now, the same item in three separate points in time, simultaneously.

The keys pulsed in unison—another magic trick. I didn't envy you, Jace, coming into all this knowledge at once, so late in the game.

Carina nodded and continued. "They are not duplicates, but the same exact key. As my life proceeds, I have been moving backward through yours. I do not recall warning you, but knowing this has happened in your past, I know where I must go next. The man you're with," said Carina, gesturing back toward the bar, "is he special?"

"To me," you replied, "yes."

"Beyond human?" she asked in a strangely skeptical tone.

"What do you mean?" you asked.

"Nothing important. Just something I sensed," said Carina with a twinkle in her eye. "He seems—familiar to me."

Carina had the key. Whether she had it before or after me, I had yet to discover. Multiple players and multiple timelines, each party racing to foil the other, and yet, there was something about her eyes. Her presence gave me the worst feeling I refused to ponder further.

"What am I?" you asked. All your memories arose from your subconscious mind, and the answer to this one question was the only one you needed to know.

It was the one question I had been digging into your timeline to uncover.

"To answer that is difficult. *Why* you are and *what* you are cannot be answered correctly by me. What I know is that you are special. There are things you can do that you should not be able to do. You are unique. I do not know why, or how, or even to what extent you are capable, or even how culpable you are for any of the things that have occurred, or potentially to occur. Malus, the two-eyed man, has plans for you. The evil he controls is like a monsoon, an uncontrollable destructive force very few can ward off. Our salvation may lie in the friends we make. A plea to rally ones who may help us. Know this, young Jacinda, the curse you bear breaks the very heart of me, an Angel, who once upon a time fell to Earth over her hatred of mankind. If I can cry sympathetic tears where once beat cold stone within my chest, others may come to our aid."

"And what happens to me, when this is all over? What will become of me?" you asked. You knew the truth but needed to hear it spoken out loud in order to believe it.

"Your life was never meant to be. Not like this. I'm afraid that win or lose this battle, your life will be gone, no matter the outcome. It is the only way," explained Carina. Her sorrow for you was clear, though not entirely sincere. She had her own motives, yet it was still more information and understanding than you ever had.

"You said you came here to offer me a gift," you said.

"I did," said Carina. "If you knew you had only a few sparing hours left, how would you wish to live them? With the knowledge of the impending doom? Blissfully ignorant, living happily with the man you love until your last moment? Or would you flee with me, to find an answer that might change the course of events? But make no mistake, eventually Malus will find you. This is your future that cannot be unwritten. He will take you. These are your choices."

Your mind raced in a million different directions, Jace. They were awful choices, and if I was you, I probably would have chosen the same.

Some of your thoughts splintered into absurdity, calling out the very idea of this conversation as a delusion, or some unfortunate drug induced trip. Others devolved into self-defeating woes, asking why you were the one stuck in the middle of all this. Yet others tackled the issue at face value, trying to rationalize and compartmentalize the damage and what could be salvaged of your ill-fated life. The choice of abandoning your love for the hopeless pursuit of help, guided by a fallen angel with her own motives, sounded like a fool's errand. And if you came across an answer, would you even want to know when it meant your own death? You thought of me and what your death would do to me—and the thought tore you apart.

No matter what, I was going to lose you, Jace. Unless you fought. If you were so special, couldn't you fight? Use whatever abilities you had to end it? You knew what you were capable of. You remembered the destruction and the complete command you had over your abilities when your mind spun out of control. If it wasn't for...

And then you remembered *me*. I'd talked you down from destroying the world. I made you stop. It was me, the man you knew, and yet, it wasn't—not yet. From your perspective, the timeline didn't make sense.

Your head hurt just imagining the tangled web of our reality.

"Malus will come after you. And those you love if you do not submit. Your memories are telling you to fight," said Carina, reading you as easy as words on a page, "but he will find a way to control you. If not by force, then by threats and fear. He is undeniable." Then she waited for your response. When none came, she prompted it. "What say you, Jacinda Moira O'Neill?"

You thought through your choices as seriously as any you'd ever made in your life. There was no precedent for a decision so consequential—in your life or in the life of any other human. How could you leave me? How could you leave your friends and your happy life? At the same time, how could you stay knowing what was to come? Could you really trust Carina? Or was she an ally of circumstance? How could you not go and try and fight and find a way to survive?

"You don't trust me," said Carina, sensing your feelings. "In your circumstance, I believe I would not trust me either."

"I only trust one person in my life with all my heart," you replied. You thought about leaving, but in your heart, you knew you could never abandon me. Your mind was made up.

Carina knew your decision without having to say it. "The only decision you have left to make is whether or not to live the coming hours with or without the knowledge of your fate."

The answer was easy. You knew that if you continued, with the information you had now, you would only end up pushing me away. And that was exactly what you were going to do. You already made the decision—to end your life.

"Give me a day. He deserves it," you said, turning away from Carina and looking in the mirror. Your eyes caught the glimmer of the key dangling on the outside of Carina's shirt. You stared at it, concentrated on it and what it meant to the love you shared.

"So be it," Carina responded with a nod. "I will help your mind to ease back the memories that have broken free of their cage, but only for one day." Carina paused, then said something that made your skin crawl. "You must do all within your power to make sure the key is no longer in your possession when you are taken. If he has you and the key, the outcome will be disastrous." Then she stepped forward to place her hand onto your shoulder and stared into your eyes through the reflection of the mirror.

"Okay," you said. "How does this work?"

"Relax. You won't feel a thing," said Carina.

"I hope you find help," you said as you began to cry.

"I will try," said Carina. "As they say, the show's not over till it's over." With that, you began to feel a warm sensation around your head. At the peak of its warmth, you felt a sharp pain and swore you heard a door slam shut.

When you finished washing your hands, you dashed out of the ladies' room and back into the bar, where you found me and Marshall bickering over something silly, as Anne listened and shook her head at our absurdity. This was your family. The people you loved most in this world.

"Are you okay?" I asked as I handed you a bottle of water.

"Yup, all set," you said, kissing me passionately on the lips. I was almost shocked that you had forgiven me so quickly, but happy that you had.

"What was that for?" I asked, taken by the exuberant smooch.

"I don't know. I just felt like I needed to show you how much you mean to me." You were safe and where you belonged.

Goddamnit, you sacrificed yourself for us, Jace! You saw the demon closing in and you wanted to protect me. You saw no other way. But why didn't you fight back? Why didn't you come to me?

There had to be another way...

XXII
hell's end

MALUS
December 23rd, 2013
Now.

Power was rarely a singularity. Often it was acquired, gathered over time and accumulated like wealth—much like the treasures of the great King Solomon, before his fall at my hands—a transformative moment in my existence. It was the day I took the first step on my current path— the day I finally grasped control of my destiny.

The spoils were laid before me. All I had left to do was to tie up loose ends. An accomplishment that would never have come to pass if not for King Solomon and the power he misunderstood.

The dead were the most powerful weapons in all existence. Harness the dead, and one could destroy kingdoms, topple governments, and even sway the pendulum of fate.

I controlled the dead. A Necromancer by title, but so much more.

The souls I owned, slain or captured by my own hand and kept as a private army, had become pieces of me. Extensions of my being. When one was suddenly destroyed, or released from my control, I took notice.

Richard Jansen was a favorite of mine. A spirit I enjoyed torturing—honing into a mean, angry psychic blast of ectoplasm—it was as easy as training a dog to fight. He was broken before I met him. And Tori Martin was exquisite—I'd snapped her spirit into a whimpering mess, willing to do anything to stop the pain.

But now they were gone. Those and the others I had collected for this occasion.

It was time I stopped underestimating them.

Tony and Jacinda—it was time I broke you both.

I knew what Jacinda was…

But Tony? Somehow, he was capable of much more than he should. Where his power came from and his ability to use it, was worrisome. It was a startling discovery to find him in Votan's Tomb. His thorny presence was always on my mind. How he managed to find me and capture his own Thread of Destiny was even more concerning. There was so much more to his story than what I knew, but a quick death with limited chance for complication was the only correct course of action.

I could not allow him to escape alive.

If he was strong enough to survive the ghastly horrors hunting him inside the halls and classrooms of the brick building, he would only escape to find me waiting for him in the courtyard. My army of dark terrors would feast on his flesh while his beloved Jacinda watched. It was the only way to destroy her resistance to my influence. Destroying her only hope, her true love, was vital.

TONY

"What's the plan, boss?" asked Maynard.

We were standing by a window on the fourth-floor landing of Hallows Hall's west staircase, staring out into the courtyard below. It looked empty, but we all knew it wasn't. Creatures lingered in the shadows just out of sight, beyond the reaches of the lamp light scattered around the courtyard. My enhanced vision could see figures standing there, but it was too dark to know what they were.

"Yeah, what's the plan, my man?" asked Montoya.

"If we're an angel, how come we can't fly?" asked Jamaal. "Can she fly?"

"I can't fly," replied Jaycie. She had replied directly to a voice inside my head. Jamaal slapped a shocked hand over his mouth in response.

"Was that even an option?" asked Maynard, confused.

"No, sorry," she said, "I was replying to—?" She gestured to Jamaal, wherever he was. In my head, I guess? I could see him standing over my shoulder, but Jaycie could hear him—all of them, actually.

"Jamaal, ma'am," he replied, and she shot me a wink meant just for him.

"Who?" asked Maynard, regripping his shotgun. "Are there more ghosts I don't know about?" He looked paranoid.

"No, it's—complicated," I said.

"Speaking of complicated," said Chappy, "how *do* you plan to get us out of here?"

A sobering chill ran up my back as I edged my way to the railing and peered down below. Even with my ability to see through most dark places, it was difficult to make out exactly what the shadows held. Something was stalking the bottom floor, taking each deliberate step toward us—a slow methodical gait.

I could hear it. Smell it. Taste it, even.

"Ever have that feeling of creeping death?" I said.

"Great song," said Maynard, and I nodded.

"So let it be written, so let it be done," said Jaycie. "I'm sent here by the chosen one."

Maynard looked confused. "You're a Metallica fan?"

"You're the one who introduced me, remember?" she replied.

"Oh," he said, "yeah, I remember. That day suddenly has context."

"Guess you don't meet many girls who scream bloody murder in public places, huh?"

Maynard sighed, and she placed a kind, forgiving hand on his arm. We didn't have time for a story, but it sounded like a memory with a vague connection to all this. What I'd give to finally understand what the hell was going on…

The stench of mildewed fur was growing ripe. It was a warning—time to leave with the kind of haste that would leave a cartoon vapor cloud in our wake. The noose was tightening by the second, and it wasn't just my neck I was worried about. I prompted the brain-trust for a plan—a really bad one if nothing else—and even Doshin, a master tactician, shrugged.

"I think—" I began to say, then paused when the doors below to the first floor swung open, and the biggest fucking wolf I had ever seen edged its way through. In horror I watched as it raised its head and greedily sniffed the air with its long snout, searching for its prey: the three of us, three and a half floors up. It had six-inch yellowed, rancid teeth and paws the size of catcher's mitts. Its smoldering yellow eyes scoured every nook and struck fear in the back of my tightening throat. Its head was easily the size of a grizzly bear's, with thick tufts of coarse matted black fur helping it cling to the shadows. If anything ever deserved to be called a beast, this creature did. "—we need to go up a floor."

They saw my expression, and without a word we vacated the landing—Jace in the lead with Maynard in his combat boots stomping up the rear. We entered the fifth and top floor, and as soon as the doors had closed, we took off running for the east staircase on the opposite side of the long hall.

Movement stopped me dead in my tracks—and I held out my arms to hold up the others.

"What is it?" Jaycie asked.

Cue horrible things.

The far door to the east stairs opened, and out swept two dozen pallid faced pregnant women with bellies that seemed almost unnaturally engorged. Their skin was splotchy like putrescence, as if their flesh was liquefying, and their eyes were wide with zombie-like attention. They smelled...*fishy*. Seriously, they *smelled* like fish, as if they had swum in a vat of ocean slime and walked directly into Hallows Hall. They were mostly barefoot and wore the most random garments for pregnant women: some wore tube tops, while others were stuffed into cocktail dresses, with a few mini-skirts and bare midriffs mixed in. Of those inappropriately dressed, they appeared to have torn or stretched their clothes to accommodate their large bellies.

Then they began to moan.

"Who and what are they?" asked Maynard. His voice sounded equally repulsed and terrified.

"The Maids of Dagon," said Jaycie, and I wasn't going to debate how she knew.

The mind can imagine all kinds of horrific things. I remember lying in my bed as a kid at night, terrified of the shadows. Every time a car passed our house with its headlights on, it partially illuminated my room, making dark shapes leap and slide across the walls. The shadows would morph and blend into creatures so ghastly and terrible, with plots so conniving and cruel, they would wait till I could no longer escape exhaustion's cold clutch and kidnap or eat me when I was fast asleep and most vulnerable.

Eventually you grow up and realize there was nothing horrible under the bed or lurking in the back of the closet under that pile of junk. I was one of the unfortunate few who came full circle and realized there really were things that go bump in the night, and there was every reason to fear the shadows and the creatures that lurked just beyond the light.

True horror, I always thought, lurked in the mind. The subconscious fear of what you couldn't quite see. I was wrong, because when true terror strikes, and you're staring it square in the face, unable to move and incapable of screaming, when one's soul truly rattles with the pillars of truth crumbling under its own weight and denial, every nightmare and every true harrowing thing you could imagine does not even come close to the reality of terror.

True terror was absolute.

Whether through ignorance or innocence, when the delusion of sanity and safety fall, one can either accept the truth and react to it or stare at the oncoming train and wait for impact. Self-preservation or death.

I looked at Jaycie, then to Maynard, and I saw two people who needed me.

I wasn't going to let them down.

The Maids filled the far end of the hall with their bloodcurdling moans, barring the east staircase from our path. The moaning was pained, like a cross between a hungry seagull and an old arthritic woman climbing stairs—they were beyond our help. Behind us, inside the other staircase, stalked a giant wolf the size of a Winnebago. *Middle*, meet *Rock* and *Hard Place*. The choice was simple: did we try and fight off a beast whose mere sight managed to send intense warning sparks of danger up and down my spine, or tiptoe past two dozen fishy pregnant women?

The answer seemed simple… at first.

One of the Maids convulsed and the others, all at once, stopped moaning and watched. I raised the gun in my left hand toward the maids—my right, aimed at the door behind us, just in case—my head on a swivel.

"Why do you think they're called the Maids of Dagon?" asked Maynard as we crept closer. His question was the kind that begged an ill-timed answer, and I didn't have a free hand to give him an irritated pop upside his head—but Jaycie did. "Ow! What was that for?"

"That was from Amanda," said Jaycie with a glare. "She'd want me to."

We were within thirty feet, sliding carefully nearer…

And then the horror came.

One by one they started convulsing, and in great red explosions their children burst forth, ripping free into the world like pimples popping from the inside out. The birthing tore the mothers to shreds; most of them didn't survive, and those that did didn't last very long. Each of their offspring were variations of the same foul creature, but none of them were at all human. They were small beasts, pale gray, each with eight long slimy tentacled arms with large, hooked suckers lining their underside. Their heads were fused to their torso, with one or two, and sometimes even three reddish yellow eyes searching immediately for food. Some of them fed on the rotten remains of their mothers, while others focused on the only viable *living* sustenance in the room.

Us.

Like a mob of ugly, slimy puppies they surged toward us, their tentacles lashing, grappling, and crawling over each other to be the first to reach fresh meat. They crawled up the walls and left a layer of gooey rancid afterbirth over every surface they touched. Mouths, like suckers lined with hooked pin teeth snapped, chuffed, and drooled.

Whether it was instinct or a disgusted involuntary reaction, I fired two shots at the nearest, putting it down with a couple flaming bullets to the head.

"Oh, what the fuck!" shouted Maynard, as he opened fire with his shotgun.

If we couldn't get to the east stairs, we were dead, either eaten by the Children of Dagon, or cornered by the slow and deliberate hunt of the great wolf.

Jaycie slipped away from my side, but she was still there. I could smell her strawberry and lavender scent. She was safe, for now, and that was all that mattered.

Maynard and I mowed the slimy creatures down. When the mob got too close, I shifted gravity and ran up the side of the walls for a different angle, gathering them to me and away from Jaycie and Maynard. Something wet and slimy wrapped around my forearm and stung like a jellyfish; its hooks sank into the muscle and pulled. Like a tug-of-war, we yanked back and forth as I fired with my free hand, then dropped from the wall to ceiling and used that leverage to whip its cephalopod body into another—swinging and smashing it like a mace.

I bashed and shot my way through six more with *Terminator*-like precision—then when I lifted my arm to pulverize the seventh, I found nothing but a limp tentacle—no body attached—I'd smashed it into a pile of flaccid mush. There were almost a dozen left, sloppily slogging forward, showing no sign of fear or reason except to gorge themselves with food, when I squeezed the triggers and heard nothing but a chorus of clicks.

I was out of ammo.

"Fuck!" I growled, shifting to the far wall. Dagon's children were in hot pursuit, chasing me in a strangely clumsy but effective way of grappling, sliding, and swinging. I underestimated them as I fled and stupidly boxed myself into a corner.

Damn.

Maynard clipped the nearest and blasted another before he too had to reload. Exactly how many shells did he have hidden inside that trench coat? I was standing on the wall, my back against the ceiling, surrounded by hungry critters—each the size of a portly eight-year-old with slobbery saliva gushing from their strange carnivorous mouth holes—

I felt the nag to give up, pulling the trigger continuously as the empty clicks became my last vestiges of hope, evaporating. I begged that a magical bullet would suddenly appear in the chamber, followed by another and another. I was desperate, I was broken, and all I fucking wanted was a cheap piece of lead stuffed into a metal casing with gunpowder so I could get the three of us out of this fucking mess!

How many times would I have my back to the wall?

How many times would I be on the retreat?

How many times did I have to face the end of everything when all I wanted was to be happy? All I wanted was for Jaycie to be safe!

How. Many. Times!?

From somewhere deep down, I pushed the flames from my gut into my chest, then down my arm. They crawled their way into my hand and exploded from the barrel of my gun with the next trigger pull. The round of pure hellfire exploded into the nearest infant monster and tore it to fiery shreds—I was no longer dependent on bullets to shoot.

Repeating the process was easy. It took only a small amount of concentration, and I sprang back into action as one of them leapt for me. The slime-ball's swipe missed and crushed the ceiling above my head; then it lost its grip and fell to the floor in a rubbery flopping mess. Maynard polished it off—placing a boot on its tentacles and blasting it to pieces.

When the coast was finally clear, and the last few critters had slithered away to feed off the remains of their brothers and sisters, I turned back and said, "C'mon, let's go."

Then I saw something that took the air right out of my lungs.

The west stairwell, back where we came from, had collapsed in on itself. Chairs, desks, and rafters were stuffed into the door-hole like it was a Thanksgiving turkey. Wires sparked and ceiling tiles dangled by loose ends, all while Jaycie stood there dusting herself off with a proud look on her face.

"Did she do that?" asked Maynard.

"That was…unexpected?" said Henry.

"Remarkable," said Chappy.

She looked at me and smiled, as if to say *look what I just did.* Then she said "whoa," and nearly fell over. I caught her before she collapsed with weak knees and a dizzy spell that made her eyes glaze over. "What a head rush."

"What are you?" The words left my mouth less like an accusation and more like I wanted to kiss her. Our embrace was romantic, and in the moment, I couldn't help but imagine her wearing white.

She looked at me, stars in her eyes, and said, "What are *you*?"

"She's got you there, my man," said Montoya.

"What a couple of weirdos," groaned Maynard, rolling his eyes. He stalked past us, reloading the shotgun, and waved for us to follow him. "C'mon. Quit giving each other googly eyes, and let's go."

Even though there were other stairwells in different wings of Hallows Hall, Jacinda had saved us in the interim. She'd prevented the wolf from catching up to us. But that wasn't the only thing we had to worry about—in the quiet, my body was collecting additional information—smells, sounds, tastes. The prognosis was fatal. I wasn't sure we were going to make it out of there alive.

Together we ventured down the east stairwell, carefully plotting how to approach every corner, and exited on the first floor. Hallows Hall was a science building with labs and lecture halls every fifty to a hundred feet. Many of the doors were closed, but a few were left open. I had Jaycie's arm over my shoulder, helping her until she could move on her own.

It was quiet. Still. Almost too still.

Then, someone sang…

"Three blind mice. See how they run. See how they run. Hahaha."

It was a woman's voice, pitchy, whiney, and off key.

"That's fucking frightening," whispered Maynard as we crept further into the hall.

"Abjectly terrifying," added Chappy.

"What are we looking for?" whispered Jaycie into my ear.

"Yeah, what's this jawn look like?" said Jamaal, his voice shouting compared to ours.

"Maintenance closet with an unmarked exit out the back," I replied.

The first floor had been through renovations, but everything appeared roughly the same as it had almost twelve years ago.

We had passed the first several classrooms when the singing continued, the voice this time closer—from behind or ahead, we couldn't tell.

"When the bough breaks, the cradle will fall, ashes, ashes, we all fall down, falling down, falling down, London Bridge is falling down... myyyyy...FFFFAIRRRR..."

"My man, I don't think that's how it goes," said Montoya.

"No, my man, that's not how it goes," replied Jamaal.

We stopped. The tune hung on the air, right on top of us. Maynard aimed his shotgun at an HVAC vent above us, while I kept both guns at the ready. The mystery woman could have been anywhere—

"LADY!"

A putrid arm swiped down from the ceiling panel and snagged Jaycie by the hair. Maynard and I shot at the same time, and the arm retracted and disappeared.

"Are you okay?" I asked her.

"Yes."

"Did you hit it?" asked Maynard.

"No," said the voice. Then she dropped from the broken ventilation system in a big crash of dust and debris and grabbed me by the throat.

She choked me while stroking my cheek with her free hand. Her touch was like acid and burned everywhere. It was the pain of leeching life, ripped from every organ at once. It was a full body pain, the kind that provided awareness about what parts had nerve endings, and others that were blessed in the circumstances to feel nothing at all. There was no scream to signify the immensity of it, nor was there any breath left to announce such torment.

She was about Jaycie's height, her platinum blonde hair encrusted with tangled dirt and filth. Her skin was as pale as death, beautiful and smooth on one side and hideously deformed and wrinkled on the other. She hid her deformity, obscured in shadow behind her mangled hair. Her eyes were big and pale, like the color of her flesh—a faded blue-violet with a hint of pearlescence. She was thin, barely more than anorexic with the dark blue lips of hypothermia, and a ratty old dress stitched of old cloth and fibers hung from her form several sizes too large. She was barefoot, with caked dirt and filth from toes to knees that looked as if she were wearing stockings. Her touch burned and inspired me with a sinister name—Hel, daughter of Loki.

Peeling her hand away from my face took the skin with it, like a hot griddle had been ripped away—my scar finally matched the rest of my face. I backed up, my eyes trained on her as she paced towards me, keeping the distance between us status quo as my wits slowly returned.

"Play with me some more! Play with me," she laughed with a full smile of rotten teeth.

"Hey," grunted Maynard, the shotgun already leveled at her face, "play with this."

The slug hit Hel in the shoulder and ricocheted through bone before exiting out her back. The impact spun her around twice and was already stitching back into place before she fell to her knees.

"Owie, owie!" she whined.

"Go!" I shouted, and Jaycie and Maynard were already running, moving past me as I protected their escape, down the hall and left into the east wing. We fled past the room where I once took bio classes, toward the strobing lights that hung above the nearest exit—the emergency message had stopped playing, but the lights were still flashing all around campus.

"Games! I love games!" squealed Hel from somewhere behind us. "Run! Tag! Red Rover, red light, I'm it!"

As we ran, we were liquid through a funnel—the evil narrowing us until it was too late. Doors closed of their own accord, blocking our escape. Hallways darkened, forcing Maynard to flee down dimly lit corridors rather than wade through complete darkness. When he stopped in front of the door beneath the flashing red glow of the emergency exit sign, waiting for the rest of us, a chill ran up my spine. It wasn't until I had my bearings that I understood why.

"That's not an exit!" I shouted. The clenching alarm in my gut warned me so.

"What?" said Maynard, his free hand slowly extending toward the release button.

I was twenty feet away with Jaycie between us—raising my gun to protect them both from the illusion—but it was impossible to protect everyone. It was impossible to be everywhere at once, to control everything. Everything was always so out of control, and every dangerous thing that jumped out of the woodwork was mine to put down.

I was always running up that hill, Jace, just like you. Climbing mountains just to exist.

For a moment, just a moment, I glanced at her—our eyes connected. The things I would do—the lengths I'd go—the miles and miles I ran and would continue to run, just to protect her…and doubt crept in. Was I good enough? Would I ever be enough?

"You try too hard, Tony," I heard her say, a memory I'd tried to forget. *"One day, maybe you'll realize you were enough."*

—but not today. Today I had to be more than enough. I had to be everything I ever was and more.

I was streaking past her and leaping through the air before I determined where to strike. One foot sprang off the wall above Maynard's head and twisted, bringing my boot down like I was stomping out a cockroach in a dark corner of my apartment. My heel struck something that resisted for a split second before cracking—the bone crushing, then collapsing to the force. The creature smacked face first into the floor, and I chased it with a fiery round to the back of its head for good measure.

"Nalusa Falaya," gasped Maynard—*"long black being."* Somewhere amongst my brain-trust was a Choctaw warrior who gasped right along with him.

However, it didn't matter what the creature was—it no longer had a face—but Maynard was mystified, if not completely frozen. Behind it was not a door. It was a mirage. An illusion. The actual door was still fifty feet away, and what existed in that span between was full of unseen horrors.

"What was that thing?" asked Jaycie. Her heart was beating three times faster than normal, and she looked flush. She was in her prime—she could run a sub-7-minute mile, so I knew it wasn't the physical effort that had her body overexerted. It was the stress.

Maynard dropped his shotgun and removed something plastic from his interior trench coat pocket, then pumped it six times in rapid succession.

"You always keep a water gun in your pocket?" I asked as he quickly drained the reservoir across the floor, walls, and ceiling tile.

Salt water. Blessed.

"Insta-U-Nat wall," he replied through gnashed teeth. "Never leave home without it."

"Red light! Green light!" shouted Hel. She was a silhouette strobing through the hall toward us—every few steps passing through a trickle of light. She was stalking us like a spry junkie pixie looking for a fresh hit.

"Will that hold?" I asked, pointing toward the saltwater wall.

"It held those zombie-angel shits, didn't it?" sassed Maynard.

"Yeah, but for how long?" I replied, as Jaycie stepped forward.

Like a mime game, Hel took two steps forward and stopped, mimicking Jaycie's stance before her. "Mother. Mother may I take four steps forward?"

"Simon says stay right where you are," said Jaycie. There was heat, and the hallway waved and bent like feverish blacktop in the dead of summer.

"Aw, mother!" shouted Hel gleefully, "that's not how this game is played." Then she took four steps forward, beyond the bending heat—disappearing into shadow and reappearing in the light beyond the boundary. Then she smiled at me. "Come now, lover. Give me more. I want more."

Hel was unstoppable. She'd gotten a taste of something she wanted, and she would not be denied more. I stepped up, sliding past Jaycie to put myself between them—I could sense Jaycie's fear, the anxiety and the overwhelming scent of doom on her perspiration. She was wavering, woozy, and whether or not that was connected to her expending energy was not something I had time to investigate.

"Stay close to Maynard," I whispered into her ear.

"Tony," she said—and her tone carried the subtext of a thousand different thoughts, concerns, and worries. I heard them all. I felt and reciprocated each and every one of them.

"We're cornered," I said. "There's only one way out of this."

"Like Hell there is," said Maynard. He strutted to my side and took aim like some kind of Dirty Harry meets Stallone badass, but when he pulled the trigger, Hel danced aside. She was fast, pushing Maynard away and swiping for my chest. She wanted to touch me, to suck more life from me—to feed.

"Get back!" I yelled. Maynard recovered and pulled Jaycie away.

When Hel attacked, she put me between her and the end of his shotgun. She was methodical, like she was playing with her food—swiping for my head to set up a lunge for my leg. All she needed was a glancing brush, and the burning sensation lit me up like the Vegas strip.

"Do something, Jaycie," demanded Maynard.

"Like what?" she said, as Hel swiped for another taste.

"I don't know! You barricaded the stairs! Why can't you drop something heavy on her?"

"I don't think I can!" she argued.

"Why not?" he asked, but when she looked at him, he knew. She looked like a Picasso portrait, stuck somewhere between two faces. She wanted to do something, but she wasn't in control. Not anymore.

"Swallow this," I growled, as I stuck my gun in Hel's face and pulled the trigger. The fiery bullet splattered her brains out, but she smiled at me as the hole closed up and the hellfire fizzled.

"I'm no Fallen, love," she said and swiped for my arms.

"I'm not your love. But you look like Hel." I name-dropped, expecting the same results I had with Mammon and Bacchus.

"Oh! Knower of names!" she said, her tone delighted. "Name magic doesn't work on me, love. But go on, shout my name. Shout my name. Shout my name! Shout it! Shout it!"

"Tony?" said Jaycie. The torment in her voice spun me toward her, and I knew something was wrong just by the tone.

Her face was flickering back and forth but rested on her own long enough to shed a single tear before it left me once and for all.

"Don't give up on me," she said. "You are the moon."

Then, she was yanked away from us, splitting Maynard and me as she flew through the air like a marionette on strings. I dove for her, but it was too late—the force whipped Jaycie away from me and beyond Hel, who stood in my way with her rotted grin, preventing me from giving chase. Jaycie hovered at the end of the hall, where two creatures silently awaited her. The puppet masters—one black with red stripes and a hideous mouth, the other white with yellow stripes and bulbous eyes—watched as they crawled around on the walls like insects.

The stairwell doors behind us opened, and out trotted that big fucking wolf, stalking into the room with its head bowed low, ready to pounce. It stalked up to the U-Nat wall and took several sniffs before chuffing angrily. It was only a matter of time.

"It's a party," said Maynard sarcastically.

"Brother, Fenrir!" said Hel to the wolf. "I found us toys to play with!"

There was no way out. We were trapped. Shadows moved. The noose was beginning to choke, and Maynard began to panic. I could hear his heart beating erratically. He shot at something that moved in the shadows, keeping it at bay as the wolf paced back and forth, waiting. Then Maynard reloaded with special slugs of his own design—made of iron, salt, and mercury.

"How'd you like my *special sauce*?" he growled, after firing off a round. Whatever he hit, it hissed and screeched and jumped back behind the wolf. He blasted anything that got within ten feet, and they didn't like his "special sauce"—not one bit.

The doors to a nearby classroom swung open, and three snake-like women slithered into the hall. Their lower bodies were scaled in bright crisscrossing black and red patterns, while their top halves appeared human, with the soft underside of humanlike flesh.

It was getting crowded. The deck was already quadruple-stacked.

I made a move—a motion to escape—but Hel caught me around the collar and yanked me to the ground. She pounced on top, her hand around my throat as she pinned me there, siphoning life away. She ate away at the flames and took the energy I needed to fight back.

"You taste so good," she cooed, the ecstasy fluttering her eyes.

I shifted and fell to the ceiling, a move that had already become my go-to, and her neck ended up below my boot. The impact with my strength and her feeble mass should have crushed her windpipe, broken her neck, and killed her instantly. Needless to say, that didn't happen, but it did offer me a moment to think. As soon as pain lit up in her eyes, I dropped to the floor and grabbed Maynard by the shoulder.

"Which way?" I asked.

"We don't have one," he said. His expression was dire—had he already given up hope?

I scanned the room. At the far end of the hall was the woman I loved, wearing someone else's face. She dangled there, arms outstretched and waiting—watching?

Malus wanted her to see this. He wanted her to see me die.

"Brother!" Hel shouted from her knees. "Brother! He tastes like sugar! Savory and sweet! Fenrir, help me! I want to eat more!"

Her calls to Fenrir scared the living shit out of me. I had faced a handful of psychotic wannabe gods, sent a few of them into the cosmic beyond, and they seemed like nothing compared to Hel's power. Perhaps the deaths of Mammon and Bacchus weren't because they were two prideful gods that made stupid mortal mistakes, but accidents. Perhaps I really didn't stand a chance against Hel. Perhaps I didn't stand a chance against any of them. The doubt crept in like those shadows on my bedroom wall slowly gliding toward my bed. The little boy who didn't want to sleep because he was too afraid of the shadows was helpless to fight back.

"If I'm going to die, I'm going to die fighting," said Maynard.

"A glorious blaze of fire and fury," I said in solidarity. "I think that's our only play." I too had resigned myself to death.

"Don't give up on me," Jaycie had said, but how was I going to get out of this?

"Sir," said Henry, choosing to speak up at the worst possible time. "There has to be another way."

Hel came at me like a cat—graceful with powerful strides, culminating in a wild slash of claws. I dodged, barely, and managed to set my feet within striking distance, then unloaded on her with a combination of fists, flaming bullets, and pistol whips. I felt her bones bend under the force of my strikes, but it wasn't enough to do any real lasting damage. She took my punch and used its momentum against me, spinning and slashing across the side of my head. Blood trickled down my face and neck, seeping into my shirt. She struck again while I was stunned, but I caught her by the arm and tried to rip it off. I bent it all the way around her back awkwardly, ignoring her painful touch until I felt her elbow and shoulder pop.

"What about the nuclear option?" I asked, referring to immolation—going Human Torch and lighting the place up.

"You'd kill Maynard," said Jamaal.

"Not to mention Jacinda," said Chappy.

Hel screamed and flailed and backhanded me off balance. Her mangled arm dangled at her side until she managed to rehinge it with a sharp snap of her wrist. It buckled and popped, then settled into the socket at an odd angle.

The playfulness within her was gone, replaced by anger and morbid desire. She came at me again, and I countered by kicking with all my strength to the inside of her right knee, where she planted all her weight. Her knee buckled with a sick crack, but that didn't stop her. Hel absorbed pain. For something so small and frail, she fought like a monster. Slashing and hacking to inflict maximum damage with every strike. There was no punching or kicking, no martial arts or anything as sophisticated. Hel was pure feral ferocity, looking to maim and slice arteries.

"What about the lightning, my man?" asked Montoya.

"Inside the building? Are you nuts?" said Jamaal.

"Same outcome. Less efficient," said Doshin.

Then what?

I fired four shots past Hel, wounding the gathered snake-women that were slithering in for the kill. The distraction gave Hel the chance to grab my jacket and toss me. The force of hitting a cinderblock wall hard enough to leave an imprint jolted my spine and may have fractured it.

The impact knocked the key free of my shirt, and it dangled in the middle of my chest like a big gleaming bullseye. I extracted myself from the wall and glanced down to find the key exposed, sparkling from a non-existent light source. Hel's pearlescent eyes glazed over it, transfixed by the sparkles. Whether or not she knew what it was, I couldn't be sure, but she wanted it. The taste of greed blossomed on the air.

"Lover, hiding presents?" she said, unaffected by our fight. Or maybe pain didn't affect her like it did me. "Give me the shiny, lover, please?"

I wrapped it in my left hand, shielding it from her eyes. "You'll have to kill me."

"Silly," Hel scoffed. "Give me the shiny!"

The key was buzzing. Vibrating. Such a small piece of metal, but it felt heavy—heavier than it ever felt before—like it was packed with enough potential energy to do enormous things.

"The key!" yelled Jamaal. "Use it!"

Celestine had called it the Key of Capricorn—the first of the four Keys of Eden—

—But we didn't know what it could do. Maybe it'd open a black hole? Maybe it would set off an explosion? End the world? Maybe it would unleash my Care-Bear Stare? Open a safety deposit box? Who the fuck knew!? I certainly didn't. And what if it didn't do anything? A great big letdown that would get us nowhere!

"Bottom of the ninth, my man," said Montoya, as the darkness around us surged.

"It's time," said Chappy.

"Two men out."

They were closing in, everywhere.

"Good luck, sir," said Henry.

"Down by three."

Was this where I was placing all my hope? Was this our great big secret weapon? A silly key *my mother gave me before she died?*

"Bases loaded."

And where did she get it, huh? Would anyone tell me how my mother fit into all this? Would anyone dare to speak her name in front of me?

"Now!" said Doshin.

I took the key and shoved it into the keyhole in my wrist.

"Maynard!" I shouted.

"Tony!" he shouted back in tune.

"Get over here, now!"

A set of yellow orbs floated nearer in the darkness, focused on me. Great tufts of waxy hair stood on end and shivered along its massive back at the power unleashed by the key. Fenrir was the largest beast I had ever seen—even seemingly larger than the Oni from Jaycie's dreamworld—standing over six feet tall on all fours. His head—nearly the size of my torso—was drooling with anticipation.

Maynard fired, keeping Fenrir at bay as Hel cackled. Her laugh sounded out of tune. She wiped stray hair from her face, then came for the key. I blocked her hand and grabbed her by the wrist despite the pain. Her other hand wrapped around my throat.

I shouted to Maynard, "Turn the key! Now!" as we tussled—the key resting within the Sharpie-keyhole on my free wrist extended as far away from the maniac as possible, waiting to be turned.

Fenrir charged and covered great lengths with every stride while the surrounding monsters closed in, like the Red Sea claiming the Egyptians.

Maynard twisted the key and I felt a sliding sensation, like I was falling as I watched Jaycie in the distance disappear in a great white flash.

Hel's eyes went wide, her body went rigid, the light sending her into a panic.

Fenrir launched himself, his massive jaws aiming to clamp down around my head and neck, while Maynard screamed at the top of his lungs.

"Fuuuuuuuuuuuuuuuuuuuuuuuck!"

The next thing I knew, we were falling into a bright space.

October 13th, 1984

Freefall. There's something about a fall that makes every sense kick into high gear. Seconds. Minutes. My inner clock sped up, and it felt like I was falling forever, tumbling and grappling with a lunatic. Hel shrieked when we slammed against something hard and her grasp on my throat loosened. We rolled off in opposite directions and fell again even harder to the tiled floor. There was a great scattering of tiny feet, and movement all around me. My eyes were having a tough time adjusting from the darkness of Hallows Hall to the bright light of the wide room.

I heard cries. Not shouts of pain, but the cries of confused and scared kids. *Where the hell was I?* I rolled onto my knees and blinked my eyes shut, even rubbed them to coax the process along. When I could finally focus, I found myself covered in glitter and Elmer's glue, lying on the floor of a room decorated with bright primary colors and tables. They looked vaguely familiar, as a memory seemed to slowly worm and wiggle its way into full recollection.

Maynard shuffled around behind me, groaning, and said, "Did I just land in paste?"

Hel thrashed about on her back, kicking and screaming. She seemed infuriated by the bright light, wounded by it even, and wailed like a tortured banshee. She rolled onto her knees, flailing, and bashed her fists onto the floor in a tantrum. The noise of frightened children suddenly grabbed her attention, interrupting her insane hysterics.

Across the way, my eyes landed on a familiar face.

"Mom?" I said.

What the fuck was going on?

"Tony, my man, where are we?" asked Montoya.

I heard a whimper, almost a whispered cry, and found it coming from a young boy who looked even more familiar to me than this room—the very pre-school I attended until—

Oh shit, it was me.

There was a high-pitched pop, and the building shook—then I watched as Byron, the painted turtle and class pet, sprouted a whole new head right in front of me from within his glass terrarium. I knew what I saw was wrong, but there was so much else wrong about the moment that I couldn't stop to consider a two-headed turtle.

"Lover," said Hel flatly, with a devilish smile and bloodshot eyes beaming with sudden horrifying joy. She knew exactly who the boy was. She could tell, by some supernatural means.

She sprawled at him—at the little me—just as I grabbed her around the ankle and yanked. Her reach came up short, but her claws scratched for little Tony, just missing as Mom snatched me up and away from harm. I was four and didn't remember any of this.

I slammed my fist into Hel's head. I felt her orbital bone crush beneath my knuckles, and she rolled away from me in pain. In the darkness she was unbeatable, but things were very different now. She rolled over and hid herself from the bright room beneath her hair, protecting her eyes.

Hel was definitely weaker in the light, a theory proven when she slid from my grasp and made a run for the nearest door.

"She doesn't like the light," I said out loud, as Maynard was peeling a paper plate full of paste from his face.

I got up and ran after her, leaping over the skewered table and past my bewildered mother—her gray eyes glancing over me like I was just some trespassing perp who'd come from nowhere and endangered the lives of the children in her care. Hel ripped the door off its hinges, then ran outside, narrowly escaping my lunge. I followed closely behind and had her in my grasp when she suddenly turned and pulled away, running through a narrow walkway behind the preschool building.

We were in the middle of my hometown. In New Jersey. In the fucking past!

Hel shouldered a white picket gate open and bolted down the sidewalk, into the bright sunlight. The shock came to her all at once and made her shiver and scream as the luminant rays enveloped her. It was midday, and early fall, judging by the color of the leaves on the nearby trees. Hel screamed at the sun and frantically searched the sky.

"Father!" she screamed and ran toward the nearby baseball fields I'd played on throughout my youth. "Father! I'm here! Help me!"

I began to catch up, each stride moving faster till I could almost grip the long flowing strands of her dirty hair. Within mere seconds we were past the baseball fields and heading towards the forest on the far side of the property. I was a blur to human eyes, moving faster than a car, moving faster than any natural living thing should move. I willed myself to be faster, and I began to inch closer to Hel, attempting to prevent her escape.

Hel needed the woods. She needed the darkness. And I needed to keep the edge.

"Do it!" yelled Jamaal.

"Now!" shouted Doshin.

I leapt, grabbed her by her hair, and pulled her down violently. We both hit the ground hard like a meteor smacking into the earth, loose dirt and fallen leaves exploding into the air all around us. We tumbled into an open hedge, just inside the tree line, before the forest thickened and the sunlight faded. She hissed defensively and crawled for the darkness, but I stopped her and dragged her back into the light—her touch siphoning and burning. We tussled and she cut me across the chest. I could smell my blood, taste the iron mixing with the scent of rotting leaves.

I tackled her, spun her down, and wrapped my arm around her neck from behind. Her teeth sunk into my bicep as I began to twist and pull, my leather jacket too thick to bite through. Her hands scrambled for a weapon, latching onto a fallen branch and driving it through my shoulder, just below the neck—but I did not let go. She tried to scream a few garbled words while she kicked and flailed for freedom, but the end was near. Hel was no god, nor Fallen. She was merely the child of one. A living breathing child in the light. As she weakened, I put my right foot into the ground below me, acquiring the leverage to—

SNAP!

Her neck broke in two and she collapsed in a heap.

I fell away from her and into a pile of leaves, then crawled until I was sitting upright against a tree and hyperventilated, allowing my body to heal.

I was damaged all over. So much so I had to strain to get the healing started, and thought I was going to black out.

"Hey," said Maynard, finally catching up, paste still stuck to his face. He'd caught me in a vulnerable moment. We escaped, but I had failed.

Again.

I was as far away from saving Jaycie as ever, and my disappointment manifested with involuntary tears.

"Let me get that for you." I didn't know what Maynard meant until his hands wrapped around the branch protruding from my shoulder, and he yanked it out with a gush of quickly congealing blood. "Thought I'd return the favor."

"Thanks," I croaked, and he sat down next to me. He did me a favor. It was easier to focus on the physical pain.

"We're in the 80s, aren't we?" he asked.

I nodded.

"We're also in Jersey, aren't we?"

I nodded again. "How'd you know?"

"The hair," he replied.

"For which?" I asked after a moment. "80s or Jersey?"

"Both." Maynard dropped something into my hand. It was the key. "Might want to hold on to that," he said. "Probably our only way back."

"Time travel," I said matter-of-factly.

"I know what you're thinking," he replied. "There's rules about this sort of thing."

"How do you know?"

"There's always rules about this sort of thing. Terminator. Back to the Future. Bill and Ted. The Butterfly Effect."

"Ack," I responded to his last entry.

"Don't mock it!" he scolded. "Think about it. Think about the damage that could be done? One small change could affect…everything."

I thought about my mom for a second, and then about Jaycie, before my mind settled on more immediate concerns.

"Want to get a beer?" I asked.

"Sure," he replied. "But what are we gonna do about her?"

I carried Hel's body deep into the woods and conjured up the flames to burn her remains. We watched the hellfire burn until there was nothing left, not even bone.

"Do you want to go home?" asked Maynard as we walked out of the woods. It was almost dark, and we were both thinking about the basics—food, shelter…toilet. But I figured he was referring to my mom.

"No," I replied, but I was lying. Still, there were some wounds I didn't need to reopen.

Maynard and I stole a car and drove to Grace Falls that night, developing a plan and working out all the details. We debated the finer points of time travel and being good stewards of the timestream. But in the end, he relented, helping me find ways to ward Jaycie's house against evil by tracking down items I could use to protect her, just like he'd done to his "lab" at the Store-It. Later, when the time came, I would hide them all inside her house on Cross Road, and in the newer one in Elm Way Acres.

Then, on a whim, I told him about Byron, the newly two-headed turtle, and how it happened right after I saw my younger self. He immediately called it a "paradox" and attempted to explain the dangers of time travel while Jamaal added extra commentary.

"If you're going to do this," said Maynard, "you have to be careful. Father Monaco, Jonah, and me have some experience in this stuff."

"Time travel?" I asked as we cruised down the interstate approaching Mercy Point, still an hour or more outside of Grace Falls.

He sighed. "I wouldn't call it that, exactly. But, listen, this goes against the very nature of…well, nature! It's dangerous. Like *Timecop*."

"I get that, Jean-Claude," I said, picking up on his reference.

"Good. Okay, so remember," he said, recapping. "No paradoxes. No Predestination, Grandfather, Bootstrap, or Let's Kill Hitler varieties. We don't know what kind of damage they could do. Stay hidden. Stay away from your past self. Go into that other world you were telling me about— the Veil. Sounds like the perfect place to hide out and watch for answers."

"Which one's the Predestination Paradox?"

"That's the one where traveling back in time becomes a part of past events."

"—a temporal causality loop," added Jamaal. "You go back to try and stop something, only to become the thing that does the jawn you're going back to try and stop."

"I think I get it."

When we arrived in Grace Falls, we rode out to Milton State, and I turned the key at the rendezvous, returning him in the exact spot where Father Monaco and Jonah Johnson were waiting. There were sirens and flashing lights everywhere as police and emergency responders surrounded the campus grounds.

"We have to go," said Jonah, nervous they might get caught. The evil had gone, but the authorities were everywhere.

"What are you going to do now?" asked Father Monaco.

I responded, "Get answers."

November 24th, 1980

As I approached the white house on Cross Road, I had no real understanding of what I was doing or what would become of me. As I walked up the side of your house toward the second story corner window that sat in the shade of a large oak tree, I had no ruminations that this was how I would spend the next twenty years of my life. I slipped behind the Veil and peered through your window as a silent watcher. You were sleeping in your crib, thirteen days after being born. Your Grammy watched you from a rocker in the corner, reading a book to a toddler with blonde hair.

I watched your life like a guardian angel. Little did I know what I would learn about you, about all the secrets you never shared with me. Secrets about how you, Jacinda Moira O'Neill, were something extraordinary.

I watched, and I watched, searching for answers.

What are you, Jace? And why?

XXIII
dark future

JACINDA
Then.

How many years had I watched your life, Jace? I watched you grow from child to adult, reliving every happy moment, until I realized the answers I needed didn't exist there. So, I concentrated on every horror and every tortured moment. I noted every clue and strange occurrence you encountered before your untimely end, hoping to find answers. Your end—I could never drag myself to endure it from this perspective. Could I watch you take your own life all over again?

During my self-imposed exile, I remained so close that I could reach out and touch your life, but I was forbidden from ever being a part of it—watching phantom moments of days gone by. I had strayed so far from my original intention—to relive these moments, to be your silent guardian, and to gather information—but to watch your light extinguished would be anguish. What good would come from witnessing your death…*again*?

Through it all, I took notice of the strange inaccuracies. I learned to attune myself with your emotions, to read them and feel them. I could even hear your thoughts behind the Veil.

The other version of me, my Echo who dissolved to ash long ago—he died in an effort to warn me, and yet I feared that no matter what choice I made, I'd never be able to willingly choose a path that separated us. If I was to fail, could I be as strong and clever as him? Could I find a way back to that night, to the next version of me, and put him on the path away from this purgatory? And if such a thing was possible, could he change history for the betterment of your life?

I knew the answer in my heart before I had even given myself the opportunity to examine it. If there was a chance to change it all, I would do it. Not for me, but for you. You deserved a happy life, one free of me and all the hell that had been brought upon you by those like me.

I was back in the game.

There were answers out there, and the two dates surrounding your "death" were two of the few places in your natural timeline I had yet to travel.

I learned a lot about you—about your psychology and your affliction. Growing up with the unconscious guilt of your sister's death, the suspicion that you had caused it in an angry moment of a child's innocent passion, and your mother's depression over being stuck with a daughter she didn't quite understand, left you searching for something—validation, love, connection—to fill your emptiness. You wanted to belong, you wanted to be loved, you wanted something more than an ordinary life. But for a young woman experiencing the harsh unsheltered reality of normal teenagerhood for the first time with such a damaged heart and suspect self-image, it was almost too much. Your heart was always in the right place, Jace, and your passion tapped into the great potential that rested within your soul—but your actions were not always for the best.

Jacinda, you could alter reality and perhaps do so much more. I found no secrets explaining why or how you obtained this ability, only that your abilities and my true past were intertwined.

Your life was a series of unfortunate events. One moment giving way to another, dominos falling in inextricable sequence, leading your life towards its own destruction.

You were never meant to be with me.

"Save her. Find a way to right our wrong," said my Echo.

That's what I came to do.

December 31st, 2008

It was after midnight.

You went back to the apartment as I drove Marshall and Anne home across town. They were too drunk to drive, and I always was the one to make sure they got home okay. It was already 2:30 in the morning, and I texted to let you know I was on my way. The entire apartment building was too quiet, so you decided to put on some music and tidy up before I got home, which included lighting a few candles to set the mood and a quick shower to freshen up.

You had almost finished rinsing off in the shower when you began to feel nauseated. It began with small shifts, like some of the bar food didn't agree with you, when the pain intensified as if an animal were clawing at your stomach from the inside. The sharp pains crippled your ability to think and sunk you onto your knees.

I was ready, Jace. It was going to be now or never.

All your previous brushes with the supernatural had been lost, forgotten intentionally using your mysterious abilities in order to keep you safe, as well as to erase the pain from the burden you carried. You had no memory of the prior hauntings. They were locked away, left behind, unloaded so that you might survive, and the world along with you. Only I, or those who existed outside of linear time, knew the truth: you had the potential to be the most powerful creature that ever existed on Earth, and you had no idea, suspicions, nor delusions of who or what you were.

In the midst of the pain, your stomach clenching, your senses pulled themselves together as you became hyper-aware of your surroundings. Each and every water droplet splash against your body felt as sharp as a needle, prickling your soft skin under its constant stream. You clawed at the fiberglass floor and gripped the shower curtain for stability while an upbeat acoustic song played off the computer in the next room. The juxtaposition between the pain and the song made you feel ridiculous, and you gripped your stomach, hoping to soothe the pain with a bit of pressure. Your eyes were teary and your mouth tasted salty, as if you were about to vomit.

If you had any understanding of what was transpiring, you didn't show it—not until the music slowed to a gradual and complete halt. Then, after a few moments of silence, the music played in reverse. It sped up exponentially, going faster and faster until it became a high-pitched wail, and the speakers shorted out with an abrupt pop. The air filled with the smell of burning wires, making your stomach lurch and groan.

The pain intensified the moment you felt the sudden disjointed feeling of your ribs expanding and contracting, pushing the poisoned contents up your stomach. You fell to your knees, gasping and heaving, when from your mouth came a patch of black, oily bile, which seemed to separate from the cascading water like wax. You threw up again, adding to the mass of rancid ichor that spread along the shower floor. Even in your dazed state, you knew this wasn't right—then, to your horror, it moved.

It spread to the edges of the stall before flattening into a perfect pool. Its surface was black as a starless night sky, mirroring your terrified face back to you, and yet something was seemingly amiss. As you contemplated your escape, out of the ichor came sticky appendages, roughly in the shape of human hands, yet incomplete, grabbing you around the wrists and neck. You tried to scream when several more grotesque hands came forth, solidifying their hold on you, a dozen of them if not more. There was no time to contemplate what their intentions were, what manner of creature it was, or even how it got into your stomach. All you knew for sure was that it meant no good, and you needed to get away no matter the cost. You pulled against its grasp with all your strength, but its grip on you was absolute. Its hands tangled in your hair and around your throat, arms and ankles, like dry ice burning your skin everywhere the sickening flesh touched you.

Rising slowly from the ichor came a featureless face. The slime contoured over its developing physiognomy, creating a pristine visage of what appeared to be a little girl. A face that you once knew well but had forgotten. The memory and the idea of her was there but just beyond reach, like forgetting a useful word mid-sentence—where the space the word should be was gone—tantalizingly close, but frustratingly far.

"You thought you could make us forget," said the little girl, and then she sang, *"but we found you."* The chilling tune made even the hot shower feel like a downpour of January sleet.

You fought back like a caged animal, grappling to free yourself as more hands groped your body, attempting to pull you into the darkness beyond the inky threshold. The air within the room seemed to vibrate as you sank lower and lower toward the girl, as she widened her jaw to consume you whole.

I motioned to leap from the Veil, arms outstretched to pull you free, ready to fight and die if I must. This was it—I was making my stand for you, Jace—but the vibrations on the air became so intense, I became locked within the Veil. I slammed my fists against the threshold, but it would not budge, and I was helpless to stop the attack.

"Let me out!" I screamed—a caged spectator. It was as if they knew I was there and purposely forced me aside. "Let me out!"

Your head plunged into the ichor, submerging as you fought against the arms dragging you under. As the shower continued, every grip slipped away, leaving little traction for leverage. I saw your body lurch, as if screaming on the other side of the portal, witnessing hellish things that no mortal eyes should ever see. You lashed back and forth against your restraints, and I still couldn't move an inch to help you, locked in place and forced to watch.

Suddenly, there was light, like the hand of divine intervention quickly followed by a flash from a burning blade, severing the hellish hands that tugged at your body. You pulled your head free from the horror and jumped from the shower stall, ripping down the shower curtain in the process. You tripped and fell, smacked your head against the floor, and knocked yourself unconscious.

The angels were watching, and for once they'd intervened, but why? Why now?

"Let me help!" I screamed.

The ichor roared with anger, then shrieked before dissolving and washing down the drain, leaving no trace of the evil behind. The vibration on the air that held me captive was released, and I left the Veil at once and rushed to your side.

You were hurt. A lump was rising on your forehead. I gently carried you into the next room and laid you onto the bed. The electricity dimmed, and the digital alarm clock by the bed started blinking random gibberish before it flashed the word "SOON"—a warning for you? For me? There was no way to know.

I was attempting to heal the lump on your head, when I heard someone coming up the hall—the past me—and I slipped away beneath the Veil.

You remembered everything, even though you didn't believe what you had seen. The evil had nearly found a way to grab you right out from underneath the watchful eyes of angels. They were watching, but how closely? Why didn't they step in sooner? Why did they let you die almost twenty-four hours from now?

The Thirteen were testing the angels and would soon find a way around them. You were the prize they sought, and the watchful angels could not stop them.

You made no mention to me of what had happened, and after a short time you began to wonder if you had imagined it all in your dreams. The ghastly things you witnessed beyond the ichor terrorized you so intensely that it began a break in your reality.

The show was over. I did not need to relive your breakdown, or the ambulance ride to the hospital where I thought I was going to lose you to an overdose. That was pain I did not wish to endure once more. But I knew where Malus would be in twenty-four hours, and I was going to stop him.

Now & Then.
January 2nd, 2007 at 6:16 A.M.

There was snow on the ground and footprints that started from the middle of the clearing like she had transported directly to this spot, then tracked toward the abandoned mill. Jaycie was already there, waiting beyond the devil door.

The past me wouldn't arrive for another half an hour. I decided to change the course of history, once and for all. If Malus was here, I'd confront him and finally end it. This was my fight, not Jaycie's. This was where I needed to be, and I wasn't going to let Jaycie end her life to save us when I was more than capable of finishing this fight myself.

As I stepped out of the Veil, the sun was rising over the horizon and silhouetting the mill. It was the setting to all my recurring nightmares— the falls rumbling in the distance, a gathering of crows on a nearby perch along the warehouse roof—I was taken back by the intense fear that gripped me. This day held a kind of biblical fear—the day my life went tumbling off the tracks forever.

My gut was always honest when I was about to do something good, or monumentally stupid. If someone were to chart my decisions in a Venn diagram, they'd find plenty of crossover between the two—most of my best decisions were stupid, by definition.

Honest Gut Reactions - Smart Decisions vs. Stupid Dumbcisions

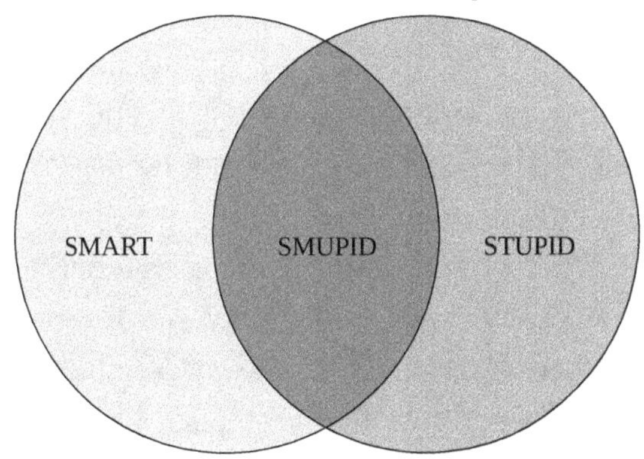

That said, most of my good decisions blew up in my face because I overanalyzed everything—but this decision may have been the worst one yet.

This decision was as blunt and direct as a being murdered by a spoon, and if I had any belief that it was going to be easy—I had none, of course—that all came to an abrupt halt when I stepped within forty feet of the barn door.

The crows admired me. They sunned themselves on the warehouse rooftop, watching my approach, and I had the strangest sensation that they were warning me. "Don't take another step, asshole," I imagined them saying. Were they spies for the Morrigan? Were they just ordinary crows? Were they something else?

When I took my next step, I received an answer.

My father had an expression. He'd often said, when remarking on an extreme level of impact, that it could "smack the taste right out of your mouth." The idiom didn't make much sense to me until that very moment, when something hit me so hard that I lost all sense of taste, sight, and hearing. I fell through the darkness and slammed onto something as hard as rock.

My shoulder shattered on impact and began mending the moment I rolled onto my back and stared up at the tiled dome ceiling. It was old tile—subway tile to be exact, and my senses were overloaded with the smell of mildew, dust, and old books.

"How did I get here?" I groaned out loud. I didn't expect an answer.

"We don't know, sir," said Henry.

I shot him a sideways glance and said, "I thought you were long gone."

Henry appeared in his old-fashioned suit and spectacles, and in blazing technicolor. The room was dark, but he was as bright as if we were standing in the sun.

"How could I leave? I am a part of you, remember?" he said.

I shrugged and stood up. I could only see Henry at the moment. The others were there, but hesitant. They were sidelined and coming to life—perhaps knocked loose by the impact. I nonchalantly checked my head, just in case I'd sustained an injury, and found it surprisingly intact—and the scar on my face felt more ragged and distorted than ever.

Interpreting my silence as a question, Henry then said, "Our dormancy was the result of your self-pity. You resigned yourself into passivity, and we faded away." He kept talking as I looked around, allowing my eyes to adjust. "Speaking in terms you might understand, when you *got up off the bench*, so did we."

"Thanks for dumbing that down for me," I said with a sarcastic smile, when I spotted someone new. "Who're you?"

He looked at ease, like he had been there all along when I dropped in—tall, wearing armor over a blood-red tunic. A Roman soldier with a crooked nose and grin.

"Markus," he said, nodding.

"Exactly how hard *did* you hit your head?" asked Jamaal.

We were standing in what appeared to be an old subway station, but it was very clearly not used in that capacity. Below us, in the space where the tracks should have been, were rows and rows of bookshelves that had been toppled and destroyed with old leather bindings and yellowed pages littering the floor. It looked like a tornado had ripped through. There were broken chairs and desks, smashed computer terminals, and what looked like an old computer mainframe that had been crushed apart when the wall collapsed.

To my left was a series of doors, each with a placard above them, from the Weapons Room—which was cleared out, I checked—all the way to the Specimen Room at the far end. It looked like some kind of laboratory until I spotted the symbol on a tattered flag. The shield and star—the symbol of Father Monaco's Patronus Lux.

"Why are we here?" asked Montoya. I looked over at him, and he smiled shyly and added, "Hey, my man."

"These books," said Chappy, "are quite interesting."

I hopped down into the *library* and grabbed the nearest book, the one that Chappy seemed the most absorbed with. Since he couldn't actually pick up the book or flatten its pages, I did it for him. The book was a leather-bound edition with only a symbol pressed into its cover—like a gemstone with ten, maybe twelve sides. It was written by someone named Robert Boyle III and I started to read aloud the first paragraph that caught my attention.

"—where twenty years prior I stood upon the precipice of a miraculous Alchemical discovery, I now realized it was only one small fraction of Alchemical fact. Alchemy was the source of all power in the natural world; from gravity to magnetism, these forces were bound by Alchemical principles. The Philosopher's Stone, whose properties could control and create many incredible things, was merely one step in the evolution of an even more powerful Alchemical Focus; a tool with which one might channel Alchemical Sorcery. The Philosopher's Stone was only the first step of three, toward the penultimate; becoming a god."

"What the fudge?" said Jamaal. His face was wrinkled up, like he'd caught of whiff of something nasty.

"Pseudo-science," scoffed Henry. "And they have the nerve to call psychology as such."

"Alchemy is merely witchcraft with a fancy name," said Markus, shaking his head.

"Perhaps," said Chappy, "but this whole room is full of books on topics just as strange and controversial. Is any of it as strange or stranger than the things we have already witnessed?"

"Good point, my man," said Montoya.

"Sorcery exists," said Doshin. "Entire cities have burned under rain like fire. I have witnessed mountain mists that decay flesh and mind, and swarms of flies that consumed cattle in a matter of moments." It was the most any of us had ever heard him speak at once, and we all took notice. "Sorcery exists."

Jamaal was wandering around the room, studying the architecture, when he said, "This place looks familiar to me."

"I thought you had an eidetic memory?" I asked. "How could you forget? You're my own personal Google."

Markus shrugged in agreement.

Jamaal shook his head. "It's bizarre hearing you say that name after everything that happened. You don't know about the Company Wars. In 2041, the three largest companies on the planet went to war over resources and workers. Those were the darkest days." His eyes glanced over the placards above the different rooms, and he saw something that made him freeze and shiver—a placard with only a symbol, like a donut, and scorch marks on the doorframe. But when we heard the screech—high pitched like grinding metal—Jamaal shivered. "We need to get out of here. Now!"

"What was that?" asked Markus, looking uncomfortable.

I grabbed at the key underneath my shirt, attempting to use its power and get back to unfinished business, when I realized it was gone.

"Where is it?" I said, searching the ground around me. "Where's the key?"

"What?" asked Montoya. "Did you drop it?"

"Was it stolen?" asked Chappy.

"I don't know," I said, feeling a panic.

"I do not see it," said Doshin.

"It doesn't appear to be in this room, sir," said Henry. "Could you have dropped it in front of the mill?"

I shrugged.

"Tony, you need to run. Run now," said Jamaal. He knew what was coming, and he was terrified. They were extensions of me, and as his fear grew, it spread into all of us. Jamaal wasn't joking around. Whatever screeched in the darkness was coming for us.

There was a hole in the wall on the far side of the room between two ruined sets of armor, and as I rushed between them and into the next chamber, I couldn't help but wonder what that room was, or what it was meant to be. Another chapter of the Patronus Lux? Did that room have anything to do with Thad and Chris? It was a far cry from the amateur arrangement of Maynard's storage unit.

The chamber beyond led to an underground tunnel with a set of rail tracks that looked like they hadn't been in use in a very long time. I chose a direction and ran.

The things, whatever they were, moved quickly. They vastly outnumbered me, and I could sense each of them as they flooded from the shadows, chasing us—although it wasn't quite chasing. They didn't run; I couldn't hear or feel their footfalls. Instead, they moved as if they were shifting in and out of existence—almost like teleportation. They hissed and screeched, and I thought one called out my name—or maybe it made me think it did? Regardless, I was looking for the first exit up and out.

The tracks led into the darkness for miles, but I spotted a metal platform ahead and shifted gravity to race there faster, running on the ceiling for the last fifty yards. The platform sat below a service entrance at the very top-center of the tunnel, with a manhole cover and thin shafts of sunlight trickling through. I slammed my shoulder into the heavy metal without slowing down—it moved but remained stubbornly in place. I did it again, and again, knocking loose whatever barricaded it from the other side.

"Put your back into it, my man!" yelled Montoya.

"For the love of Christ," growled Markus, "hit it with all you've got!"

I slammed it again, starting in a squat and launching my whole body straight up into the metal—I was running out of time. Each slam dislocated my shoulder and cracked a collarbone, the injuries healing before my next attempt. I gritted my teeth through the pain and kept hitting it, the rubble blocking my escape audibly tumbling. The next thrust shifted the weight on the other side, and I almost broke through when something grabbed my leg and pulled.

When I fell into the darkness, I was instantly engulfed in wickedness. The beings were comprised of absolute evil. There was no conscience or remorse, no morality or empathy—the things that snagged me were creatures of absolute negativity. One of them got inside my head and bounced around through my thoughts, spying on my personal demons and laughing at my loss, my broken heart, my suffering, before finding secrets that made it squeal. My skull felt like it was splitting, a pulsing ache behind my eyes. In an effort to pull free, I grabbed and punched at everything. If I was going to go down, consumed by these things, I was going to make it as foul an experience as possible. I was scrambling to stay alive—there was no strategy or nifty planning—I was being mauled by things that were darker than shadow, things with milky white eyes and straw-like hair. They were hideous creatures that were as brutal as they were ugly. My hands ignited, and the creatures quickly extinguished them. It was a scramble, and when my hands groped across a length of chain, I fought back like the hourglass of my life were grains away from ending. With a snap of my wrist, I lashed the chain and swung, forcing them away.

Despite their darkness, they still felt pain.

I rolled onto my feet as the thing inside my head kept probing. The others watched and waited for me to make a move.

"Get outside! Get into the light," shouted Jamaal.

I sprinted up the wall, returning to the exit, and clawed my way through before they could regroup and drag me back down into the darkness. Through the heavy metal covering was an alcove beneath ruins—like a building had fallen onto its side. It was an office, and although I was abiding the gravity status quo, running along the floor, it appeared as if I was moving on the walls. I ran toward the glimmer of light as the thing continued to claw inside my head and dove through what was left of a plate glass window into the blistering sunlight beyond.

The creature hissed and screamed, then fled my mind and scrambled back into the darkness, howling as it went. I rolled around in the dust and squeezed my eyes shut as the migraine began to subside.

"What the fuck was that?" I shouted, hoping Jamaal had answers.

"Tony," he said, "I think we have bigger problems."

I opened my eyes and saw the sky. It wasn't blue.

"Hail Mary," said Chappy under his breath. "Where are we?"

"This," said Markus, "is incorrect. This is blasphemous."

Doshin sat back, watching our surroundings, while the rest of us studied the sky and the ruins.

"This isn't right," said Montoya. "Why is the sun like that, my man?"

It was like an eclipse, only it wasn't. The sky was a shade of violet, like the blue we were used to had mixed with the radiant red light that burned from the edges of the sun. The sun's center was black—like an eclipse, but different. It wasn't like the sun was being blocked, but rather, like the sun itself had become a black hole.

"The quasar," said Jamaal absentmindedly.

"Jamaal, where are we, my man?" asked Montoya.

"Jamaal?" asked Henry.

"Home," he finally said. "I'm home."

"What do you mean?" I asked.

"Welcome to the 90s," he said.

"The 90s?" I asked. This didn't look like grunge, JNCO jeans, and episodes of *Friends*.

"The 2090s," he clarified. "Welcome to my time."

It wasn't just the sky that was different. It was everything. We were standing amidst a wasteland—skyscrapers sheared in half, surrounded by rubble and dust and decay. There was no life there, nothing that grew—only death and concrete. At the center of it all, I spotted a familiar sculpture in the jagged shape of a lightning bolt attached to a kite and key. Behind it was the twisted metal shape of what was left of the Ben Franklin Bridge, and a leaning church steeple. I knew it well. Saint Augustine's Church on Fourth Street—a block away from the cemetery where I'd disappeared into the funerary mist and wound up in the penitentiary cell moments later.

"We're in Philly," I said. "Philadelphia."

"The Company Wars weren't the only bad thing that happened in the 21st century," explained Jamaal. "Climate change. Pandemics. Food shortage. Overpopulation. Natural disasters. All the while, sea temperatures kept warming and rising. Scientists warned us, but politicians never listened—cashing in before checking out, leaving a ruined planet for the next generation."

Then he chuckled, but we were too rapt by his story to stop him.

"It began here. In the middle of the city," he continued. "First the *Event* happened. Then, a few years later, people started dying in their sleep while dreaming. Others were snatched at night, in the dark, never to be seen again. There was mass hysteria, and the cities were abandoned, then became war zones—Boston, New York, Philadelphia. They created New Delphia—a mega-city that spanned from New York state to Baltimore. We built an eastern wall and twenty-four-hour lights across the entire border keeping those things out, but people still went missing."

"When?" I asked. "When does all this happen?"

"First reports of people gone missing started in 2015," said Jamaal. "Two men, John Monks and Michael Graves were the first to go missing. I researched all the official reports. Wrote my whole thesis on it."

"John Monks?" Were all my old friends swept up in this mess? Why did it feel like we were in the middle of everything? "And the Event? What was that?"

"Tony," said Doshin, interrupting my thoughts. "The sky moves."

At first, I thought something was lost in translation, until I followed his eyes and spotted a glimmer. The sky was shifting—almost rippling. I was still holding the chain and wrapped the first length of it around my wrist and fist, ready for a fight.

"What is that?" asked Markus. He began walking toward it, squinting into the violet light.

As I tracked the glimmer across the sky, a crow landed on a nearby pile of rubble and squawked.

"What the—?" I said, questioning the absurdity of its arrival. Had the crows followed me? There wasn't a living thing in sight, not even a blade of grass or pesky weed—no ants or gnats. Nothing—except this bird.

"That's odd," Chappy agreed just as the glimmer unloaded.

The sky lit up like a nuclear blast. Fire and fury rained down on my position like a laser- targeted missile. When it hit, I ran, jumped, and scurried to get as far away from the blast as possible. The ignition withdrew all the oxygen from the air, sucking in large chunks rubble. I held on, grappling to an exposed piece of rebar, when a flash of a metal blade snapped it.

I went tumbling into the inferno.

XXIV

the crescent moon

TONY
August 12th, 2093
Far From Now.

"He should be ash."

"Should be, but he is not."

"How is that possible?"

"Shall we apprehend him?"

"The Raptor has broken our laws. He has put the stability of this realm in jeopardy. Death is the only permissible action."

"Were those our orders?"

"The Voice has spoken."

"Then he shall die."

I was still smoldering when I heard the footfalls—booted steps, the gentle clang of metal. The heat and fire burned me alive—the agony was immense. But at this point, let's be real, I had felt worse. I couldn't breathe within the blast—the oxygen was sucked from the air throughout a six-block radius. I could only fight to stay alive like a cockroach in nuclear fallout—now, however, I was playing possum.

"Put the traitor out of his misery."

They didn't know what hit 'em.

The chain was still glowing red hot when I whipped the nearest one across the helmet. The glittering specimen of metal and majestic white wings, like shards of crystal, was otherworldly—and I took great pleasure dinging it straight-up the side of its perfect armored head and cracked it like the Liberty Bell. I spun and whipped for their legs; they dodged at first, reeling back onto their heels, until I caught another with a blistering lash across the temple. The fiery lance that had been aimed at my chest was tossed aside and fizzled into smoke as they backed away from me.

And that's when I got my first clean look at them.

They were angels, no doubt.

Their armor was a combination of thick black leather and metal plates the color of platinum, woven together with interlocking, overlapping pieces—like a pangolin crossed with a human-sized tank. The armor appeared pliable despite being metal—it bent and contorted to the wearer's every move. Around the head was a dark gray hood connected to a helmet that fully masked their faces. The mask had long vertical slits for the eyes and covered the nose and mouth completely, leaving nothing but shadow over the slightest bits of exposed face. Upon their helmets were nine interlocking circles chiseled into the foreheads—and my chain had just scratched one of the rings clean off.

There were six of them. Each with weapons that crackled and burned, and every set of wings was unique, like a fingerprint or a snowflake. They staggered backward while I continued swinging my red-hot chain like a wild man at a rodeo looking to 'rassle him up some cattle. I must've looked hideous—I could see the sinew and tendons in my hands. The flesh had burned right off—but I was too amped up to feel it. I felt like I could have demolished an entire construction site with my bare hands, or joined Dr. Teeth and the Electric Mayhem as a replacement for Animal on the drums—

—You choose the more aggressive of the two.

One of the angels attempted to out-flank me. I swung my chain for the angel's head, and to my surprise he caught it—but it was his surprise when I yanked him off balance toward me and unloaded three to four fast combinations of lefts and rights that broke both hands and sent the angel sprawling backward.

"Do not touch him!" one of them shouted. "He is a Powers." They were speaking a language I had never spoken but could understand. Their words came to me like a conversation with friends. It was succinct and graceful, older than Latin, but similar. It was the first language, my instincts told me.

I grabbed the disarmed angel with the broken helmet, his flaming lance nothing but smoky vapor, and ripped the mask from his head. When I put my hand around his throat and growled into his pale face— his auburn hair and eyes smoldering like hot embers—all at once the name came to me. But before I could speak it, something walloped me, like I was being struck with a cartoon mallet.

Slamming into a pile of rubble when traveling at high speeds crushes every bone in your body. My lungs collapsed and several organs smashed—except the only one that mattered—my heart. My anger raged, and with it came the internal flames that stitched and healed every broken part and slid them back into place. I was almost mobile when the rubble shifted. A great big hand made of rebar and concrete wrapped five enormous fingers around me, knocking the air from my newly inflated lungs.

The un-masked angel strode forward with a smile—I could sense the connection from him to the concrete hand, as if he was controlling it.

"The Raptor," he said, speaking in English. "How the mighty fall." He stared at my face, fascinated by my scar, then torqued his lance as if to viciously drive it through my left eye.

I pulled against the concrete, gasping for a breath—and with a single inch, I inhaled.

"Zephon," I said.

His face turned cold and the concrete hand crumbled away, dropping me to my knees as his lance slid forward, grazing me across the side of the head. His name dissolved his magic, leaving him only one choice—to fight mano a mano.

Zephon was fast. He belonged to an Authority of Warriors, and he knew how to kill all manner of creatures, but with the chain wrapped around my left arm and my right hand pulling the gun from my crispy belt, I was daring him to prove it.

I was daring them all to prove it.

Zephon flinched—or maybe, I imagined it—the guy had one of those squirrelly faces that was either flinchy or just asshole—so I shot him through the arm. My hellfire bullet ripped right through his fancy metal suit, clipping him below the shoulder. Then, just because, I winked at him with what little I had left of my eyelids as he painfully buckled over.

Each and every one of them thought twice—I could smell their hesitation like smoke and mint—though there was a good chance the smoky fragrance was just me.

Wings flapped.

Lances and swords were drawn.

The static on the air crackled, and I began to reach out and grab it as I cued up a snappy retort—something about fried angel being the other white meat. I was going to electrocute the fuck out of these motherfuckers.

Then Zephon's lance struck me in the leg, and I went down onto one knee quicker than being put into a sleeper hold by The Rowdy One, Roddy Piper.

"STOP!" yelled a commanding voice. Three figures stepped out of the Veil, two in blood-red armor—a third in blue. "Who ordered this? Who ordered you to drop him into the Underground?"

"Metatron," said one of the masked angels. "His Voice willed it so."

There was a sigh. Then the angel in the blue armor said, "Stand down."

"Why?" answered Zephon, angling his lance once again at my left eye like he was lining up a cue ball. "The traitor deserves to die. At least let us toss him into the Unbecoming until his grace fails and his flame wilts."

"Zephon, stand down," commanded the superior. A quick glance through the Veil revealed a gleaming halo above their heads—but the halo above the one in the blue armor was like a brilliant crown.

A second lance entered my sight and gently lifted Zephon's away from my face.

"Zephon, we do as we are told," said a calming voice from someone new.

"We *were* told! We have orders!" yelled Zephon.

"We had orders," said another. "We have new orders now. We do as we are told."

"I know, Midael," sighed Zephon. "My Prince, I am sorry." Zephon stood back, and a second armored creature moved into view, blood-red feathered wings tucked behind his back.

"It is not I you should apologize to, brother," said Midael, his red wings bristling.

"Do not distress, Zephon," said the superior. "I understand your anger. Please, help him to his feet."

Two hands—one from Midael, the other from Zephon—reached down and took hold of my forearms, then lifted me to my feet. I realized I was surrounded by nine of them—the two who spoke, four who stood guard, and the three who came to my aid. They seemed out of phase with this world, like they could evaporate at any moment, yet they appeared as solid as stone. But there was something that did not seem right about them—like there was something to be seen just below the surface—as if I could scratch it away with a coin to reveal my prize.

Then I saw it.

—crows! It all of a sudden made sense. They were masquerading as crows. They were always there, watching.

The superior stepped forward. His armor was accented with gold, same as the tips of his great feathered wings, which were twice the size of the others. One of the nine rings engraved into his helmet was filled with gold, while the others remained unfilled. His hand, completely en-cased in a metal gauntlet, reached up and turned a switch at the side of his helmet, which clicked and released, allowing him to retract it like a hood, resting behind his head.

In front of me stood a handsome man with bright golden eyes and long, sandy brown hair. He had a well-trimmed beard and looked no older than me—early thirties—but with a perfectly shaped crescent moon tattoo around his left eye, in the same place as my own crescent scar.

"Paradoxes are not permitted, no matter how honorable the intention," he said to me. His kind smile was full of warmth, though tainted with distrust. "You look very different in this form."

"You know who I am?" I asked. It seemed like a dumb question to everyone but me, the way they each turned their heads to look at the other. I felt like I should have introduced myself to an anonymous group for amnesiacs—*Hi, I'm Tony, I'm an angel, and I have no idea who I truly am.*

"Don't you?" he asked, but it seemed almost sarcastic. It was so damn frustrating being the only one who knew nothing about my identity. "If it was not for your grace, or at least the portion you command, we would never have recognized you."

Staring at him, I realized this man, the angel in front of me, was more powerful than anything I had yet encountered.

"Zephon, Midael, Tristian, Valum, Serien, Galxese," said their leader, then gestured to the red-armored angels, "Eris, Sagitarii—say hello to your Fallen brother. Show him we mean no harm." One by one they removed their helmets, and each of them were nothing less than perfect, and nothing less than complete and total blanks in my memory.

Zephon had a shock of tightly cropped auburn hair which flickered and shifted like fire, with a similar tattoo of a crescent moon around his left eye. He had a fair complexion, and a pair of auburn eyes that smoldered at the sight of me.

Midael was a blonde man with a square jaw, taller than the others, with a four-pronged star tattooed across the middle of his forehead. He had kind eyes and a nasty scar across his chin and lips that ended at the top of his nose.

"Brother," said Tristian with a nod. His tattoo was a flame upon his forehead, and his dark chocolate complexion stood out against his gray eyes. He was bald and built like a tank.

Next to Tristian was Valum, with a water drop tattoo on his right cheek, just below his eye. He had dark hair and could have been confused for any typical young townie drinking beers at Down the Hatch.

Beyond them, at the back was Serien, a woman with long blonde hair and the tattoo of the *sun*?—a circle within a circle—on her forehead. She was stoic and somber and reminded me so much of Amanda with the way she leaned and glared.

The final member of the first group, Galxese, removed his helmet and nearly took the warmth from my beating heart. His skin was so pale, it was nearly as white as bleached bone. His eyes were equally colorless, except for a light gray ring which defined the iris, with a black pinprick of a pupil in the center. His hair was long and as black as the deepest darkest night, and he was clean-shaven, without a single crease or wrinkle on his glassy skin. He wore a somber expression with a sickle tattoo that bent around his right eye. He looked like the embodiment of death.

Every single one of them was a stranger.

Lastly, the two in blood-red armor removed their helmets, but there was something about *them* that struck me as familiar—

The one with the vacant blue eyes was Eris, with long black hair and a pale complexion. She had a circle tattooed into her forehead—a ring, my instincts told me, depicting no beginning and no end. She shoved the point of her lance into the ground and rested against it, almost indifferent to the events transpiring around her—and yet there was something about her—*an emotion?*—I picked up from the slightest cues in her body language. She was fighting an internal battle.

Sagitarii was next, with light blonde hair and bright gray eyes. His complexion was as dark and deep as caramel. His tattoo was that of a downward pointed sword at the center of his forehead, which also resembled a cross. He glared at me bitterly, somewhere between sadness and anger.

"I haven't the slightest idea who any of you are," I explained. "But you two feel familiar." Eris and Sagitarii exchanged glances I couldn't decode.

"When one falls," said the leader, "the knowledge of the next world is stripped from the Fallen's consciousness, as are all the secrets and the hidden paths to return home. We do not need to hide behind pseudonyms, like Fallen, burying our identities. We all know names, including yours."

"Then why not tell *me?*" I asked. "Do you all speak in riddles?"

He gave me a thin smile and continued. "Perhaps with your full grace, you could defeat your brothers and sisters here," he said, suggesting those in the platinum and red armor around him, "but you might not fare so well if you attempted to extinguish my flame."

"And who are you?" I asked.

"I am Gabriel, your Archon and your Prince." The name quickened my pulse. Even the most uneducated knew his name.

"The Archangel," said Chappy. "It means *God is my strength.*"

"Yeah, I don't care what it means," said Montoya. "If he raises his fist, we go loco on this cabrón."

"You bear my mark," he said. "You were a member of the Crescent Moon. You once served to protect and guard Empyrea. You see amongst you members of the Star, the Sun, the Rain, the Flame, the Sickle, the Sword, and the Ring. There are many others, separated into Choirs. My helmet displays my rank, a Prince of the First Circle of Empyrea." He pointed to the golden circle on his helmet next to the empty platinum ones. He paused and gave me a penetrating stare, studying my face and emotions. I could feel all their senses trained on me, eyeing me up like I was a piece of IKEA furniture without instructions.

"Empyrea?" I said aloud, then answered my own question—"Heaven."

Gabriel nodded, then said, "Tony, you have put us into a difficult predicament." If he knew my true name, why didn't he use it?

"I came to end this," I said. "I can end Jacinda's suffering by killing Malus."

Zephon scoffed, and Eris winced.

"And how might you accomplish that?" asked Zephon.

"With this," I said, holding up the gun I had infused with hellfire. Midael spun his lance in my direction, and I aimed it at his heart the second he twitched.

"Stop," said Gabriel, and Midael lowered his lance.

"The Raptor has created a Divine Device," argued Midael. "He continues to sin. Effortlessly. Shall he not be punished?"

"Death is the only viable punishment," said Zephon.

"They keep calling us that, my man," said Montoya. "The Raptor?"

"The Unbecoming would be too polite a punishment," growled Valum, groping his lance. They all wanted me dead, except—

"No," said Eris quietly. When Zephon opened his mouth to argue, she said "No!" once again, silencing his retort. "We are all brothers and sisters in the eyes of The One. Our mission, what bonds us together, is real—preventing the Omens. However, what bonds us—" She gestured between her, myself, and Sagitarii. "—is blood."

Sagitarii hung his head and wept.

"You defend The Raptor?" asked Midael. The look on his face was blasphemous.

"Powers defending Powers," groaned Zephon. "Since their beginning."

"What is The Raptor?" I questioned. "Like the dinosaur?"

"Ignorance is sin, traitor," spat Zephon.

"In Latin," said Chappy, "raptor could mean *abductor, plunderer, robber…*"

"Or *thief*," finished Markus.

Was that it? Was that my crime? Did I rob them?

"Our laws stripped him of his memory," said Eris. "His knowledge is of Earthly things. Spare us all your righteousness."

"Righteousness?" scoffed Midael. "Is it righteous to stop this from happening?" Midael then pointed to the sky toward the eclipsed sun.

When Eris had no response, I asked, "What happened here?"

When Zephon motioned to reply, Gabriel held his hand up to stop the bickering. "This," said Gabriel, "is the future."

"What happened?" I asked again.

"Would you be so kind, Tony, to come with me?" asked Gabriel. "I believe we are in need of a private chat." His tone was not as friendly as his words suggested. Although he was asking, I had the implicit feeling it was not an invitation as much as an obligation. "Eris, maintain order. We will not be long." Then he turned to me. "Follow."

After a few short steps guiding me away from the group, I could feel them vanish, leaving us alone. Despite the fact that I was in the presence of a being that went beyond celebrity, to a level of renown that was beyond anything any human had ever encountered, I did not feel intimidated. In fact, I felt at ease.

After we had walked toward the fallen tower of St. Augustine's Church, he turned to me with words on his mind, but stopped and changed his approach. "You must be in some kind of pain."

I hadn't noticed it, but at the mention of my physical being, I could sense all the damage done across my body that my ability to heal was struggling to fix.

With a wave of his hand, not only was I healed and strong, but my clothes and my dearly departed leather jacket were back, brand new, as well as all the contents in its pockets.

"Magic?" I asked.

"Miracle," he replied. "Alchemy, to be exact."

"Lead into gold?" I questioned.

"Something like that," he said. "I instructed the universe to provide you new flesh and clothing. Now, the cloth you wear will heal, just as your body may heal the injuries you sustain."

"Wow, really?" I asked. He nodded. "Thanks."

"The secrets of the universe are more akin to computer code than magic. We call them miracles, but there is a science behind it. A method of bonding tags and handles with variables and constants. You or I cannot fathom the complexity of it. We know only but a small fraction."

So, Gabriel knew Java? Huh.

"If you can perform miracles, how come there's so much bad? Where's God in all this? How could any of this happen?"

"The One," he replied, "God, as you call them, vanished a long, long time ago. And miracles are small in nature. If we were able to go back and perform miracles to repair every event that transpired, course-correcting the future away from this unfortunate outcome, then we would be guilty of that which you have been condemned."

"Was that my crime? Was that what I did to start all of this mess?"

"No," said Gabriel. "I speak of only the crimes committed since you began to interfere with time."

"I don't understand," I said. "I thought I was making things right."

"This key," he said, opening his palm where it rested, still attached to the chain, "as all holy keys do, performs two tasks. The first is to unlock that which it has locked. The second, is to give its wearer the ability to go wherever they must travel. Between realms. From one point in the galaxy to another. Or through time and space."

"You say that like I abused it," I said.

I was still upset they had stolen it, and now Gabriel was rubbing it in my face like a parent scolding a misbehaved child.

"Tony, my man," whispered Montoya into my ear. "Look at the key."

It was pulsing. There was another key close by—hidden beneath Gabriel's armor?

"Snatch it," said Markus. "Snatch it and run." Even if his voice did represent a small portion of my subconscious, I was too fearful, too overwhelmed to listen.

"This world is built upon principles. Physical laws that when stacked, one upon the other, create an order that must be upheld. If that order is ever subverted, the stacks begin to topple. When that happens, it is inevitable that this will occur," he said, gesturing to the sky. "The Black Sun is a portent of the end."

"Are you saying that I am the cause of this?"

"Indirectly," he said, "yes." He saw my face contort with rage and attempted to calm me down. "Time is one of the few things that must be constant. Rearranging time, fixing time, interfering in time's natural progression, is like detonating explosives to the support structure of any building."

I spun away from him in disgust, then turned back when the words in my throat caught up to my anger. "What am I supposed to do? Am I supposed to sit back and let it all happen?"

Instead of answering me with anger, he smiled and said, "I never expected you to do that."

"Then what do you want from me?"

"You do not remember this," he said, "but you made me a promise.

You promised to right your wrongs. I gave you that chance because I believed you were truly repentant for your crimes."

"Then why are you stopping me now?"

"Because there is the right way and the wrong way. If you topple the natural order of things to fulfill your promise, this will be our fate."

"Are you saying that this," I said, gesturing to the destruction, the city I once called home, "is all avoidable?"

"Yes and no. If you travel the righteous narrow path, this specific outcome will be avoided. It still exists, just as we have observed. There are many paths, Tony. Outcomes unquantified."

"But I can't use the key to right my wrongs? I can't use it to give Jacinda a better life?" I asked, and he nodded. "You're tying my hands behind my back."

"No," he said, "Penance is never easy! It can appear insurmountable, but it is possible if one dares."

"All that suffering," I said as the emotions began to overwhelm me, "and I can't do a damn thing to prevent it."

"Your suffering is part of your penance," he said.

"I wasn't talking about me!" I screamed. "I don't give a damn about me!" I kicked at the dirt like there was something there, the anger and frustration and sadness reaching a point where my body shook. "Jacinda—she doesn't deserve this."

"And Marshall. Amanda. Tori. Anne. Brad. What do they deserve?"

"Better than me."

"And Richard Jansen?"

"Why is that even a question?"

"You killed him."

"To prevent him from raping the woman I love!"

"I understand why you did it," said Gabriel, "but did he deserve to die?"

"Yes!"

"Could you have prevented it without death?"

I suddenly felt the world around me stretch, like I was being pulled through the silky membrane of a bubble. When we pushed through, we were standing in the middle of a playground, watching kids run and play on various multi-colored slides, swing sets, and jungle gyms. There was a thick forest on the side with what looked like a small-town elementary school on the other. It had a well-groomed garden of flowers leading up to an entrance where a handful of adults, most likely teachers, stood watching the kids run and scream like crazy little maniacs.

"Do you know where we are?" he asked.

"No, not at all," I responded after taking a few seconds to look for clues. As we discussed, a handful of older kids separated from the pack.

"I brought you here for a reason. You murdered a man you hold responsible for the actions he took to hurt the one you love. This is wrong. If you wanted to hold a single man accountable for the pain endured by the one you love, you would look no further than your own reflection," said Gabriel.

He pulled no punches, and the guilt poured on in waves.

"Do you see the young boy over there," he asked, breaking me away from my thoughts. He could sense the downward spiral inside me and needed to keep me on target. "The large one with the flaxen hair?" he asked.

"Yes," I said with a nod. He was taller than the other boys, no older than six, maybe seven. He wore expensive clothes and was clearly the ringleader, giving orders to the others.

"Do you believe there are bad people in this world?" he asked.

"You mean like nature versus nurture?" I asked him to clarify.

"Yes."

"I think most people are good-intentioned. Nobody believes they're the villain. They all do what they do because of outside forces which have shaped the way they think and act," I explained.

"No matter how innately rotten a person may seem, nurture is always the correct answer. Tabula rasa. Humans all begin the same. However, temptation comes to some earlier than others." The ringleader and his group of six surrounded a group of three smaller boys who were happily playing in a large sandbox. The ringleader sent two others to distract the teachers while he and his squad took care of business. Within the next few seconds, I witnessed the larger boy punch and kick sand in the faces of each of the three smaller boys. It was sickening to see small kids behaving so violently. All three of the small boys screamed for help and cried until the teachers heard them, and then the bullies scattered to avoid being caught. It was cruel and efficient. It was also one of the most fucked-up things I had ever seen, which was saying a lot about the level of disturbed I felt watching it.

"There is the man you murdered," said Gabriel, nodding toward the kids.

"That makes perfect sense," I said, shaking my head. "It figures Rick was always a bully."

"No. Him," said Gabriel, pointing to the small boy who was wiping the tears and sand from his eyes.

"I almost don't believe it," I said, baffled by such a strangely different young Rick Jansen. After studying the kid, I could almost see it. The features were the same, just young and most importantly, uncorrupted.

"There's more you need to see," he told me, and the scenery changed in an instant, dissolving like sand in the wind.

A house in a nice neighborhood, surrounded by other houses of the same size, came into focus. It was a middle-class neighborhood, sometime in the mid-80s.

"Are you the ghost of Christmas past?" I joked, feeling like Ebenezer Scrooge.

"Dickens was an intelligent man and a brilliant writer. It is said that imitation is the greatest flattery, is it not?" he replied with a smirk. I had the feeling Gabriel wanted to like me but didn't quite know how to let go of all that had transpired.

"That is what they say," I added.

"Richard Jansen grew up here, from age two until age seven. Rick was born out of wedlock, a mistake that turned to a labor of love for his parents. They worked very hard those first few years after his birth, giving him everything they could, which was not very much."

Without taking a step we were suddenly standing in the backyard, where a swing-set rocked shakily in the cold winter wind. Little Rick was on his knees in the corner of the lot by a wooden fence that surrounded the back yard. He seemed to be breathing heavily, huffing like he had just finished running laps around the yard. We approached him slowly, Gabriel leading me.

"The lonely, the outcast, are tempted more easily than others," said Gabriel. "A whisper on the wind, a mind open to dark seduction, an offering of friendship and power, can cause a tiny rift to open in such a young malleable mind. Like a seed being planted."

When he mentioned whispers, I could hear the slight words, hardly discernible, like escaping breath slipping and drifting on the air.

"A young boy, alone in the world, who was fated to one day have ties to a certain young woman who held a powerful secret. Do you think this was a coincidence?"

Gabriel's question had no sooner left his lips when I was finally able to peer over little Rick's shoulder and see his blood-soaked hands—and the tiny, mangled body of his pet rabbit on the ground below him. He looked to be in the midst of a trance, anger and hate pulsing through his body, stinking the air around him with pungent odors.

"Somewhere, beyond our view, a great evil pressed its vile will upon the boy's impressionable soul. The outcome was unquestionable. Innocence lost, and corruption spread. The boy was a perfect target," explained Gabriel.

The house faded and we moved again, shifting through time. A moving van was parked outside, and a slightly older, bitter Rick was carrying a small box of his belongings.

"Your friends will write you," Rick's mom said sweetly, trying to lift his spirits about their move.

"No, they won't. I don't have any friends," he responded bitterly.

Gabriel then continued, "In a surprising turn of events, Rick's father came into a sum of money that would change their lives. He packed his family up and moved them back to Grace Falls, where he was born."

Like hitting the fast-forward button, the world around us moved at unnatural speed, highlighting Rick's ascension from prey to predator.

Then, when I felt I had it all figured out, Gabriel showed me something new.

"When Jacinda had accepted Rick into her heart, the trap was sprung, and so started a series of tests," he said. The scene repainted itself and slowed. "Malus recognized the danger. He tested her abilities. Tested our careful watch. Without Rick in her life, their opportunities to take her were limited."

We were standing on the side of a narrow country road near the bottom of a hill, which led into a thick wooded area. It was night, and the only light was coming from the crescent moon above us. I could hear small creatures scurrying through the tall grasses, searching for food. It seemed like a strange place for the next leg of Gabriel's tour. Crickets chirped and the wind blew just as Gabriel began to speak.

"Do you know where we are now?" he asked, motioning toward the paved road.

"I have no idea." I shoved my hands into my pockets to help cure a rush of anxiety.

"Good. You will be reminded shortly. Just watch, and whatever you do, stay calm."

I was trying to grasp the meaning of his last few words when the crickets stopped chirping all at once. The animals stopped scurrying. The wind swirled into one big burst, then calmed to a dead silence.

Then something moved. Something from within the woods. A small snap of a twig, followed by the rustling of leaves, preceded a shadowy figure strolling from the forest.

He wasn't alone.

"No," I said in disbelief, and the fires inside me exploded with rage. It was Malus. Gabriel put his hand on my shoulder, and the cold metal of his gauntlet dug into my skin. My hands balled into fists, shaking with the ferocity of a space-plane re-entering Earth's atmosphere.

The others—the Thirteen?—stood silently, concealed by the forest shadows, waiting patiently. Behind us, from high atop the hill, I heard a rumble which progressively grew until a pair of headlights flashed over the top of the incline. The red Mustang, traveling faster than what was lawful or safe, swerved erratically.

When the car got within thirty feet of us, Malus stepped into its path. Even through the bright headlights and the darkened windshield, I saw

Rick's eyes flare into a panic. Just before the inevitable impact, the car suddenly stopped—its inertia deadened, and the motor shut off—completely disobeying physics.

Rick's body tore through the windshield, slicing pieces off and tossing him fifty feet in the air. He rolled and skidded for another twenty after he landed.

I was sure Rick was dead. Nobody could have survived such brutal trauma, but then there was a miracle. He twitched and spasmed as he choked on his own blood, attempting to breathe.

Malus stalked toward him, each step deliberately placed.

"Pick him up," said Malus, and a tall, robed figure flipping a gold coin stepped out of the shadows and lifted him by the neck. I recognized the robed beast—Mammon, the Fallen I'd torched after he killed Marshall and Anne.

Rick spasmed and kicked, but not to defend himself. He was irreparably damaged and didn't have the kind of ability to heal as I did.

"Where are you going, Richard?" asked Malus.

Rick looked like he had pulled the pin but forgot to throw the grenade. Half his face was missing, and the other half didn't seem to know where he was. Bones jutted from his mangled legs and chest, broken and splintered through the skin.

"Hey! I'm talking to you!" Malus growled and thrust his clawed hand deep into Rick's side. What he did inside there, I don't know, but the look on Rick's face was one of absolute agony. Malus left his hand inside Rick, and asked him again, "Where are you going, Richard?"

"H-h-h-h-home," he whispered.

"I instructed you never to leave Jacinda unattended on nights of the crescent moon, did I not?" Malus snarled.

"Y-yes," Rick squealed.

"What was that?" screamed Malus.

"Yes," replied Rick firmly.

"You disobeyed me," said Malus calmly, before turning to the shadows. "Devour him."

There was a great hiss, and I watched helplessly as twelve insidious monsters scrambled from darkness and ate Rick's flesh, like ravenous zombies, until he was nothing but a gnarled carcass. When there were no more parts left worth devouring, they slunk back into the darkness and left Malus alone with him.

"Tsk, tsk," he said, kneeling down to pat Rick's fleshless cheek. "I need a more obedient slave. Not a fucking cunt who runs when he's not getting his way." The air grew cold, and the pile of bones on the ground began to steam. "You're mine, and you'll always be mine." The bones began to tremble. "Rise."

The bones, held together by stringy tissue, miraculously got up off the pavement. It was one of the most harrowing things I had ever witnessed. Bits of gristle and cartilage hung from it; bile and mucus dripped and oozed from the remnants of Rick's clothing.

Reaching out with his left hand, the one wearing the intricate silver ring, Malus swiveled his hand around his wrist, as if reeling back time, and watched as the flesh returned to Rick's bones. Bit by bit, he regenerated, becoming whole once again. First the tendons, attaching bone to cartilage, then muscle, arteries and veins. Finally the skin grew back, first pink and raw, followed by a darker, more durable layer, and hair. Rick was a shaking sweaty mess, his eyes wide with horror and his complexion sickly pale with the look of a man who had just gone through the worst torture humanly imaginable.

"Am I dead?" he croaked. Rick's voice sounded like it had never been used before. Raspy and dry, like gargling razor blades.

"Somewhere in between," Malus replied. "I'll show you." With a few flicks of his wrist, Malus tore Rick apart at the seams. His scream cut off when his throat became disconnected from his lungs. His arms and legs each went in a different direction, while his head and torso splintered. Within seconds Malus had put him back together again, like some deranged game of Humpty Dumpty, with each part slowly shifting along the ground like magnets attracted to the other pieces.

Once together, Rick didn't stop screaming for a full ten minutes, as Malus paced around him. Although I struggled with my hatred for Rick, I couldn't help but feel sad for him.

"I own you. Do you understand?"

"Yes!" screamed Rick.

"Yes, master?" questioned Malus.

"Yes, master!" Rick screamed before his indiscretion was punished again.

"Good." Malus laughed.

He walked toward Rick's Mustang and swung his hands around as if bored with what he was seeing. A light breeze picked up, and the glass from the windshield reassembled itself into a perfect pane. After another simple gesture, the car slid to the side of the road and onto the grass just beside Gabriel and me.

It was an awesome show of power. Power that appeared to be only a small fraction of what he was capable of.

"I want you to get into your car and wait for her. When she comes, take back what's yours. I'll be watching."

Rick quickly hobbled into his car and sat down, while the surrounding evil vanished. Malus was there one second, gone the next.

The crickets began to chirp once again, and the forest life resumed. I walked over to the Mustang and peered through the open window at Rick, studying him, looking for damage or a sign of what had transpired. There was nothing there I could see, except for the panting and the distant look of trauma.

"Your enemy is a Necromancer. He controls the dead," said Gabriel. "A powerful one. More powerful than Azrael, the Angel of Death. No harvester can match his might; no reaper can break his will."

"Is that what Malus was? When he was an Angel? A harvester of souls?" I asked.

"No. He was not."

"Will you tell me more?"

"No, I will not."

We waited silently for several minutes, and I expected Gabriel to show me more. The night, the setting, it all looked familiar. Then it hit me.

"This was the night of the Labor Day Fair. The night Jacinda kissed me on the Ferris Wheel."

Gabriel nodded.

Soon after, we heard the cawing of nearby crows, followed by the headlights of an incoming car approaching the top of the hill.

"I was here," I said pointing. "How come we can't see me standing there? Aren't we behind the Veil too?"

"We are behind the Veil," said Gabriel. "But you are here. You are not there. You are an outside observer. You have much to learn about time."

"And if the past me left the Veil? Would we then see me?"

"Yes."

"That makes literally no sense!"

"Paradoxes can destroy the world. Be glad it is near impossible for one to exist."

Jacinda's tiny red car slowed and pulled up behind Rick's Mustang. The car's engine shut off, but the headlights stayed on. She sat behind the steering wheel, wondering, questioning, before she finally got out and paced over to Rick's window.

"Rick?" said Jaycie. "Are you okay?"

"Why are we here?" I asked. "I don't want to see this again." It was bad enough to have witnessed it once.

"I brought you here to show you that Richard Jansen, although a man rife with sin, was still just a man," said Gabriel. "He, alone, was never capable of the evils against you and Jacinda. He never acted alone, but under the direct influence of evil." Rick started his Mustang and revved it, then released her hair as he peeled out, kicking up dirt and grass onto Jaycie. "Richard was always a pawn. A means to an end. He was not your true enemy."

It was a hard pill to swallow. As much as I knew Malus was the true evil behind all the pain and suffering Jaycie had been through in her life, I wanted an easier target. Someone to pay for all the pain. But that only made me a murderer.

I watched Jaycie cry on her knees as the crows watched overhead, knowing for the first time that they were her guard. Ever watching.

"How was I supposed to know?" I asked. "Did I murder an innocent man?"

"Free will, Tony," said Gabriel. "Malus tormented Rick Jansen. He tortured him physically and mentally for years, but even Rick knew the difference between right and wrong. Free will, Tony. We always have a choice."

Then the world around us changed once again, and we were standing in a field, seemingly in the middle of nowhere. The sky was overcast, and the tall brown grass was swaying on a cold breeze. The skeletal forest beyond signified mid-winter. It appeared as normal a place as any, similar to the fields outside the small New Jersey town I grew up in—but something was amiss. I couldn't place a finger on why, just that the entire place felt hollow.

"Where are we?" I asked.

"Follow me," said Gabriel as he led the way through the tall grass. We had paced several steps in complete silence when he asked me the weirdest fucking question of all time. "Do you enjoy chicken soup?"

Like I said, it was the weirdest fucking question of all time, considering the context.

"I do on occasion," I said. He could tell from my tone that I was confused.

"What do you like in your chicken soup?" he asked. Was Archangel Gabe a chicken soup snob? Or was he gearing up for an extreme metaphor?

"I don't know," I responded. "Chicken, obviously. Rice. Carrots. Potato. Maybe some salt and pepper."

Out ahead of us, a quarter mile away was an empty road. There were no cars, nothing, just me and Gabriel in the field, walking and talking about fucking soup.

"Imagine a pot of chicken soup cooking. You add your ingredients. You add your chicken, some rice, carrots, potato and seasoning. You mix it up, and once it is done heating, you pour yourself a bowl and sit down to eat. Every bowl of soup should have the same ingredients, correct?"

"Yeah." I was beginning to think he had gone full Arthur Fonzarelli and jumped the shark on water skis.

"Every bowl of soup has constants, like broth, seasoning, and ideally, plenty of rice. However, would it be possible to dish out equal portions of chicken, potato, and carrot in every bowl?"

"Possible? Yes. Probable? No, not at all."

"Exactly. Even if the ingredients poured into every bowl change—specifically, the ratio of each individual part—you still have chicken soup."

"Is there a restaurant up ahead? Are you hungry? I'm confused."

"You were not supposed to kill Rick Jansen, Tony. Rick's destiny was to live three and a half more years. He would go to jail. He would be released under a combination of good behavior and his father's money. Eventually, he would re-engage in the conduct that put him in jail, and he would die, right where we are standing."

We were about twenty paces from the road when Gabriel stopped.

"What does that have to do with chicken soup?" I was growing angry, and I felt like I was being dicked around to make me feel more guilty about the decisions I had made. Yeah, I murdered a piece of shit. But I did it because I couldn't stand back and let him do something so awful to the woman I love! How come they couldn't see that?

"Every action we take is like pouring a new bowl of soup," continued Gabriel. "Sometimes we get mostly chicken. Other times potato. Sometimes we get an even ratio. And other times still, we ladle a full bowl with only one single orange carrot."

"What does that have to do with anything!?"

I heard the distant rumble of a motor from down the road.

"For you and I, for Rick Jansen, when we do not have time-altering tools at our disposal, like one of the Keys of Eden, we may only get one bowl to pour for every decision we make," he explained, as I saw the heat rising from the blacktop despite the cold. The same familiar blurry wave I had witnessed in those strange moments of Jacinda's life—the strange moments when things appeared to change.

"Where are we?" I suddenly asked, feeling ill.

"January 25th, 2005. The day Jacinda found the single carrot in her bowl."

As the red Mustang crested the hill, the sound of its motor raging into high speeds stole away the entire span of my attention. I never even heard the semi-truck coming the other way until it passed me by and made an almost immediate impact—a head-on collision that sent the truck veering off the road and the Mustang lurching into the air before tumbling no less than fifteen times, settling in tall grass nearby. Rick Jansen was immediately ejected and hit the ground thirty feet away. His body was folded up and cut to hell. The truck's trailer unhooked and flipped, spilling a few thousand cans of chicken soup into the field across the street.

The wreckage was on fire, and I was dumbfounded. Should I help him? Should I call an ambulance? But he was already dead, wasn't he?

"What are we watching? How many times has Rick flown through his car window?" I questioned. "He died. I shot him."

"A time remnant," he explained. "You see, when you cheated the natural order of time, the great Cosmic Scales—think of them as the balance between good and evil—toppled over and weakened the structural integrity of all existence in the Third Dimension—our world. This timeline never got to exist, like a stranded island floating further and further away from our own timeline."

I saw something through the smoke. At first, I thought it was just the fire, or the red paint of the wrecked Mustang, but then I saw it more clearly—the crimson hair in the passenger seat, a woman beginning to stir.

It struck me like I was falling. My stomach sank and my heart skipped into arrythmia.

"I don't understand!" I shouted, as tears flooded my eyes. I wanted to help her, to rush her away to safety, but would Gabriel let me? Would it even matter? This was a *What if?*—not the actual timeline—this was a never-was, and my heart, conscience, and mind were each going in different directions, shouting different orders I was paralyzed to act upon.

"Jacinda tried to change her destiny. She changed the outcome multiple times, until she came across a more favorable fate, one that ended right there, in the passenger seat of Rick Jansen's car."

The broken Rick on the ground unfolded himself and wheezed—his lung was punctured and collapsed, and integral parts of him refused to work, but he still got to his feet like a boxer by the count of nine. He spun around, loopy, blood running down his face, and found her in the passenger seat. She was rousing slowly, then spotted him as he limped his way toward the car. Jaycie tried to open the Mustang door, but it was stuck. She tried again, over and over, but Rick kept getting closer.

"After breaking up with you," continued Gabriel, "knowing that you would never leave her, Jacinda ran away once again. She did not wish to put you in harm's way. She was protecting you and broke your heart."

Rick stumbled closer as Jaycie began to panic. He pulled a gun from his belt, and I stepped forward, when Gabriel put a hand on my chest to stop me—his touch took the nerve from my heart and pacified me into becoming a watcher only.

"With his resources, Rick tracked her down. She fled and searched for you, even driving all the way to your hometown, when he abducted her."

I knew the field looked familiar. We were only five miles outside of where I grew up.

"Rick was taking her to Malus, when this occurred."

"Rick, no," whimpered Jaycie. "You can't take me to him. You can't!"

"I have to!" Rick shouted. A gurgle of blood erupted from his mouth.

"No," she said calmly. "No, you don't." Then she looked around her and coughed. The oil was burning, creating a thick black noxious smoke. "Is he here?"

Crows landed on the telephone lines above. Three at first, then five or more.

Rick looked like he was caught in a lie. "No, he's not here. Not now."

"Kill me, Rick," she said. "Do it now, before he finds us."

"No," he replied, shaking his head.

It was shocking. All of it—and I found myself rooting for Rick to do it. To be merciful to the woman I loved so she could be at peace.

"How many times?" I asked. "How many times had Jacinda rewritten her destiny?"

"Countless," replied Gabriel. "There is no way to know for certain. We are part of the soup. She is the one pouring the bowl." Then he turned to me. "This outcome ended her misery. In her last moments, Jacinda was able to reach Rick's humanity, momentarily steering him away from the evil he served."

"Please," pled Jaycie. "Don't let him get me."

"How was Jaycie allowed change her destiny without a paradox?" I asked, as if I was appealing to Gabriel's better nature to step in and stop this from happening.

"Jacinda was acting within accordance of the law. She was not cheating time. She was molding it," Gabriel explained.

Then Rick's resolve cracked. The darkness in his heart wilted, and he lifted the gun and shot her. I saw her death, a different one, and it hurt just the same. The devastation was so intense that I had to look away. I couldn't bear to see any more of it.

The crows cawed loudly overhead. There were dozens of them.

Rick then stumbled away toward us, lifted the gun to his own head, and shot himself. He died at our feet, right in the spot Gabriel had pointed out to me.

"Was she free?" I asked, choking on the grief.

"She found a way to be at peace. A peace that was stolen from her when you cheated the natural order of time. The timeline you created by murdering Rick kept you together, but in the end, it brought catastrophe. It brought forth the world of Jamaal's future, as well as allowing Jacinda to fall into the clutches of the one creature who'd haunted her all her life."

"What was I supposed to do?" I cried. "What am I supposed to do now?"

Gabriel's consoling hand rested on my shoulder. "I think you know how this will end."

Of everything he had said, these words were perhaps the most meaningful. I was in over my head. Gabriel expected me to fail. *"Your suffering is part of your penance,"* he had said. *"Penance is never easy!"* However, I hadn't planned on surviving. The plan was to free Jaycie and provide her a long and happy life. This wasn't about me. It hadn't been for some time.

"Jacinda can alter reality," I said. "She can change her fate. I saw her step into the Veil before she was ten, and I watched as she defended herself by inadvertently tossing a boy into the path of a mini-van with nothing but a thought. I witnessed her ending the whole world, her rage spinning out of control as she broke the Earth apart in anger, then undid it all in a single blink of an eye. I went searching for answers, but I only have one question. What is Jacinda? What is the Omega?"

Gabriel sighed, as if he had finally resigned to answering one of my questions, a secret he did not wish to divulge. "Locked within Jacinda's soul is the Holy Dyad—the Godly powers of Creation and Destruction," he said, then paused as his words sunk into me like aloe into burned skin. "Tony, Jacinda is the Omega. She is the maelstrom, the coming cataclysm. Jacinda is The One. She is...*God*."

"Huh... *Huh*?"

To be continued in

The Third Book of Cataclysm:
THE PALE DEMON

a letter from the author

Hello Friends!

Thank you for reading **THE OMEGA!**

I started writing this book nearly 14 years ago, and at the time I had no idea what it would become. I hope you'll continue this journey with me through the next two parts: **The Pale Demon**, and **Cataclysm**.

In the meantime, please go to your favorite book site and leave a review. Reviews, especially written reviews, are the lifeblood of every author. A book's success is dependent on reviews and referrals from readers just like you.

If you enjoyed **The Raptor** and **The Omega**, please go and review—tell your friends, your family, your neighbors, your cats, your dogs, your Social Media friends, and anyone who's willing to listen.

Thank you for continuing this journey with me.
G.A. Finocchiaro

THE OMEGA

G.A. Finocchiaro lives in the suburbs of Philadelphia, where he ponders why people give their dogs human names. Its weird. Stop it. Go back to unimaginative Spot or Fido, just don't call them Steve or Rebecca.

Check out his website: http://www.gafino.com
Follow him on Twitter: @G_A_Fino
Follow him on Facebook: https://www.facebook.com/GAFinocc
Sign up for his Newsletter: http://www.gafino.com/Newsletter/

THE OMEGA